KT-233-655

The Twenty-Three

SWANSEA LIBRARIES

0001435699

ALSO BY LINWOOD BARCLAY
FROM CLIPPER LARGE PRINT

No Safe House
Broken Promise
Far From True

The Twenty-Three

Linwood Barclay

W F HOWES LTD

This large print edition published in 2017 by
W F Howes Ltd
Unit 5, St George's House, Rearsby Business Park,
Gaddesby Lane, Rearsby, Leicester LE7 4YH

1 3 5 7 9 10 8 6 4 2

First published in the United Kingdom in 2016
by Orion Books

Copyright © NJSB Entertainment Inc., 2016

The right of Linwood Barclay to be identified as
the author of this work has been asserted by him
in accordance with the Copyright, Designs and
Patents Act, 1988.

All rights reserved

A CIP catalogue record for this book is available
from the British Library

ISBN 978 1 51008 075 1

Typeset by Palimpsest Book Production Limited,
Falkirk, Stirlingshire

Printed and bound in
T J International, Padstow, Cornwall
Printforce Nederland, Culemborg, Netherlands

CITY & COUNTY OF
SWANSEA LIBRARIES

Cl.	
Au	Pr.
Date	Loc.
No.	

For Neetha

CHAPTER 1

I know I won't be able to get them all. But I hope
I'll be able to get enough.

DAY I

CHAPTER 2

Patricia Henderson, forty-one, divorced, employed at the Weston Street Branch of the Promise Falls Public Library system as a computer librarian, was, on that Saturday morning of the long holiday weekend in May, among the first to die.

She was scheduled to work that day. Patricia was annoyed the library board chose to keep all of the town's libraries open. They were slated to close on the Sunday, and on the Monday, Memorial Day. So, if you're going to close Sunday and Monday, why not close for the Saturday, too, and give everyone at the library the weekend off?

But no.

Not that Patricia had anywhere in particular to go.

But still. It seemed ridiculous to her. She knew, given that it was a long weekend, there'd be very few people coming into the library. Wasn't this town supposed to be in the midst of a financial crisis? Why keep the place open? Sure, there was a bit of a rush on Friday as some customers, particularly those who had cottages or other weekend places, took out books to keep them occupied through to Tuesday. The rest of the weekend was guaranteed to be quiet.

Patricia was to be at the library by nine, when it opened, but that really meant she needed to be there by eight forty-five a.m. That would give her time to boot up all the computers, which were shut down every night at closing to save on electricity, even though the amount of power the branch's thirty computers drew overnight was negligible. The library board, however, was on a 'green' kick, which meant not only conserving electricity, but making sure recycling stations were set up throughout the library, and signs pinned to the bulletin boards to discourage the use of bottled water. One of the library board members saw the bottled water industry, and the bins of plastic bottles it created, as one of the great evils of the modern world, and didn't want them in any of the Promise Falls branches. 'Provide paper cups that can be filled at the facility's water fountains,' she said. Which now meant that the recycling stations were overflowing with paper cups instead of water bottles.

And guess who was pissed about that. What's-his-name, that Finley guy who used to be mayor and now ran a water bottling company. Patricia had met him the first – and, she hoped, *last* – time just the other evening at the Constellation Drive-in. She'd taken her niece Kaylie and her little friend Alicia for the drive-in's final night. Kaylie's mom

– Patricia's sister, Val – had lent her their minivan, since Patricia's Hyundai was too cramped for such an excursion. God, what a mistake that turned out to be. Not only did the screen come crashing down, scaring the little girls half to death, but then Finley showed up, trying to get his picture taken giving comfort to the wounded.

Politics, Patricia thought. How she hated politics and everything about it.

And thinking of politics, Patricia had found herself staring at the ceiling at four in the morning, worried about next week's public meeting on 'Internet filtering.' The debate had been going on for years and never seemed settled. Should the library put filters on computers used by patrons that would restrict access to certain Web sites? The idea was to keep youngsters from accessing pornography, but it was a continuing quagmire. The filters were often ineffective, blocking material that was not adult oriented, and allowing material that was. And aside from that, there were freedom-of-speech and freedom-to-read issues.

Patricia knew the meeting would, as this kind of meeting always did, devolve into a shouting match between ultraconservatives who saw gay subtext in *Teletubbies* and didn't want computers in the library to begin with, and ultra-left-wingers who believed if a kindergartner wanted to read *Portnoy's Complaint*, so be it.

At ten minutes after five, when she knew she wasn't going to get back to sleep, she threw back the covers and decided to move forward with her day.

She walked into the bathroom, flicked on the light, and studied her face in the mirror.

'Ick,' she said, rubbing her cheeks with the tips of her fingers. 'ABH.'

That was the mantra from Charlene, her personal trainer. Always Be Hydrating. Which meant drinking at least seven full glasses of water a day.

Patricia reached for the glass next to the sink, turned on the tap to let the water run until it was cold, filled the glass, and drank it down in one long gulp. She reached into the shower, turned on the taps, held her hand under the spray until it was hot enough, pulled the long white T-shirt she slept in over her head, and stepped in.

She stayed in there until she could sense the hot water starting to run out. Shampooed and lathered up first, then stood under the water, feeling it rain across her face.

Dried off.

Dressed.

Felt – and this was kind of weird – *itchy* all over.

Did her hair and makeup.

By the time she was in her apartment kitchen, it was six thirty. Still plenty of time to kill before driving to the library, a ten-minute commute. Or, if she decided to ride her bike, about twenty-five minutes.

Patricia opened the cupboard, took out a small metal tray with more than a dozen bottles of pills and vitamins. She opened the lids on four, tapped out a calcium tablet, a low-dose aspirin, a vitamin D, and a multivitamin, which, while containing vitamin D, did not, she believed, have enough.

She tossed them all into her mouth at once and washed them down with a small glass of water from the kitchen tap. Moved her upper body all around awkwardly, as though her blouse were made of wool.

Patricia opened the refrigerator and stared. Did she want an egg? Hard-boiled? Fried? It seemed like a lot of work. She closed the door and went back to the cupboard and brought down a box of Special K.

'Whoa,' she said.

It was like a wave washing over. Light-headedness. Like she'd been standing outside in a high wind and nearly gotten blown over.

She put both hands on the edge of the counter to steady herself. *Let it pass,* she told herself. *It's probably nothing. Up too early.*

There, she seemed to be okay. She brought down a small bowl, started to pour some cereal into it.

Blinked.

Blinked again.

She could see the 'K' on the cereal box clearly enough, but 'Special' was fuzzy around the edges. Which was pretty strange, because it was not exactly a tiny font. This was not newspaper type. The letters in 'Special' were a good inch tall.

Patricia squinted.

'Special,' she said.

She closed her eyes, shook her head, thinking that would set things straight. But when she opened her eyes, she was dizzy.

'What the hell?' she said.

I need to sit down.

She left the cereal where it was and made her way to the table, pulled out the chair. Was the room spinning? Just a little?

She hadn't had the 'whirlies' in a very long time. She'd gotten drunk more than a few times over the years with her ex, Stanley. But even then, she'd never had enough to drink that the room spun. She had to go back to her days as a student at Thackeray for a memory like that.

But Patricia hadn't been drinking. And what she was feeling now wasn't the same as what she'd felt back then.

For one thing, her heart was starting to race.

She placed a hand on her chest, just above the swell of her breasts, to see if she could feel what she already knew she was feeling.

Tha-thump. Tha-thump. Tha-tha-thump.

Her heart wasn't just picking up the pace. It was doing so in an irregular fashion.

Patricia moved her hand from her chest to her forehead. Her skin was cold and clammy.

She wondered whether she could be having a heart attack. But she wasn't old enough for one of those, was she? And she was in good shape. She worked out. She often rode her bike to work. She had a personal trainer, for God's sake.

The pills.

Patricia figured she must have taken the wrong pills. But was there anything in that pill container that could do something like this to her?

No.

She stood, felt the floor move beneath her as though Promise Falls were undergoing an earthquake, which was not the sort of thing that happened often in upstate New York.

Maybe, she thought, *I should just get my ass to Promise Falls General.*

Gill Pickens, already in the kitchen, standing at the island, reading the *New York Times* on his laptop while he sipped on his third cup of coffee, was not overly surprised when his daughter, Marla, appeared with his ten-month-old grandson, Matthew, in her arms.

'He wouldn't stop fussing,' Marla said. 'So I decided to get up and give him something to eat. Oh, thank God, you've already made coffee.'

Gill winced. 'I just killed off the first pot. I'll make some more.'

'That's okay. I can—'

'No, let me. You take care of Matthew.'

'You're up early,' she said to her father as she got Matthew strapped into his high chair.

'Couldn't sleep,' he said.

'Still?'

Gill Pickens shrugged. 'Jesus, Marla, it's only been a little over two weeks. I didn't sleep all that well before, anyway. You telling me you've been sleeping okay?'

'Sometimes,' Marla said. 'They gave me something.'

Right. She'd been on a few things to help ease the shock of her mother's death earlier that month, and learning that the baby she'd thought she lost at birth was actually alive.

Matthew.

But even if her prescriptions had allowed her to sleep better than her father some nights, there was still a cloud hanging over the house that showed no signs of moving off soon. Gill had not returned to work, in part because he simply wasn't up to it, but also because child welfare authorities had allowed Marla to take care of Matthew only so long as she was living under the same roof as her father.

Gill had felt a need to be present, although he wondered how much longer that would be necessary. All the evidence suggested Marla was a wonderful, loving mother. And the other good news was her acceptance of reality. In the days immediately following Agnes's jump off Promise Falls, Marla maintained the belief that her mother was actually alive, and would be returning to help her with her child.

Marla now understood that that was not going to happen.

She filled a pot with hot water from the tap, set it on the counter instead of the stove, then took a bottle of formula she'd made up the day before from the refrigerator and placed it in the pot.

Matthew had twisted himself around in the chair to see what was going on. His eyes landed on the bottle and he pointed.

'Gah,' he said.

'It's coming,' Marla said. 'I'm just letting it warm up some. But I have something else for you in the meantime.'

She turned a kitchen chair around so she could sit immediately opposite Matthew. She twisted the lid on a tiny jar of pureed apricots and, with a very small plastic spoon, aimed some at the baby's mouth.

'You like this, don't you?' she said, glancing in her father's direction as he scanned his eyes over the laptop screen. He appeared to be squinting.

'Need glasses, Dad?'

He looked up. Gill suddenly looked very pale to her. 'What?'

'You looked like you were having trouble looking at the screen.'

'Why are you doing that?' he asked her.

Matthew swatted at the spoon, knocked some apricots onto his chair.

'Why am I doing what?' Marla asked.

'Moving around like that.'

'I'm just sitting here,' she said, getting more apricot onto the spoon. 'You want to bring that bottle over?'

The pot with the bottle in it was sitting

immediately to the right of the laptop, but Gill appeared unable to focus on it.

'Is it funny in here?' he asked, setting down his mug of coffee too close to the edge of the island. It tipped, hit the floor, and shattered, but Gill did not look down.

'Dad?'

Marla got out of the chair and moved quickly to her father's side. 'Are you okay?'

'Need to get Matthew to the hospital,' he said.

'Matthew? Why would Matthew have to go to the hospital?'

Gill looked into his daughter's face. 'Is something wrong with Matthew? Do you think he has what I have?'

'Dad?' Marla struggled to keep the panic out of her voice. 'What's going on with you? You're breathing really fast. Why are you doing that?'

He put a hand on his chest, felt his heart beating through his robe.

'I think I'm going to throw up,' he said.

But he did not. Instead, he dropped to the floor.

Hillary and Josh Lydecker had been frantic for four days.

They had not seen their son, twenty-two-year-old George Lydecker, since late Tuesday. Now here it was Saturday morning, and they still had no idea where he was.

Early Wednesday morning the family was supposed to have flown out to Vancouver to visit

Josh's relatives. When George left the house Tuesday evening, he had promised to be home early so that he could get in at least a few hours of sleep before the taxi came for everyone.

His parents were not shocked when he failed to get home at a decent hour, but they were surprised he didn't make it home at all. It would have been just like George to show up at the house as the rest of his family was putting their bags into the cab, grinning stupidly, weaving slightly, saying something like, 'Told ya I'd be here.'

But that had not happened.

George had always been their wild child – their daughter, Cassandra, sixteen, was a perfect angel, at least so far – with a reputation for getting into trouble, most recently at Thackeray College, where he had, among other things, turned a professor's Smart car onto its roof (no real damage done, but still) and put a baby alligator into Thackeray Pond. He drank too much, even by the standards of college-age boys, and often acted impulsively without considering the consequences. He thrived on risk. Back when he was in his teens, he was caught twice wandering the halls of his high school in the middle of the night when the facility was supposedly all locked up.

'What has he done?' Hillary kept asking her husband. 'What has that damn fool done?'

Josh Lydecker kept shaking his head. For the first two days, he kept saying, 'He'll show up. He will. The dumbass is sleeping it off somewhere, that's all.'

But by day three, even Josh had come to believe that something serious had happened.

The morning of the first day, Hillary had called all of George's friends, including Derek Cutter, to see if anyone had seen him. She got George's sister, Cassandra, to spread the word via social media so that everyone they knew could be on the lookout for George.

Nothing.

By the afternoon, Hillary wanted to bring in the Promise Falls police. Josh had objected at first, still believing George would turn up. He was also worried that whatever was delaying George's return might not be something they wanted the police to know about. Although he did not share this thought with his wife, it occurred to him that maybe George and his buddies were celebrating the end of the Thackeray school year by engaging the services of prostitutes. Maybe they'd gone to Albany and were doing God knew what.

But Hillary called the police anyway.

They took down all the relevant information. But a young man who liked to party hard, who had a history of mischief, was not exactly a high priority for the local police. And it wasn't as though they had nothing to do. There'd been some crazy shoot-out at a Laundromat the other day, and it hadn't even been a week since some nutcase

16

had blown up the drive-in on the outskirts of Promise Falls and killed four people.

Whoever'd done that was still out there.

The Lydeckers had not just sat around doing nothing the last four days. They'd been out every day, driving around town, going out to the college, popping into local bars, checking back in with George's friends. They felt they had to be doing something.

They'd been back to the police, too, who were finally starting to take this more seriously. On Thursday, they sent around a detective named Angus Carlson. He sat down with the parents and Cassandra, made notes. He even took Cassandra aside later, said he wondered if she might know anything about her brother that she wouldn't want to say in front of her parents. Something that might help him find George.

'Well,' she'd said, 'he likes to break into people's garages and look for stuff.'

'Do your parents know about that?'

Cassandra had shaken her head no. Said maybe she should tell them.

Carlson had made a note.

And now here it was, Saturday morning. Hillary and Josh in the kitchen, Cassandra upstairs in bed. Hillary had been down here since five, making a pot of tea, and then drawing up a list of things they should do today in their search for George.

The list, so far, read:

- call Detective Carlson, update
- call friends again. D. Cutter
- check places George might explore, abandoned factories, Five Mountains park, drive-in disaster
- make flyers with George picture, put up around town, call printer

When Josh entered the room, Hillary had turned on the kettle to make another pot of tea. She showed her husband the list.

'Okay,' he said wearily. 'I'd been thinking about Five Mountains. I could imagine him looking around there, now that it's closed down. It'll probably be all locked up. I could call the management, or maybe get the detective to do that.'

'George would find a way in, even if it was locked. You know what he's like. He's always sneaking into things.'

Josh hesitated. 'About that. Cassie told me something, last night.'

'Told you what?'

'Sometimes . . . sometimes George breaks into places. Not like a school or something, just goofing around. He looks for unlocked garages, gets in, takes stuff.'

'He does not,' Hillary said angrily. Her face had become flushed, and beads of sweat had sprouted on her forehead.

'I'm just telling you what she said. I think . . . at first I didn't want the police brought in, in

18

case George had done something stupid, but I'm past that. We should ask them if there have been any break-ins. Of garages. Maybe that would be a lead to finding out what – Hillary, are you okay?'

'Seriously?' Hillary said. 'I've had three hours' sleep this week. Now you're saying my son is a thief, and you ask if I'm okay?'

'I'm just saying, you don't look good.'

'I can't sleep, I'm worried sick about what's happened to my baby, I feel like I'm going to have a heart attack, and—'

Hillary's cell phone, which was on the table next to her cup of tea, vibrated. A text.

'Oh my God, maybe it's George!' she said, and dived for the phone, snatched it up, looked at it with puzzlement. 'It's Cassie.'

'Cassie?' Josh said. 'She's upstairs.' He hesitated. 'Isn't she?'

Hillary, her face crumpling, turned the phone to her husband.

The text read:

I think I'm dying

Ali Brunson said, 'Hang in there, Audrey. You're going to be fine. You just have to keep it together a little bit longer.'

Of course, Ali had said that many times in his career as a paramedic, and there were many of those times when he hadn't believed it for a second. This looked as though it was turning into one of those times.

Audrey McMichael, age fifty-three, 173 pounds, black, an insurance adjuster, resident of 21 Forsythe Avenue for the last twenty-two years, where she lived with her husband, Clifford, was showing every indication of giving up the fight.

Ali called up to Tammy Fairweather, who was behind the wheel of the ambulance, and racing it to Promise Falls General. The good news was, it was early Saturday morning and there was hardly anyone on the road. The bad news was, it probably wasn't going to matter. Audrey's blood pressure was plummeting like an elevator with snapped cables. Barely sixty over forty.

When Ali and Tammy had arrived at the McMichael home, Audrey had been vomiting. For the better part of an hour, according to her husband, she had been complaining of nausea, dizziness, a headache. Her breathing had been growing increasingly rapid and shallow. There had been moments when she'd said she could not see.

Her condition continued to deteriorate after they loaded her into the ambulance.

'How we doing back there?' Tammy called.

'Don't worry about me. Just get us to church on time,' Ali told her, keeping his voice even.

'I know people,' Tammy said over the wail of the siren, trying to lighten the mood. 'You need a ticket fixed, I'm the girl to know.'

The radio crackled. Their dispatcher.

'Let me know the second you clear PFG,' the male voice on the radio said.

'Not even there yet,' Tammy radioed back. 'Will advise.'

'Need you at another location ASAP.'

'What's the deal?' Tammy asked. 'All the other units take off sick? They go fishing for the weekend?'

'Negative. All engaged.'

'What?'

'It's like an instant flu outbreak all over town,' the dispatcher said. 'Let me know the second you're available.' The connection ended.

'What'd he say?' Ali asked.

Tammy swung the wheel hard. She could see the blue *H* atop Promise Falls General in the distance. No more than a mile away.

'Something going around,' Tammy said. 'Not the kind of Saturday morning I was expecting.'

Whenever Tammy and Ali got the weekend morning shifts, they usually started them with coffee at Dunkin's, chilling out until their first call.

There'd been no coffee today. Audrey McMichael, it turned out, was their second call of the day. The first had been to the Breckonwood Drive home of Terrence Rodd, an eighty-eight-year-old retired statistician who'd called 911 after experiencing dizziness and chest pains. Tammy had pointed out that he lived right next door to where that Gaynor woman had been murdered a few weeks ago.

Terrence never made it alive to the ER.

Hypotension, Ali thought. *Low blood pressure.*

And here they were again, with another patient experiencing, among other things, dangerously low blood pressure.

Ali raised his head far enough to see out the front window just as Tammy slammed on the brakes and screamed, 'Jesus!'

There was a man standing in the path of the ambulance, halfway into their lane. 'Standing' was not quite accurate. More like stooping, with one hand on his chest, the other raised, palm up, asking the ambulance to stop. Then the man doubled over, and vomited onto the street.

'Goddamn it!' Tammy said. She grabbed her radio. 'I need help!'

'Drive around him!' Ali said. 'We don't have time to help some geezer cross the road.'

'I can't just – he's on his knees, Ali. Jesus fucking Christ!'

Tammy threw the shift lever into park, said, 'Be right back!' and jumped out of the ambulance.

The dispatcher said, 'What's happening?'

Ali couldn't leave Audrey McMichael to tell him.

'Sir!' Tammy said, striding briskly toward the man, who looked to be in his late fifties, early sixties. 'What's wrong, sir?'

'Help me,' he whispered.

'What's your name, sir?'

The man mumbled something.

'What's that?'

'Fisher,' he said. 'Walden Fisher. I don't feel . . . something's . . . not right. My stomach . . . just threw up.'

Tammy put a hand on his shoulder. 'Talk to me, Mr Fisher. What other symptoms have you been experiencing?' The man's breaths were rapid and shallow, just like those of Audrey McMichael and Terrence Rodd.

This is one serious clusterfuck. That's what this is, Tammy thought.

'Dizzy. Sick to my stomach. Something's not right.' He looked fearfully into the paramedic's face. 'My heart. I think there's something wrong with my heart.'

'Come with me, sir,' she said, leading him to the back of the ambulance. She'd put him in there with Audrey.

The more the merrier, she thought, shaking her head, then wondering, *What next?*

Which was when she heard the explosion.

When Emily Townsend had her first sip of coffee, she thought it tasted just a tiny bit off.

So she dumped out the entire pot – six cups' worth – as well as the filter filled with coffee grounds, and started over.

Ran the water for thirty seconds from the tap to make sure it was fresh before adding it to the machine. Put in a new filter and six scoops of coffee from the tin.

Hit the button.

Waited.

When the machine beeped, she poured the coffee into a cup – a clean one; she'd already put the first one into the dishwasher – added one sugar and just a titch of cream, and gave it a stir.

Brought the warm mug to her lips and tentatively sipped.

Must have been her imagination. This tasted just fine.

Maybe it was her toothpaste. Made that first cup taste funny.

Cal Weaver was having breakfast – if you could call it that – in a room adjacent to the lobby of the BestBet Inn, which sat on Route 9 a quarter mile from the exit off 87, halfway between Promise Falls and Albany.

He'd been here most of the week.

It wasn't a surveillance or any other kind of private detecting gig that had brought him to the lovely accommodations of the BestBet (*Free Wi-Fi!*). It was, however, the only affordable hotel close to Promise Falls that had any rooms available. He'd booked himself in here while he looked for a new place to live. Someone had firebombed the bookstore below his apartment and while his place had not burned to the ground, it was not a place where anyone could stay. The smell of smoke was overwhelming, and power had been cut to the building.

Cal was not going to stay with his sister, Celeste,

and her husband, Dwayne. His presence would aggravate the tensions that already existed between his sister and his brother-in-law. The man did road repairs for the town, and with all the recent budget cuts, he was getting very little work.

So Cal found a hotel.

The BestBet advertised a free breakfast, and it was true what they said. You get what you pay for. The first day, when Cal came down, he was thinking he'd get a ham and cheddar omelet with home fries and brown toast. So he was dismayed when he found that his breakfast choices consisted of single-serving cereals in sealed plastic containers, hard-boiled eggs (preshelled, which he supposed was at least something), day-old muffins and donuts, bananas and oranges, containers of yogurt, and – praise the Lord – coffee.

The only time any hotel employee showed up was to make sure there was coffee in the tall, aluminum urn.

Miracle of miracles, it was drinkable.

He'd grabbed a free copy of the Albany paper in the lobby and was leafing through it, sitting at a table by the window so he could watch the traffic go by on 9, washing down a dry blueberry muffin with his paper cup of coffee. He'd already refilled it twice.

He hadn't expected to find any Promise Falls apartment-for-rent listings in the paper, and he was not disappointed. And since there was no longer a *Promise Falls Standard*, he'd turn to the

Net after breakfast to see whether any new places had come online.

His cell rang.

He reached into his pocket, checked out the caller.

Lucy Brighton.

It was not the first time she'd tried to reach him since he'd last seen her earlier in the week. He'd taken a couple of her calls, but had ignored the more recent ones. He knew what Lucy was going to say, what she was going to ask him. It would be the same thing she had asked him the time before.

What was he going to do?

He still didn't know.

Should he tell the police what he knew? Should he call up his old friend Promise Falls police detective Barry Duckworth, and tell him he knew who had murdered Miriam Chalmers?

Cal knew he probably should. But he wasn't sure that it was the right thing to do.

Because of Crystal, Lucy's eleven-year-old daughter. The girl Lucy was raising on her own, ever since her husband, Gerald, had skipped off to San Francisco and rarely been seen since.

Cal didn't know what would happen to Crystal if her mother went to prison. Lucy's father, Adam, had died in that bombing at the drive-in. Her mother had died years ago.

Was justice served if it left a young girl without her mother?

And was that Cal's problem? Wasn't that something Lucy should have thought of before she—

The phone continued to ring.

The so-called dining area of the BestBet was not busy, but the handful of others having breakfast had glanced furtively in Cal's direction, wondering whether he was ever going to answer his damn phone.

He tapped the screen, declined the call.

There.

Cal went back to reading the paper, which had been following the recent events in Promise Falls pretty closely. The police still hadn't made any headway in finding out who'd toppled the drive-in screen. There was a quote from Duckworth, that police were pursuing several leads and hoped to make an arrest shortly.

Which sounded, to Cal, like they were nowhere.

His phone rang. Lucy again.

He couldn't let it ring another dozen times. Either he declined the call right now, or he answered it.

He tapped the screen, put the phone to his ear.

'Hey, Lucy,' he said.

'It's not Lucy,' a young voice said.

'Crystal?' Cal said.

'Is this Mr Weaver?'

'Yes. Is that you, Crystal?'

'Yes,' she said flatly.

Crystal was, Cal had quickly learned, an odd,

but incredibly talented, kid. She was constantly creating her own graphic novels, withdrawing into her own imaginary world. Her interactions with others, beyond her mother, were hesitant and awkward, although she had warmed to Cal after he'd shown an interest in her work.

Was Lucy using her own daughter to ensure that Cal didn't go to the police? Using her to gain sympathy? Had she put her daughter up to making this call?

'What's up, Crystal?' he asked. 'Did your mother ask you to call me?'

'No,' she said. 'She's sick.'

'I'm sorry to hear that. Has she got the flu?'

'I don't know. But I think she's really sick.'

'I hope she gets better soon. Why'd you call, Crystal?'

'Because she's sick.'

Cal felt a shiver. 'How sick is she, Crystal?'

'She's not moving.'

Cal stood up abruptly from the table, kept the phone to his ear as he started heading for his car. 'Where is she?'

'In the kitchen. On the floor.'

'You need to call 911 right now, Crystal. You know how to do that?'

'Yes. Everybody knows how to do that. I did that. Nobody answered. Your number was in her phone, so I called you.'

'Did your mother tell you what's wrong?'

'She's not saying anything.'

'I'm on my way,' he said. 'But keep calling 911, okay?'

'Okay,' Crystal said. 'Good-bye.'

Before Patricia Henderson decided to try to get herself to the hospital, she dialed 911.

She figured when you called 911, someone answered right away. First ring. But 911 did not respond on the first ring, nor did it respond on the second.

Or the third.

By four rings, Patricia was thinking maybe this was not the way to go.

But then, an answer.

'Please hold!' someone said hurriedly, and then nothing.

Patricia's symptoms – and there were more than a few – were not subsiding, and she did not believe, even in her increasingly confused state, that she could wait around for some 911 dispatcher to get back to her.

She let go of the receiver, not bothering to place it back in the cradle, and looked for her purse. Was that it, over there, *waaaay* over there, on the small table by the front door?

Patricia squinted, and determined that it was.

She stumbled toward it, reached into the bag for her car keys. After ten seconds of digging around without success, she turned the bag over and dumped the contents onto the table, most of them spilling onto the floor.

She blinked several times, tried to focus. It was as though she'd just stepped out of the shower, was trying to get the water out of her eyes so she could see. She bent over at the waist to grab what appeared to be her keys, but was snatching at air, some three inches above where her keys lay.

'Come on, stop that,' Patricia told the keys. 'Don't be that way.'

She leaned over slightly more, grabbed hold of the keys, but tumbled forward into the hallway. As she struggled to get to her knees, nausea overwhelmed her and she vomited onto the floor.

'Hospital,' she whispered.

She struggled to her feet, opened the door, made no effort to lock, or even close, it behind her, and went down the hallway to the elevators, one hand feeling the wall along the way to steady herself. She was only on the third floor, but she still possessed enough smarts to know she could not handle two flights of stairs.

Patricia blinked several times to make sure she hit the down instead of the up button. Ten seconds later, although to Patricia it might as well have been an hour and a half, the doors opened. She stumbled into the elevator, looked for G, hit the button. She leaned forward, rested her head where the doors met, which meant that when they opened on the ground floor a few seconds later, she fell into the lobby.

No one was there to see it. But that didn't mean there was nobody in the lobby. There was a *body*.

In her semidelirious state, Patricia thought she recognized Mrs Gwynn from 3B facedown in a puddle of her own vomit.

Patricia managed to cross the lobby and get outside. She had one of the best parking spots. First one past those designated for the handicapped.

I deserve one of those today, Patricia thought.

She pointed her key in the direction of her Hyundai, pressed a button. The trunk swung open. *Oops.* Pressed another button as she reached the driver's side, got in, fumbled about getting the key into the ignition. Once she had the engine running, she took a moment to steel herself, rested her head momentarily on the top of the steering wheel.

And asked herself, *Where am I going?*

The hospital. Yes! The hospital. What a perfectly splendid idea.

She turned around to see her way out of the spot, but the upraised trunk lid blocked her view. Not a problem. She hit the gas, driving the back end of her car into a Volvo owned by Mr Lewis, a retired Social Security employee who happened to live three doors down from her.

A headlight shattered, but Patricia did not hear it.

She put the car into drive and sped out of the apartment building parking lot, the Hyundai veering sharply left and right as she oversteered in the manner of someone who'd had far too much to drink, or was texting.

The car was quickly doing sixty miles per hour

in a thirty zone, and what Patricia was unaware of was that she was heading not in the direction of the hospital, which, ironically, was only half a mile from her home, but toward the Weston Street Branch of the Promise Falls Library system.

The last thing she was thinking about, before her mind went blank and her heart stopped working, was that when they had that meeting about Internet filtering, she was going to tell those narrow-minded, puritanical assholes who wanted what anyone saw on a library computer closely monitored to go fuck themselves.

But she wouldn't get that chance, because her Hyundai had cut across three lanes, bounced over the curb at the Exxon station, and driven straight into a self-serve pump at more than sixty miles per hour.

The explosion was heard up to two miles away.

Now that he was working as a publicist and campaign manager for Randall Finley, owner of Finley Springs Water as well as the former mayor of Promise Falls on the comeback trail, David Harwood was bringing home free cases of bottled water every day. The stuff was coming into the house faster than he – and the others under his roof – could consume it.

David's son, Ethan, drank mostly milk anyway, but David was tossing a bottle a day into the lunch Ethan took to school. With his parents, who were living with him and Ethan until the rebuilding of .

their kitchen was finished, it was a mixed bag. David's mother, Arlene, was drinking the stuff at every opportunity, forgoing the water that came out of the tap. It was her way of showing support for David in his new job, even if she hadn't been very happy at first that he was working for Finley, a man whose predilection, at least once a few years back, for underage prostitutes had tarnished her opinion of him.

David's father, Don, however, did not share his wife's contempt for the former mayor. As the ex-mayor himself had said to David, and Don could not have agreed more, if everyone in the world refused to work for assholes, there'd be almost total unemployment, and there were a lot bigger assholes out there than Finley. Don's enthusiasm for Finley, however, did not extend to his product. Don viewed bottled water as the ultimate rip-off. The very idea of paying for what came out of the tap for next to nothing was ridiculous to him.

Not that David disagreed.

'They've already got us paying for TV when it was free when I was a kid,' Don railed. 'And they've got these deluxe radio stations you have to subscribe to. Good ol' AM radio's good enough for me. Christ, what next? They gonna put in a coin slot on our upstairs toilet?'

When David came downstairs and opened the refrigerator, he found more space than he was expecting. 'You're really guzzling these down,' he said to his mother, who was already there fixing breakfast for Don. David swore they must get up at three in the morning. He'd never managed to beat them downstairs.

'I'm using them to make the coffee,' she said.

Don, his finger looped into the handle of his mug, looked up from the tablet he was struggling to read the news on. 'You what?'

Arlene shot him a look. 'Nothing.'

'You made this with that bottled stuff?'

'I'm just trying to use it up.'

He pushed the mug toward the center of the table. 'I'm not drinking this.'

Arlene turned, put one hand on her hip. 'Is that so?'

'That's so,' he said.

'I didn't hear you complaining about the taste.'

'That's not the point,' he said.

Arlene pointed to the coffeemaker. 'Well, you're more than welcome to pour that out and make yourself another pot.'

Don Harwood blinked. 'I never make the coffee. You always make the coffee. I always measure it out wrong.'

'Well, today's a good day to learn.'

They stared at each other for several seconds before Don retrieved the cup and said, 'Fine. But I want to go on record that I'm opposed.'

'I'll send CNN a tweet,' his wife said.

'I swear,' David said.

'You better not,' Arlene said. 'What do you have

34

going on today with our God-help-us possible future mayor?'

'Not much,' David said. 'Looks like it's going to be a quiet day.'

His father's head went up suddenly, like he was a deer listening for an approaching hunter. 'Do you hear that? Must be a helluva fire somewhere. Been hearing those sirens all morning.'

Those sirens woke Victor Rooney.

It was a few minutes past eight when he opened his eyes. Looked at the clock radio next to his bed, the half-empty bottle of beer positioned next to it. He'd slept well, considering everything, and didn't feel all that bad now, even though he hadn't fallen into bed until almost two in the morning. But once his head hit the pillow, he was out.

He reached out from under the covers to turn on the radio, maybe catch the news. But the Albany station had finished with the eight o'clock newscast and was now on to music. Springsteen. 'Streets of Philadelphia.' That seemed kind of appropriate for a Memorial Day Saturday. On a weekend that celebrated the men and women who had died fighting for their country, a song about the city where the Declaration of Independence had been signed.

Fitting.

Victor had always liked Springsteen, but hearing the song saddened him. He and Olivia had talked once about going to one of his concerts.

Olivia had loved music.

She hadn't been quite as crazy about Bruce as he was, but she did have her favorites, especially those from the sixties and the seventies. Simon and Garfunkel. Creedence Clearwater Revival. The Beatles, it went without saying. One time, she'd started singing 'Happy Together' and he'd asked her who the hell'd done that. The Turtles, she'd told him.

'You're shittin' me,' he'd said. 'There was actually a band called Turtles?'

'*The* Turtles,' she'd corrected him. 'Like *the* Beatles. No one says just *Beatles*. And if you could name a band after what sounded like bugs, why not turtles?'

'So happy together,' he said, pulling her into him as they walked through the grounds of Thackeray College. This was back when she was still a student there.

The better part of a year before it happened.

Three years ago this week.

The sirens wailed.

Victor lay there, very still, listening. One of them sounded like it was coming from the east side of the city, the other from the north. Police cars, or ambulances, most likely. Didn't sound like fire trucks. They had those deeper, throatier sirens. Lots of bass.

If they were ambulances, they were probably headed to PFG.

Busy morning out there on the streets of Promise Falls.

What, oh, what could be happening?

He wasn't hungover, which was so often the case. A relatively clear head this morning. He hadn't been out drinking the night before, but he did feel like rewarding himself with a beer when he got home.

Quietly, he'd opened the fridge and taken out a bottle of Bud. He hadn't wanted to wake his land-lady, Emily Townsend. She'd hung on to this house after her husband's death, and rented a room upstairs to him. He'd taken the bottle with him, downed half of it going up the stairs. He'd fallen asleep too quickly to finish it off.

And now it would be warm.

Victor reached for it anyway and took a swig, made a face, put the bottle back on the bedside table but too close to the edge. It hit the floor, spilling beer onto Victor's socks and the throw rug.

'Oh, shit,' he said, grabbing the bottle before it emptied completely.

He swung his feet out from under the covers and, careful not to step in the beer, stood up alongside the bed. He was dressed in a pair of blue boxers. He opened the bedroom door, walked five steps down the hall to the bathroom, which was unoccupied, and grabbed a towel off one of the racks.

Victor Rooney paused at the top of the stairs.

There was the smell of freshly brewed coffee, but the house was unusually quiet. Emily was an early riser, and she put the coffee on first thing.

She drank at least twenty cups a day, had a pot going almost all the time.

Victor did not hear her stirring in the kitchen or anywhere else in the house.

'Emily?' he called out.

When no one called back, he returned to his room, dropped the bath towel on the floor where the beer had spilled, and tamped it down with his bare foot. Put all his weight on it at one point. When he'd blotted up all the beer he believed was possible, he took the damp towel and placed it in a hamper at the bottom of the hallway linen closet.

Back in his room, he pulled on his jeans, and found a fresh pair of socks and a T-shirt in his dresser.

He descended the stairs in his sock feet.

Emily Townsend was not in the kitchen.

Victor noticed that there was an inch of coffee in the bottom of the pot, but he decided against coffee today. He went to the refrigerator and pondered whether eight fifteen was too early for a Bud.

Perhaps.

Sirens continued to wail.

He took out a container of Minute Maid orange juice and poured himself a glass. Drank it down in one gulp.

Pondered breakfast.

Most days he had cereal. But if Emily was making bacon and eggs or pancakes or French toast – anything that required more effort – he was always quick to get in on that. But it did not appear that his landlady was going to any extra trouble today.

'Emily?' he called out again.

There was a door off the kitchen that led to the backyard. Two if one counted the screen door. The inner door was ajar, which led Victor to think perhaps Emily had gone outside.

Victor refilled his glass with orange juice, then swung the door farther open, took a look at the small backyard through the glass of the screen door.

Well, *there* was Emily.

Face-planted on the driveway, about ten feet away from her cute little blue Toyota, car keys in one hand. She'd probably been carrying her purse with the other, but it was at the edge of the drive, where, presumably, she had dropped it. Her wallet and the small case in which she carried her reading glasses had tumbled out.

She was not moving. From where Victor stood, he couldn't even see her back rising and falling ever so gently, an indication that she might still be alive.

He put his juice glass on the counter and decided maybe it would be a good idea to go outside and take a closer look.

CHAPTER 3

Duckworth

I have a routine for getting on the scale in the morning.

First of all, I have to be in the bathroom alone. If Maureen's in there and sees me step on the scale, she'll peer around and take a peek, say something like, 'How's it coming?'

Of course, if it were coming along well, I wouldn't mind her sneaking a look, but the odds are it won't be going well at all.

Second, I have to be naked. If I have so much as a towel wrapped around me, once I've seen the readout on the scale, I'll tell myself I should allow five pounds for the towel. It is, after all, a thick one.

I can't have had anything to eat, either. On rare occasions, I'll have some breakfast before attending to my morning ablutions. Those days, I do not bother to weigh myself.

Once those three conditions have been met, I'm ready to actually step on the scale.

This must be done very slowly. If I pounce on

the thing, I fear the needle will shoot up too quickly and stick there. Maureen will wander in later and ask if I'm really 320 pounds.

I am not.

But if I'm being honest with you, I'm at 276. Okay, that's not exactly true. It's more like 280.

Anyway, I put one hand on the towel rack as I step on, not just to balance myself, but to give the scale a chance to prepare for what's coming. Once I've got both feet planted firmly on it, I carefully release my grip on the bar.

And face the music.

Maureen, in the kindest, most supportive way, has been trying to get me to lose a few pounds. She hasn't expressed the slightest disapproval about how I look. She claims to love me as much as ever. That I'm still the sexiest man she's ever known.

I'm grateful for her lies.

But she says more fruit and vegetables and grains, and fewer donuts and ice cream and pie, might be good for me.

She doesn't know the half of it.

I've been to the doctor. Our regular GP, Clara Moorehouse. Dr Moorehouse says I am borderline diabetic. That my blood pressure is dangerously high. That I am carrying extra weight in the worst place a man can – on my gut.

It really hit home for me the other day, at the drive-in. A woman who served over in Iraq as a bomb deactivator was helping us out, trying to

41

figure out how the explosive charges had been rigged to bring the screen down, and it was all I could do to keep up with her as she moved about the rubble like a mountain goat scaling a cliffside.

I was out of breath. My heart was pounding.

Which I told Dr Moorehouse yesterday.

'You have to make a decision,' she told me. 'No one can make it for you.'

'I know,' I said.

'Do you know why you do it?' she asked.

'I like to eat,' I said. 'And I've been under a lot of stress lately.'

That made her smile. 'Lately?' she said, looking at me. 'Did this just happen in the last week or so?'

She had me there.

The truth was, I *had* been under a lot of stress lately. Not that it had anything to do with what I was or was not eating. But in the twenty years I'd worked for the Promise Falls police – the anniversary had slipped by this month largely unnoticed – I had never had a month like this one.

It had started with the horrific murder of Rosemary Gaynor. And then there were some strange goings-on around town. Everything from dead squirrels and a Ferris wheel coming to life all on its own to a college predator and a flaming bus.

As if all that weren't enough, that bombed drive-in.

And then there was Randall Finley, the son of a bitch.

He was running for mayor again and looking for

whatever dirt he could get on anybody. The current mayor, the chief of police, *anybody*. I'd learned that he'd gone so far as to blackmail our son, Trevor, who was driving a truck for Finley's bottled water company, into telling him things Trevor might have heard me talking about around the house.

I wanted to kill the asshole.

Maybe, I told myself, I'd be better equipped to deal with all this bullshit if I weren't lugging so much weight around.

Today had to be the day.

After I'd weighed myself, I shaved. I don't always bother on a Saturday, but I decided to make an effort. Either my blade was too dull or the shaving cream too loaded with menthol, because my cheeks and neck felt like they'd been set ablaze. I patted my cheeks thoroughly with a towel, which helped. I dug an oversized red T-shirt out of one drawer, and some old purple sweatpants I hadn't worn in years out of another. Then I went into the closet for my running shoes. When Maureen came upstairs and into the room and saw me, she said, 'What's going on? You look like a down-on-his-luck superhero.'

'I'm going to do a walk this morning,' I said. 'A mile or two. I don't have to go in this morning. I'm taking a day.'

I needed a month.

'I just put on the coffee,' Maureen said.

'I'll have some when I get back. And don't bother

making me any breakfast. I'll just have a banana or something.'

She eyed me slyly. 'You can't do it this way.'

'Can't do what?'

'I mean, the walk, that's a good idea. Go. But you have to eat more than a banana for breakfast. You have nothing more than that and by ten you'll be inhaling six Egg McMuffins. I can help you with this. I can—'

'I know what I'm doing,' I said.

'Okay, okay, but if you try to do too much too fast, you'll get discouraged. You have to do these things gradually.'

'I don't have time to do them gradually,' I said. I hadn't meant to say that.

'What do you mean?' Maureen asked.

'I'm just saying, I need to make a change. I might as well do it.'

'What happened between yesterday and today?'

'Nothing.'

'No, something's happened.'

Maureen had acquired over the years, as if by osmosis, some of my skill at spotting a lie when it was being told.

'I said, nothing.' I looked away.

'Did you go see Dr Moorehouse?'

'Did I what?' God, I was terrible at this.

'What did she say?'

I hesitated. 'Not a lot. Just, you know, a few things.'

'Why did you go see her? What prompted it?'

'I . . . the other day, I felt – I was a little, you know, short of breath. At the drive-in. Climbing over stuff.' Also, recently, at Burger King, but I did not see the point in mentioning that particular incident.

'Okay,' Maureen said slowly.

'And she said that maybe I might want to start thinking about maybe considering some slight changes to, you know, my lifestyle, as such.'

'As such,' Maureen repeated.

'Yeah.' I shrugged. 'So, that's what I'm doing.'

Maureen nodded slowly. 'Okay. Terrific.' She surveyed me, head to toe. 'But you're not going out like that.'

'Like what?'

'Those pants. Dear God, you look like you were shot and left to die in a vat of grapes.'

I looked down. 'They are a bit purple.'

'There must be something else. Let me look.' She brushed past me and went into the closet. I could hear her moving clothes back and forth on the racks. 'What about – no, not that. Maybe—'

My cell phone rang. It was plugged in next to the bed, still charging. I went over, saw who was calling, detached the cord, and put the phone to my ear.

'Duckworth.'

'Carlson.'

Angus Carlson. Our new detective, bumped up from uniform because we were shorthanded. As I recalled, he was working today.

'Yeah,' I said.

Maureen stepped out of the closet, a pair of gray sweats in her hand. How could I have missed those?

'You need to come in,' Carlson said. 'Everybody and his dog is getting dragged in here.'

'What's going on?' I asked.

'The end of the world,' Carlson said. 'More or less.'

CHAPTER 4

Whenever David Harwood dismissed something his father heard, he regretted it later. If Don heard an odd rattle under the hood of David's car, he got it checked out. That time, years ago, when David was just a kid, and Don heard something in the ceiling no one else had noticed, it turned out they had raccoons in the attic.

So when Don said he'd been hearing a lot of sirens, David walked out of the kitchen, through the living room, and out onto the front step of the house.

There was, in the distance, not just a siren but a chorus of sirens. At least two, maybe three. Maybe even more than three.

He scanned above the trees, looking for smoke, but they soared too high in his older part of town for him to see very far. But something was up. Even though David no longer worked for a newspaper, he still had a reporter's instincts. He had to know what was going on.

He ran back into the house, grabbed his car keys from the hall table. Arlene spotted him, asked, 'Where you off to?'

'Out,' he said.

Before he dropped into the seat of his Mazda, he stood and listened, trying to pinpoint just where the sirens were coming from. One sounded as though it was off to the east, but another seemed to be coming from the west.

Did that make any sense? If there'd been a major accident, wouldn't all the sirens be coming from one place? Had two or more accidents happened almost simultaneously in different parts of the town? But then again, ambulances could be on their way to a single scene, approaching from disparate locations.

Didn't matter, he decided. If what he was hearing was, in fact, ambulances, they'd all be headed to the same place: Promise Falls General.

That's where he would go.

He did a quick glance up and down the street before he started backing the car out of the driveway. He had the rear wheels on the street when he heard a blaring horn. A blue van, coming out of nowhere, swerved, tires squealing, and went screaming past at, David guessed, nearly seventy miles per hour on a residential street where the limit was thirty.

The van was headed the same way David was going. It made a fast left turn at the next intersection, nearly going around on two wheels.

David tromped on the accelerator. As he was coming out of the neighborhood, the hospital a couple of miles ahead of him, he saw smoke.

Rounding another corner, he saw three fire engines and flashing lights at the Exxon station, which was ablaze, the charred remains of a car visible straddling the island where the pumps stood. It looked to David as though the car had plowed straight into one of them. Was this what all the fuss was about? An explosion at the gas station?

He heard a siren approaching from behind him. He glanced in the mirror, saw an ambulance bearing down on him. He swerved over to the curb, screeched to a halt, figuring the emergency vehicle would be stopping a safe distance from the gas station.

But it raced right past the fire.

David took chase.

As the hospital came looming into view, he saw, crammed outside the emergency entrance, at least a dozen ambulances and enough flashing lights to give someone with photosensitive epilepsy a seizure. David ditched the car along a No Parking stretch on a street that bordered the hospital, and ran.

Back in the day, he'd have had a notebook in one hand and very likely a camera in the other. In a strange way, he felt naked. But even without those tools of his trade, he still had his observational skills, and one thing immediately struck him.

It was generally accepted procedure for paramedics to bring a patient into the ER, confer with admitting staff, make sure the person they'd brought in was being looked after, before departing.

That wasn't what David was seeing.

Two paramedics from the ambulance that had passed him moments earlier were pulling out a woman on a stretcher, taking a few seconds to tell a doctor standing at the back of the vehicle what was wrong with her, then jumping back into the ambulance and taking off, tires squealing, siren engaged.

David ran past the cluster of ambulances into the emergency ward.

Bedlam.

All seats were taken, half with people waiting to be seen, the others occupied by desperately worried family members. There were moans, people crying, others shouting for help.

A man in his sixties struggled to stand and vomited on the floor in front of him. Several seats to the left of him, a woman in her thirties who'd been breathing rapidly suddenly stopped. A man with his arm around her screamed, 'Help! Help!'

In addition to paramedics and hospital staff, there were uniformed police pitching in, but David could see a kind of helplessness in their eyes, as though they were overwhelmed and didn't know what to do.

He spotted a woman with a child no more than six who was doubled over in pain. 'What's happened?' he asked.

The woman's eyes brightened briefly with hope. 'Are you a doctor?'

'No.'

'We need the doctor. When are we going to see

the doctor? How long do we have to wait? My girl is sick. *Look* at her!'

'What's wrong with her?' David asked.

The woman shook her head frantically, ran her words together hurriedly. 'I don't know. Kathy seemed fine, and then all of a sudden she just started feeling faint and she started breathing really fast and getting dizzy and—'

'Mommy,' Kathy whimpered, 'I think I'm going to be . . . The room is all weird.'

'How fast?' David asked.

'It was, like, out of nowhere. She's a perfectly healthy child! I've made sure she's had all her shots and—' She stopped herself, as if she'd just thought of something. She reached into her purse and came out with her phone. 'Why can't I get service in here? My husband is in New York on business and I can't—'

'Which part of town do you live in?' David asked.

'What?' she said.

'Where do you live?'

'On Clinton,' she said. 'Near the school.'

David definitely knew where that was. His girl-friend, Samantha Worthington, sent her son, Carl, to that school.

'I hope the doctor comes soon,' he said, and moved down a few seats to where a man was sitting, leaning over, elbows on knees.

'Sir?' he said.

The man looked up. His eyes were glassy and lacked focus.

'What?'

'What's your name?' David asked, thinking he recognized the man.

'Fisher,' he said, struggling to swallow. 'Walden Fisher.'

David hadn't worked on the Olivia Fisher murder case but followed it closely online while he was working at the *Boston Globe*. There'd been several pictures of the dead woman's parents, and he believed this man was Olivia's father. Not that he was going to bring up the fact.

'You need to give me something,' Fisher said. 'I think . . . I think maybe I'm gonna pass out.'

'I'm sorry. I'm not a doctor.'

'. . . throat's raw . . . throwing up . . . heart going a hundred miles an hour.'

'When did this happen?'

'. . . morning . . . breakfast. I felt okay. Had some coffee . . . started feeling funny. Stomach feels like it's doing backflips.' He gave David a desperate look. 'Why aren't you a doctor?'

'I'm just . . . not,' he said. David asked him the same thing he'd asked the mother of Kathy. 'Where do you live?'

Fisher mumbled an address, which was nowhere near where Kathy and her mother lived.

'Do you know any of these people?' he asked, pointing to all the others waiting to be seen. Maybe, he thought, they'd all been to the same fast-food restaurant the night before. Some mass case of food poisoning.

Someone collapsed onto the floor. A woman wailed.

Fisher said, 'Should I? Is it my birthday?'

David was no epidemiologist, but it wasn't stopping him from trying to figure out how all these people from all corners of Promise Falls would come down with similar symptoms at exactly the same time. Something in the air, maybe?

Had some coffee . . . started feeling funny.

Bad coffee? How could everyone in town suddenly get bad coffee? David glanced back at the sick girl.

She was too young to drink coffee. But—

David went back to the little girl's mother, who was trying again to get reception for her phone. 'What did she have for breakfast this morning?'

The woman, who was busily scratching her hand, looked up, tears in her eyes. 'What?'

'What did Kathy have?'

'Nothing. She never eats breakfast. I try to get her to eat something, but she won't.'

'Nothing to drink?'

The woman's eyes danced. 'Orange juice.'

David hadn't asked Fisher whether he'd had orange juice in addition to his coffee. Had the town's grocery stores taken in a shipment of contaminated juice? Was it like that scandal years ago when someone tampered with some headache medicine? But even if that was the case, was it likely that everyone would start drinking it at the same time?

But David still asked, 'What brand?'

'I don't . . . remember. It was frozen.'

'Frozen?'

'Concentrate. I mixed it up this morning.'

Water. Water to mix up the orange juice. Water to make the coffee.

David spun around, looked for someone in authority. There were so many nurses and doctors attending to people it was difficult to tell who was running the show. Maybe no one was.

Agnes would have been.

David thought briefly of his aunt, Agnes Pickens, who used to be in charge of this hospital, right up until she took her own life a couple of weeks earlier by jumping off Promise Falls.

Agnes, sadly, had turned out to be a pretty bad person. But right now, David conceded, this place needed her.

Someone nudged David out of the way. A man in his late twenties, pale green operating scrubs top and bottom, stethoscope around his neck. And a surgical mask over his mouth to protect him from whatever everyone in here might have.

David suddenly felt very exposed. Why hadn't it occurred to him that what everyone in this room had could be extremely contagious? God, maybe some airborne contagion had been dropped on the town that morning. Promise Falls was already on edge about a possible terrorist attack after the drive-in came crashing down earlier in the week. There'd been no real evidence so far to suggest terrorists had done it – Promise Falls, a terrorist target, *really*? – but only a few days later, this?

The man knelt down before Kathy and said, 'I'm Dr Blake. What's your name?'

Kathy, who appeared to be fading, did not answer. Her mother said, 'Kathy. Her name is Kathy. I'm her mother. What's happening? What does everyone have?'

The doctor, at least for now, ignored the question. He was looking into Kathy's eyes, then putting his stethoscope to her chest.

'Hypotension,' Dr Blake said.

'Hypertension? High blood pressure? That's ridiculous in a child her age that—'

'*Hypo*, not hyper. Low blood pressure.'

'Why?' David asked.

The doctor whirled his head around. 'I don't know,' he said.

'Could it be the water?' David asked. 'Some sort of contaminant?'

The doctor hesitated a moment, thinking, his eyes taking in the room. 'It's the best explanation I've heard so far,' he said. 'That might account for the rashes.'

'Rashes?'

'A lot of people are complaining of skin irritation.' He said to the mother, 'Bring your girl this way.'

'How many?' David asked.

'How many what?' the doctor said. Turning his head away from the child and her mother, he said, 'Sick or dead?'

David had meant sick, but whispered, 'Dead.'

'More than I can count,' he said under his breath. 'Dozens, more every minute.'

The woman scooped Kathy into her arms and followed the doctor to one of the curtained examining areas.

'Jesus,' David said, and dug into his pocket for his own phone. He wasn't surprised to see that he had no bars.

He ran out of the emergency ward, where ambulances and private cars continued to arrive with a steady stream of patients. He dialed home.

'Yes?' his mother said.

'Don't drink the water,' David told her.

'What are you talking about? I thought the bottled water was way better than the other—'

'No, from the tap! Don't drink it! It may be poisonous!'

Arlene shouted, not to David, 'Don't drink that! It's David! Don't drink that!'

David said, 'Tell me Dad hasn't had any of it.'

'He just made a new pot of coffee to make a point, the old fool.'

'Don't drink anything out of the tap. Don't even brush your teeth with it. In fact, don't even let it get on your skin. Tell Ethan! Start phoning everyone you know and tell them not to drink the water.'

'What is it? What's in the water?'

'I don't even know if I'm right,' he said, 'but right now, it's the one thing that makes sense.'

'Are you going—'

'Mom! Call people!'

He ended the call, stayed on his list of contacts, thumbed through them.

Marla Pickens. His cousin. Newly reunited with the baby she had not known she had.

Matthew.

David had a mental image of Marla making up formula for the child. He called the home number.

It rang several times. David was about to give up when someone picked up, then dropped the receiver.

'Hello?' he said.

More fumbling, then, 'Where are you?' Marla said, her voice shaking. 'I called ten minutes ago!'

'You called me?'

A half-second pause. 'David?'

'Yeah. Marla, listen, I might be wrong about this, but I think there may be something wrong with the—'

'I think he's dead!' she screamed.

Dear God, Matthew.

'Marla, I'll hang up. You call 911 and—'

'I called ages ago! No one's showed up! I can't wake him up!'

Why couldn't David's uncle Gill just drive Matthew to the hospital? 'Get your dad to drive Matthew to the hospital! Don't wait for the—'

'It's not Matthew! It's Dad!'

Just then, as if on cue, David could hear a baby crying in the background. He felt an overwhelming sense of helplessness. Judging by what he'd just seen in the hospital, if Gill looked dead to Marla, he probably was. David didn't know what he could do for Gill if he were there, but he could at least give Marla, who'd already been through so much this month, some support. And along the way, stay on the phone and tell anyone else he could think of that they should not—

Sam.

Samantha Worthington and Carl. He had to warn them. It was barely nine o'clock on a Saturday morning and chances were they weren't yet up. He hadn't talked to Sam in a couple of days, but had been intending to phone her today, see if she wanted to get together that evening. David had been thinking maybe he could even find a way to get her son to have a sleepover at his house with Ethan. He'd planned to push his mother into the role of babysitter, which would allow him to have an even better sleepover with Sam at her place.

That, however, was no longer the priority.

David said to Marla, 'Keep calling 911. I'm on my way. And whatever you do, don't drink the water. It's—'

He thought he'd heard a click. 'Marla?'

She'd gotten off the line.

Fine. He had to call Sam. David brought up her number, tapped it. She had no landline, but her cell was usually close at hand.

The phone rang.

And rang.

By the fourth ring, David was starting to panic. Suppose she and her son had risen early? Suppose they'd both had water from the tap?

Six rings.

Seven.

He ended the call, opting for a text instead.

He typed: CALL ME!

Waited for a response, for those three little dots to indicate Sam was composing a reply.

Nothing.

He added: DONT DRINK TAP WATER

As David ran for his car, he saw an unmarked police car wheel into the hospital lot, brakes screeching as it came to a halt.

Detective Barry Duckworth behind the wheel.

CHAPTER 5

Randall Finley had been up early, taking their dog, Bipsie, for a walk, and now sat on the edge of his wife's bed. He put a gentle hand to her forehead, which felt warm and clammy, and asked, 'How did you sleep?'

She shifted her head on the pillow to take him in, blinked her eyes so slowly, it was like watching two garage doors close and open.

'Okay,' she said weakly. 'Help me up.'

He got an arm under hers, shifted her forward slightly on the bed into a sitting position, propping pillows behind her.

'That's perfect,' she said.

'I think you look good today,' he said, sitting back down. 'Well rested.' Finley looked at the collection of pills, water bottle, reading glasses, and a Ken Follett novel big enough to chock a jetliner's tire, set down open somewhere in the middle, the spine cracked.

'Still working your way through this,' he said.

'I really like it, but every time I start, I forget what I read last, so I have to go back.' She forced a smile. 'I like it when you read to me.'

He had taken to reading her a chapter every night when he got home. 'I don't have anything on today,' he said. 'Maybe I can read a chapter this morning and another in the afternoon.'

'Okay,' she said. 'How about you? How did you sleep?'

'Oh, you know. I never sleep that good.'

'I thought I heard you up in the night. Did you go out after you left me?'

'I don't think so,' he said. 'Maybe just for a bit of air.'

Finley heard a car door close outside. 'That must be Lindsay,' he said. The home care worker Finley had hired not long after his wife became ill. In addition to tending to Jane Finley's needs, she made meals, cleaned the house, ran errands.

'Isn't this the holiday?' Jane asked.

Finley nodded.

'You should have given her the weekend off.'

Finley shrugged. 'Well, you never know. Something might come up. They might need me at the plant. If I have to take off in a hurry, she's here for you.'

Jane pressed her tongue to the roof of her mouth, pulled it away, making a soft clicking noise. 'My mouth is so dry.'

He reached for the half-empty bottle of Finley Springs water on the bedside table, uncapped it. He held it to her mouth, tipped it far enough to give her a few drops.

'That's good,' Jane said. 'So, no campaigning today?'

'I'm not sure. So many people are away, gone to their cottages, or working on their gardens, doing spring cleaning. I don't think anyone's going to pay much attention to a gasbag like me today.'

She reached out a weak hand and touched his arm. 'Stop that.'

Finley smiled. 'I know what I am, sweetheart. And I'm good at it.'

That made her laugh, but the chuckle then sent her into a coughing fit. Finley got a hand behind her back and leaned her forward until she was done.

'You done?' he said, easing her back.

'I think so. A bit of water went down the wrong way when I laughed.'

'I'll try not to be so hilarious,' he said.

'The thing is,' Jane said, 'you're not the gasbag you once were.' Another small smile. 'You're a better man than you used to be.'

He sighed. 'I don't know about that.'

'I thought I heard something, just as I was waking up. Sirens?'

'I was in the shower, and I had the radio on in the bathroom,' Finley said. 'I didn't hear—'

He cut himself off, listened. 'I think I hear one now.'

'Just so long as they're not coming for me,' she said.

Finley patted his wife's hand, stood. 'I'm going to go down and see Lindsay.'

'Would you ask her to make me some lemonade?'

'Of course. But you're going to have some break-fast, aren't you?'

'I'm not very hungry.'

'You need to eat.'

Jane's eyes misted, and with all the strength she had, she gripped his hand and squeezed. 'What's the point?'

'Don't say that.'

'It's only a matter of time.'

'That's not true. If you keep your strength up, no one can say how long . . . you know.'

She released his hand, dropped hers down to the comforter. 'You want me to hang in long enough to see you redeem yourself.'

'That's ridiculous,' Finley said, frowning. 'I want you to hang in, period.'

'You've already redeemed yourself in my eyes.' A pause. 'Although I might need those glasses.'

That brought Finley's smile back.

'I'll be back up in a little while, read to you,' he said.

'Morning,' Lindsay, a wiry woman in her late sixties, said to Finley as he came into the kitchen.

'Hi,' he said.

'How's Jane doing this morning?'

'Tired. But fine. She'd love some lemonade.'

'About to make up a new pitcher. Think she's up to any breakfast?'

'She says no, but I think you should take her up something, anyway. Maybe a poached egg? On toast?'

63

'I can do that. How about yourself?'

He thought a moment. 'I guess I could be talked into the same. But make it two eggs.'

'Coffee?'

He nodded.

Lindsay grabbed an oversized measuring cup from the cabinet and filled it from the Finley Springs cooler in the corner of the kitchen. She poured it into the coffeemaker, added a filter and some ground coffee, and hit the button.

'Don't know what's happenin' out there today,' she said.

'Hmm?' he said, reading messages on his phone.

'Must have seen five ambulances on the way into Promise Falls today.' Lindsay lived out in the country, about five miles outside the town.

Finley slowly looked up from his phone.

'How many did you say?'

'Five, six, seven. I kind of lost count.'

Finley looked at his watch. 'All in the last half hour or so?'

'Well,' she said, going into the refrigerator for eggs, 'that's when I was coming in.'

Finley went back to his phone, brought up David Harwood's number. It rang several times before he picked up.

'Yeah?' David snapped. Finley could hear a car engine in the background.

'David, it's—'

'I know who it is. Don't have time to talk, Randy.'

'I need you to check something for me. Lindsay says—'

'Lindsay?'

'You haven't met her. She's our—'

'I'm hanging up, Randy. All hell's breaking loose and—'

'That's why I'm calling. Lindsay says there are ambulances all—'

'Go to the hospital and see for yourself.'

'What's happened?'

When there was no reply, Finley realized that David had already ended the call.

'Don't worry about those eggs for me,' Finley said to Lindsay. 'And would you be good enough to tell Jane that I had to head out? I think something's come up.'

CHAPTER 6

Duckworth

It was the kind of scene one might expect to find if a jet had crashed outside of town. Except there was no jet, and the people waiting for treatment were not suffering from cuts and bruises and severed limbs.

But that didn't make things any less chaotic.

I didn't need long to take in the scene. Dozens of patients in various stages of distress. Some, on the floor, were clearly already deceased. People vomiting, writhing, scratching their arms and legs. Children crying, parents shouting for help.

The doctors and nurses were going flat out. I hated to stop anyone in the midst of treating all these cases, but I needed to get a sense of what was going on, and fast.

I pulled out my police ID long enough to get someone's attention, but then I spotted someone whose eyes and glasses I thought I recognized above the surgical mask. After all, I'd seen her only yesterday.

'Dr Moorehouse?' I said.

Hair was hanging down over her eyes and those brown-framed glasses were askew. She was looking off in another direction, moving past me.

'Clara!' I said.

She stopped, turned. 'Barry.'

Even with the lower half of her face covered, she managed to look terrified, and professional, at the same time.

'Give it to me fast,' I said. 'What are we dealing with?'

'Similar symptoms across the board. Nausea, headache, vomiting, severe drop in blood pressure. It escalates. Seizure, cardiorespiratory arrest. Hypotension. On top of all that, some patients are scratching their skin off.'

'Food poisoning?'

'I don't think so. I mean, not food. But something ingested. Something they've come in contact with.'

'All at once? From all over the town?'

Clara looked me in the eye. 'Not just all over town. All over this hospital. We've got current patients on every floor with the same symptoms. Started happening first thing this morning.'

'How can that be? What spreads that fast?'

'I'd look at the water.'

'The town water supply?'

She nodded. 'Something got into the drinking water. Fuel spill, maybe. Chemical spill. Something like that.'

I asked, 'What can you do for them?'

Her lips were set firmly before she spoke. 'Right now, it appears absolutely nothing.'

'How many?'

'They're stacking up like planes over the airport. Dozens dead. We're likely going to be in the hundreds soon. I have to go, Barry. Get the word out. Fast as you can.'

'Have you seen Amanda?' I asked. Amanda Croydon, Promise Falls' current mayor.

'No,' Clara said. 'I *have* to go.'

I let her.

As I turned around, someone familiar bumped into me.

'Carlson,' I said.

'Shit, sorry,' Angus Carlson said. 'When did you get here?'

'Just now. What do you know?'

He consulted a small notebook in his right hand. 'No one was getting sick last night. Earliest anyone started feeling ill was around six this morning. Symptoms pretty much the same across the board. Dizzy, sick to stomach, shallow but rapid breathing.'

'It could be the water,' I told him.

'Yeah,' he said, his voice shaky. 'Common element seems to be the drinking water from the tap. Even if it was boiled, like for tea. Seems like it's hitting older people more, but that may just be because older people get up earlier.'

That made sense. I noticed Carlson's trademark black humor wasn't in operation this morning. No sick jokes today. The man was clearly shaken. It was fair to say neither of us had ever seen anything like this.

The water. I had to call Maureen.

'You called those close to you?' I asked. 'In case they haven't heard?'

He nodded. 'I called my wife, told her.'

'What about your mother?' I'd overheard him, at the station, talking to her on the phone.

'Yes, yes, I called her, too,' he said. 'Everyone's on high alert.'

I looked beyond Carlson, saw yet another person I knew, but this wasn't a doctor or one of the staff. It was Walden Fisher sitting in one of the ER waiting room chairs, nervously chewing a fingernail.

'Ah, shit,' I said.

'What?' Carlson asked, glancing over his shoulder.

'Walden Fisher.'

'Fisher?' Carlson said with, I thought, some recognition.

'Like he hasn't been through enough. You remember the Olivia Fisher murder.'

'Of course.'

'That was his daughter. And his wife passed away pretty recently. I'm gonna talk to him. Keep asking around, find out anything else you can.'

I broke away, expecting to approach Fisher on my own, but Carlson chose to follow me.

'Mr Fisher,' I said.

He looked up, blinked a couple of times, and seemed to be searching my eyes, as though trying to place me. 'Detective . . .'

'Duckworth,' I said, helping him. 'And this is Detective Carlson.'

'Mr Fisher,' Angus Carlson said, nodding respectfully. 'How are you managing?'

Fisher's eyes moved slowly to Angus. 'How am I managing? I feel like I'm goddamn well dying, that's how I'm managing.'

'What happened?' I asked.

He shook his head slowly, more a gesture of bewilderment than a negative. 'I don't know. They found me throwing up in the middle of the street – nearly got run over by an ambulance. They brought me here. I'd had some coffee and then started feeling weird. Why are we all sick? What's happening?'

'Everyone's trying to find out,' I said. 'Has a doctor seen you?'

'No. I've been sitting here forever.' He laid a hand on his chest. 'My heart's been going like crazy. Feel.' He reached out, took my wrist, placed my palm on his chest, and held it there. Despite his condition, his grip was surprisingly strong. I felt flannel under my fingertips, and an erratic thumping. I didn't exactly have a medical degree, but what I was feeling didn't feel good.

'Whaddya think?' he asked me.

I didn't know. If I dragged someone over here to check him out, I'd just be taking a doctor from another patient who might need more immediate attention, and as bad as Walden Fisher was, there looked to be other people in the ER who were in

70

worse shape. I rested a hand on his shoulder momentarily and said, 'They're seeing people as fast as they can.'

Good ol' Barry Duckworth. Always knows just what to say. Turned out Carlson was better at this than I was.

He went down on one knee so he was at eye level with Fisher and said, 'I just wanted to say, I was in uniform back when your daughter, Olivia, was taken so cruelly.'

Walden Fisher's sick eyes widened slightly.

'So I wasn't actively involved in the investigation, but I followed it closely, and it's a terrible thing that no one has yet been brought to justice for that crime.'

'Um . . . yes,' Walden said.

'I just . . . I just wanted to say I'm sorry for your loss.' Carlson glanced awkwardly my way, as if hoping I'd rescue him from a conversation he was now thinking he shouldn't have gotten into. He stood, gave a nod first to Fisher and then me. 'I'll let you know if I hear anything,' he said, then struck off in the pursuit of more information.

This wasn't the same Angus Carlson I'd encountered earlier in the month. The one who couldn't stop making corny jokes about dead squirrels. Maybe a move up the ranks, even temporarily, was actually making the man less of a jerk, because that was how he'd impressed me initially.

We'd see.

I got out my phone, saw I had no signal. It had

been my experience that you could get a signal in most parts of the hospital, but not in the ER, where you needed one the most. Rather than go back outside, I went into the nursing station and found a landline. One of the nurses looked at me, but gave me a permissive nod when I flashed my badge. As if she had time to worry about me.

I needed to call Rhonda Finderman, the Promise Falls police chief. But sometimes the personal trumps the professional. I dialed home.

'Hello?' Maureen said. She must have been alarmed, seeing the hospital show up on her caller ID.

'It's me,' I said.

'Are you okay?'

'Yes. Listen. Have you had any water from the tap today?'

A pause. 'I was just making myself some tea.'

'Don't. There may be something in the water supply making people sick. Call Trevor and warn him. Then start going up and down the street. Wake people up if you have to.'

'Is it bad?'

'It's bad.'

'I'm on it,' she said.

'Wait,' I said. 'Run some water from the tap, see if it's giving off a whiff of anything. But don't put your hand in it.' If there was, as my doctor had speculated, diesel fuel in the water, it would surely give off a smell.

'Hang on.'

Maureen was gone about fifteen seconds. Then, 'Nothing. Ran it a good thirty seconds and nothing.'

'Okay. Now start—'

'I'm gone,' she said, and hung up.

I loved her so much.

Now I could make the call to my boss. I had her office, home, and mobile numbers in my cell. I dug it out again, brought up the numbers I had for her, and entered her cell into the landline.

Finderman wasn't very crazy about me these days. She was the subject of the comments Trevor had heard and passed along to Randall Finley, who made them public when he announced he was running for mayor again.

I'd forgiven Trevor, but not Finley.

It all found its way back to me, and Finderman was pissed. But this wasn't the day to let grudges get in the way of work.

She must have seen the hospital's name come up on her caller ID, because she answered with an alarmed 'Yes?'

'It's Duckworth,' I said. 'I'm at the hospital.'

'I'm heading there.'

'We have to get the word out. The town's drinking supply may be contaminated.'

'Ferraza's on it.' Angela Ferraza, the department's public relations person. 'She's putting out a release to TV, radio – it's on the Web.'

'Not enough,' I said. 'You need people going door-to-door. Wake everyone up. You need every fire truck with a loudspeaker going up and down

73

the streets. You need every person you can find getting on phones. The full emergency plan.'

The town had drafted one of those in the wake of September 11, but no one had thought much about it since.

'I get it,' Rhonda said. I was getting under her skin. She didn't want anyone telling her how to do her job.

'And CDC,' I said. The Centers for Disease Control and Prevention, outside of Atlanta. 'The state health department. Everyone.' I had a thought. 'Is Homeland Security still sniffing around town?'

They had parachuted in after the drive-in screen came down and killed four.

'They've cleared out. Even though the guy hired to bring it down swears he didn't do it, they think he did. Which means there could still be charges and lawsuits galore, but it's not a terrorism matter.'

I had no reason, at least not yet, to think what was happening now was terrorism. It could be an accident of some kind. A failure to treat the water properly. I remembered a case from years ago, north of the border, where a small town's water supply was contaminated with E. coli from farm runoff. The people who ran the treatment plant didn't have a clue what they were doing, and people died. But it was incompetence, not terrorism.

'You think it's a terrorist act?' Rhonda asked.

'I have no idea what it is. I need to talk to

whoever's in charge of the treatment plant. Do you know who that is?'

'No.'

'Leave it with me,' I said, and ended the call before she had a chance to hang up on me herself.

I thumbed through the contacts on my own phone, found the city hall number, and dialed it on the hospital's phone.

An almost immediate pickup. 'Hello—'

'This is Detective Duckworth. Put me through—'

'—you have reached the offices of the town of Promise Falls. We are currently closed. Our hours are—'

'Fuck.'

The recorded voice droned on. '—Monday to Friday from nine thirty a.m. to four thirty p.m. If this call is concerning a power outage, please call Promise Falls Electric at—'

I hung up. I'd been dumb enough to think that in the middle of an emergency like this, someone would be at the town hall fielding inquiries, even if the mayor was out of town. I wanted the name of whoever ran the water plant and I wanted it now. I might be able to find it by searching the town's Web site if any of the computers around here connected to the Internet, and if they didn't, I'd have to go outside and try to do it on my phone.

It occurred to me I might have a number on my phone that would put me in touch with someone who'd know off the top of his head.

I scrolled through recent incoming calls on my cell, found one from a couple of weeks earlier. I was pretty sure I had the right one. I entered the number into the hospital phone.

He picked up on the third ring.

'Hello?'

'Randy?' I said.

'Who's this?'

'Barry Duckworth.'

'Barry!' he said loudly, almost cheerfully. He knew I hated him, and yet he greeted me like an old friend, the bastard. 'What in Sam fuck is going on?'

'Who runs the water plant?'

'The what?'

'I'm wondering if it would be the same person who did the job when you were mayor. Who had it then?'

'Why don't you tell me first why you need to know?'

I could almost picture him smirking on the other end of the line. Randy always had an angle. *Sure, I'll help you, but you help me first.*

It wasn't that I didn't want to tell him what was going on. The whole world would know what was going on in very short order. I just didn't want to take the time. But it struck me that it would take less time to fill him in than argue.

I gave him the broad strokes – that the town's water might be deadly.

'Goddamn,' he said. 'Makes me glad I use

nothing but my own springwater at home. How the hell could something like that happen?'

'A name, Randy.'

'Garvey Ottman. At least, he was in charge when I ran the show. I haven't heard anything to the effect that he isn't still.'

'Know where I can reach him?'

'Tell you what,' Finley said. 'I'm already up and out. Heard all those sirens, wanted to find out what was going on. I'll try to track him down for you, get back to you the moment I find him.'

'Okay,' I said, willing, right now, to accept his assistance. 'I'm heading out there in the meantime.'

'Glad to help,' Finley said. 'I call you at this number?'

I didn't think I would be staying here that much longer. 'No,' I said. 'Call my cell.' I knew he had the number already.

'I'll get back to you ASAP.' He ended the call.

At that moment, I happened to glance at a bulletin board fixed to the wall above where I'd been using the phone.

There were nurses' schedules, hospital notices about handwashing, a photo of what looked to be several off-duty nurses grouped together at a bowling alley.

All smiling happily.

A promotional calendar from a local flower shop was pinned to the upper right corner, with boxes big enough that social events were scribbled on them. 'Book club' and 'Marta's Bday.' For today, someone had scribbled 'Bridge.'

That was when I noticed what today's date was. It was the twenty-third of May.

CHAPTER 7

Joyce Pilgrim had been thinking seriously of quitting her security job at Thackeray College only a couple of weeks ago, and now here she was, running the department.

Strange, the way things turned out.

Her number one reason for quitting was her boss: Clive Duncomb.

Where to begin?

Even before he'd put her life at risk by using her as bait to catch a campus predator, she couldn't stand the man. Mr Macho. Talking about his days with the Boston PD like he was the toughest cop that city had ever seen. Which led Joyce to wonder, *If you were such hot shit in Boston, what the hell are you doing running security for a small college in upstate New York? What did you do that you had to get out of Boston and disappear to a place like this?*

Joyce had had her suspicions, many of them focused on Duncomb's wife, Liz, who, rumor had it, was not exactly from Beacon Hill. More like the Combat Zone. Okay, so maybe it had been a few years since the Combat Zone's heyday of strip clubs and whorehouses, but just because they'd spruced up the area didn't mean there was no more prostitution. Liz had found a way – and a stable of women – to meet the demand. The supposedly incorruptible cop had been taken by her charms, and before their misdeeds caught up with them, they'd bailed on their respective lives and built new ones here in Promise Falls.

But just because people move, it doesn't make them different people.

Clive never passed up an opportunity to tell Joyce how she looked. Was she working out? Was she on a diet? Those pants sure fit nice. He'd tried to get through the door at the same moment she did, the back of a hand inadvertently touching her breast. The other numbnuts she worked with told her not to worry about it, that Clive didn't mean anything by it – that was just the way he was.

And then came the guy in the hoodie.

Attacking women on campus, dragging them into the bushes. None of the female students had been raped or beaten, but that didn't exactly put anyone at ease. The next attack, they feared, could be worse.

The assaults would *escalate*.

So rather than bring in the local cops, Duncomb decided they'd run a sting operation themselves. He persuaded Joyce to walk late at night along a wooded path, just daring the son of a bitch to show up. He tried to talk her into dressing up like a hooker – boots and fishnets, the whole nine yards

– but Joyce pointed out to him that ladies of the evening had not been their guy's victim of choice.

Fine, Duncomb said, clearly disappointed. He told her he and the rest of the security team would be watching closely, that she had nothing to worry about, which of course was total bullshit, because the guy did show up, did drag her into the bushes. The funny thing was, once he had her pinned to the ground, he'd told her she had nothing to worry about, that it was all for show, that—

And then Duncomb had burst through the bushes and put a bullet in the guy's brain.

Joyce took a leave.

She'd pretty much made up her mind not to come back. She'd have a complete nervous breakdown working for that idiot. No way she was ever working for that trigger-happy asshole again.

And then something crazy happened.

The asshole died.

Clive Duncomb was killed. Run down – deliberately, it turned out – by one of the college's professors. Details were sketchy – the whole thing was still under investigation by the Promise Falls cops – but Clive, his wife, and this English professor and his wife, who'd been killed when that drive-in came crashing down, were part of some sex club.

Well, there's a shocker.

It would have been more surprising, Joyce thought, if Duncomb *hadn't* been mixed up in something like that.

Anyway, the day after Clive had been killed, a call came from the office of the president of Thackeray College. Would Ms Pilgrim be available to come in for a private lunch?

Not really up to it, she'd said.

The president, she was told, would very much like to speak with her. They would send around a car.

And so they did. A limo. A driver in a suit and tie. Came around and opened the door for her and everything. The driver pointed out to her that between the seats were bottles of water and a choice of snacks. Peanuts, chocolate bars, mints.

For a ten-minute ride!

The president's private chef prepared lunch in a small, private dining room down the hall from his office. Filet mignon.

Joyce tried to remember whether she'd ever had filet mignon before.

He made his pitch. He wanted her to become the new chief of security.

'Not a chance,' she told him.

He told her that the college had made a serious error in judgment when it had hired Clive Duncomb. They had not done a thorough enough background check. They had been dazzled by his time on the Boston PD, had assumed a man with that kind of experience would be a perfect candidate.

'We could not have been more wrong,' the president said.

Duncomb's failure to bring the Promise Falls police into the hunt for the campus predator had created massive liability problems for Thackeray. The parents of the boy he'd shot dead, Mason Helt, were launching a multimillion-dollar suit against the school. If the police had been brought in, it was unlikely Duncomb would have been running his own sting operation.

Joyce did not mention that she herself had been wondering whether to bring a suit against the college for what Duncomb had put her through.

'You've got a clear head,' the president told her. 'You're smart, you're responsible, and I think it would be sending a strong message that someone like you—'

'A woman,' Joyce Pilgrim said.

'That someone like you was taking over.'

Joyce took a bite of her filet. 'How much?'

Once her salary had been sorted, she agreed to take the job.

On a Saturday morning, especially the Saturday morning of a long holiday weekend when the college was pretty much deserted until September, save for a few dozen students who were taking some summer courses, one would not have expected the head of security to be in her office.

But because Joyce was new to the position, she was trying to get herself up to speed. She'd been familiarizing herself with every aspect of the college. Getting to know the staff, at least those who were here. She wanted to completely revamp all the security protocols before students returned in the fall.

Plus, she was getting caught up on e-mails and phone messages. She'd barely gotten started and already she was feeling behind. She was sitting at her desk, on the computer, when the phone rang.

'Security,' Joyce said.

'This is Angela Ferraza, Promise Falls police. Who's this?'

'Joyce Pilgrim.'

'Ms Pilgrim, there's reason to believe Promise Falls' water supply may have been contaminated, constituting an emergency health hazard. You need to get word out to everyone to not drink the water.'

'What's happened?' she asked.

'No time to explain. Check our Web site later for further details. I've a million more calls to make.'

Ferraza hung up.

Joyce kept the phone to her ear, entered the extension for the college infirmary. She had her doubts anyone would even be there, but someone picked up on the third ring.

'Hello?' a woman said.

'It's Joyce Pilgrim in security. Who's this?'

'It's Mavis. How ya doin', Joyce?'

'Hey, Mavis. Didn't know if I'd find anybody there.'

'Place is deserted, but as long as there're kids here somewhere, someone's gotta be here. I'm getting a lot of reading done.'

'So you haven't had any sick kids wandering in this morning?'

'Nope. Why?'

'We got word there's something wrong with the municipal water system. Some kids might show up sick.'

'Doubt that'll happen anyway,' Mavis said.

'Why's that?'

'The college isn't on the town's water system. Town's got its own reservoir, has for years. Same source of water that feeds Thackeray Pond.'

'Just the same, in case – what do they call it, the aquifer? – in case it's something that could get into both water supplies, be aware, okay?'

'Got it.'

'I'm sending out a mass e-mail and text, putting it up on the Web.' The college had the e-mail addresses and phone numbers for all its staff and students and could send out messages to everyone in an instant.

She gave herself a mental kick for not knowing the college didn't rely on the town for water. What did she think was going on, exactly, in the pumping station at the north end of the campus?

Duh.

When Joyce got off the phone with Mavis, she sent out the mass e-mail, but not before phoning her husband, Ted, at home and telling him not to drink what came out of the tap. They had a house out in the country, and their water came from a private well. But what if the source for that well was the same as the one for the town?

Better safe than sorry.

The light on her phone had been flashing the whole time she'd been sitting here, and she figured now was a good time to get caught up on a few things.

The first two calls were job applications. Joyce made a note of their names and numbers. Clive's death, and her promotion, had left a vacancy in the ranks, and she wanted to start interviewing the following week. She might have more than one spot to fill, given that some of the existing staff made Inspector Clouseau look like Sherlock Holmes.

The third, which had come in the night before, shortly after ten, went like this:

'Oh, hello. My name is Lester Plummer, in Cleveland. Our daughter, Lorraine, is attending Thackeray and has opted to stay to take a couple of summer courses, and . . .'

His voice faltered. He cleared his throat and continued. 'Lorraine is taking two courses, and staying in residence, and the thing is . . . I'd like you to call me the moment you receive this. Please.' He provided a number and hung up.

Lorraine Plummer. Joyce recognized the name immediately. She was one of the three students who'd been attacked by Mason Helt. Joyce had spoken to her after the incident, before Clive had come up with his plan to catch the guy. While the young woman was shaken up by the incident, it hadn't traumatized her to the point that she wanted to go home.

Maybe that had changed.

Joyce entered the student's name into the computer. She was, as her father had said, still at school. She'd kept her room in Albany House, one of several residential buildings scattered across the campus and, like all the others, close to empty. Joyce was betting Lorraine didn't have to worry about late-night parties keeping her up, or having to wait to use any of the shared showering facilities.

Maybe the fallout from being attacked was only hitting Lorraine now. Maybe living in a nearly deserted dorm was freaking her out. Maybe her parents were calling to see if she could be moved. Or maybe they were looking to sue the college, and this was an exploratory call to pry incriminating details from Joyce.

She wondered whether the Plummer family was looking to blame her for things that were clearly, to her mind, her dead predecessor's fault.

Only one way to find out.

Joyce returned the call. Someone picked up on the first ring.

'Hello?' A woman.

'It's Joyce Pilgrim, Thackeray College security. A Lester Plummer left a message last night?'

'My husband. Lester! It's the college!' A few seconds later, Joyce could detect an extension being picked up.

'I'm on,' he said. 'Who'm I talking to?'

Joyce told him. 'What can I help you with?'

'We haven't heard from Lorraine,' the man said. 'She—'

His wife cut in. 'This is Alma. I'm Lorraine's mother. We usually talk to her once a week or so. We called her Thursday night and didn't get her, and left a message on her cell, but she didn't call us back yesterday so—'

The husband: 'It's not like her not to call. But we thought, maybe she just didn't get around to it, or maybe—'

Maybe there was a boyfriend, Joyce thought.

'But we tried again last night,' Alma said, 'and we still couldn't get her, and there are hardly any of her friends around to get to check in on her and—'

'Why don't I pop by and tell her you're worried about her?' Joyce offered.

'No!' the mother said. 'I mean, yes, check in on her, but don't tell her we asked you to.'

'She'd be so embarrassed,' Lester Plummer said.

'But could you call us back after you see her? Would you be able to do that?'

'Of course,' Joyce said. 'I'll be in touch.'

She hung up and decided she might as well stroll over to Albany House now. As she came out of the admin building, she could hear sirens off in the distance, somewhere downtown.

It was a funny thing about Thackeray. It butted right up against Promise Falls, but was its own

88

community. A small town of its own, with its own president and governing body, its own set of rules and bylaws.

Even its own water supply, as it turned out. Which, today, from what Joyce had gathered during her short chat with Angela Ferraza, was a good thing.

She didn't bother taking a car to get to Albany House. It was only a five-minute walk. She entered the residence, headed for the stairs. Joyce was still thinking the reason Lorraine's family might not have heard from her was a boyfriend. When they said students went off to university for an education, well, that was definitely understating it. This was the time most young people lived on their own for the first time, when they didn't have their parents snooping on them.

No one waited up for you when you went to college.

When she came out of the stairwell at the second floor, it hit her right away.

The smell.

'Jesus,' she said aloud.

It got much stronger as she headed down the hall, and by the time she reached the door of Lorraine Plummer's room, she had pulled her jacket over the lower half of her face.

She banged on the door. 'Lorraine? Lorraine Plummer? It's security! Joyce Pilgrim. We spoke a couple of weeks ago.'

No reply.

'No no no no,' Joyce whispered to herself, and reached into her pocket for the collection of keys designed to get her into any room on the entire campus.

As she looked down to insert the key into the lock, she saw, peeking out from under the bottom of the door, the edge of a puddle of something dark, almost oil-like.

Joyce turned the key and pushed the door open.

It took everything she had not to scream. Screaming, she told herself, was not becoming of a security chief.

Shouldn't have come back. Shouldn't have come back.

CHAPTER 8

David hit the brakes hard out front of the Pickens home, leaving a short strip of rubber on the street. He got out of the car and ran to the front door, not bothering to knock or ring the bell.

'Marla!' he shouted.

'David!' she called back. He followed her voice to the kitchen, but he didn't immediately see her. Matthew was strapped into his high chair over by the table, twisting himself around to try to see what was going on.

David came around the island, which had blocked his view of Gill Pickens, as well as Marla, who was kneeling over him. Gill lay on his side, eyes closed, a small puddle of vomit on the floor next to his head.

'Let me see him,' David said, edging Marla out of the way. He kept Gill on his side to avoid any risks of choking, and placed his head sideways on the man's back.

'What are you doing?' Marla asked.

'Shh!'

He held his own breath while he listened.

91

He sat up. 'He's not dead. There's a faint heart-beat. We have to get him to the hospital.'

'I called three times for an ambulance,' Marla said.

'Gill!' David said. 'Can you hear me at all? We need to get you out of here!'

A barely perceptible moan. David wasn't sure, even with Marla's help, that he could get his uncle all the way down to the street to his car. He took in the sliding glass doors that led from the kitchen to the stone patio. He was pretty sure he could drag Gill as far as that.

'Is it a heart attack? He's in good shape! He works out.'

'It may be the water,' David said.

'What?'

'Didn't you hear what I said on the phone? The water may be poisoned.'

Her eyes, already red from crying, went wide with fear. She looked over to Matthew in his chair. 'Oh my God. Oh my God.' She put a hand to her mouth. 'I gave him his bottle. The formula, it's mixed with water from the tap.'

But Matthew, at least so far, was showing no ill effects. He wasn't crying, wasn't throwing up.

To be on the safe side, though, David thought the baby should go to the hospital, too.

'I'll be back in a second,' he told Marla. 'Unlock those doors.'

He ran from the house, down to the street, and got behind the wheel of his car. He steered it up the driveway, then veered onto the grass and drove the car down between the Pickens house and the one next to it, flattening blades of grass, putting ruts in the sod along the way.

Once past the house, he turned hard left and brought the car right onto the flagstone patio.

Marla had the sliding doors open, Matthew now in her arms. David leapt from the car, opened a back door, then ran into the kitchen and dropped onto his haunches by Gill's head. He got his arms under Gill's and slowly lifted him to the point where David was standing, and his uncle stretched out in front of him. He dragged the man out of the kitchen, eased himself into the back of the car first, pulling Gill in with him as he shifted across the rear seat. David opened the door on the other side to get out.

'Come on,' David said to Marla, who exited the house, not bothering to close the doors, and got into the passenger seat, clutching Matthew, gently touching his head to her shoulder.

'What will happen to him?' she asked as David turned the car around on the patio and drove back down between the houses.

He didn't look her way, but he was pretty sure she was talking about her baby and not her father.

'When did you give him his bottle?' he asked.

'In the last hour.'

'He seems fine.'

'I – I don't know. I mean, he seems okay.'

David, first of all, didn't know for sure the water

was to blame. But assuming it was, he had no idea how long it took for symptoms to develop once it had been consumed. Everyone seemed to be getting sick this morning.

'When did you make it up?' David asked, glancing in the mirror for any signs of life from Gill as he sped toward the hospital. He had a bad feeling that even once they got Gill there, he might not get the attention he needed in time. But where else was he to go? He knew off-duty medical staff would be getting called in, that more help would be at Promise Falls General than even a few minutes ago.

'Make up what?' Marla asked. 'Don't you believe me? You don't think my father's sick?'

Marla had become so accustomed to people questioning her honesty, and sanity, that she'd misheard the question. 'When did you make up the bottles of formula?' David asked, taking a second to look at her.

'Oh,' she said, shifting Matthew from one shoulder to the other. 'It was . . . it was yesterday. In the afternoon? I think it was the afternoon. I made up half a dozen bottles.'

'Not today.'

She shook her head.

'Not this morning,' David pressed.

'No! It was yesterday.'

'Okay,' he said. 'What about you? Have you had any water this morning?'

More thinking. 'I haven't even brushed my teeth

yet.' She craned her head around and said to her father, 'Dad? Can you hear me? I love you.'

'I need you to do something for me,' David said, handing Marla his cell phone. 'Call up the recents.'

She took the phone, looked at the screen. 'Okay,' she said.

'See the one that says Sam? Call that number.'

'Who's he?'

'Just call it. Whoever answers, tell them not to drink the water. It might be a woman. It might be a boy.'

Marla made the call, put the phone to her ear. 'It's ringing,' she said.

David's grip on the steering wheel tightened while he waited. 'Still ringing,' she said. 'That's eight rings.'

'Are you sure you touched the right number?'

'Sam. Yes. That's the one. Ten rings. Who is this guy?'

'It's not a guy,' he said. He took one hand off the wheel, ran it over the top of his head, pulling on his hair at the same time, trying to release the tension any way he could. He put the hand back on the wheel.

'Twelve rings. Wait. It's going to message.'

'Never mind,' he said. David had already sent a text. He couldn't see the sense, right now, of a voice mail. All Sam would have to do was look at her phone to see she'd missed several calls from him. 'You can hang up.'

Marla ended the call and was about to return the phone when it started to ring in her hand. It startled her and she let out a short scream.

'Is it Sam?' David asked.

'I don't think – hello? No, no, you have the right number. This is David's phone. He's driving. This is Marla.' She said to David, 'Someone wants to talk to you.'

'Who is it?'

Marla said, 'Who's calling? Randy who?'

'No,' David said angrily.

'He can't talk to you,' Marla said. 'We're on our way to the hospital. My father is—' Marla listened a few more seconds, then handed the phone to David. 'He says it's really important.'

'Jesus,' David hissed as he grabbed the phone. 'This has to wait, Randy.'

'Listen! This is big! The town's water may be—'

'I know!'

'—poisoned. David, do what you have to do. Help that woman's father.'

'It's my uncle,' David said.

'Christ, I'm sorry,' Randall Finley said. 'How is he?'

David glanced in the mirror again. 'Not great.'

'What can I do?'

For once, David thought his employer sounded sincere. But then again, Randy was good at pretending to care when he didn't give a shit.

'Nothing,' David said.

'I want to help. Not just you, but everyone. It's

96

in my power to make a difference here, to do something good.'

'What are you—'

'I'm calling everyone in. I'm cranking up production. We're going to distribute thousands of bottles of water. We'll drop them off in the middle of town. In the park, next to the falls. There's a crisis and we're going to—'

'Exploit it,' David said.

'No!' Was that genuine hurt David was hearing? 'I just want to do the right thing. I swear. Go. Save your uncle and call me later. In the meantime, I'm moving forward on—'

David didn't hear the rest of it. He'd ended the call, but instead of putting the phone away, he gave it back to Marla.

'Go into the contacts. Hit "home," then hand it to me.'

Marla did so.

David listened for the rings. His mother picked up before the third.

'Mom,' David said, 'I need you to get yourself to Promise Falls General.'

'I'm fine,' Arlene said. 'I didn't drink anything from the tap and I didn't let your father have that pot of coffee he made.'

'That's good, that's good, but that's not it. I may need your help. Dad can stay home, be there when Ethan wakes up, tell him not to drink anything. Or take a bath. Like I'd need to talk him out of that.'

'Oh, okay. I'm on my way.'

'What kind of help?' Marla asked once David had put the phone away.

'It's crazy there,' he told her. 'There may be questions to answer, forms to fill out, and you've got your hands full with Matthew. She can help with that.'

He didn't have the heart to tell her what he was really thinking: that if Gill wasn't already dead in the backseat of the car, he very likely would be by the time they got to the hospital, and David was going to need his mother there to help Marla get through it. She was going to go to pieces. If she couldn't pull herself together, she wasn't going to be able to look after Matthew.

Arlene would be a great help there.

And David didn't want to spend a moment longer at the hospital than he had to. He had to get to Samantha Worthington's place.

He had to know whether the woman he was falling in love with and her young son, Carl, were already dead.

CHAPTER 9

Duckworth

In the car, heading toward the town's water pumping and treatment center, I called home again. No answer. But I had asked Maureen to start banging on the neighbors' doors to warn them about possible water contamination, so it made sense she wasn't in the house.

I was betting she'd taken her cell with her. I tried that number, and she answered on the third ring.

'Did you get Trevor?' I asked.

'Yes,' she said, sounding out of breath. 'I woke him up. And then he called me back a few minutes ago to tell me he's being asked to come into work.'

'What? Finley called him in?'

'I don't know if it was him specifically, but he's going in, on his day off – he *had* to come in.'

It didn't take long for me to put it together. If the water wasn't drinkable, there'd be an increased demand for the bottled stuff from Finley's uncontaminated spring. The son of a bitch was going to use this crisis to make himself a small fortune.

I wondered how much he'd hike the price. The opportunistic bastard could probably charge whatever he wanted once the shelves of all local grocery stores were cleared of every other brand of bottled water.

As much as Randy's exploitation of what was shaping up to be the biggest tragedy in the history of this town infuriated me, it wasn't my problem. I had no doubt that trying to rip off the citizens of Promise Falls would backfire on him and very likely deep-six his hopes of getting the mayor's job back.

Maureen said, 'You there?'

'Yeah. Just thinking. How's it going on the street?'

'I feel like I'm doing collections on a paper route, banging on all these doors. I think I interrupted Stan and Gloria in the middle of you-know-what, and poor old Estelle probably thinks her nightie is long enough to hide her business, but she's mistaken.' She paused, then said worriedly, 'There're a couple houses where I didn't get any response at all.'

I knew what she was thinking. 'Maybe they're away.'

'I hope so. You know that old man who lives alone down on the corner?'

'Which end?'

'Going south. The house with the red shutters. He's got that old Porsche in the garage. I think he used to be a dentist – his wife died years ago?'

I knew the house. 'Yes.'

'I couldn't raise anyone there.'

'Just hit all the houses you can, and then maybe go back,' I said. 'And I need another favor.'

'Shoot.'

'Find Amanda Croydon. She's apparently out of town. She needs to be here. Maybe someone else is trying to track her down, but there's so much going on I just don't know. If you can find her, tell her to call me.'

'On it. Anything else?'

'All for now. If you hear anything, call.'

The phone rang again before I could put it away. 'Yes?'

'Ottman's already there,' Randall Finley said. 'At the plant. He's waiting for us.'

'I don't need you to be there,' I told him.

'I'm trying to help you out here, Barry.'

'I know exactly who you're helping out.'

'What's that supposed to mean?'

I put the phone back into my pocket.

Coming into view ahead of me, hovering over the horizon like some massive unidentified flying object on stilts, was the Promise Falls water tower. That meant I was close to the water plant, a sprawling two-story cinder-block structure. It sat in the shadow of the tower, and was hidden by enough trees that the town's administrators felt they didn't need to spend an extra dime on making the building even remotely attractive.

Beyond the water plant was a reservoir fed by

various tributaries. The water was treated in the plant to make sure it was free of E. coli and other contaminants, then pumped high up into the tower. From there gravity did the rest, channeling water through a vast network of mains across Promise Falls.

I sped down the driveway, parked near the main entrance, where three other cars were parked. There was a white Ford pickup, a blue Chevy Blazer, and a rusting, yellow Pinto that was a piece of crap even when it was brand-new back in the 1970s. I hadn't thought there were still any of those on the road.

As I got out from behind the wheel, I heard another car roaring into the lot. Finley's Lincoln.

I headed straight into the plant without waiting for him. There was no one in the reception area, so I kept on going, through a door that read AUTHORIZED PERSONNEL ONLY, and standing by a large panel of dials and readouts was an unshaven man in a red-and-black flannel shirt. I put him at around forty, and when he saw me, he said, 'Who are you?'

I showed him my ID. 'You Ottman?'

He nodded.

'What the hell is happening?'

'That's what I'm trying to figure out now.' He pointed farther into the plant, a cavernous space filled with oversized pipes and tanks and conduits whose purposes were a mystery to me. There was a young woman in jeans, a dark sweater, and a hard hat, with some kind of device that reminded me of Spock's tricorder in her hand.

'I've got Trish trying to sort it out now. She came on shift a couple of hours ago.'

'Is it the water that's making everyone sick?'

Ottman grimaced. 'Best guess, yes.'

'Garvey!'

We both turned. Randy stuck out a meaty hand and shook Ottman's. 'Mr Finley, good to see you.'

'Always Randy to you,' he told the man, and clapped a hand on his shoulder like they were old buddies from way back. 'What in the fuck has happened?'

'I was just telling the detective here we don't exactly know yet. We've got to run tests on the water, check the records, see that everything that's supposed to be done was done. We test the water every twelve hours. Last time would have been noon yesterday. So that would have meant another test last night, at midnight.'

Before I could say anything, Randy jumped in. 'Was that done?'

Ottman looked as though he didn't want to have to answer that one. 'I don't know,' he said.

'What do you mean?' I asked. 'You keep records, right?'

'That's right. But the overnight guy didn't do that.'

'Who's that?'

'Tate.'

'Tate Whitehead?' Finley asked.

Ottman nodded.

'Jesus,' Finley said. 'That guy's got the IQ of a lug nut. You've got him in charge of our drinking water?'

Ottman frowned. 'I put him on nights because the responsibilities are minimal. He does a couple of tests, checks that things are running the way they should, and if there's a problem, he lets me or someone else know and we send in the troops to deal with it.'

I asked, 'Why didn't Whitehead do the midnight check?'

'I don't know,' Ottman said.

'Did you ask him?'

He shook his head. 'I don't know where he is. The dumb bastard knocked off early. He's supposed to be relieved by Trish, but she says when she got here at six, he was gone.'

'He do that a lot?' Randy asked. 'Fuck off early?'

Ottman was looking increasingly pained. 'He's done it before. But he punched in last night at nine. He was here.'

'So for all you know,' I said, 'he left right after that. He might never have done the midnight check, let alone made a record of it. So if the water was contaminated, it wouldn't get caught in time.'

'In theory,' Garvey Ottman said.

Finley was slowly shaking his head. 'Garv, tell me Tate's not still drinking.'

'I thought he had it under control,' the water

plant manager said. He rubbed a hand over his mouth. 'Oh my God, this is horrible. If that dumb bastard did this, I swear, I'll kill him with my bare hands.'

'You might have to take a number,' I said. I was astounded the lives of thousands of people could depend on the judgment of an incompetent drunk. 'Let's say something got past Tate. What could it be?'

'First thing I'd look at is contamination in the reservoir,' he said. 'Maybe a fuel spill, or runoff, upstream, from a farming operation, like effluent from a pig farm or something like that. But I've done a quick test on the water in the reservoir and it checks out. I mean, it's not perfect. The reservoir water never is, because that's what gets treated before it gets pumped up into the tower.'

'I need an address for Tate Whitehead,' I said.

'Sure, I got that in the office here,' Ottman said. 'But the thing is, his Pinto's still out there in the lot.'

I turned on my heels and headed back outside to check the rusting, yellow heap I'd noticed earlier. I hadn't taken a close look at the car and I wondered whether Tate might be inside, maybe sleeping one off.

I made a visor out of my hand to peer through the side glass. The interior matched the exterior. Not in color, but the upholstery had as many holes as the fenders, springs and stuffing visible. I saw something else I didn't like the look of.

I tried the driver's door and was not surprised to find it unlocked. It creaked painfully on its hinges as I swung it wide. On the floor in front of the passenger seat were several empty beer bottles.

Ottman was approaching with a slip of paper. 'Here's Tate's address and phone number.'

I took the paper from him and pointed down into the footwell. 'That's the kind of guy you had looking after the safety of every man, woman, and child in this town.'

'Jesus,' he said. 'I didn't know, really.'

'You never walked by his car? You never noticed this? You never noticed alcohol on his breath?'

'It's just, I mean, the thing is, Tate's hours and mine, they never really overlap. He comes in after I go home, and he leaves in the morning before I get here.'

'When's the last time you even saw him?'

Before Ottman could answer, Finley, surveying the mess in the car, made a disapproving clucking noise with his tongue.

'This is very bad, Garv. Very bad.' A shake of the head. 'Things weren't like this when I was running this town.'

Here we go, I thought.

'And where the hell is Amanda?' Finley asked. 'This town is rudderless.'

'This all works really well for you, doesn't it?' I asked him. 'Just the kind of catastrophe you've been waiting for.'

'My God, Barry, how could you?' he said. 'I know you don't think much of me, but I had no idea you thought that little.'

'Maybe you've got enough campaign material now that you don't need to keep leaning on my son.'

'Barry, now, come on—'

'And I'm guessing profits are about to go way up. Am I right? Getting Trevor and everyone else in on their day off? Ramping up production? What's the price on a case of bottled water about to go up to?'

Garvey Ottman, his eyes moving back and forth between us, must have wondered what the hell was going on.

Randy's face almost looked like it was going to crumple. I was shocked to think I might have wounded him. He'd always seemed to me to be immune to offense.

'You have no idea,' he said, his voice free of rancor. 'Yes, I'm increasing production. Like never before. And within the next few hours, we'll be handing out those cases of water to the folks of Promise Falls, absolutely free. You know something, Barry? I feel sorry for you. To be that cynical. To assume your fellow man has no goodness in him whatsoever.'

I didn't know what to say, but I knew what I was thinking. I'd misjudged his actions, but I was less sure that I had misjudged his motives. Handing out free water in the middle of this disaster was likely to score him points with potential voters, so long as he didn't blow his own horn too hard.

That would be the challenge for Randall Finley.

'Well, there's a first,' Randy said. 'Detective Barry Duckworth without a comeback.'

He turned to Garvey. 'Give our friend here as much help as you can, and if you find Tate, or if there's anything I can do for you, let me know.'

Then, back to me. 'If you want to find Tate Whitehead, I'd start there.' He pointed into the wooded area that separated the plant from the highway. 'Probably propped up against a tree blitzed out of his mind.'

He gave us both a nod, got back in his Lincoln, and drove out of the lot.

Garvey looked at me, then tilted his head in the direction of the trees. 'That's actually a pretty good idea,' he said.

We made our way into the woods.

CHAPTER 10

Cal knew something was up as he was driving into Promise Falls.

He saw two ambulances, each coming from a different part of the town, heading in the direction of the hospital. Driving down one street, he saw uniformed police officers running from house to house, banging on doors.

Two blocks from Lucy Brighton's house, he eased off the accelerator when he saw a red Promise Falls Fire Department pumper working its way down the street, lights flashing. But the truck wasn't racing to a scene. Cal thought he heard something being broadcast, so he powered down the window, pulled over to the curb, and listened as the truck rolled past.

'Do not drink the tap water!' blared from a speaker mounted behind the front grille. The firefighter behind the wheel had a mike in his hand.

'This is an emergency! Do not drink water from the tap!'

Cal turned on the car radio, tuned it in to the Albany news station.

'—reports coming in of hundreds of people

becoming ill in Promise Falls this morning. The town has issued an emergency statement urging citizens not to drink town water. Information is sketchy at this time, but people are already reporting on social media that – and we have to point out that this information has not been confirmed by us – that there have been multiple fatalities. If you live in or near Promise Falls, you are being warned not to drink the water, although there has been no statement so far regarding what kind of possible contamination there may be. We're going to be staying with this story all morning and will be updating with any details the moment we have them.'

Cal got out his phone and called his sister, Celeste. The phone had barely finished one ring when he heard, 'Cal?'

'Yeah,' he said. 'You know about the water?'

'Yeah.'

'You and Dwayne okay?'

'We're okay. We haven't had any to drink yet. Dwayne heard about it from a neighbor. What about you?'

'I have to go,' Cal said. 'I'll check in with you later.'

When he arrived at the Brighton house, eleven-year-old Crystal was sitting on the front step, dressed in pink pajamas. She had a clipboard with some paper on it resting on top of her knees, a pencil in one hand. She was busily drawing when Cal pulled into the driveway, and the sound of

110

his car prompted her to raise her head. But she didn't get up.

Cal walked briskly to the front door and said, 'Crystal, what's happening?'

'Nothing,' she said.

'Has the ambulance been here?'

'No. I kept calling, like you said, but it didn't come.'

'Where's your mother?'

'She's in the bathroom.'

'Upstairs?' he asked.

The girl nodded, returned to working on her drawing. Cal glanced down, saw that she was drawing what looked like thunderclouds.

He walked into the house, called out, 'Lucy?' He went up the stairs, two at a time, to the second floor, past the guest bedroom, where he and Lucy had spent the night together so recently, and stopped at the bathroom door.

It was closed. He wondered if Lucy had done that for privacy, or if Crystal had, because she didn't want to have to see what had happened in there. He turned the knob, eased the door open.

Lucy Brighton was seated, more or less, on the floor, dressed in pajamas and a housecoat, her arms hanging limp at her sides, palms turned up, hands resting on the tile floor, her head lolled over onto her right shoulder. Her back was leaned up against the tub, her legs splayed open toward the toilet.

The room was high with the smell of vomit and other bodily fluids.

Cal was certain Lucy was dead, but he needed to be sure. He turned his head back toward the hall, took a deep breath, then entered the room and knelt next to her body. He put two fingers to her neck, just below the jaw, feeling for any sign of a pulse. There was none.

'Goddamn it,' he said.

He stood, looked into the toilet, which had not been flushed and was awash with what he guessed had been the contents of Lucy's stomach. He glanced at the items on the countertop. Toothbrush, tube of Crest squeezed in the middle, an empty water glass with droplets still clinging to the inside.

Cal backed out of the bathroom and closed the door. Propped himself up against the wall for ten seconds to draw some fresher air into his lungs.

He thought immediately of Crystal. If the town's water supply was deadly, had she had any? But she had sounded fine on the phone, and seemed fine – at least physically – for the moment. So he decided to take a couple of minutes and do a walkabout of the house.

His real focus was the kitchen. The coffeemaker light was still on, and there looked to be maybe half a cup still in it. There was a mug on the table, maybe half an inch of coffee remaining in it. On a plate, a half-eaten piece of toast.

More vomit on the floor.

Cal went back outside, sat down on the step next to Crystal.

'Do you feel sick?' he asked her.

'I feel sad.'

'I know. But do you feel sick in your stomach, like you're going to throw up?'

'You think I caught what Mom got?'

'I just want to make sure you're feeling okay.'

'I guess. My hands are a little itchy.'

'What have you had to eat or drink today?'

'Nothing.'

'Nothing at all? Not even a glass of water?'

'Nope.'

Cal felt he could relax, a little, where the girl's health was concerned. 'Tell me what happened,' he said.

Crystal was shading the underside of a cloud. Without stopping, or looking at Cal, she said, 'I heard Mom making funny noises, so I got out of bed. She was in the kitchen, saying she felt sick, but I should go back to bed. So I did, but then it was worse, so I came down again, and she was on the floor and she wasn't saying anything and that was when I called 911.'

'Okay. Then what?'

'Nobody answered. So then I found Mom's cell phone and I called you and then you came.'

'What happened between the time you called me and when I got here?'

'Mom kind of woke up, and crawled up the stairs. I watched her the whole time and told her that you were coming. And she went into the bathroom. Where she was sick again, but this time she tried to get it into the toilet.' Crystal stopped moving her pencil and became very still. 'And then she just kind of sat back, and then she didn't get sick anymore.'

Cal slipped his arm around the girl and held her tight. She allowed him to pull her into him.

'Did you close the bathroom door?' Cal asked her.

'Yes,' she said quietly. 'Did you see her?'

'I did.'

'Is she totally dead?'

'Yes,' Cal said. 'I'm sorry.'

Crystal said nothing for several seconds. Finally, she turned her head toward Cal and said, 'I don't know how to pay the bills.'

'You what?'

'I don't know how to do those things. Mom paid the bills, like for electricity and her Visa and stuff, online. I could probably figure it out, but I don't know if she had passwords.'

'Don't worry about that,' he said, tightening his grip on her.

'If I don't pay the bills, I won't be able to live here. Isn't that right?'

'All that will get sorted out, Crystal. Your dad will help do that.'

'He's in San Francisco. I think, anyway.'

'We'll get him up here to help you.'

'Mom said he was hard to find.'

'Still, it can be done. Do you have other family, a little closer? Aunts or uncles or grandparents?'

Cal felt her head moving side to side. 'Nope.'

'What about on your father's side? What about his mother and father? Are they still alive?'

'I don't think so. I never met them.' She paused. 'I have an idea.'

Cal closed his eyes.

'Did you get to move back into your apartment again after that fire?' she asked.

'No.'

'Then you could live here and you could figure out how to pay the bills and then I wouldn't have to move out of my house.'

Cal rubbed his hand on her arm. 'Let's just take everything one step at a time, okay?'

'Okay,' she said.

'But in the meantime, until your dad gets here from San Francisco, I'll make sure you're okay.'

'I don't want to live here now,' she said. 'I don't want to go inside.'

'Of course not,' he said.

'What happens to my mom? Do you take her away?'

'No. But people will come.'

'Are you sleeping in your car?'

'What? No.'

'I thought you were sleeping in your car because of the fire.'

'No, sweetheart. I'm in a hotel.'

'Can I stay with you?'

Crystal would have to stay with someone until her father showed up, *if* he showed up. But Cal wasn't sure of the appropriateness of her living with him at the BestBet. He thought of Celeste and her husband, Dwayne. He could be a bit of an asshole, but Celeste would take good care of the girl, and be tolerant of her eccentricities.

'I'll make sure you have a place to stay.' Cal wondered if she'd ever set foot in her own home again.

'I guess there's one good thing,' Crystal said.

'What's that?'

'My mom won't ever have to go to jail.'

Cal felt his heart skip a beat. 'What's that again?'

'I heard her talking to someone on the phone. That she might be in trouble. I was really scared she'd go to jail.'

A lawyer, Cal figured. Lucy had been talking to someone, just in case Cal finally decided to go to the police with what he knew.

A fire engine, blaring a warning from behind its grille, had rounded the corner and was slowly making its way up the street.

'Are you okay sitting here while I go talk to them?' Cal asked Crystal.

'I'll draw.'

'That's good.'

'When you come back, could you go into the house and get some things for me?'

'Yes,' he said, giving her a kiss on the top of her head before he went to talk to the guy behind the wheel of the fire truck.

CHAPTER 11

Victor Rooney dialed 911 twice after finding his landlady, Emily Townsend, dead in the backyard of her house. But when no one answered the second time, he figured, what the hell, it wasn't like they were going to be able to do anything for her anyway.

He turned on the radio in her kitchen and found the local news. Plenty of talk about what was happening in Promise Falls.

'That is some serious shit,' he said to no one in particular, reaching into the fridge for a carton of Minute Maid orange juice. He unscrewed the cap and drank straight from the container. That was the sort of thing Ms Townsend frowned upon, but it was hardly going to upset her now.

Victor took the carton of juice with him as he stepped out the front door and dropped into one of the wicker chairs on the porch. Lots of activity for a Saturday morning, that was for sure. Neighbors helping sick family members into cars, racing off down the street. Others going house to house, banging on doors. People milling in groups, talking.

Judging by what Victor had heard on the radio, the hospital was the center of excitement.

He went back inside, leaving the half-empty carton of orange juice on the table just inside the door where Ms Townsend left her keys, and went back up to his room. He was glad to have skipped his usual shower this morning. He wouldn't have wanted any water to have accidentally dribbled into his mouth. He sat on the edge of the bed, pulled on a pair of sneakers, and grabbed the keys to his van.

He parked two blocks from the hospital and hoofed it over.

Even before he wandered into the emergency ward waiting room, he could see the mayhem playing out before him. Paramedics and nurses and doctors all being run off their feet. People puking their guts out. People collapsing.

He'd never seen anything like it. Promise Falls, he bet, had never seen anything like it. Upstate New York had never seen anything like it.

Ever.

'Out of the way!' someone shouted, and Victor Rooney spun around to find himself in the path of two paramedics wheeling a gurney toward the sliding ER doors. There was a teenage girl strapped to it, hands clutched to her stomach. Trailing the gurney were a man and a woman, presumably the girl's parents.

The woman said, 'You're going to be okay, Cassie! You're going to be okay!'

Victor stepped out of their way, then followed them, as though slipping into their jet stream, and entered the ER.

He stood to one side, cast his eye about the room. There had to be seventy to a hundred people in here. And that was just the ones he could see. Those beds in the examining area, behind the sliding curtains, were likely all full, too.

It took only a few seconds for him to spot someone he knew.

Walden Fisher, the man who'd nearly become his father-in-law.

'Christ on a candlestick,' Victor said.

Walden was seated in one of the waiting room chairs, doubled over, elbows on knees.

'Walden,' Victor said under his breath.

The man looked up suddenly and when he saw who it was, his mouth opened in surprise.

'Victor,' he said, putting his hands on his knees and starting to make the effort to push himself up.

'No, stay there,' Victor said. He'd have taken a seat next to him, but they were all filled with people waiting to see a doctor.

'Whoa,' said Walden, settling back into his chair. 'Even trying to get up, things start spinning. I'm pretty light-headed. How sick are you?'

'I'm fine,' Victor said.

Walden appeared puzzled. 'What are you doing here? Did you bring someone in?'

The younger man shook his head. 'No. But my landlady's dead. Found her in the backyard. I just wanted to come up, see what was going on.' He paused, added, 'It's all over the news.'

'What are they saying?'

'Might be something in the water,' Victor told him.

'Jesus. You didn't drink any?'

Victor shook his head. 'Guess I was lucky. What about you?'

'I . . . I had coffee. I made a pot. Never used to do it. Beth always did it, but now I make it. I got real sick, and my heart started doing weird things.' He gazed about the room. 'Some of these people, they're real bad.'

'Maybe you didn't drink enough,' Victor said.

Walden gave him a look. 'Whaddya mean by that?'

'Nothing. I'm just saying, maybe you didn't drink enough to get as sick as these other people. What did you think I meant?'

Walden waved a weak hand at him. 'Nothing, nothing.'

'There anything I can do for you?'

Walden found enough strength to nod. 'Get someone to see me. I'm just sitting here, like I'm invisible or something. I'm gonna be dead before they know I'm here.'

Victor said, 'Okay. Hang on.'

Victor interrupted three nurses and two doctors who were in the middle of treating other patients before he found someone who'd give him some attention. 'Are you a nurse or a doctor?' he asked a woman whose arm he'd grabbed hold of.

'I'm Dr Moorehouse,' she said.

'No one's looked at that man,' Victor said, pointing at Walden.

Moorehouse took a breath, headed for Walden, knelt in front of him. 'Sir? How are you doing?'

'Not so hot,' he said. She asked his name, and he told her. She asked him several other questions. How long he'd been here, what he'd had to eat and drink this morning, how he was feeling now compared with when he'd gotten to the hospital.

The doctor listened to his heart, shone a tiny beam of light into his eyes. 'I can't admit you,' she said. 'You're sick, but we've got way worse.' She tipped her head toward Victor. 'This your son?'

'No,' Walden said.

'I'm a friend,' Victor said.

'He should be looked at, but we're swamped here. I'd suggest you take him to Albany, get him checked out there.'

'Albany?' Walden said.

'Hospitals there are taking people,' Dr Moorehouse said. 'We're not equipped to handle something this big.'

'I can do that,' Victor said. 'Can you handle that, Walden? Can you make it to Albany?'

Walden patted his chest, as though diagnosing his ability to travel. 'I guess.'

'Take care, Mr Fisher,' the doctor said, and went off to look at someone else.

Victor helped Walden Fisher to a standing

position. 'I'm parked a few blocks away. Can you walk it?'

Walden let go of Victor's hand to test his balance. 'I think so.' But he took the younger man's elbow as they left the ER.

Halfway to the van, Walden asked to stop. He leaned forward, rested his hands on his kneecaps.

'You gonna be sick?' Victor asked.

'Just a wave of something,' he said, then stood, tentatively. 'I think it's over.'

When they reached the van, Victor opened the passenger door for Walden and helped him into the seat. Victor ran around, got in, and said, 'I'm telling ya, what a clusterfuck. You know?'

Walden said nothing.

'Kind of takes your mind off it, though,' Victor said.

Walden turned his head. 'Kind of takes your mind off what?'

'All this shit that's happening. Kind of takes your mind off the fact that it's been three years.'

Walden stared at him.

'You know. Three years since Olivia—'

'Of course I know,' Walden said, his voice stronger than it had been up to now. 'Nothing ever takes my mind off that. Ever.'

'Okay, well,' Victor said, and turned the key. The van sputtered to life. He put the vehicle into drive, checked his mirrors, and pulled out into the street. 'You have to wonder, though.'

'Wonder what?'

'Whether any of them died today. The ones that did nothing.'

Walden turned away, looked out his window, chewed on the middle fingernail of his right hand.

'Forget Albany,' he said. 'Take me home. If I die, I die.'

CHAPTER 12

Duckworth

'How long has Tate Whitehead worked for the town?' I asked Garvey Ottman as we wandered through the treed area between the water treatment plant and the highway.

'Long as I can remember,' Ottman said. 'Twenty-five years, maybe.'

'Has he always had a drinking problem?'

Garvey was scouring the bushes to the left and right, pretending, I thought, not to hear. If Whitehead had failed to do his job properly because he was hammered, resulting in the deaths of God knew how many Promise Falls residents, Ottman had to know there was a good chance it was going to come back on him.

'I said, has Tate had this problem a long time?'

'I guess it's all in how you define "problem," you know?' Ottman said.

'Let me help you with that,' I said. 'Did Whitehead come to work drunk?'

'Like I told you, our shifts didn't really overlap.'

I stopped trudging through the tall grass, turned,

124

and raised a hand in front of the man. 'Cut the bullshit,' I said.

Ottman blinked. 'What do you mean?'

'You're in charge of this plant. You telling me you don't keep track of the people you don't actually see? You have no mechanism in place to make sure they do their jobs?'

'Well, sure,' he said defensively. 'Like, if Tate was having a problem overnight, he'd leave me a note, ask me to check it out, that kind of thing.'

'You saying Tate would have to e-mail you to say he was too drunk to chlorinate the water or whatever the hell you do with it, and maybe you'd like to look into that?'

'No, of course not, he wouldn't say that. But if there was a technical problem, he'd let me know.'

'How would you know if Tate was performing his duties while under the influence? He worked the plant alone overnight. How would you know?'

'The guy he relieved would see him, and then whoever relieved him in the morning, like Trish this morning.'

'If I asked Trish if he was ever drunk when she came in for her shift, what would she tell me?'

A hesitation. 'She might say it's happened once or twice.'

'And you know this because she passed that along to you?'

Another damning hesitation. 'She might have mentioned something at some point.'

'And when she did, what did you do about it?'

'Look, Detective – Duckworth, is it?'

I nodded. I was grateful to have stopped for this discussion. It gave me a chance to catch my breath after stepping over all the brush and debris.

'Tate Whitehead drinks. A lot of people drink. I think the odd time, the dumb bastard came out and had a beer in his car when he was supposed to be doing his job. But I've never – and I swear to God I'm telling you the truth here – I've never known him to not do what he was supposed to do. You think Tate's the only guy on the town's payroll who drinks on the job? What about the cops? You want to tell me you never worked with a cop who had a drink during his shift, or got smashed when it was over, and maybe showed up the next day pretty hungover?'

I said nothing. He was right about that, of course.

'If the town fired everyone who drank too much, there wouldn't be enough people left to get things done,' he said.

'Be sure to tell that to the lawyers,' I said.

'Lawyers?'

I scanned the woods. 'I don't think he's out here. And yet, his car's still here.'

'Maybe he got a taxi.'

'Hmm?'

'If he finished his shift drunk, maybe he had just enough smarts not to try and drive himself home.'

I supposed that was possible, although it had been my experience that good judgment did not

126

typically follow heavy drinking. But Ottman had given me Tate's home address, so it wasn't going to be long before I found out for myself.

'I want to ask you about Finley,' I said.

'Randy? What about him?'

'You seem to be friends.'

Garvey Ottman shrugged. 'I know him.'

'He also seemed to know about Tate Whitehead. That he's got a problem.'

'Let me tell you something about Randall Finley,' Ottman said. 'Lot of people, they think he's a big asshole. And maybe he is. But when he was mayor, he never acted like he was too good for regular people. He used to come by here all the time. And not just here. You ask them at the fire department, or even the guys who pick up the trash. He'd go visit those people, shoot the shit with them. He came by here lots, into the plant, talking to people, asking what they did, how everything worked. Like he really cared, you know? So when people say Randall Finley is a jerk, I say you don't know the guy.'

'He came by here a lot?' I asked.

'When he was mayor.' The man nodded. 'And even after, the odd time, if he was driving by, he'd just pop in. I hear he's running again.'

I nodded.

'Well, he's got my vote. I mean, he's not even the mayor right now, but he's up here, trying to help out. Where's Amanda Croydon? You see her here?'

'I hear she's out of town,' I said, although I didn't feel much like defending her. She needed to get her ass back, and fast. 'I'm going to swing by Tate's house, see if he's there. In the meantime, if you see him, if he shows up, I want you to call me immediately.'

I gave Ottman one of my cards. He looked at it, tucked it into his shirt pocket.

'Okay,' he said.

As I worked my way back through the trees to the parking lot, my cell phone started to ring. It was the station.

'Duckworth.'

'Yeah, Barry, Chief here.'

Rhonda. She usually identified herself to me by her first name. Was the more formal tone related to her being pissed off with me, or was the gravity of the town's situation prompting a more official approach?

'Hey,' I said.

'Where are you?'

'Water plant. The overnight guy who monitors the place is apparently a drunk and nowhere to be found.'

'Terrific.'

'I'm going to see if I can find him at home.'

'Something else has come up.'

Jesus. What the hell else could happen? Half the town had been poisoned, and I was still working the drive-in bombing from a few days ago. Had a truck carrying radioactive waste rolled over on the bypass?

'What is it, Chief?'

'We've got a homicide.'

'They might *all* end up being ruled homicides,' I said. 'We could have hundreds of them.'

'I'm not talking about the poisonings. This is out at Thackeray. They're not hooked up to the town water supply.'

'Thackeray? Hasn't everyone gone home?'

'Summer student.'

'Christ. Send Carlson.'

'I tried. I can't reach him.'

He was probably still in the hospital ER, unable to get calls on his cell.

I sighed. 'I'll try to get out there ASAP. What do we know so far?'

'Not much,' Rhonda Finderman said. 'Just that it's a young woman, and it's bad.'

CHAPTER 13

David figured Gill was dead.

Every time he glanced in the mirror to see how his uncle was doing, there was no movement from the man. Not so much as an eye blink. The man was sprawled across the seat, and Marla was up front next to David, Matthew in her arms. She was turned sideways, her back to the door, maintaining a constant chatter with her father.

'Hang in, Dad. Just hang in. I love you. Matthew loves you. We need you. You need to be strong. You need to be there for us. We need you so much.'

David was almost as worried for Marla as he was for Gill. She'd been through so much in the last month. Implicated, and ultimately exonerated, in a murder. Found out her baby was alive, but lost her mother.

Perhaps most devastating of all was learning her mother had conspired to let her believe her baby had died. At first, Marla'd been unwilling to comprehend it. The betrayal was more than she could handle. But in the weeks since, reality had

130

slowly set in. The credit for that, David felt, rested in large part with Gill, who had patiently and delicately led Marla toward the truth.

Marla needed him. David was wondering how she'd cope if she lost her father now. He feared a complete mental collapse. Which would be horrible enough for Marla, but what about Matthew? Who'd look after him if his mother became incapacitated? And for how long?

David was pretty sure he knew the answer to that question. He and his parents would do it, for as long as they had to.

When he got to the hospital, he nosed the Mazda right up to the ER doors, navigating around several ambulances like a fish working its way upstream. He told Marla to wait with her father while he ran in to find a doctor or a nurse or even a goddamn orderly who could take a look at his uncle.

He spotted a woman with the proverbial stethoscope hanging around her neck and a mask across her mouth and nose heading across the crowded waiting room.

'My uncle!' he said, positioning himself right in front of her. David knew there was no way he was going to get any help for Gill without being in someone's face.

'What about him?' the woman said.

'He's in the car, just outside. I don't know if he's still alive or not.'

The woman's entire body seemed, for half a

second, to wilt. She glanced toward the door, then back toward all the waiting patients, a gesture that suggested to David that she had no idea whom to look at first, or whether the order in which she saw people was going to make any difference.

'Show me,' she said.

David led the way, asking, 'What's your name?'

'I'm Dr Moorehouse. Your uncle?'

'Gill Pickens.'

She reached out and grabbed him by the elbow. 'Gill? Agnes's husband?'

David nodded. At the car, Marla had the back door open and was leaning over her father, talking to him, while balancing Matthew on her hip.

'Marla,' David said, pulling her out of the way.

The doctor squeezed in. 'What's he had this morning?' she asked. 'To eat, to drink?'

'Just coffee, I think,' Marla said.

'Symptoms?'

'He got dizzy and he started throwing up and then he passed out,' she said. 'Can you help him?'

The doctor nodded, more to herself than her audience, as though she'd heard this many times already today. She held up a hand, a 'no more questions' gesture, as she put the stethoscope to Gill's chest.

She listened for several seconds. David steeled himself for the worst.

'This man is alive,' the doctor said. She pulled herself out of the car, stood, and shouted over the roof at a couple of paramedics who appeared to be, at least for several seconds, idle.

'I got a live one here!'

They ran toward the car, one pulling a gurney behind them. They maneuvered Gill out of the car and onto it while David and Marla watched, barely breathing.

'Oh my God,' Marla said under her breath. 'Oh my God, oh my God. You're going to be okay! They're going to fix you up, Dad!'

She started to trot along after them, following them into the building, but Dr Moorehouse turned and said sharply, 'Wait.' Gill was whisked away down a hallway that was already jammed with patients on gurneys.

David caught up to her. 'Come on, Marla. Come on. Let's go outside.'

As they exited the building someone yelled, 'David!'

It was his mother, Arlene. She was running up the driveway. David raised his palms, trying to get her to slow down. The last thing he needed was for her to fall down and break her wrist. He ran ahead to meet her.

'I had your father drop me off down the street,' she said, huffing. 'There's so much traffic he didn't think he could get any closer. Ethan's with him.'

'Great.'

'How's Gill?'

David filled her in, walking slowly to force her to do the same. When Arlene reached Marla, she gave her niece a hug and kissed Matthew on the cheek.

A paramedic said, 'That your car?'

David whirled around, admitted that the Mazda was his.

'Get it the hell out of here.'

David said to his mother, 'Can you hang in here with Marla now?'

'Of course,' she said.

'I have to go.'

Arlene nodded. 'Go.'

David got behind the wheel and carefully steered his way back to the street. Once he was clear of the hospital, he pulled over, got out his phone again, and tried Samantha Worthington's cell.

Still no answer.

He felt physically ill. He feared the worst – that Sam and her son, Carl, were both already dead.

He had to get there. David put the phone back into his pocket, took his foot off the brake pedal, and floored it.

He raced through the streets of Promise Falls to reach Sam's place, a narrow row house sandwiched in between several others. The Mazda screeched to a halt out front of her house. David got out so quickly he didn't bother to close the driver's door.

He leapt up the stairs to the front door, rang the bell, and pounded on the door at the same time.

He put his mouth close to the crack where door met jamb. 'Sam!' he shouted. 'Sam! It's David!'

No one came to the door. He couldn't hear or sense any movement on the other side.

There was no point in calling the police to enter the premises and see if they were okay. The cops were too busy. He was going to have to do it himself. At least he wasn't worried that he'd be looking down the barrel of a shotgun, like he was the first time he'd knocked on this door.

David turned the doorknob and pushed, but the door did not budge. The house was locked up.

'Shit.'

He'd have to break it down. He took two steps back, turned sideways, then ran into the door with his shoulder.

'Son of a bitch!' he said. His shoulder felt as though it had dislocated, and for all his effort, the door was still locked.

He rotated his shoulder to make sure he hadn't done any serious damage, then set his eye on the closest window, which was low enough that he could crawl into the house if he could open it. He stepped between some shrubs and the foundation to get in front of it, tried to raise the glass, but it was no good.

David slipped off his jacket, wrapped it around his lower right arm, then rammed his elbow into the glass. Better luck here than with the door. The glass shattered. He cleared more of it away with his protected arm, then reached in, found the lock, slid it open, then raised the glass.

No alarms rang. Sam did not have a security system. That's what the shotgun was for.

He brushed away the glass fragments, then hoisted himself up onto the sill and tumbled into the house, headfirst.

He rolled into the living room.

'Sam!' he shouted.

He went to the kitchen first. No dishes out, nothing in the sink. No pot of coffee on the go.

The two bedrooms were upstairs.

David bounded up the steps two at a time, went into Carl's bedroom first. No Carl, and the bed was made.

Same story in Sam's room. Everything looked in order, pillows in place.

The good news was, he hadn't found Sam and Carl in the house dead. But the bad news was, he hadn't found Sam and Carl in the house.

Where the hell were they?

It hit him then that he didn't remember seeing Sam's car out front. He went to the bedroom window, which looked out onto the street.

Sam's car was not there.

He did recall, from an earlier visit, seeing the edge of a suitcase under Sam's bed. He dropped to his knees and lifted the bed skirt.

The suitcase was gone.

He came back downstairs and thought to look for one last thing. Something Sam always kept in the closet by the front door.

He opened it, pushed aside some coats hanging in the way.

This was where Sam kept her shotgun, and it was not there.

As he closed the closet door, he began to feel light-headed. He turned and rested his back against the door, and as the events of the morning overwhelmed him, he put his face in his hands and began to sob.

CHAPTER 14

'Let's go, let's go, come on, people, let's go! Move it, move it!'

Finley was standing on the loading docks at Finley Springs Water, acting as a traffic cop as forklifts delivered pallets of bottled water from deep inside the plant to the open doors of the panel vans. There were vans backed up to each of the three doors, and others waiting to take their place once a space was created.

Shortly after his first phone call with David, he'd gotten on to his foreman to start rounding up every one of the company's twenty-two employees. Those who'd gone out of town for the weekend, if they could be reached on their cell phones, were ordered to get their asses back as fast as possible.

Four employees couldn't be raised on their cells or home phones.

'They might be sick, at the hospital,' the foreman said.

Finley had to agree that was possible. But getting in as many as they did allowed Finley to put the plant into full production, and get every truck on the road.

Trevor Duckworth was one of the first to arrive, and Finley had greeted him warmly.

'Good to see you,' he said, clapping his hand on the young man's shoulder. 'I was just helping your dad get a handle on what's been happening.'

'Uh-huh,' Trevor said.

'I was giving him some info on the water plant, what might have gone wrong.'

'Great.' Trevor cocked his head. 'How do you know your own water supply isn't going to make everyone sick?'

Finley's head recoiled, as though he'd been struck. 'What the hell are you talking about?'

'Where does the town water come from? Doesn't it come from springs and stuff in the hills around Promise Falls, just like your water? If the problem's at the source, wouldn't all this stuff be bad, too?'

Trevor waved a hand at the hundreds of cases of water.

'Don't be ridiculous,' Finley said. 'That's just nuts.'

'Is it?'

'Yes. My water is one hundred percent pure and drinkable. I just know it. I know it in my gut.'

Trevor did not look convinced.

'Fine, I'll prove it to you,' Finley said. He took a few steps over to the closest pallet load, used both hands to rip a small hole in the plastic casing that held two dozen bottles together, and pulled one bottle out. He twisted the lid, heard the distinctive crack of the plastic seal being broken, tipped the bottle up to his mouth, and started drinking.

Once he'd downed nearly half the bottle, he glared at Trevor Duckworth and said, 'There. You want one?'

'When was it bottled?' Trevor asked.

'What?'

'All the problems started this morning. When was that bottled? Maybe anything bottled before today is safe, but—'

'Fine, for fuck's sake,' Finley said. He turned and bellowed, at no one in particular, 'Get me a fresh bottle! From this morning!'

A young woman scurried off, returned in thirty seconds with a plastic bottle, and handed it to her boss.

'Let's try this,' he said, going through the same ritual again, cracking the lid, drinking half the bottle this time.

'God, I'm gonna have to take such a piss,' he said, wiping his mouth with the back of his hand. 'That water tasted absolutely perfect. Cool, fresh, no aftertaste. Not a hint of anything wrong with it.'

Trevor shrugged. 'Okay, then. Which truck you want me to drive?'

'Just help load them all – then I'm going to give everyone their instructions.'

Finley took out his phone, thinking it was time to bring in David Harwood.

He needed the man's help now more than ever. He'd hired Harwood to do his publicity, help run his mayoral campaign, but every time Finley had instructions for him, the guy had some fucking crisis. Finley couldn't recall ever knowing someone with so many problems. All that shit years ago with his wife, then more recently this thing with his cousin and the baby. God almighty, it was a fucking soap opera with him.

Granted, he had to cut David and everyone else in this town some slack today.

Good thing he'd been sending David home with plenty of free bottled water. If he hadn't, Finley might have lost his right-hand man this morning. But David was not the only one. He'd been sending all his employees home, lately, with free cases of water. Told them that if they worked for the company, they had to demonstrate brand loyalty.

Went to the company's integrity, Finley told them.

Finley'd overheard one of the drivers gripe recently that they weren't drinking Finley water; they were 'drinking the Kool-Aid.'

The irony of that comment hit hard today. It was the good people of Promise Falls, who'd been foolish enough to have faith that their local officials would look after them, who'd drunk the Kool-Aid.

Finley had been very clear with Lindsay that any water she took up to Jane was to be of the bottled variety. Even the coffee or tea, or even lemonade, was not to be made from what came out of the tap. The rules had been put in place some time ago. How would it look, he'd told Lindsay one time, if it got out he didn't drink Finley Springs Water?

It'd be like Henry Ford getting caught driving around in an Oldsmobile.

Finley took out his phone and entered David's number. One ring, two . . . three . . . four . . .

'Hello.'

'David?'

Finley wasn't sure. It didn't sound like David, unless David had suddenly come down with a terrible cold or something.

'Yeah, this is David. What is it, Randy?'

'You okay? You sound funny.'

David cleared his throat. 'I'm fine.'

'You got a second?'

A pause at the other end of the line. Finally, 'Yeah, go ahead.'

'You sure?'

'I said go ahead.'

'I'm about ready to drop hundreds of cases of free water right downtown. But people need to know it's there. Plus, I'm about to give a little rallying-cry, pep-talk kind of thing here at the plant. I'd like you to be here. There needs to be a record of all this. Could be very helpful in the coming months.'

When David didn't say anything right away, Finley said, 'I'm doing a good thing here, David.

142

I know you think it's all self-promotion, and I won't deny there's an element of that, but I have an opportunity here. I have an opportunity to help people. I have an opportunity to actually do something good.'

A pause. Then, 'I'm on my way.'

Finley broke into a grin. 'That's what I want to—'

David had already hung up.

The trucks were loaded and ready to go, but Finley had not yet given the word for them to move out. He was waiting for David to show up. He wanted his pep talk recorded. He could have gotten anyone here to film him on a smartphone, but Finley didn't just want David to record it – he wanted David to *hear* it.

It was important, Randall Finley realized, that David actually believe in him. It was an extension of his philosophy about his employees drinking his bottled water. If David was going to be telling the good folks of Promise Falls that Finley was the man to lead them into the future after the next election, it needed to come from the heart.

Okay, maybe that was expecting too much. But David was not going to be effective if people thought he was just mouthing the words, that he was nothing more than a paid mouthpiece.

'We need to go,' Trevor said, leaning up against the back doors of one of the trucks.

'Another minute,' Finley said. 'We just need to—'

There was David. Running up a short set of concrete steps, coming into the plant through the loading dock.

'Okay,' Finley said. 'I want to say a few words to everyone before you go.'

He took a breath. 'This is turning into one of the darkest days, if not *the* darkest day, in the history of Promise Falls. We're witness to a tragedy of immense proportions. I thank God all of you are okay, but it's very likely people you know, perhaps even loved ones, are in the hospital now, waiting for treatment.'

Finley tried to see David out of the corner of his eye, make out whether he had his phone out and was getting all this.

'What we have today is a chance to make a small difference in people's lives. To bring them something life-sustaining.' A pause. 'Water. So simple and yet so fundamental to our survival. It's like air. We take it for granted, but when we don't have it, we can't go on. People have been stunned to learn this morning that what is coming out of their taps may be poison. And until this horrible state of affairs has been dealt with, we're going to step in and do what we can by offering free, safe, pure drinking water. I don't care what it costs me. There're thousands and thousands of dollars of product in those trucks, but I don't care. Some things are more important than money. Being a good citizen counts above all.'

Finley snuck another look at David. Phone out.

Thank God.

Finley continued. 'We're going to drive over in a convoy and set up along the street next to the park downtown, by the falls. I think word'll spread quickly of what we're offering. And remember, you're not just there handing out free water. You're there to offer hope, a comforting word, a shoulder to cry on.'

Someone muttered, 'Fucking hell.'

'Okay, so, off we go!' Finley said.

As the workers of Finley Springs Water piled into the trucks and began to drive off, Finley walked over to David, whose eyes were red and bloodshot, and said, 'You get that?'

'Yeah.'

'You look like shit. What the hell happened to you?'

'I'm fine.'

'What about whoever it was you were taking to the hospital?'

'My uncle. He was alive last I saw him.'

Finley gave David a friendly punch to the shoulder. 'That's good, then, right?'

'Sure.'

'We need to head downtown, and we need to let the media know what I'm doing.'

'I'll start making some calls.'

'Well, make them on the way. Time's a-wastin'. We'll go in my car.'

'You need to be careful,' David said.

Finley cocked his head. 'Careful?'

'Of how you play this.'

'Not sure I'm following you, David,' Finley said.

'You don't want to look like you're taking advantage. Like that night the drive-in screen came down. Acting like you wanted to help people, but not until the camera was on.'

'You misjudge me. You're as bad as Duckworth.'

'Duckworth?'

'Never mind. What would you have me do, David? I have an opportunity here to genuinely help people in a crisis. You saying I should do nothing? For fear it would make me look opportunistic? Wouldn't that be just as cravenly political?'

'I'm not saying that.'

'Well, what the fuck are you saying, David?'

David shook his head. 'Fine, do what you want. Go save Promise Falls.'

Finley grinned and gave David a pat on the shoulder. 'Why don't we?'

CHAPTER 15

Duckworth

As critical as it was for me to get out to Thackeray College, I was determined to make a stop along the way at Tate Whitehead's house. I was in the early stages of this poisoned-water investigation – we still didn't know what was actually wrong with the water supply – but Whitehead was a so-called person of interest in what might end up being a mass murder.

In my mind, that trumped one dead student right now.

Garvey Ottman's note had led me to an address in the downtown. There's a block of two-story houses in Promise Falls that were built nearly a hundred years ago that most developers in town want to get their hands on so they can tear them down and build condos and retail shops, although in this real estate market it was hard to believe that was smart business sense. Off the top of my head, I knew Frank Mancini, who had bought the Constellation Drive-in property, wanted this block.

The homes were linked together in groups of

six, with sagging porches, rotting handrails, missing shingles. No one wanted to put any money into fixing these places, figuring they'd all be sold and razed.

I parked in front of 76 Prince Street – not even a hundred years ago would these addresses have been deemed suitable residences for visiting royalty – and went to the front door. Finding no doorbell, I banged on the door with the side of my fist.

I heard movement in the house, and fifteen seconds later a thin, silvery-haired woman opened the door a crack.

'Yeah?' she said, showing some brown teeth.

I showed her my ID. 'I'm looking for Tate Whitehead.'

'He's not here.'

'Do you know where he is?'

'Probably at work,' she said. 'At the water treatment plant. They're having some problem up there, case you haven't heard. Fire truck was driving around telling everybody not to drink the water. Check at the plant.'

She started to close the door, but I put a hand up to stop it. 'Are you Mrs Whitehead?'

'I am.'

'When did you last talk to your husband?'

'Last night 'fore he went to work.'

'What time would that've been?'

'Around nine, I guess. My husband works the overnight shift there. Sometimes I fall asleep before he goes, but I heard him leave last night.'

'And when does he usually get home?'

'Around six thirty, most nights. Well, mornings, actually.'

'Most?' I asked.

'Mostly, yeah.'

'If he's late getting home, why would that be?'

She eyed me suspiciously. 'What's all this about? If you want to talk to him, just go up there.'

'Has your husband called you since he left for work last night?'

Mrs Whitehead blinked a couple of times.

'Doesn't that seem odd to you?'

'Why would that be odd? He never calls me from work. That's when I'm sleeping.'

'His shift ended several hours ago. Wouldn't he call you if something kept him at work?'

She blinked again, as if I were out of focus.

'But I know what's going on,' she said. 'I heard about it on the radio and from that damn fire truck making all that noise.'

'The point I'm trying to make,' I said, 'is if Mr Whitehead knew there was a problem with the water, wouldn't he have called to tell you himself, rather than waiting for you to find out from the radio or someone else?'

That gave her pause. She looked at me quizzically. 'Why *didn't* he call me?'

'That's my question.'

'I mean, we've had our ups and downs, but I don't think he'd want me to drink bad water and drop dead. He needs me. He doesn't know the first thing about how to take care of a home.'

Looking around, I wasn't that sure Mrs Whitehead did, either.

'Can you tell me any places where your husband might go to, you know, unwind after work? A place to get a drink?'

Her eyes narrowed. 'Tate stays out of the bars.'

Perhaps he didn't need them, considering he had a fully stocked Pinto.

'What about friends? Buddies he likes to hang out with?'

'He doesn't really have any friends,' she said. ''Cept me.'

'Could you give me his cell phone number?'

'Tate doesn't got a cell phone. He had one a long time ago, but he was always losing it. So he stopped having one. Cost too much anyway. Have you been to the plant? Wouldn't it make more sense to just go there and talk to him?'

'He's not there,' I told her.

'He's not?'

I shook my head.

She looked around me, cast her eyes up the street in both directions. 'I don't see his car. He's got a yellow car. A Pinto. He's kept that thing running for years. It's never blown up or anything.'

'His car's at the plant,' I said.

She was starting to do something funny with her mouth, working her jaw around anxiously, maybe chewing on the inside of her cheek.

'What is it?' I asked.

'Nothin'.'

'It's important we find him, Mrs Whitehead. You already know what's going on, with the water. Something bad's happened. I think your husband might be able to shed some light on that. I need to speak with him.'

'Sometimes . . . sometimes if there's not a lot to do, and it's pretty quiet on that shift, sometimes he'll take a little break.'

'A break.'

She nodded.

'Where might he take this break?'

'There's a room down in the basement of the plant. Where they keep extra pipes and tools and things for when they have to do repairs. He might be there.'

'Does he go down there to have a drink?'

'I didn't say that,' Mrs Whitehead said.

'May I use your phone?' I asked.

My cell would have worked just fine, but I wanted to get into the house and see for myself whether Whitehead was here.

'Uh, okay,' she said, stepping back to let me in. 'It's in the kitchen.'

I walked through a living area furnished with items that might have been bought at the time the house was built. In the kitchen, I noticed just one plate with half a piece of toast on it. An empty glass looked as though it had had orange juice in it. Looked as though Mrs Whitehead had breakfasted alone.

I found a phone on the counter and dialed Garvey Ottman.

'Yeah. Duckworth?'

'Yeah.' I described the room where Mrs White-head said her husband liked to disappear to during his shift. 'You got a room like that?'

'Yup.'

'Have you looked for Whitehead there?' I asked.

'No, why would I?'

'Can you check it out?'

'Hold on, okay? I'll head down there now.'

I could hear hurried, echoing footsteps as Ottman ran through the plant, then down what sounded like a metal stairway.

'I'm almost there,' he said. 'How'd you hear about this?'

'Mrs Whitehead,' I said, and gave her a weak smile, 'is with me, and she said he sometimes goes down there for a break.'

'Jesus, the son of a bitch,' he said. 'Okay, I'm here. Hang on.'

I heard a loud, rusty squeak. Some more noises, as though Ottman was moving some things around.

'Shit,' he said.

I felt my pulse quicken. 'What? Is he there?' I pictured him passed out, surrounded by empty bottles.

'No,' Ottman said. 'He's not.'

I left a card with Tate Whitehead's wife and got her to promise – for what that was worth – to call me if he showed up. From there, I headed to Thackeray College. I'd phoned ahead, to the security office once run by Clive Duncomb, and was put through to the new boss of that department, Joyce Pilgrim. I'd already met her, back when I was looking into Duncomb's fatal shooting of Mason Helt, the lead suspect in a series of campus assaults. Duncomb had used Joyce as bait to flush out the predator, and the plan had worked all too well.

She told me which student residence to meet her out front of, and moments later I found her there, standing at the building's entrance.

'I called ages ago,' she told me as I walked up. She was pale, drawn, and her voice was shaking.

'We've kind of had our hands full,' I told her. 'Are you okay?'

'Huh? Yeah, yeah, just a bit shook-up.'

She led me into the building and up a flight of concrete stairs. This was a newer, more modern building for Thackeray, a school that went back to the late eighteen hundreds.

'Who's the victim?' I asked as we were halfway up.

'Lorraine Plummer,' Joyce Pilgrim told me.

I knew the name. 'She was one of the ones Mason Helt attacked.'

'That's right,' Joyce said.

'Why was she here? Isn't school over?'

'It is, but there are some summer classes. But of the students taking them, a lot of them live in town. Hardly any in the residences, at least not this one.

We've got a couple of students on the third floor, at the other end of the building. Lorraine's the only one, through the summer, living on the second floor.'

'So who found her?'

Joyce told me about the call from the family, who had not heard from their daughter for several days.

'Any idea when it happened?' I asked.

'I'm no expert on that kind of thing,' she said, 'but it's been a while, I'm pretty sure of that.'

You try to go into these things with an open mind. You don't prejudge, preguess. But, looking back, I'd clearly been expecting something different from what I found.

I had in my head that what I'd be looking at was a sexual assault that had escalated to a homicide. Girl living alone, maybe she meets a boy at some local bar, invites him back to her dorm room, and things get out of hand.

I'd seen that kind of thing before.

The killer wouldn't have to worry about someone hearing what was happening, given that the building was nearly empty.

That part I had right.

As soon as we came out of the stairwell and into the hall, I had a sense of what we were dealing with. The smell was overwhelming, and it hit me hard because I was gulping air after just the one flight.

God, one lousy flight of stairs and I was winded.

I stopped, reached down into my pocket where I kept a small tube of Vicks VapoRub.

'What are you doing?' Joyce asked.

'You'll want some of this, too.'

I put a dab on my finger and rubbed some on between my nose and upper lip. The strong menthol smell would mask the stench.

Joyce let me put some on her finger so she could do the same. 'Wish I'd had this earlier.' Embarrassment washed over her face. 'I threw up.'

'Nothing to be ashamed of,' I said.

Even before we reached the door, I could see the blood that had seeped out below it. The door was closed. Before I could ask, Joyce told me she had closed the door when she'd gone down to wait for me.

'You've touched the handle?' I asked her.

Her face fell. 'Yes.'

Even so, I managed to turn the knob with my fingernails, just in case some usable prints remained. I nudged the door open with my elbow.

It was not as I had imagined. It was much, much worse.

Lorraine Plummer was stretched out on the floor, slightly on her right side, her dead eyes open, lips parted. I had a view of a bloated tongue, and her skin was bluish in color, indicating she had been dead for some time. She was dressed in a T-shirt and a pair of stretchy workout pants, and covered in blood below the waist.

I glanced back at Joyce Pilgrim, thinking I would

have to tell her to stay out in the hall, but it wasn't necessary.

I got as close to the body as I could without stepping in blood – all of which looked dried – then knelt down for a few seconds, which was no picnic for my knees. I wanted a closer look without actually moving or touching the body. Given what was going on in town, I wasn't likely to see a medical examiner or a forensics team here for a long time.

It was difficult to tell exactly how she had been attacked, and I'd have to wait until Lorraine Plummer was on an autopsy table with all the blood washed away to be sure, but I was able to make out the wound that was the apparent cause of death.

Someone had sliced across the young woman's abdomen. The cut ran, roughly, from just above one hip bone to the other. But along the way, it curved down slightly.

I felt a wooziness that was not directly related to the stench in the room. I had seen this individual's handiwork before. Once, in person, when I'd investigated the murder of Rosemary Gaynor. And a second time, when I had seen autopsy photos from the Olivia Fisher homicide.

The slice that looked like a smile.

CHAPTER 16

The driver of the fire truck told Cal Weaver there were so many casualties from whatever was making people sick that he couldn't even guess when officials might get to Lucy Brighton.

Cal took the man's suggestion to leave a detailed note on the door. He walked back to Crystal, still sitting on the front step with the clipboard and sheets of paper she was drawing on.

He sat down next to her and said, 'Do you have a clean sheet there?'

Crystal slipped one out from underneath and put it on the top. Cal took the clipboard and pen from her and wrote at the top of the page 'NOTICE' and underlined it three times.

In bullet form, he indicated that the body of Lucy Brighton was in the home, in the upstairs bathroom. He wrote that the only other resident of the house, Crystal, age eleven, was safe and with him. He put his name and contact information at the end, adding that he had a key to the house and would return to let the authorities in.

'Where would I find some tape?' Cal asked Crystal.

She told him which kitchen drawer to look in. Also, he was going to get in touch with her father. Where would he find that information?

'All that stuff is in my mom's phone,' she said.

Cal nodded. He'd find the phone and bring it along. 'You trust me to pack a bag for you?' he asked Crystal.

'Okay.'

'You have a suitcase or anything somewhere?'

'There's a backpack in my room.'

'You have any prescriptions or anything like that you take that I need to pack?'

The girl shook her head. Cal had already decided he'd buy the girl a new toothbrush. He wasn't going back into, or taking anything out of, that bathroom unless it was absolutely necessary.

'I'll be as quick as I can,' he said.

'I need clothes to put on now.' She was still in her pajamas.

'Okay.'

He went into the house and found Lucy's phone right away, on the kitchen table. In a drawer he found a roll of duct tape. He located her purse up in her bedroom and took a set of keys so he could lock up the house when they left. Finally, Cal went into Crystal's room and threw some tops and pants and socks and underwear into a red backpack. He kept one change of clothes separate. On her dresser was the collection of markers he'd recently bought her. He grabbed those, too.

He came out the front door, set the backpack

next to Crystal, taped his sign securely to the front door, tossed the roll of tape back into the house, locked the door, and pocketed the keys.

'Have you had any breakfast?' Cal asked Lucy's daughter.

'No,' she said.

'Are you hungry?'

'Kinda.'

'Let's go get something to eat,' he said, resting a light hand on her shoulder.

'Okay.'

She stood and they walked to Cal's car. Once inside, he handed her a top and some pants and suggested she put them on over her pajamas. They drove to Kelly's, the downtown diner, where they got a seat by the window. Crystal ordered French toast with extra syrup and powdered sugar.

Cal, out of habit, ordered coffee.

'We can't do coffee,' the waitress said. 'You see anybody in here drinking coffee? You haven't heard what's going on?'

'What was I thinking?' he said.

'People dying all over the place,' she said.

Cal, catching the woman's eye, gave her a cautious nod toward Crystal, who had her head down. But the waitress missed the signal, and said, 'Can't do tea, neither. Want a milk?'

'No, thanks,' he said. 'Have you got bottled water?'

'Yeah, that local stuff.'

Cal thought. 'Could you pour some into a mug and nuke it and toss in a tea bag?'

The waitress sighed, as if this were the biggest imposition she'd encountered in her career. 'You'll get charged for the water, and for the tea.'

'I'm good for it,' Cal said.

'And I hope you aren't expecting our fine china. We don't know if it's safe to wash the dishes. We're doin' paper plates and plastic cutlery.'

'No problem.'

'What about you, kid? Anything to drink?'

Crystal raised her head. 'Milk, please.' A pause, and then, 'I know all about what happened. My mom is dead.'

The waitress was stunned into silence.

'She drank the water and she threw up and then she died in the bathroom,' Crystal said, as though describing what she'd studied in school the day before.

'I – I'm sorry.' She looked back at Cal. 'I'm so sorry. Your wife?'

'No.'

The waitress took another look at Crystal, as though puzzling over why she didn't appear more upset.

'Can I have that tea?' Cal asked.

The waitress disappeared. Crystal resumed working on her drawing while Cal opened the list of contacts on Lucy Brighton's phone.

'What's your dad's name again?' he asked her.

Without looking up, she said, 'Gerald.'

'Not Jerry?'

Her head went back and forth. Cal found Gerald

Brighton quickly under the *B*s. 'You okay here for a couple of minutes? I'm going to give your dad a call.'

'Okay.'

He slid out of the booth, went out onto the sidewalk, and stood where he could keep an eye on Crystal through the glass. He e-mailed Gerald Brighton's contact info off Lucy's phone to his own, brought it up on the screen, and hit the number.

It rang five times before going to voice mail. 'Yeah, hey, you've reached Gerald Brighton. Leave your name and number and maybe, just maybe, if you're really lucky, I'll get back to you!'

A pause. Cal said, 'Mr Brighton, this is Cal Weaver, in Promise Falls, New York. I need to speak to you about your wife, Lucy, and daughter, Crystal. It's urgent.' He gave his number, ended the call, and went back inside.

Crystal said, 'No answer, right?'

'Yeah,' Cal said, slipping into the booth.

'He doesn't usually answer his phone.'

'What did your mother do when she had an emergency and needed to get in touch with him?'

'She always leaves – she always left a message and he calls back later sometimes if he feels like it.'

The waitress returned with a paper cup of boiled bottled water and a tea bag. 'French toast is almost ready, sweetheart,' she said.

Cal bobbed the tea bag up and down in the water. 'Talk to me,' he said to Crystal.

She looked up. 'About what?'

'I just wondered how you are. Which I guess is a pretty dumb question.'

'I feel things,' she said. 'But I don't know how to show them.'

'I get that.'

She turned the clipboard around so he could see what she had been working on. The clouds, even darker now, as though heavy with rain.

'They're about to burst,' Crystal said.

Cal's heart felt connected to a fifty-pound anchor. 'So they are.'

The waitress set Crystal's French toast in front of her. 'You need anything, let me know,' she said.

Cal and Crystal didn't say another word to each other during breakfast.

'Whose house is this?' Crystal asked when Cal stopped the car.

'My sister and her husband live here,' he told her. 'Her name is Celeste and his name is Dwayne. She's very, very nice.'

'What about Dwayne?'

'He's okay.'

Crystal seemed to perceive some meaning there. 'Is he a douche?'

Cal, for the first time in days, laughed. 'A bit. But he's had a rough time lately. He's got a paving company and he does a lot of work for the town, but they've been cutting back, so he hasn't had much work.'

'Oh.'

'But that's just between us.'

'Do you live here, too, since the fire?'

'No.' She looked at the house, then back at him, then at the house again. 'Come on,' he said. 'Grab your backpack and I'll introduce you.'

They went to the door together. Celeste showed up seconds later.

'Hey, who's this?' she asked, bending at the waist to get face-to-face with the unexpected visitor.

'This is Crystal,' Cal said.

'How are you, Crystal?' Celeste asked, extending a hand.

Crystal said, 'My mom's dead.'

'Can we come in?' Cal asked while his sister struggled for something to say.

'Um, yes, yes, come in,' Celeste said. 'Crystal, would you like something to eat or drink?'

'I just had French toast with syrup.' She paused. 'And milk.'

'Why don't you watch TV or draw while I talk to Celeste?' Cal said. Crystal walked into the living room, grabbed a remote, and plopped down on the couch as Cal and Celeste excused themselves to the kitchen.

Cal filled her in.

'Oh God, that's horrible,' Celeste said.

'I haven't heard anything back from her dad yet. And even if I do, he's in San Francisco and it's probably going to be a day or two before he gets here.'

'What are you asking?'

'I can't have her stay with me at the hotel. It just doesn't look right. Strange man who's not her father.'

'She can stay here,' Celeste said without hesitation.

'Dwayne won't mind?'

Celeste sighed. 'He minds just about everything these days.'

'Where is he?'

'Out in the garage doing God knows what.' Celeste's eyes moistened.

'What's going on?'

'It's just . . . more of the same. The more worried he gets about losing work, the more withdrawn he gets. He goes out without telling me, is gone for hours. When he comes back, I ask him where he's been and all he says is "out." I don't know what to do. I try to boost his spirits, tell him things are going to turn around, but nothing much seems to work. And now, God, given what's happened today, I don't know what the future holds for this town.'

'Me, neither,' Cal said.

'They said on the radio that there might be more than a hundred dead. Just for starters. And there may be lots of people sick or dead they don't even know about yet.'

Like Lucy, Cal thought.

'How does a town get over something like this?' she asked.

'I can't worry about the whole town,' Cal said. 'Right now all I'm worried about is Crystal.'

'She seems kind of . . . forgive me, but she seems kind of weird. And I don't mean just because of her mom being dead. There's something—'

'I know. Just be patient with her.'

'Of course. But is there anything I should know—'

The door that led from the kitchen to the backyard opened and Dwayne came in. 'Hey,' he said. 'Cal.'

'Dwayne.'

'Thanks for the heads-up about the bad water, but we already knew,' he said.

Celeste added, 'Dwayne knew before anybody.'

Dwayne stepped in quickly. 'I was out for a walk before Celeste even woke up. Ran into someone on the street who told me. Came home, made sure Celeste knew before she was even out of bed.'

'Lucky thing,' Cal said.

Dwayne nodded. 'Yeah.' He heard the television going and peered around the corner into the living room. 'Who's the kid?'

Celeste brought him up to speed.

'She's gonna stay with us?' Dwayne asked.

Cal said, 'Not for long, I hope. I'm trying to get in touch with her father. Once he gets here . . .'

Dwayne shook his head. It was clear he didn't like the idea, but he said, 'I guess. As long as it's just her.'

Cal went back into the living room. Crystal

had tuned the TV in to, of all things, the Weather Channel.

'Why are you watching this?' Cal asked.

'I like weather,' she said.

Cal told her she would be staying with Celeste and Dwayne until her father could get to Promise Falls.

Crystal asked, 'Both of us?'

'No,' Cal explained. 'I'll stay in my hotel.'

Cal noticed the child's face starting to look brittle. 'No,' she said. 'I can't stay here without you.'

'Celeste and Dwayne are very nice. You'll—'

'No!'

Cal had never heard the child raise her voice before. He'd never really seen her emotional on any level.

She stayed sitting perfectly rigid on the couch, hands clasped together on her lap atop the clipboard, and screamed: 'No! No! No! No! No! No!'

Celeste and Dwayne rushed into the room, Dwayne saying, 'What the hell?'

Cal slowly sat down beside Crystal, put his arm around her, and pulled her close. 'Okay,' he said softly. 'Okay.'

As Crystal stopped screaming, Cal glanced over at his sister.

'Sure,' she said, nodding encouragingly, a broad smile on her face. 'We've got lots of room! Cal can stay here, too.'

'On the couch,' he said. 'I'll be fine right here.'

Dwayne turned and went back into the kitchen, where, seconds later, they could hear the pop of a beer can opening, then the back door opening and closing.

CHAPTER 17

Hillary and Josh Lydecker were among the throngs of people crowding the Promise Falls General Hospital ER and adjoining hallways. Doctors were now looking at their daughter, Cassandra, whose symptoms were pretty much the same as everyone else's.

The Lydeckers had made a trip to the hospital chapel and prayed quietly for their daughter to pull through.

But they prayed for their missing son, George, too.

They were heading back to the ER from the chapel when Hillary spotted the detective who had been to their house after they'd reported George missing.

'Detective!' Hillary called out. 'Detective Carlson!' She started running down the hall, her husband right behind her.

Angus Carlson had been talking to one of the doctors when he heard his name called out. He turned, saw the Lydeckers, and said to the doctor, 'Thanks, we can talk later.'

He waited for the Lydeckers to close the distance

between them, then said, 'Hello. Why are you here? Who's sick? Is it George? Has George turned up?'

Hillary, nearly out of breath, said, 'Cassie.'

'Your daughter,' Carlson said, remembering.

'Yes. She's very sick.'

'I'm sorry,' he said. 'It's hit so many people.'

'Is there any news about George?' Josh Lydecker asked.

Carlson's lips pressed tightly together before parting. 'I'm afraid I don't have any.'

'Cassie told us,' the father said. 'About what George has been doing.'

Carlson waited. 'You mean—'

'Breaking into garages,' Hillary said. 'She said he does it all the time. That he breaks in, that he steals things. I can't believe he would do that. Is it true?'

'According to your daughter, yes. I've asked to be notified of any garage break-ins, see if they might be connected at all to your son's disappearance, but there haven't actually been any such occurrences in the last week, at least none that have been reported to the Promise Falls police.'

'So what else are you doing to find him?' the woman asked.

Carlson said, 'Well, right now, as you can see—'

'But before all this happened,' the father said. 'What have you been doing?'

'We've put out a description to all officers, I've

spoken to George's friends, I've looked for any activity on his cell phone, and—'

'Have you searched?' Hillary Lydecker asked. 'Have you gone door-to-door? Have you – I don't know – searched people's basements and . . . and abandoned buildings, someplace where he might have fallen and gotten hurt, or—'

Carlson reached out a comforting hand to the woman's arm. 'We can't just search random houses, ma'am, without cause. We're doing what we can, believe me.'

'How can this be happening to us?' she asked. 'One child missing, now the other sick? What did we do? Why would God do this to us?'

Carlson said, 'That's out of my area, I'm afraid. But if I hear anything about your son, believe me, I will be in touch. I hope your daughter's going to be okay.'

He made his way outside the hospital so he could use his cell phone. He'd learned a few things since Duckworth had left, and felt it was time to update him. He made the call.

'Duckworth.'

'Carlson, sir.'

'Where've you been? Finderman was trying to reach you earlier.'

'Why?'

'She was going to send you out to Thackeray, but I got pulled off and had to take the call.'

'You know there's no cell coverage in the ER. What happened at Thackeray?'

'Homicide.'

'What? Who?'

'Student named Lorraine Plummer. She was one of the ones—'

'I interviewed her,' Carlson said. 'I remember. What happened?'

'Later. Why are you calling?'

'I'm still at the hospital. Story's not really changing. Same symptoms with everyone. Number of people coming in has slowed. Guess the word's getting out. Local and state health officials already all over it, taking samples, looking for E. coli, like maybe there's sewage or animal waste in the water, but it's not like they can tell you immediately whether that's the cause or not. It takes several hours to do the tests on the water to confirm what it is.'

'Is that their best guess?' Duckworth asked.

'They're kind of hedging. The symptoms they're seeing are not totally consistent with E. coli. So they're not issuing a boil-water advisory. Like, if they were pretty sure it was E. coli, they'd say if you boil the water, that'll kill the bacteria, and then it's safe to drink. But lots of people, they *had* boiled the water, and they still got sick.'

'The overnight guy at the water plant – shit!'

'What?'

'Why didn't I think of that?' Duckworth said. 'Maybe he's one of the ones who got sick.'

'Say again?'

'Find out if someone named Tate Whitehead has been admitted.'

'I'm going back in. I'll get back to you.'

Carlson ended the call and reentered the hospital. A paramedic told him a list of patients' names was being kept at the admitting desk, on paper and on computer. Carlson saw a nurse behind the desk. Early twenties, fair-skinned, black hair that would have fallen to her shoulders if she didn't have it pulled back into a ponytail.

Carlson gave her the name.

'Whitehead,' she said. 'Whitehead.' She looked up, shook her head. 'Nothing. Maybe he's sitting out there and hasn't checked in with us.'

'Thank you,' Carlson said.

He was about to step away when the young woman looked at him, her eyes filled with fear, and said, 'Eighty-two.'

'Excuse me?'

'Eighty-two people have died. And the number just keeps going up. I feel . . . I feel—'

'Scared,' he offered, and she nodded. 'What's your name?'

'Sonja.'

'Sonja what?'

'Sonja Roper.'

'Sonja, everyone's scared. I know I am. We're scared for ourselves and our loved ones.' Amid the chaos, he smiled. 'Do you have children?'

'No,' she said. 'Soon, I hope. My boyfriend – his name is Stan and we're going to get married in the fall – and I really want to have kids. He's missed all this, lucky him. He's a pilot for Delta and won't be back till Monday.'

'When you see what's going on here, does it make you rethink that? That the world is too dangerous and unpredictable a place?'

Her eyes moved down to the desk as she thought about that. 'I don't know. I don't think so.'

'Sonja!' someone shouted. 'We need you!'

'I have to go,' she said, and flew away from her desk.

Carlson took a position in the middle of the ER waiting room and shouted loud enough to be heard over the chatter: 'Is there a Tate Whitehead here?'

The noise dropped slightly for several seconds, people glancing at one another, waiting to see if someone would step forward.

One man raised a weak hand.

'Mr Whitehead?' Carlson said.

'No. But I know him, and he ain't here. Haven't seen him.'

Carlson went back outside to give Duckworth the news.

CHAPTER 18

The convoy of ten Finley Springs Water trucks lined up on the shoulder of the road that ran past the park at the foot of the waterfall in downtown Promise Falls. Randall Finley had trailed behind in his Lincoln, figuring he would give his employees a few minutes to get things set up before he made his appearance.

Sitting in the passenger seat, David Harwood had been making some calls along the way, getting in touch with the same news outlets he'd alerted to Finley's campaign announcement a few days earlier. He'd made that announcement in this very same spot, there at the park. Even if that news conference hadn't gone as well as Finley had hoped – inevitably, reporters had brought up his involvement years before with that underage prostitute who'd later died – he liked this park for events. The falls always made a great backdrop, and the park was centrally located.

David was still on the phone, but this call didn't sound like it was to one of the news organizations.

'Sam,' he said, lowering his voice. 'Please call. I went by your place, to warn you about this whole water thing. Where'd you go? How could you leave without telling me? Please, please get in touch. I love you. I—'

'David, we're here,' Finley said.

'I have to go,' David said. 'I'll try again later.' He tucked the phone into his jacket.

'What the hell was that?'

'Nothing,' David said.

'Come on. You got a problem, you can tell ol' Randy.'

David shot him a look. 'You're not someone I'd go to with my personal problems.'

Finley shrugged. 'Have it your way. But I've got a big shoulder to cry on if you need it.'

David opened the door as the Lincoln came to a stop.

'First thing we gotta do is get the signs up,' Finley said. Before leaving the plant, he'd had posters made up that read FREE BOTTLED WATER to be plastered on the side of the trucks. 'Just make sure they don't put them over the logo.' By that he meant the Finley Springs Water markings on the sides of each of the panel vans.

'Sure,' David said, closing the door.

Finley muttered, 'It's so hard to get good help these days.'

He got out of his Lincoln and strolled up the street past his trucks. They'd been parked with half a car's length between them so the back doors could be opened up and flats of water handed out from there.

As he was walking by the third truck, he saw Trevor swinging open the back doors.

'Not yet,' Finley told him.

'But I'm all set to—'

'Not yet,' he repeated. There were no news crews here yet. How much death and mayhem could they film at the hospital? There was another important part of the story happening right here.

'David!'

Harwood had been helping to put a sign on one of the trucks and taking questions from drivers of passing cars who were already slowing, powering down windows to ask if free water was really being handed out. He stopped what he was doing and ran over to Finley.

'How long's it going to take for the press to show?' he asked.

'They'll get here when they get here,' David said.

'Oh!' Finley shouted, pointing. 'Look!'

A news van with an NBC logo emblazoned on the side was working its way up the street. 'This is good, this is good,' Finley said. 'National coverage.'

But the van didn't slow, and went right past the convoy of trucks.

'What the fuck?' Finley said, turning on David. 'Run after them!'

'They're heading for the hospital,' he said. 'Did you not hear anything I said to you before?'

Finley ignored him. A car had stopped and a woman who looked to be in her eighties was slowly getting out from behind the wheel.

'You have drinking water?' she asked.

'That's right,' David said.

'Oh, please, could I get some?'

'Not yet!' Finley whispered. 'There's no one here!'

David got out his phone. 'You do it. Get a case out of the back and give it to her. I'll get pics.'

Finley gave that a second's thought. 'Okay, fine, that'll have to do for now. But tweet it or Facebook it or whatever it is you do soon as you get the shot.' He put on a smile and strode toward the woman. 'You bet we have water for you,' he said, opening the closest van's rear door.

'This is wonderful,' she said.

'It's pretty heavy,' he said, grabbing a case and lugging it toward her car. 'You have someone to help you when you get home?'

'I can take them in a few bottles at a time,' she said.

David put the smartphone up to his eye, grabbed some pictures.

'You look familiar to me,' the elderly woman said.

'I'm Randall Finley,' he said.

'Oh, you,' she said. 'I remember you.'

'You want to open the back door and I'll just put this on the seat there?'

'You used to be the mayor,' she said.

'Hope to be once again, too,' he said. 'But that's not what this is about today. This is about helping people like you.'

'Do you still use prostitutes?' the woman asked.

'Okay, there you go!' he said once he'd put the water in the backseat. He held the front door open for her.

As she slipped back in, she said, 'I'm sure it was you.'

'I think you have me confused with someone else,' he said. 'You're thinking of the former attorney general. That was quite the scandal.'

'Oh,' she said. 'You might be right.'

He closed the door and waved her on. Shaking his head, he said to David, 'If the stupid old bat can be fooled that easily, she shouldn't be behind the wheel. Tell me you couldn't hear the question on the video.'

'I can always change the sound, dub music over it, something.'

'People need to move on about that shit,' Finley said. 'Oh, here we go.'

Another news van was coming down the street, but it was from a local station in Albany, and instead of continuing on in the direction the NBC van had taken, it stopped.

'Action!' Finley said under his breath. 'Get those doors open! Let's go. Move it, move it, move it!'

At which point the back doors of all the vans were swung wide. Cases of bottled water were put on display on the sidewalk and nearby picnic tables in the park. Soon, the road was jammed with cars. People were getting out, helping themselves to cases of water – 'One case per family for now!' Finley shouted – and tossing them into their trunks.

Before long, Finley found half a dozen micro-phones in his face.

'Why are you doing this?' one reporter asked.

'Why?' Finley responded. 'I think the question if I weren't here would be, why not? I'm in a unique position to be able to help the people of Promise Falls in their hour of need.'

'What's this costing you?'

Finley shrugged. 'No idea. Thousands, probably. But I really don't give a rat's ass.' He chuckled. 'Can I say that on TV?'

'Didn't you just announce your intention to run for mayor again?'

Finley shook his head, waved the question off. 'That may be true, but that has nothing to do with why I'm here today. This is not a day for politics. This is a day for helping, for pitching in. And tomorrow will be a day for healing.'

He looked past the news crews, wondering where David was. It would be all he could do not to give the man a thumbs-up if he caught sight of him.

There he was. Sitting on the edge of one of the picnic tables, on his cell phone.

Later, after the reporters had left, and most of the water had been given away, Finley joined David at the table.

'I'd call that a success,' Finley said.

'You mean that you were able to help out people with drinkable water?'

Finley smiled. 'That, too.' He patted David on the back. 'What say I give you a ride back to the plant so you can get your car? Then I'm going to slip away for a while. Regroup, gather my strength. We can talk later in the day, do some strategizing.'

'Sure.'

'Sounds like a plan. You get hold of that Sam person you were looking for?'

'No,' David said.

'That a man or a woman?'

'A woman.'

He nodded, pleased. 'Well, that's a relief. Not that I got anything against queers. I sure as hell don't. I just don't know if I'd want one running my campaign.'

David asked, 'How did you do it?'

'How'd I do what?'

'How'd you ratchet up production so fast? It's only been a few hours since people started showing up at the hospital, since the outbreak. It normally takes that long to get the plant up and running, doesn't it? And you'd have to be getting all your people in. I just don't know how you did so much in such a short amount of time.'

Finley looked over in the direction of the falls, as though taking in its natural beauty.

'The water was already bottled,' he said. 'It was mostly a question of getting it all into the trucks. I upped production in the last week.'

'Why'd you do that?' David asked.

'You know. Summer's coming. Increased demand. Employees taking holidays. Just wanted to get ahead of things, that's all. Who could have guessed it would turn out to be so fortuitous?'

CHAPTER 19

Duckworth

I put in a call to my friend Wanda Therrieult, the Promise Falls coroner, but she wasn't answering. The bodies were probably already stacking up in the morgue like firewood before the winter. I left her a message that I needed her, but wasn't hopeful I'd hear back soon.

I'd have to do the best I could with the Lorraine Plummer investigation on my own.

Careful not to stand in the pool of dried blood, I surveyed things from the door to her dormitory room. There did not, first of all, appear to be signs of a struggle. The computer chair at her desk was not knocked over. Papers and books had not been tossed about. The couple of posters that hung on the wall – one was for the movie *The Girl with the Dragon Tattoo*, the Hollywood version with Daniel Craig; the other a Mahatma Gandhi quote that read, in an elegant typeface, 'Be the change you want to see in the world' – were not askew, as one might expect them to be if a person had been thrown up against the wall.

The door showed no signs of being forced. No splintered wood, no obvious scratches. There was no peephole installed in the door that would have allowed Lorraine to see who might be knocking on her door.

Of course, Lorraine might not have had a knock at the door. She might have brought her killer to the room. A boyfriend, maybe. Someone she'd just met. Either way, the lack of any real disruption to the room suggested Lorraine might have known her killer.

Known him well enough, at least, to allow him into her room.

I had a terrible feeling that the man who'd killed Olivia Fisher and Rosemary Gaynor had struck again.

So much for Bill Gaynor. And so much for Clive Duncomb.

I'd been looking at both of them as possible suspects. I didn't yet know of a connection between the dead security chief and Rosemary Gaynor, but Duncomb had had a motive for killing Olivia Fisher.

Gaynor, on the other hand, had links to both victims. He was married to one, of course, and there was a motive. There was a hefty life insurance policy on Rosemary, and her husband had debts. His alibi – he'd supposedly been in Boston at the time of her murder – wasn't airtight. He'd also been the insurance agent for the Fisher family, and therefore had known Olivia.

But Bill Gaynor was not magical.

He couldn't have slipped out of prison to do this to Lorraine.

I'd taken in the room, so now I focused on Lorraine herself. Wanda would be the one to determine with any degree of certainty whether Lorraine had been sexually assaulted, but it didn't appear to me that she had. Her clothes were intact. Her top had not been pulled up; her pants had not been pulled down.

This didn't look like a so-called crime of passion. It struck me as more ritualistic, especially given that this was the third Promise Falls woman I knew of to have been attacked in this way.

Now I turned my attention to the bed itself.

The covers were rumpled, but not turned down. Sitting atop them was an open laptop, the monitor dead. I figured Lorraine had been dead several days, so the laptop had probably run out of charge. I'd want to see what she'd been working on. Maybe she'd been sitting on the bed, doing something on her computer, when someone came knocking on the door.

There was something caught in the folds of the blanket. Something shiny.

I tiptoed around the body on the floor and approached the bed from the foot. I pulled lightly on the blanket until the item that had caught my eye revealed itself.

A cell phone.

I grabbed it delicately by the edges, aware that

the screen and the back side might contain finger-prints other than Lorraine's. I moved it over to the desk, set it down, and pressed the home button with a fingernail.

Nothing happened. The phone was dead.

Inches away, already plugged into the wall, was a charging cord. Again, careful not to leave my mucky fingerprints all over the phone, I worked the charger into the base of the phone and waited for the screen to come to life.

Please, please, please, I thought, *do not be password protected.* Despite warnings from the tech industry that everyone should have a four-digit password to get into their phones, many still did not bother. Some required a fingerprint.

I glanced at Lorraine's body, dreading the thought of having to position her dead finger onto the phone.

I got lucky.

The phone's main screen, displaying all its various apps, materialized. The first thing I noticed was that she had several phone messages awaiting her. Given what Joyce Pilgrim had told me, they were probably from her frantic parents.

She also had a text message awaiting her. I tapped on the message app and up came a conver-sation with someone named Cleo.

Her last message to Lorraine Plummer had been simply: K.

What I guessed she meant by that was 'okay.' Certainly took a lot less effort to type and got the message across.

184

There had been conversation leading up to that, a back-and-forth between Cleo and Lorraine.

Cleo: Did u hear about Bmore?
Lorraine: What?
Cleo: He got arrested. Ran down someone with his car
Lorraine: Holy shit
Cleo: Yeah
Lorraine: Hate to think of this first but what about essay
Cleo: Yeah I know
Lorraine: GTG someone here

'I've got to go,' Lorraine was saying. Someone was there. Was the door open? Was there a knock? A recorded phone call would have told me more, but what I had here was pretty good. Lorraine had sent that text at 12:21 a.m. on May 21.

Then, at 12:22 a.m., Cleo had texted: K.

Lorraine had not returned that text. If she had a visitor, it was no surprise she hadn't texted back right away. But she might have texted Cleo later to tell her who'd dropped by.

Lorraine had never texted Cleo, or anyone else, again.

I needed to know who'd come to visit Lorraine Plummer at 12:21. I also needed to find out who Cleo was. Still trying to be careful not to smudge the screen, I opened the contacts file and looked for anyone named Cleo.

185

I found her in the *G*s. Cleo Gough. I got out my own cell phone and entered the number, put the phone to my ear, and took the opportunity to walk out into the hall.

There was a pickup on the fifth ring. 'Hello?'

'Is this Cleo Gough?'

'Who's this?'

'I'm Detective Barry Duckworth with the Promise Falls police.'

'What? Who?'

I repeated it for her. 'Okay,' she said in the same tone in which someone might say 'Whatever.'

'I need to speak with you, Ms Gough.' I had pronounced it *goff*. 'Am I saying that right?'

'Yeah,' she said cautiously.

'Are you on the Thackeray campus?'

'Uh, not exactly. How do you know I go to Thackeray?'

'I understand you're a student there. You took Professor Blackmore's class?'

'Is this about that? About him running down that guy with his car? I don't know *anything* about that. What would I know about that?'

'Where are you right now, Ms Gough?'

She hesitated. 'I live just off campus. I guess I could meet you in like ten minutes or something. There's a Dunkin's like half a block from here.'

I wondered whether that was the best place for me to meet Cleo, or anyone else for that matter. I'd been doing so well lately when it came to donuts.

'Okay,' I said. 'Tell me which one.'

186

She did.

I said, 'I'll be the guy who looks like a regular customer.'

Joyce Pilgrim had posted herself outside the building. When I came out, I asked her how extensive Thackeray's system of surveillance cameras was.

'We have them, although we don't have them everywhere,' she said. She looked more pulled together than when I'd last seen her.

'What about around here?'

She pointed. 'There's one down the street, near the athletic center. Another one up that way by the library.'

'What about this building?'

'None in the hallways or directly outside.'

'But to get here, someone would have to go past one of those other cameras.'

Joyce nodded slowly. 'Probably.'

'How long does your security system hold on to video?'

'A week.'

So there was time. I told her my hunch about when Lorraine Plummer had been killed. I wanted to know who showed up on any surveillance cameras in the hour leading up to that time, and the hour after.

'I'll see what I can do,' she said. 'You got a number where I can reach you?'

We exchanged contact information. 'Ms Pilgrim,'

I said, 'I am completely and totally counting on you here. I don't know how much you know about what else is going on in Promise Falls today, but Putin could drop a nuclear bomb on Thackeray today and we wouldn't be able to get to it for a week.'

'I get it, Detective,' she said.

'Are you going to be okay?'

Her eyes met mine. 'I've got a job to do, just like you.'

I parked in front of the Dunkin' Donuts that Cleo Gough had directed me to and went inside. A young woman seated by the window who appeared to be watching everyone who came in the door raised her head when she saw me. I definitely looked like a patron.

She was early twenties, stick thin, with alternating streaks of black and blond hair.

'You the cop?' she asked.

'I am.'

'I wanna see some ID.'

'That's smart.' I got mine out and gave her plenty of time to examine it.

'Okay,' she said. 'There are a lot of sick fucks out there, you know.' Sitting there, she seemed to recoil in her seat, even though I'd passed the initial test.

'You want something?' I asked.

She shrugged. 'Black coffee, I guess.'

'Anything to eat? I'm buying.'

Cleo shook her head. I went to the counter, ordered two coffees.

'Haven't you heard?' the kid behind the counter asked.

'Oh, yeah,' I said.

'All I can give you is something bottled. Water, juice, milk, anything like that.'

I called over to Cleo to ask what she might like instead. 'Orange juice.'

'Make it two,' I told the kid. I surveyed the wondrous baked offerings. It was past noon, and I'd had nothing since breakfast. This was not a case of my treating myself to something I shouldn't have. This was a matter of basic survival. And I did not have to get a donut. There were sandwiches.

'A ham and cheese on a bun,' I said. 'And that strawberry and vanilla sprinkle thing you've got there. Actually, two of them.'

If today had taught me anything, it was that we could end up dead at any minute. Delayed gratification did not seem like an option at the moment.

The kid put everything on a tray. Once I'd paid, I took it and sat down opposite Cleo. She looked disapproving as I handed her the juice.

'That's terrible for you,' she said. 'Not the sandwich so much, but the other stuff. It's no wonder you're—'

She stopped herself.

'Fat?' I said.

'I wasn't going to say that.'

'That's okay.' I smiled, bit into the sandwich. 'God, I'm so hungry. I've been going all day. Guess you heard about the water thing.'

An eye roll. 'Seriously? Like, people getting sick everywhere? Of course I heard.'

I nodded. 'Good. I was working on that, then got sidetracked with something out at Thackeray. So you don't live on campus?'

'No.'

I had to wait a minute before my next question. I had a mouth full of ham and cheese. I dabbed the corner of my mouth with a napkin.

'You have a friend named Lorraine Plummer?'

A shrug. 'I guess.'

'You guess she's a friend?'

'I have a class with her. We don't hang out, but I know her.'

'Well enough to text with her.'

'Yeah,' Cleo said very slowly, stretching the word out.

'When's the last time you were texting with her?'

'I don't know. A few nights ago.'

'About Professor Blackmore? About his class? You take that class?'

'Yeah.' A nod. 'Except there is no class now. He's in jail or something.'

'You haven't been in touch with Lorraine since then?'

Her head went from side to side. She opened her juice, took a sip. 'So?'

'I just wondered why you hadn't been in touch with her since then.'

'Why?'

'Yeah,' I said.

'Because I didn't need to. The next morning, I decided to go back home for a couple of days.'

'Where's home?'

'Syracuse. I figured, what with Professor Blackmore getting arrested and everything, that class was toast, and I only had one other class, so I decided to blow it off and come back last night.'

'Why come back now? It's a long weekend. Why not come back Monday night?'

'Two days is all I want to spend with my mom and dad.' She did something funny with her mouth. 'Mostly I went home to see if they'd give me some money. They gave me five hundred, so then I came back.'

That was believable. I could remember Trevor's time in school. His most brilliantly argued pieces of writing were not his essays, but pleas to Maureen and me for more funds.

I was almost finished with the sandwich. I'd been glancing at the two donuts, the sense of anticipation building.

'Do you know Lorraine well?'

'Is she in some kind of trouble?'

'I just wondered how well you know her.'

'Not that well, like I said. I'm not going to say anything else until you tell me what's going on with her. Like, she's totally not the kind of person to do drugs or anything like that, so if that's what you think, you're totally wrong.'

I could not bring myself to eat a donut while telling Cleo a friend of hers – even one who was

191

not that close – was dead. I pushed the tray off to one side.

'A couple of nights ago, shortly after you finished texting with Lorraine,' I said, 'someone came to her room.'

'I know. She said she had to go.'

I nodded. 'That's right. Do you have any idea who it was?'

'No. Not a clue. What happened? Did something happen?'

'Yes. Cleo, someone killed Lorraine Plummer. I think whoever did it was the person who interrupted her chat with you.'

She set down her juice. 'That's – no, that's crazy.' Her eyes started to well with tears. 'How do you know this? You're wrong.'

I shook my head slowly. 'I wish I were.'

'How? Who?'

'That's why I'm here talking to you. To find out who.'

'Oh God,' she said, putting a hand over her mouth and looking out into the parking lot. 'Thackeray is so totally fucked.'

I leaned in slightly. 'What?'

'I mean, come on. They had this perv attacking girls, and he gets shot, and then the security boss or whatever he was is run over by my fucking professor? What the hell's *wrong* with that place?' She shook her head forcefully. 'I'm done. I am never setting foot on that campus again. The place is totally nuts. This whole *fucking* town is nuts. Did you hear about what happened at the drive-in?'

'Yes,' I said.

'And then today you can't even drink the water without dropping dead. I mean, what the hell is going on?'

'You're right,' I said, keeping my voice low and calm. 'You're absolutely right. There's been a lot of strange stuff going on these past few weeks.' And she didn't even know about the squirrels, or the mannequins on the Ferris wheel, or that goddamn bus.

Or that anonymous phone call I'd had the other day from someone congratulating me on putting things together.

'And now, there's this, with Lorraine,' I said, hesitating, not wanting to share more than I should, or overspeculate. But I said, 'Maybe, in some way, it's tied in to some of the other things that have been going on.'

'How?'

'I don't know. It's just kind of a feeling I have. But right now, this second, I want you to concentrate on Lorraine. Did she have a boyfriend?'

Cleo tried to focus. 'Um, uh, not that I know of. She might have, but I don't know.'

'Can you think of anyone she might have been seeing, if not recently, then going back a ways?'

'I can't, I just—'

She stopped suddenly, as though she'd just remembered something.

'What?' I asked.

'The other day when I saw her, she did say something weird.'

'What did she say?'

'Just – she said she met this guy who was really cute, but he was off-limits.'

'Did she say who he was?'

'No.'

'A student at Thackeray?'

'She didn't say that, either.'

'What did she mean by this guy being off-limits?' I asked.

'He was married,' Cleo said. 'The guy was married. It was sort of like a crush.'

'When did she tell you this?' I asked.

She shrugged. 'I don't know. In the last few days?'

'What day?'

She shook her head. 'I have no idea. It was just something she said recently.'

Suddenly, she gathered up her purse, stood, and said, 'I'm outta here. I'm quitting this school, and getting out of this town. Fuck it, I'm done.'

'I just had a couple more questions about—'

'No, I mean it. I'm *done*. I'm going back to Syracuse, even if it means living with my nutso parents.'

With that, she walked briskly out of the Dunkin's.

I put in a call to Joyce Pilgrim.

'Still no coroner or anyone else here,' she said without even saying hello.

'Lorraine was interested in a married man,' I said. 'She was having an affair?'

194

'Not sure about that. She was interested in him, but felt he was off-limits. I don't know if she had something going with him or not.'

'Professors aren't supposed to have relationships with their students,' Joyce said.

I thought, *Yeah, and they're not supposed to give them roofies and include them unwittingly in their* lifestyle *sex parties, either.* But I already knew *that* had happened. And, according to further interviews I'd had with Professor Peter Blackmore, they'd happened with Lorraine Plummer, although not recently.

Could Lorraine have been referring to Clive Duncomb or Blackmore? Or even the writer, Adam Chalmers? All three were married, and at the time of her death Lorraine was unaware – I had not yet interviewed her about this, and had still been sorting out how to tell her she was a sexual assault victim – just how despicable those three men were. It was possible she'd made her comment to her friend Cleo about being interested in a married man before the deaths of Chalmers and Duncomb, and the arrest of Blackmore.

So it could have been one of them she was referring to.

But it couldn't have been any of them who killed her. Only Blackmore was alive the night of her murder, and he was in custody.

Which would mean that her comment about having a crush on a married man was a lead that was going to go nowhere.

Still.

'You there?' Joyce asked.

'Yeah,' I said. 'When you're talking to people about Lorraine, ask them about who she might have been seeing. Married, unmarried, student, professor. Whatever.'

'What am I now?' Joyce Pilgrim asked. 'A detective?'

'Just ask, okay?'

'You want me to be a coroner, too? 'Cause there's still been no one here to look at the body. I'm waiting out front of the building for someone to show up. I can't exactly check that security video while I'm killing time here.'

'I'll make another call,' I said, thanked her, and put the phone down on the plastic tray, next to the two donuts.

I hadn't taken a bite out of either of them yet. They seemed to be taunting me, daring me to eat them.

To show I was weak.

My phone, which had been out of my hand for only about thirty seconds, started to ring.

It was Garvey Ottman, at the water treatment plant.

'Hello?' I said.

'Duckworth?'

'Yeah.'

'We found Tate.'

CHAPTER 20

Randall Finley was talking all the way back to the water plant about what David should do next, but the former reporter was not listening.

He was thinking about Samantha Worthington.

He really hadn't stopped thinking about Sam since he'd broken into her house and found out that she had left. Where had she gone? Why had she packed up and taken off? Why hadn't she called to let him know what she was doing?

Was he wrong in thinking that there was something there? Had he misjudged things? Had he been an idiot to think that Sam had feelings for him? David knew his feelings for her were genuine. He was, he believed, in love with this woman. Pretty funny, considering that the first time he had met her, she had a shotgun pointed at his head.

It was one of those things they'd worked through.

It had gotten worse before it got better. For a period of time, Sam had believed David had betrayed her, that he was helping her former in-laws, Garnet and Yolanda Worthington, in their bid to take Carl away from her and raise him themselves. Seemed pretty paranoid, David had thought at first, but he soon realized how obsessed the parents of her ex-husband, Brandon – who was serving time in prison for bank robbery – were about getting Carl. They'd even sent a nutcase by the name of Ed Noble to kidnap him at school.

David had foiled that. Ed Noble had been arrested, and so had Garnet and Yolanda – all three charged with kidnapping. Ed Noble was up for attempted murder. They weren't going to be a problem for a very long time. And Sam's ex-husband, Brandon, remained in prison.

Sam's life was starting to approach normalcy, and she seemed ready to do what normal people did.

See one another. Go out. Have fun.

Sleep together.

It was early in the relationship, but David was sure there was a real connection here.

Not that he hadn't been wrong before.

Years earlier, there was another woman David set out to rescue. Her name – at least the name she gave him at the time – was Jan. But Jan turned out not to be who she claimed to be, and things ended, as they say, badly.

It was a long time before David could trust anyone. Not just a woman he might be interested in, but anyone *at all*. The number of dates he'd had in the last five years could be counted on the fingers of one hand. There had been a couple of women in Boston, one a coworker at the *Globe*.

But there hadn't been anyone since he'd returned to Promise Falls.

Not until he'd found himself looking down the barrel of that shotgun.

What was wrong with him? he kept asking himself. Why was he drawn to women who had more problems than the entire cast of *Orange Is the New Black*? What was it his dad said, quoting one of his favorite crime writers? 'Never sleep with a woman who has more troubles than you.'

His father really nailed it once in a while. And yet, David had not been very good at following his advice.

He had to know what had happened to Sam.

He'd failed to find any trace of where she'd gone at her house, but he hadn't had a chance to check her place of work. Sam managed a Laundromat in downtown Promise Falls. Was there even a chance she might be there today? Was it possible she'd moved out of her house for some reason but hadn't quit her job?

It occurred to him there was someone who might know.

Once he was back in his own car, he phoned home. His father answered.

'David?'

'Hi, Dad.'

'People are dying all over the place,' he said. 'I feel like I should be doing something, but I don't know what.'

'You're looking after Ethan, right?'

'Yup.'

'That's doing something. Have you heard anything from Mom?'

'She called from the hospital a little while ago. She's still there with Marla and the kid.'

'Matthew,' David said.

'Yeah, right. Matthew. Sounds like it's still touch and go for Gill, but at least he's still among the living.'

'Dad, can you put Ethan on?'

'Huh? Sure, hang on.'

Seconds later, Ethan said, 'Dad?'

'Hey. You okay?'

'Poppa is letting me drink all the Coke I want,' he said. 'Nana' and 'Poppa' were his names for Arlene and Don.

'Isn't that great,' David said. 'Was Carl at school yesterday?'

'Nope,' Ethan said.

'You didn't see him around at all?'

'Nope.'

'How about the day before?' That would have been Thursday. David had spoken with Sam on the phone around lunch. He had told her he would call her on Saturday about doing something that evening.

'Uh,' said Ethan. 'I think so. Yeah, he was at school on Thursday.'

'Did you talk to him?'

He hesitated. 'Maybe.'

'What about?'

'Nothing.'

'This is important, Ethan. What did you guys talk about?'

'Well, we talked about how it was kind of weird that you and his mom were boyfriend and girlfriend. He said . . .'

'What did he say?'

'Don't be mad.'

'I won't be mad,' David said.

'He said that when he had a sleepover at my house, you were doing it to his mom at her place.'

David closed his eyes wearily. 'Did Carl say anything about going away?'

'No.'

'Nothing about his mom and him moving or going on a trip or anything like that?'

'No.' A pause. 'Are you mad about the other thing?'

'No, Ethan. You take care of yourself. I'll check in later.'

'Do you want to talk to Poppa?'

'No, thanks.'

He tossed the phone onto the seat next to him and headed for the Laundromat.

David got a space right out front, and was encouraged when he saw the OPEN sign in the Laundromat window. Below that, however, was a hastily scribbled sign that read: 'USE AT OWN RISK WATER WARNING.' He jumped out of the car and ran inside.

Despite the warning, there were three customers in the shop. One man was standing at a folding table, taking clothes out of a nearby dryer. A woman was loading washing into a machine, and a second woman was killing time, reading a copy of the *New York Times*. A couple of the machines had signs taped to them saying that they were out of order.

One of the machines had bullet holes in it. David knew all about that. That detective, Cal Weaver, had been here when Ed Noble showed up to kill Samantha. Shots had been fired, but Sam had not been hurt.

Shook-up, though. Big-time.

There was an office at the back where Sam often hung out when she wasn't tending the machines. The door was closed. David walked briskly from one end of the place to the other, turned the knob on the door, and stepped in without knocking.

'What the hell do you want?'

It wasn't Sam asking. It was a thin, balding man in his seventies, sitting at a desk.

'Who are you?' David asked.

The man reared back. 'Who am I? Who the fuck are you, busting into my office?'

'I'm sorry,' David said. 'I was looking for Sam. Samantha Worthington.'

'Yeah, well, she ain't here, is she?'

'Do you know where she is?'

'Who wants to know?'

'I'm David Harwood. We – we were kind of going out. Who are you?'

'I *own* this place. Sam runs it for me. Or she did.'

'What's going on?'

'Maybe you can tell me,' he said gruffly. 'She calls me Thursday afternoon and says she won't be coming in anymore. I tell her, "What the fuck are you talking about?" She says she's quitting. I say okay, but I need two weeks' notice. She says she's leaving right now.'

'What do you mean, right now?'

'Like, right fucking *now*. She calls me from this desk, says she's walking out the door soon as she hangs up the phone.'

'Why?'

The owner raised his shoulders. 'Damned if I know. So I had to get down here right away and I don't even live around here. I'm in Albany, for Christ's sake. This place is my pension. I own it – she runs it and looks after it. And then, just like that, she takes off on me. Goddamn her, anyway. I don't need this kind of shit at my age. As if that wasn't bad enough, the water's poisoned or something. I'm tellin' people to put in extra soap.'

'She must have said something,' David persisted. 'About why, or where she was going.'

'I didn't ask her where to send her last check because damned if I was going to pay her if she was going to leave me in the lurch like this. I gotta find someone else to run this place. I can't do it. I got a bad ticker. You need a job?'

'No.'

'Know anyone who does?'

David shook his head.

'Go try her at home,' the man said. 'Maybe she's there. You see her, tell her thanks a bunch from me.'

'Already been there,' David said. 'No sign of her. And she's not answering her phone.'

'So maybe you two weren't the item you seem to think you were,' the owner said, 'if she took off without letting you know where she was going.'

That wasn't what he wanted to hear, but it was what he'd been thinking.

'Maybe it's you she was running away from,' the man said, and laughed.

'I just don't understand,' David said.

'Any man says he can understand how a woman thinks is living in a fool's paradise,' the man said.

'Sorry to have bothered you,' David said, backing out of the office. 'Uh, you probably shouldn't be letting these people wash their clothes with this water.'

The owner shrugged. He said, 'Maybe the other guy will find something out. You can find out from him.'

David stopped. 'What other guy?'

'The guy who was in here yesterday asking around for her.'

David immediately thought of the private detective. 'Was his name Weaver? Cal Weaver?'

The man shook his head. 'No, that wasn't it. What was the name he gave me? Hang on. Oh yeah. Brandon. That was it.'

David felt a chill. 'Are you sure?'

'Yeah, Brandon. Nice guy. Wanted to find Sam, but mostly he was looking for the boy.'

CHAPTER 21

O nce he was back at his place, he didn't go
into the house. He wanted to check the
garage first.

He used his key to unlock the side door. He'd
been making sure the door was pulled closed since
his carelessness a few nights ago, when he'd
thought he'd locked it, but had failed to pull it
tightly into the jamb.

That boy had gotten in.

Well, not exactly a boy. A young man. A check
of his wallet turned up a driver's license in the
name of George Lydecker. A Thackeray College
student.

Stupid bastard.

Thought he'd sneak in and steal something. But
when the man caught him in the act, George
wasn't stealing anything. He was trying to figure
out what was in all the clear bags.

Hundreds of them, piled in a heap in the center
of the garage floor. All filled with something white
and powdery looking. They'd been hidden under
a tarp, but curiosity had gotten the better of
George, and he had pulled it back.

The dumb kid figured it was cocaine.

If it had been cocaine, the man wouldn't have come into the garage wearing a gas mask, would he?

The bags were all gone now. The same could not be said for George. After the man had stabbed George with a croquet post, sprinkled the body liberally with lime, then rolled it up in plastic sheets secured with duct tape, he'd dragged the body to a corner of the garage and hidden it behind some boxes.

Couldn't have George telling anyone what he'd seen.

Not just the bags of chemicals.

Those squirrel traps on the shelf, for example.

Or the random leftover limbs from some mannequins.

The various items that had been used to assemble the bombs that brought down the drive-in.

The man couldn't keep the body here indefinitely. Once it, and the other incriminating items, were disposed of, he'd have to give the garage one hell of a vacuuming. Eliminate any chemical traces.

Only now was he starting to think about how to cover his tracks. He'd been so consumed with the mission that he'd never given a lot of thought to evading capture.

There was once a time when he'd thought he didn't care about being found out. Once he'd made his point.

Only now, he wasn't so sure he was finished. Many had died, there was no doubt about that. But was it enough?

Maybe I'm not done.

CHAPTER 22

Cal Weaver said to Crystal, 'You okay here if I go into the kitchen and talk to my sister?'

Crystal, sitting on the couch, her eyes alternating between the Weather Channel on TV and the drawing she was working on, said, 'Are you going away?'

'No. Just to the kitchen. And even if I do have to go somewhere, I'll be coming back here.'

'Not your motel.'

'No. But I have to go back there to check out, get my stuff.'

'Can I come with you when you do?'

Cal nodded. 'Maybe. We'll talk about that. And I'm going to try to get hold of your dad again.'

Crystal said, 'It's going to be sunny all weekend.'

'Isn't that great?' Cal said. He patted the girl's knee, got up from the couch, and went into the kitchen.

'The poor thing,' Celeste said. Even though Cal and Crystal had recently eaten, Celeste had thrown herself into making sandwiches. 'I can't tell you how many times I've gone to get a glass of water and had to stop myself.'

'Yeah,' Cal said.

'Have you been able to get in touch with her father?'

'Not yet.' Cal put a hand on his sister's arm. 'I'm sorry about all this.'

'What?'

'About imposing. I thought it would just be the girl, for a while, but now it's both of us.'

'It's okay,' Celeste said.

'I know Dwayne's not happy about it.'

Celeste bit her lip, turned away, took a jar of mayonnaise from the refrigerator. 'Yeah, well, that's tough for him.'

'I know you guys are already under a lot of stress, and now—'

Celeste turned swiftly. 'What do you know, really?'

'Excuse me?'

'You think you know what goes on between him and me, but you don't know anything.'

She opened a drawer quickly enough to make the contents rattle, grabbed a knife, and began slicing a tomato.

'What don't I know?' Cal asked. 'Is there something I *should* know? Something you want to let me in on?'

She had her back to him as she sliced. The knife was hitting the cutting board with a *thwack!* each time it came down.

'Shit!' she said, dropped the knife, and grasped the hand that had been holding the tomato. Blood was dribbling from a cut on the side of her index finger.

'Here,' Cal said.

He grabbed some paper towels, wrapped them around her finger.

'I can't believe I did that,' Celeste said.

'Just hold it for a minute, then we'll have a look.'

Celeste held both hands to her chest, her head down, as though trying to fold in on herself.

'You need to talk to me,' Cal said.

'*I* need to talk to *you*?' she said. 'How many times have I tried to get you to open up about Donna and Scott?'

'That's not what we're doing right now,' Cal said. 'We can get into that another time.'

'That's what you always say. But aren't you hurting? Aren't you hurting more than any of us? You keep everything bottled up inside. I can feel this anger coming off you all the time, like you're on a low boil.'

'There's nothing I can do about what's happened,' Cal said. 'It's over. Donna and Scott are gone and I can't bring them back. But we can deal with whatever's going on with Dwayne, between the two of you. But if you want to avoid facing that, then by all means, keep bringing up my wife and son.'

Celeste needed a moment. Then, 'He's . . . he's not the same.'

'What do you mean? Since he stopped getting work from the town?'

A nod, but then a shrug. 'I think it started even before that. He's been getting – I don't know . . . more distant. We don't even . . . we're not close like we used to be. We hardly ever . . .'

'Okay.'

'He's, like, "everyone's all against me." Thinks everyone is taking advantage of him. It's always everybody else's fault. He didn't use to be this negative about everything.'

'It's gotta be work,' Cal said. 'That has to be getting him down. If I was in his shoes, I'd be worried sick. Things'll turn around sooner or later.'

'It's not just . . . I can't talk about it.'

Cal pulled Celeste toward him, hugged her. 'Come on. This is me. When have we ever not been able to talk about stuff?'

From the living room, Crystal shouted: 'Rain Tuesday!'

Celeste said, 'It's hard for me to say the words.'

'Just say them.'

'I . . . I wonder if he's seeing someone.'

Cal loosened the hug to put some space between them. He looked her in the eye and said, 'What are you talking about?'

'He's away so much. He says he's going out and I ask him where and he just says "out." Like to the bar or something. And he's gone a long time.'

'Maybe that's all he's doing.'

'I don't think so. One time, he said he'd been

out drinking, but I didn't smell anything on his breath at all.'

Cal smiled. 'First time a guy's been in trouble for coming home sober.'

Celeste allowed herself a short laugh, and sniffed. 'Maybe I'm crazy. Maybe I'm imagining it. But he's so tense. Not just about not working, but he just seems more secretive. I get this feeling that he's hiding something from me. What's he going to hide if not an affair?'

'You're jumping to conclusions. Unless there's someone you actually suspect.'

'No, there's no one I'm aware of. I mean, Dwayne had a girl working for him at the office, where he keeps the trucks and the paving equipment and everything, but he had to let her go, and honestly, if he'd want her instead of me – she's got a face like a train crash – I wouldn't know what the hell to make of it. But if he's not fooling around on me, then where the hell is he going?'

'Have you talked to him? Have you sat him down and hashed it out?'

'I've tried, but he just brushes me off. Says he's working through some stuff.'

'Maybe he is.'

Celeste forced a laugh. 'I don't suppose I could hire you?'

'What?'

'You know, to follow him around, see what he's up to.'

'That's a joke, right?' Cal said.

She nodded. 'Of course it's a joke.'

'Because that's just wrong on so many levels.'

'Of course it is,' she said. 'I'm sorry I even said it. As a joke.'

'It's okay. You're just under—'

Cal's cell phone started to ring. He dug into his jacket, pulled it out. 'It's him,' he said.

'Who?'

Bringing his voice down to a whisper, he said, 'Crystal's dad. I'll take it outside.'

He tapped the phone, held it to his ear, and, while heading out the back door, said, 'Hello?'

'This Mr Weaver?'

'Is this Gerald Brighton?'

'Yeah. Who are you?'

'I did some work for Lucy and in the course of things got to know her and Crystal,' Cal said, standing in the driveway along the side of the house.

'This about Lucy's dad getting killed in that drive-in thing? That was terrible, and I meant to get up there, but I just wasn't able to get away. You a lawyer or something sorting all that stuff out? Because if there was something left to Lucy, I think I may be entitled to some of that.'

Cal said, 'I have some bad news for you, Mr Brighton. Have you been watching the news today?'

A pause. 'Not really.'

'We've been dealing with something of a catastrophe here in Promise Falls. The water supply's been contaminated.' Cal took a breath. 'I'm afraid Lucy is dead.'

A beat, then, 'What?'

'Lucy died this morning,' Cal told him. 'I'm sorry.'

'What about Crystal? Is Crystal okay?'

'Crystal didn't consume any water and did not require medical treatment. She's not sick. But she was in the house with her mother when she died. I think she's pretty traumatized by what's happened.'

'Oh Jesus.'

'When can you get out here?' Cal asked.

'Uh, well, let me see. . . .'

'Crystal needs you.'

'Sure, I know. I'm just trying to get my head around this news, you know? Are you totally sure about this? The police haven't called me or anything.'

'I'm sure, Mr Brighton.'

'Where's Crystal now?'

'She's in my care.'

'And who are you again?'

'I'm a licensed private investigator, Mr Brighton. If you need some references or reassurances about me, I can provide—'

'No, no, that's okay. So she's with you.'

'That's what I said.'

'And she's okay.'

'Yes.'

'Thing is, I might have a little trouble coming

up with the airfare. I'm kind of maxed out on my cards. I mean, I want to be there. I do. I want to look after Crystal. I just don't know how fast I can get there. You know what I'm saying?'

'Find a way,' Cal said.

'I'll have to ask around, see if I can scrape up the cash. But Crystal's okay, right? I mean, she's not in any immediate danger.'

Cal used his free hand to make some space between his collar and neck. It was feeling hot.

'Mr Brighton, forgive me for sticking my nose in where it might not belong, but your daughter just lost her mom, and she's a very special little girl who needs all the support she can get right now, and if you don't get your ass on a fucking plane and get out here and take some responsibility for this situation, I will personally fly out there and dangle you off the Golden Gate Bridge. Are you hearing me?'

'Yes,' Gerald Brighton said. 'I hear you. Let me, uh, let me see what I can do and I'll get back to you.'

'I look forward to your call,' Cal said, and slipped the phone back into his jacket.

He heard a noise to his right. Dwayne was coming out the side door of the freestanding double garage that sat on the back corner of the property. He took a set of keys from his pocket, inserted one into a lock, turned it, then put the keys back where he'd gotten them.

He turned and saw Cal standing there.

215

'You been watching me?' he asked.

'I just got off the phone,' Cal said.

'Let me guess,' Dwayne said. 'You're inviting some more people to stay over at my house. Well, why the hell not?'

He started walking Cal's way.

'I'm not the enemy,' Cal said.

'Who said you were?'

'I care about Celeste and you. If there's anything going on I can help you guys out with, just tell me.'

Dwayne kept on walking, past Cal and toward his truck.

'Thanks very much, but I got everything under control,' he said. Then Dwayne opened the door, hauled himself up into the driver's seat, backed the vehicle onto the street, and drove off.

CHAPTER 23

Duckworth

'I haven't touched him,' Garvey Ottman said. 'I mean, other than to drag him out and put him there. Which I guess, technically, is touching him.'

We were standing at the edge of the reservoir behind the treatment plant in the shadow of the water tower. It was a large man-made pond with a concrete bottom, a kind of gigantic kids' wading pool. It was fed by streams and nearby rivers; then from here water moved through the treatment plant and, finally, was pumped up into the tower, where simple gravity delivered it to all the homes and businesses of Promise Falls.

Tate Whitehead's body was resting, faceup, dead eyes open, on the concrete walkway that encircled the reservoir. His clothes were still drenched. According to Ottman, he had only pulled him out of the water about half an hour ago.

'I didn't try to do nothing like mouth-to-mouth,' Ottman said. 'I mean, it was pretty obvious he was dead. If I thought he'd had any life in him,

I'd have done something, or at least called an ambulance. Maybe it's just as well he was dead, 'cause no ambulance was likely to get here anytime soon anyway. But I woulda done it if I had to.'

'It's okay,' I said. 'You're right. He's very dead, and likely has been for several hours. Tell me about finding him.'

'Okay, so, I came out here to take some samples. I've been taking samples at each step of the process to see where the trouble might be, you follow me?'

'Yes.'

'Because if the water in the reservoir is okay, then the contamination, whatever it is, must be further along.'

'I get that.'

'But if it was from farm runoff or that kind of thing, and got into the river upstream of here, I'd find traces in the reservoir.'

'Tate,' I said, nodding my head in the direction of the body.

'Right. So I'm out here, and I see something dark just under the surface, right about there, where the bottom slopes up some, and I get close and I can see it's a person, and I'm thinking, holy shit. So I run and grab a pole to pull him in a bit, then step in and haul him out.' He pointed to his rubber boots. 'I had these on.'

It was good to know Ottman hadn't ruined a pair of shoes.

'You know what I think?' Ottman asked.

'What do you think?'

'I think he must have come out here to hoist a few, lost his balance, hit his head on the edge when he was falling in, and went unconscious and drowned.'

'Maybe,' I said, kneeling down next to the body. 'Help me turn him to the side some.'

He knelt down next to me and we gently rolled Tate Whitehead over a quarter turn, far enough that I could get a look at the back of his head. It was a pulpy, bloody mess. The skull had been cracked open.

'I don't think it played out the way you just said,' I told Ottman.

'Jesus,' he said. 'You see that? How the hell would he hurt his head that bad falling in? You'd have to fall out of a tree headfirst to bust your noggin like that.'

I stood. 'Stay here,' I told him.

I began a slow clockwise walk around the edge of the reservoir. Beyond the concrete walkway was a strip of well-maintained lawn, and then trees were beyond that. This was not the forested area we had searched earlier. That had been on the other side of the building, by the parking lot. At the time, I'd been thinking Whitehead would have been close to the booze supply in his Pinto.

I kept my eyes down, scanning the reservoir's edge as well as the walkway. It took nearly five minutes, and I was about three-quarters of the way around – I should have gone counterclockwise – when I saw what I was expecting I might find.

A few drops of blood.

I got down on my knees for a closer look.

'What is it?' Ottman shouted over to me.

Half a dozen drops within a few inches of the edge. Whitehead's attacker had probably been hiding in the nearby trees. When Whitehead passed, probably somewhat under the influence and an easy target, his assailant came at him from behind, bashed him in the head, and pushed him into the water in one swift motion. Otherwise, there would have been more blood on the walkway.

I stepped off the concrete walkway and into the nearby grass, scanning the ground. It didn't take long to find what I was looking for.

A large rock, half again as large as a closed fist. There was what looked to be blood and hair on it.

I did not touch it.

'What'd ya find?' Ottman shouted.

I walked back to where he had remained standing over the body.

'D'ja find something?' he asked.

'So let's say Tate here went into the reservoir early in his shift. There would have been no one else here throughout the night?'

'That's right. The place kind of runs itself, with minimal supervision.'

Once Whitehead was dead, his killer, or killers, had hours to do whatever they wanted in the treatment plant.

'What have your samples shown so far?'

Ottman, glancing at the body, said, 'Can we talk someplace else? I can't keep looking at this. I'm feeling queasy.'

I motioned him a few feet away, by the trees.

'The sample,' I said.

'Okay, well, it takes time, but the water here is looking pretty good. Since you've been gone, we've had the state health authorities here collecting samples of their own. They're testing the reservoir, they're testing the water once it's been treated before it pumps up to the tower, and they're testing all over town.'

'What have they found?'

'Don't know yet,' he said. 'You can't do an instant test on E. coli.'

I was starting to think this had nothing to do with E. coli. I was starting to think it had a lot more to do with dead squirrels and painted mannequins and a flaming bus and a Thackeray student in a hoodie, and, worst of all, at least until today, the bombing of the drive-in theater.

Not to mention the murders of Olivia Fisher, Rosemary Gaynor, and now Lorraine Plummer.

While I believed the three women had been murdered by the same person, I didn't know that they were connected to the other incidents. I didn't even know, with any certainty, that all those other incidents were connected to one another.

But something told me they were. Something told me that everything that had been going on

221

in Promise Falls the last month – and stretching back three years – was somehow related.

We had a serial killer and a madman on the loose. All wrapped up, it seemed, in one person.

Or not. Maybe we were dealing with a group of people. Some kind of cult. If Mason Helt had been part of this, well, he was dead, and there was still shit happening, so that definitely meant we had been dealing with, at least at some point, more than one person.

Clive Duncomb was dead, too. And Bill Gaynor was in jail awaiting trial. Their names had been linked, one way or another, to events of the last month, but they couldn't be linked to Lorraine Plummer's death, or the poisoning of the water supply.

I needed to go back to the beginning. Square one.

Olivia Fisher.

My phone rang. I looked at the readout, saw who it was.

'Wanda,' I said.

'Sorry for not getting back to you sooner,' Wanda Therrieult said. 'I don't suppose I have to explain.'

'You getting help?'

'So far I've got three medical examiners coming in. A lot of the bodies will have to be autopsied elsewhere. They've become our number one export. So what's this about a dead female at Thackeray?'

'Yeah, well, that's all I had at the time when I

called. Now I've got another possible homicide at the water treatment plant. A man. Neither of them poisonings.'

'Christ, Barry. What the hell is going on? These things connected?'

'The body at the water plant, I'd say, is definitely connected to the poisonings. But the body at Thackeray, that may be related to something else.'

'What?'

'You be the judge.' I didn't want to tell her I believed Lorraine Plummer was killed by the same person who'd killed Rosemary Gaynor and Olivia Fisher. I didn't, as they say, want to lead the witness.

'Where do you want me first?' Wanda said.

I told her to head out to Thackeray. The sooner she got there, the sooner Joyce Pilgrim could move on to reviewing the security tapes.

As I put my phone away, I heard, 'Hey!'

Garvey Ottman and I turned. Coming out of the water plant door was Randall Finley.

'What the hell is he doing here?' I asked.

'He asked me to give him a call if anything happened,' Ottman said.

'You don't take orders from him,' I said. 'He's not the mayor. He's not anything, except a pain in the ass.'

Ottman opened his palms to me, a 'What was I supposed to do?' gesture.

Finley was striding quickly toward us, but as soon as he saw Tate's body, he stopped.

'Goddamn, so there he is,' Finley said. He looked at me. 'What have we got here?'

'This is a crime scene, Randy. Get out.'

'Looks like someone bashed his brains in. Jesus, Barry, this looks like it was deliberate. Like it's a murder!'

'Thank you, Randy,' I said.

'Oh, man, that's a lunch tosser if I ever saw one.' He took a step closer to the body. 'He was a dumb ol' drunk, but he didn't deserve that.'

'Randy, step away.'

'I just wanted to see what—'

'Now!' I moved toward him. I was reaching around into my pocket where I kept a pair of plastic wrist cuffs.

The moment he saw them, he said, 'Whoa, hold on there! What the hell you think you're doing?'

'Trying to preserve what's left of this scene that hasn't already been trampled on.'

'Okay, okay, I'm going, I'm going.'

'That way,' I said, pointing back to the plant. 'Both of you.'

Once we were all inside the building, Finley started poking a finger in my face. 'You know what I'd like to know? I'd like to know what the hell kind of progress you're making here. Looks to me like not much!'

I said to Ottman, 'Show me the process. How you treat the water once it comes in from the reservoir.'

'Yeah, I can—'

'Christ in a Chrysler, Barry,' Finley said. 'You got a dead guy out there and dead people all over town and you want an engineering lesson?'

To Ottman, I said, 'Give me a moment.'

I approached Finley, slipped a friendly, conspiratorial arm around his shoulder, and said, 'There're things I can't say in front of Garvey that are for your ears only.'

'Oh?' he said, no doubt flattered to finally be brought into the loop.

I led him toward a metal industrial door with a strong handle.

'I'm putting you under arrest.'

'You're what?'

'Give me your hand.'

'I will not—'

I grabbed his wrist, slipped half of the plastic cuff over it, and cinched it tight.

'You son of a bitch,' he said.

'Stand here, put your hands down there.' When Finley started to resist, I said to him, through gritted teeth, 'I am not fucking around here, Randy.'

I put the other half of the cuff through the door handle before slipping it over his other wrist and cinching it as tight as the other one.

'What's the charge?' Finley asked.

'Being an asshole in a water treatment plant. It's an environmental statute. Fecal contamination.'

'You're making a big mistake, Barry. A very big mistake.'

'Not as big as the one you made when you

blackmailed my son,' I said, leaning in close to his ear. 'I'd rather just take my gun out and shoot you, but the paperwork would be murder. And I have a lot of other things on my plate right now.'

As I walked back in Ottman's direction, Finley yelled, 'I'll sue your ass off! That's what I'll do! You haven't heard the fucking last of this!'

'You want to show me now?' I asked Ottman.

'Yeah, sure, right this way.'

CHAPTER 24

Gale Carlson decided to go out.

Even before catastrophe struck Promise Falls that morning, she'd had no real plans. It might have been a long holiday weekend for her – the dental clinic, which was usually open Saturday mornings, had closed Friday at five and wasn't to reopen until nine Tuesday morning – but her husband, Angus, was scheduled to work through the weekend. While being bumped up to detective had been good news, being the new guy in the department meant he was at the bottom of the list for getting the weekend off.

He'd started at six that morning, and Gale had no idea when she would see him again. She had every expectation he'd be doing a double or even a triple shift. He, and every other cop and paramedic and doctor and nurse in town. She'd been watching the news – all the major networks were carrying the story within a couple of hours – and seen interviews with people at the hospital, some still waiting to see a doctor, others weeping at the loss of a loved one. There was footage of that goofball who used to be mayor handing out free water down by the falls, the same brand of bottled water Gale kept in the fridge. And then they went live to a news conference, where the interim head of Promise Falls General, flanked by a doctor and the chief of police, was giving the grim news.

So far, 123 people were dead.

It was one of the worst disasters in the state's history. After 9/11, a few airplane crashes, and the Triangle Shirtwaist Factory fire in New York in 1911, which had claimed 146 lives, this was it.

Nearly three hundred people were being treated for symptoms of hypotension, which – Gale didn't catch all of it – had something to do with low blood pressure.

One quote in particular, from the hospital's head doctor, caught Gale Carlson's attention.

'Whatever has affected these people is resistant to any kind of treatment we can offer. There appears to be nothing we can do.'

Either people made it, or they didn't. Survival appeared to depend on how much water they had consumed. Only half a cup of coffee? You probably lived. A large glass of water? Probably not. If you'd had a shower or washed your hands, your skin probably felt like it was crawling, but that wasn't likely to kill you. And while there was little doubt the drinking water was the cause, the source of the contamination remained a mystery.

Dozens of patients had been transferred to hospitals in Albany and Syracuse, and a handful had even been sent to New York City. The local emergency staff had been stretched far beyond their capabilities.

If there was any good news, it was that most people had now gotten the message. The number of people coming to the hospital for treatment in the last couple of hours had dropped off considerably. As bad as it was, it could have been worse, Chief Finderman pointed out. Had this happened on a regular workday, and not on the Saturday of a long weekend, far more people would have been up early, and consumed the contaminated water.

'Oh!' Gale had said while watching the conference when she caught a brief glimpse of her husband walking past the camera.

She wanted to phone him then, ask how he was doing, but she knew this was the wrong time to bother him. She felt she'd been bothering him a lot lately, and watching what Angus had to deal with, she felt awash with guilt.

Maybe her husband was right. Maybe this was no world to bring a child into. Although that had never been his argument, exactly. It wasn't the state of the world that worried him. It was the quality of parenting, and what he'd endured as a child was certainly not the best.

But Gale knew she would make a wonderful mother, if only given the chance. She'd spent hours on the Internet Googling 'my husband does not want a baby,' and been inundated with stories from marriage-counseling and parenting sites. Gale was hardly alone. Millions of women were married to men who did not want to become fathers.

Sometimes what Gale really wanted was just one good book, instead of being overwhelmed with online material. Given that she was going stir-crazy at home, she decided to take a walk downtown.

A walk would do her good. She'd have her phone with her should Angus need to get in touch.

She had a destination in mind.

There was a bookstore in the Promise Falls Mall, but there was a used bookstore downtown where she loved to browse. Although the manager stocked mostly fiction, he also had a nonfiction section and, within that, some books on parenting and psychology.

Maybe she'd find something there, something that would help her persuade Angus that they should take that leap of faith.

Get pregnant.

And after all, it wasn't as though the baby-making process was without its fun. At least, most of the time.

Gale grabbed her purse. She stepped outside first to see whether she needed a jacket, but it was a pleasant, late-spring day, temperature in the midseventies. No jacket required.

She and Angus lived in a small two-story house not far from the central business area of Promise Falls. When they first moved here from Ohio, they'd often walked down to the park by the falls, but the novelty of that had worn off. Gale found she strolled down there more frequently on her own, especially when Angus had to work evenings. That had been a regular occurrence when he was in uniform, and likely would still be the case now that he was a detective.

She thought she might go down there today, after her bookstore visit.

Gale set herself a steady pace. It didn't take long before she had walked the several blocks to her destination.

She was taken aback by what she found.

There were sheets of plywood where the windows of Naman's Books used to be, and the brickwork was stained with soot. She'd had no idea that there had been a fire here. When had that happened?

'Oh, no,' she said under her breath. There were enough bookstores, used and new, going out of business without one having to go up in smoke.

She thought she heard noise inside, things being shuffled about, and noticed that the glass door, which had been covered over with cardboard on the inside, was ajar. She peeked inside.

'Naman?' she said.

'Hello?'

'Naman, what on earth has happened?'

The owner of the store appeared in the sliver between the door and the jamb, one dark eye taking Gale in.

'It is you,' he said, and opened the door wide

enough that she was able to see him. The corner of his mouth went up in an attempt at a smile. 'One of my best customers.'

'I didn't know,' Gale said. 'What happened?'

'A fire,' he said.

'When?'

'A few nights ago.'

'How did it happen?'

He shook his head, suggesting he did not want to talk about it.

'Come on,' Gale said. 'Tell me.'

'Some guys in a truck. They drove by, threw something through the window. A what-do-you-call-it. Cocktail. Molotov cocktail. A bottle on fire. It broke the glass and landed in the books and the fire started.'

'Oh my God,' she said, peering in to try to see the damage. 'I'm coming in.'

'It's not safe.'

'It's okay,' she said. 'I'm tough.'

He stepped back to allow her to come in. He had set up two spotlights on stands so he could see what he was doing.

'They haven't turned the electric back on yet, so I am running extension cords out back, borrowing power from a neighbor. It's not as bad as it was. It was all wet after the fire department came, water in the basement, thousands of books wet and ruined. I have a Dumpster out back for the stuff I cannot save. But I am going through, book by book, seeing what is salvageable.'

'This is horrible. Did they catch the people who did it?'

Naman shook his head.

'Why would someone do this?'

'They called me a terrorist,' he said.

'Oh, Naman.'

'They see a different kind of name out front, and suddenly I am the kind of guy who would blow up a drive-in theater. Good thing they already set the store on fire, or they would be back today to blame me for what has happened to the water.'

'Those kinds of things, they bring out the ugly side of people.'

'Yes,' he said.

'I don't know what to say. Do you want me to ask my husband if they are having any luck tracking them down?'

'Your husband?'

'He works for the police. He's a detective now.'

'I don't think you ever mentioned that before,' Naman said.

'Maybe not.'

'I think I would have remembered.' He glanced upward. 'The man who had the apartment upstairs, he was a private detective. Not with the police, but working for himself.'

'Really?'

Naman nodded. 'But he is gone. I don't think he will come back. Anyway.' He went over to the counter, where he'd been sorting books into boxes. 'What were you looking for today? I mean,

I am not open, but if I have what you want and it is a little water-damaged, I would give it to you for free.'

'I was looking for . . .' Her voice trailed off.

'What?'

'It's kind of personal.'

'Oh.'

She laughed. 'But if I'd found it, I'd have been bringing it up to you to pay for, so . . .'

'What kind of book?'

'Just . . . advice about marriages. The different things that couples go through.'

'You don't have to tell me.'

She laughed again. 'It's not *that*.'

'I didn't say anything.'

'But I know what you were thinking. It's just, Angus – that's my husband – and I can't seem to agree on whether to start a family. I want to, and he's hesitant.'

'Oh. I don't know if I have any books like that. In good condition, or damaged. You know, you should go to the bookstore in the mall, maybe. Or look online.'

'I guess. I just – I've always liked coming here. I love books, and old books. I love the smell of them.'

'They all smell of smoke now,' Naman said sadly.

'Are you going to reopen?'

'We'll see. I have to clean up first.'

'I should let you get back to it. I'm so sorry.' Gale turned and, as she took a step toward the door, stumbled over something. 'Stupid me,' she said, bending over and picking up a book that had clearly been drenched by the firefighters. It had dried, and expanded to twice its original thickness.

'Guess this is one for the Dumpster,' she said. She looked at the title. *'Deadly Doses: A Writer's Guide to Poison.'*

'I'll take that,' Naman said, extending a hand.

Gale gave it to him. 'Guess you won't want that one around when you've got nutcases accusing you of awful things.'

She offered an awkward chuckle.

'No,' said Naman. 'I guess I don't.'

CHAPTER 25

David Harwood went straight home.

His father was in front of the TV in the living room, watching CNN. 'They just had something on Promise Falls,' Don said as his son walked through.

David wasn't interested. He was headed for the kitchen, where he kept a laptop tucked at the far end of the counter. He grabbed it, set it up on the table, and sat himself down.

He heard someone bounding down the stairs. A second later, Ethan was in the kitchen.

'Did you find out what happened to Carl?' Ethan asked. 'Did he drink the water and get sick?'

'No,' David said, opening a browser and tapping away with his fingers to fill in the search field. His eyes were on the screen. 'I mean, not that I know of.'

'Why were you asking if he was in school?'

'Ethan, I'm doing something here.'

'What about his mom? Did she drink the water?'

'Ethan!' David snapped. 'I'll talk to you later.'

Ethan frowned, turned, and walked out of the kitchen.

David had entered 'Brandon + Worthington + Boston + bank.' He figured adding 'bank' would narrow the search down, pinpoint stories about the Brandon Worthington who had been sentenced to prison for bank robbery.

Up popped some stories. The initial arrest, a short story about his sentencing. David knew, from his brief experience working at the *Boston Globe*, that trials were not covered the way they once were, because there weren't enough reporters to go around. It was only the more sensational cases that made the papers once they went to court. But Worthington's case had attracted some attention because there was an interesting element to it: His father worked for the bank he'd robbed. Not the same branch, but the same financial corporation.

Brandon was also mentioned in more recent stories about the arrest of his parents in the brief kidnapping of Carl by Ed Noble. Also, they were being investigated for their involvement in Noble's failed bid to kill Samantha Worthington at the Laundromat. That had ended in a shoot-out with Cal Weaver, and Noble's arrest.

The shit Sam had been through with these people, David thought. A bunch of total lunatics. Willing to do anything to separate Sam from her son, to take him away and raise him themselves.

But these stories contained no new information for David. This was all ancient history, if something that had happened only a few days ago could be called ancient. What he was looking for was something much more recent. Something that would explain why the owner of the Laundromat would say someone named Brandon had been by looking for Samantha.

He narrowed the search to the last seven days.

And up popped an item from a news station in Boston. A segment called 'Hank Investigates,' which he remembered from his time there. Hank, a woman reporter, was always digging into something, and this time it was the ineptitude of local corrections officials. The story was that after Garnet and Yolanda Worthington had been arrested, they were brought back to Boston to be arraigned, and shortly after that, Yolanda had what appeared to be a heart attack.

She was admitted to hospital, at which point Brandon, who was being held in Old Colony Correctional Center in Bridgewater, made a request for a supervised release so that he could see his mother. Yolanda's condition was, for a period of time, deemed critical, and there were fears this might be Brandon's last chance to see his mother in person.

A supervised release was approved.

Just before going into the intensive care unit to see his mother, Brandon asked his escort for his cuffs to be removed. Was it right, he'd asked, that his mother, in what might be the last time she would ever be with her son, see him in handcuffs?

The cuffs were removed.

Brandon was allowed to enter the ICU

unaccompanied. After all, his police escort figured, there was only one way out. The officer took a seat just outside the ICU entrance. Gave Brandon ten minutes.

According to the police, Brandon was behind a curtain, talking to his mother, when a male, uniformed orderly came in to check on her. Brandon saw an opportunity. He put the man in a choke hold, and in ten seconds the orderly had slipped into unconsciousness.

The orderly did an on-camera interview. 'He was about my size, but man, he was strong. Hooked his arm around my neck, and brother, I was gone.'

Brandon stole his uniform and walked out the ICU door, right past the cop.

He hadn't been seen since.

His mug shot was displayed on-screen, and the public was asked to call the police if they spotted him. 'Police advise that this man should not be approached,' the news reporter said. 'He is believed to be dangerous.'

David watched the segment a second time, wondering if he'd missed anything. Like, where the police thought Brandon might be headed, and why.

Nothing.

But he was pretty sure they knew. And he was betting someone with the Boston PD, or the prison system, had given Samantha a heads-up.

No wonder she'd vanished.

David wondered if the local police had been notified, if they were watching for him. He got out his phone and brought up the cell phone number he had for Barry Duckworth. He knew the detective would have his hands full this morning with the water contamination, but he didn't care.

Duckworth answered on the fourth ring.

'Duckworth. David?'

'Yeah, it's me.'

'If this is about your boss, I don't care.'

'Randy?'

'If you're looking for him, he's handcuffed to a door at the water treatment plant.'

'What?'

David felt as though the chair beneath him were swaying. He thought about his earlier conversation with Finley, about how lucky it was that he'd been cranking up production in the days leading up to this disaster.

Was it possible?

Could Randy have somehow—

'I don't understand,' David said. 'What's he done? Because – I don't know if this means anything, but he cranked up production before—'

'He's been getting in the way, that's what he's been doing. You've got some smarts. You need to talk to him, get him to back off.'

'Getting in the way where?'

'Everywhere I go, pretty much, but especially out here at the water plant. He thinks he's back

240

in the mayor's office and I've got news for him. He's not.'

'Okay, okay, but that's not why—'

'Make it fast, David.'

'Do you know about Brandon Worthington?'

'Who the hell is—'

'You know about Garnet and Yolanda Worthington? They hired that idiot to grab Samantha Worthington's kid, and then at the Laundromat—'

'Right. I know. Carlson – Angus Carlson – he worked on that, but I know what you're talking about. Brandon's the son? The one who's in jail?'

'He's not anymore.'

'He got released?'

'He escaped.' David quickly gave Duckworth the details from the news video. 'I think he's in Promise Falls.'

'I'm sure Boston PD've been in touch. Look, David, if you see him, call me. But I'm up to my ass in alligators.'

'I'm worried about Sam and Carl. I think they're on the run and—'

'David, I have to go.' Duckworth ended the call.

'Well, thanks a fuck of a lot,' David said.

'I heard that,' said Ethan from the living room.

Phone still in hand, David tried Sam's number yet again. If only she'd pick up. She had to see who was calling. If she'd just answer, he could tell her he knew why she'd fled, that he knew Brandon was out of prison and looking for her, that he would help her in any way he could.

241

No answer after ten rings.

A text, he thought.

He typed: Know about Brandon, why you left. Please let me help. Call me when you can.

He hit send. Looked to see that the text had been delivered, and it had. While he stared at the phone, hoping for those three little dots to indicate she was writing back, he wondered where she might have gone.

He didn't know what other family she might have. He seemed to recall her mentioning that her parents were no longer alive, so she couldn't hide out with them until this passed over.

Until Brandon had been caught.

It was looking as though Sam was not going to get back to him, so he put the phone down on the table.

Maybe, he told himself, he should stop worrying. It was possible Sam had things in hand, that she was dealing with this situation the best she could. When she'd gotten word that Brandon was out, she'd packed Carl and herself up and hit the road. Given all she'd been through with Brandon's parents and Ed Noble, the smartest thing to do was get out of town.

'I wasn't the priority,' David said to himself.

And why should he be?

Once Brandon had been apprehended, she'd come back, and they'd pick up where they left off.

Sure.

But did it put her in *that* much jeopardy to answer his phone call? To respond to a text?

Unless . . .

Unless she was expecting a trick. The Worthington clan had tried to pull fast ones on her in the past.

Could she be thinking Brandon had found David? That he had his phone, and was pretending to be him in a bid to find out where she and Carl were?

Was that a reach?

But then, suddenly, another scenario occurred to David.

Sam wasn't answering because Brandon had already found them.

CHAPTER 26

Duckworth

I felt like I was back in high school chemistry class.

With Tate Whitehead's body still out by the reservoir waiting for a forensic examiner to come God knew when, and Randy Finley cuffed to a door by the entrance to the water treatment plant, Garvey Ottman gave me a quick tour of the place at the same time as he offered up a course in Water Filtration 101. I'd been interrupted with a call from David Harwood, but once that was out of the way, Ottman was able to continue.

'Water treatment is really only about eighty years old,' Ottman said, 'and it wasn't until Congress passed the Safe Drinking Water Act in 1974 that it became the law of the land that the water coming out of the tap had to be one hundred percent drinkable.'

He was leading me through parts of the plant I'd never seen before. Huge water-filled basins divided into different compartments the size of a school gymnasium.

'There are six basic stages water goes through before it comes out of your tap,' he said. 'There're pretreatment and screening, which is basically what happens in the reservoir. As the water moves from there into the plant, there're coagulation and flocculation, then—'

'Flock what?'

'Flocculation. Coagulation and flocculation remove suspended particles in the water that survive the screening process. These particles get stuck together into clumps called floc. In the sedimentation stage, the floc settles to the bottom, where it can be collected and separated from the water and—'

'So all the crud, all the bad stuff in the water, it sinks? Like cigarette butts and stuff like that?'

'More than that. Larger things like butts, they should get caught in the screening process, but there are plenty of things in thc water that count as solids that are too small to see. It's that stuff that we get rid of here. Then, at filtration, which is the next stage, the remaining impurities are removed.'

Ottman threw some other words around. Aeration. Chlorination. Fluoridation.

'Fluoridation?'

'Fluoride,' he said. 'For teeth. It gets added in one of the last stages. Then the water gets pumped up into the tower, ready to go. So the pumps don't have to be going all the time. They run a lot overnight, refilling the tower from town water usage during the day. So, when everyone gets up in the

245

morning, when the demand for water is at a peak, what with everyone having showers and cooking and all that kind of thing, there's plenty in the tower, and the delivery system is as simple as flowing downhill.'

Now we were moving from chemistry to engineering. Neither had been among my top subjects in school. But I was trying my best to get my head around everything Ottman was telling me.

Even though we were well into the plant, surrounded by tanks and massive pipes, I turned to face the reservoir and said, 'So let's say, even if something really bad got into the reservoir, then there's a whole slew of steps along the way, before that water comes out of the tap, where the contamination would be caught and neutralized.'

'Like to think so,' Ottman said. 'Tate's not able to defend himself, so I have to say, even if he fucked up somewhere, this system is so well automated, it practically runs itself. Even if he failed to make a few checks in the night, chances are the water would still be fine.'

But it was already looking obvious to me that Tate's only fuckup was getting himself killed. He didn't do anything to the water. He was killed so someone else could.

'So, given all these steps, and all the safeguards, if you were going to add something to the water that would make people sick – that would kill them – you'd have a better chance doing it at the tail end of the process.'

Ottman nodded. 'Yup. That makes sense.'

'What about putting something into the tower?'

'Seriously?'

I nodded. 'Yeah. What?'

'Have you *seen* that thing? I can't imagine lugging something up there. And even if you could climb all that way, there's no way to dump something in that I can think of. No, you'd want to do it down here, let it get pumped up there.'

'So where, then?'

Ottman shrugged. 'Is that where you're going with this? Someone deliberately put something in the water?'

Far from us, an angry, echoing shout: 'Let me go!'

Ottman glanced that way. 'Randy sounds pretty pissed about—'

'Don't worry about him,' I said. 'So if you wanted to add something into the system, where would you do it?'

'I don't know. Maybe into the chlorine or fluoride tanks.'

'Take me there.'

We continued on farther through the plant to more tanks and pipes and other things I didn't understand.

'This here's the fluoridation area,' Ottman said.

Something I'd noticed the moment I'd walked into this place the first time was how spotless it was. All the floors, every pipe, every pane of glass, were sparkling clean.

But where we were standing now, I noticed

something on the floor. I felt it underfoot first, the tiniest bit of grit. I stopped, turned my foot around so I could see the sole.

It looked like salt. I licked my index finger, then touched it to some of the grains on my shoe to get a better look.

'I wouldn't taste that if I was you,' Ottman said.

'Don't worry,' I said. I brought my finger up to my eye. 'You have any idea what this is?'

'Nope,' he said. He looked down at the floor. 'But there're a few granules of it around in this area. Like someone was carrying around a huge bag of table salt with a pinhole rip in the bottom.'

'My finger feels kind of itchy,' I said.

'Shit,' Ottman said. 'You need to wash it off. No telling what it might be.'

He steered me immediately toward a door with a male symbol on it. A men's room.

'It feels kind of like when you handle fiberglass insulation,' I said. 'All irritated.'

Ottman led me quickly to a sink, turned on the tap full blast. 'Get it under there. Put on lots of soap. Keep washing it.'

'What the hell is it?' I asked.

'Just keep running water on it,' he said, tension in his voice.

'Do you know what it is?' I was running water on the finger, soaping it up, then sticking it back under the tap. The itchiness was subsiding.

'Not for sure. I mean, I might be completely wrong,' Ottman said.

'What's your best guess?'

'What were the symptoms?' he asked.

'A burning finger.'

'No, I mean, what were the main symptoms of all those people going to the hospital?'

There were so many, it was hard to remember them all. I said, 'Throwing up, dizzy, low blood pressure. Vision problems. I think someone said hypertension. No, not hypertension. Hypotension. A big drop in blood pressure.'

Ottman was shaking his head, almost in wonder. 'You'd need so much of it.' He seemed to be talking more to himself than to me.

'So much of what?'

'And it would probably take a long time. You put it in too fast, it might explode on you,' he said.

'For Christ's sake, what the hell are you talking about?' I asked, still holding my finger under the tap. Then it hit me. 'And if the water's bad, what the hell am I doing holding my finger under the tap?'

He looked at me and turned off the tap. I thought I saw fear in his eyes.

'We need to get out of the building,' he said. 'We need to get out now.'

'Ottman, tell me what's going on.'

'You got some way to get Randy out of those cuffs?'

'A sharp knife, heavy-duty scissors,' I said. 'They're just plastic. There's no key.'

'Let's go.'

We left the men's room, Ottman grabbing my arm to keep me from going anywhere near those salty-looking granules.

'It could be in the air,' he said. 'There might be more of it around than what we saw on the floor.'

I decided to stop asking him what he was talking about. We'd get out of the building first. He'd already reached into his jacket for a pocketknife. He had the blade out as he walked briskly toward Finley.

Finley's eyes went wide when he saw the knife. He must have been wondering whether Ottman intended to set him free or kill him. There must have been some relief as Ottman shouldered Finley's body out of the way, allowing him access to the man's wrists.

Finley said to me, 'You're in a lot of trouble, my friend.'

I said, 'Soon as he cuts you free, get out of the building as fast as you can.'

'What?' He seemed to gulp. 'Jesus, is there a bomb?'

'No,' Ottman said. He cut through the cuffs. 'Go.'

The three of us started for the door, Ottman pausing long enough to pull a fire alarm switch on the wall. A high-pitched clanging commenced.

'There're still some people in there,' he said.

We made it outside to the parking lot. I couldn't say for the others, but my heart was pounding.

'Ottman,' I said. 'Tell me.'

He took a couple of deep breaths. 'I could be wrong about this, but I think what was on the floor there could be sodium azide.'

'What's that?' I asked.

'A fucking catastrophe.'

CHAPTER 27

Cal Weaver was looking for something to drink in his sister's refrigerator when his cell phone rang. It was someone from the Promise Falls police who had seen the note he'd posted to the door of Lucy Brighton's house. Cal had indicated that he had a key, and the police wanted to get inside.

'I have to go out,' Cal told Celeste.

'You taking Crystal with you?' she asked.

Cal shook his head. He definitely did not want Crystal to see her mother's body being taken out of that house.

He went into the living room to talk to her.

'Does your sister have any paper I can draw on?' she asked, looking up from her clipboard.

'I think so. Why don't you ask her?'

Crystal started to slide off the couch, but Cal put a hand on her knee to stop her. 'In a second. I have to talk to you.'

'What about?'

'I have to let the police into your house. They just phoned me. They saw the note I left on the door.'

'Oh.'

'You can stay here, okay?'

'How long will you be gone?'

His shoulders went up and down. 'I don't know. I'm also going to go to my hotel and get my stuff so I can stay here. With you.'

She looked at him, her face devoid of emotion. He was trying to read her, trying to figure out what she might be thinking.

'Okay,' she said, then continued her slide off the couch and walked into the kitchen to ask for paper.

It took him ten minutes to get to Lucy Brighton's house. There was a Promise Falls police car in the driveway, two cops in the front seat. Cal edged his car over to the curb, got out, and approached them.

'You Weaver?' the one behind the wheel asked.

Cal told them what he knew. The call from Crystal, where he found the body. He gave them Gerald Brighton's number, but could not guarantee when, or if, the man would show up.

'The kid still with you?' the same cop asked.

He nodded.

There wasn't anything else they needed from him at this time, so he got back in his car with the intention of heading to the highway that would take him south, out of town, to his temporary home. He figured he could be packed and checked out in less than twenty minutes, be back to his sister's place by late afternoon.

His phone rang just as he was about to turn the key in the ignition.

'Weaver,' he said.

'Mr Weaver, my name's David Harwood?'

Making it sound like a question, as though Cal was supposed to ask, 'Okay, is it really?' Instead, he said, 'How can I help you?'

But then he realized he recognized the name. Harwood was the guy who'd rescued Carl Worthington when Ed Noble snatched him from his school at the end of the day. Sam had called Cal for help first, but when he couldn't get there in time, she had called David Harwood.

'I'm a friend of Sam Worthington's. I—'

'I know who you are. Thanks for getting to the school when I couldn't.'

'Have you heard from her?'

'No. I mean, we spoke after what happened at her place of work a couple of times, but I haven't heard from her lately.' The hairs on the back of Cal's neck started to rise.

Sam and her boy drank the water.

'Shit,' Cal said. 'Have you been by the house?'

'Yes,' David said. 'It's not about what's going on. Not about the water. The house is empty – her car is gone.'

'Okay,' Cal said, his hairs settling down. 'Then what's this about?'

'Do you know about her ex-husband?'

254

'Just lay it out for me, David.'

David brought him up to speed. Brandon Worthington escaping custody. Sam not answering her phone. It was all news to Cal.

'Call the police,' he advised.

'I did that,' David said. 'They've got their hands full at the moment.'

'So have I,' Cal said, then thought that sounded too dismissive. 'Look, Sam probably got word that he was out, took off with her kid for a few days. Not telling anyone, not taking your call, that might be the smartest thing she could do.'

'Maybe,' David said. 'But what if the reason she's not answering is because he's already found her? This guy, he was in for robbing a bank. And you already know his parents are lunatics, that they sent Ed Noble to kill her.'

'I was there.'

'I *know*. So you see what I'm saying? I'm not worrying for nothing.' The man's voice was breaking. 'There was a time, maybe, when I was able to handle this kind of stuff. But not anymore. I feel helpless. I want to help her, but I don't know what to do.'

Cal closed his eyes, leaned his head up against the headrest, thought of Crystal. Until her father showed up, she was his responsibility. He couldn't go charging off to help this Harwood guy find Sam. Not now.

'You said you've been to the house?'

'Yes,' David said quickly, sounding encouraged that Weaver was taking the time to ask questions.

'See if you can get inside, see if—'

'I did that. It looked like they'd packed up.'

'What did the neighbors say?'

David didn't answer right away. 'Shit,' he said finally. 'I didn't even talk to them.'

'Start there,' Cal said. 'Let me know how it goes.'

He felt bad, ending the call, but there was only so much he could deal with. He'd promised Crystal he wouldn't be long. Right now, he believed she needed him more than Harwood did. David had reason to be concerned about Samantha and her son, Cal knew, but he also knew Sam was no fool. If she'd heard her ex-husband was on the loose, then she'd have done what she had to do and gotten out of town.

Cal hoped David was wrong in thinking Sam wasn't answering her cell because Brandon had already found her. But hadn't Harwood been a reporter once? Cal recalled hearing that he was. So let him nose around, use the same basic skills Cal would have employed.

Cal turned on the engine. It was time to check out of his hotel.

Before long, he was at a T intersection, about to make a right, when he saw a familiar vehicle approaching from the south.

It was Dwayne, in his pickup truck.

Cal's brother-in-law blew past, Dwayne's focus

on the road ahead. He never glanced in Cal's direction, didn't notice the car.

Cal wasn't sure what made him decide to turn left, in the opposite direction of the hotel.

He told himself he wasn't actually following his brother-in-law. Not in any *surveillance* kind of way. It wasn't as though he'd set out this afternoon to tail Dwayne.

It just happened.

Dwayne drove by, and Cal decided to see where he might be going. Told himself that if Dwayne pulled off the road to go into a 7-Eleven to buy a Slim Jim, he might just follow him in, strike up a conversation, see how the guy was doing. Maybe see if he wanted to go for a beer.

Tell him something like, 'Look, I'm sorry that little girl and I have crashed at your place, but I really appreciate it, and we're going to get out of your hair as soon as possible.'

Yeah. Maybe something like that.

Cal told himself he was definitely not following his brother-in-law even though Celeste was worried he might be seeing another woman. Was that something Cal really wanted to stick his nose into? Okay, maybe a *little*. This *was* his *sister* they were talking about. *You go messing around on my sister and that's likely to piss me off.*

But then again, they were all adults. And if there was one thing Cal had learned from his years working with the police and as a private investigator, there were usually two sides to every story.

He hadn't heard Dwayne's. Maybe he had some serious complaints about Celeste, and maybe he didn't. It was possible whatever story Dwayne had to tell was bullshit.

Maybe whatever problems there were in his marriage were one hundred percent his fault.

Cal wasn't sure he wanted to know. He had no wish to be mediator. If their marriage was in trouble, they should talk to a marriage counselor.

Cal had enough problems of his own to work through without taking on anyone else's.

Except for Crystal's, of course.

He'd look after her until her father showed up. *If* he showed up. If he was honest with himself, he'd admit that he was hoping Crystal's father would take his time getting here.

Cal liked Crystal. He found her quirkiness endearing, even challenging in a way, and there was a mix of vulnerability and toughness about her. Maybe his feelings had something to do with losing his son. There was a part of him that yearned to care for someone, to—

Dwayne made a turn. He was heading downtown.

Cal decided to stick with him. But he held back, keeping at least one other car between himself and Dwayne. The kind of thing he did when he *did* have someone under surveillance.

Okay, he thought, *so maybe I am following him. Just for a few blocks.*

If he did see Dwayne meeting another woman,

what would he do then? Reach under the seat for his camera with the telephoto lens? Show the shots to his sister? Unlikely. But he might, just might, take Dwayne aside at that point. Tell him he knew. Tell him to get his fucking house in order.

Once they were well into the business district, the truck's brake lights came on. Then the right blinker. Dwayne rolled the truck over to the curb, killed the engine.

Cal drove on, eyes forward.

He checked the passenger door mirror, saw Dwayne get out of the truck and cross the street. Once on the other side, he walked in the same direction Cal had been driving. Cal saw an open spot at the curb and wheeled into it, sat there and waited for Dwayne to come up parallel to him on the opposite side of the street.

Dwayne slowed as he neared a bar, Cal thinking he was going to go inside. But instead, Dwayne disappeared into a narrow alleyway between the bar and a shoe store.

'What the hell?' Cal said.

He had to ease the car ahead a length to get a better view down the alley. Dwayne was heading in from the street, and another man was approaching from the back. They stopped in the middle.

Cal settled back in his seat and reached under the passenger seat from behind. He pulled out the camera with the telephoto lens. The one he often used when he was doing work like this for hire.

It wasn't so much that he wanted to take a picture. But the camera was as good as, or better than, a pair of binoculars.

He quickly wrestled the camera out of its case, took the lens cap off, and brought the camera to eye level.

The guy meeting Dwayne was mid-forties, short, about 250 pounds. Jeans and a black Windbreaker.

They were talking.

Nodding.

Then the other guy reached into his pocket, handed something to Dwayne.

Click.

It was just reflex, hitting the shutter button when he did. Because if this were a real job, this might be evidence of something. Of money changing hands. A thick wad of it, too, it looked like to Cal.

CHAPTER 28

Gill Pickens was faceup on a gurney that hugged the wall in a hallway some distance from the emergency ward, somewhere between radiology and the cafeteria, but he was not alone. The ER, and the adjoining examining rooms, had not been able to accommodate the huge influx of patients, and there was no space in any of the hospital rooms, so the spillover had left the sick languishing throughout the building. Patients lined both sides of the hallway, which resulted in a lot of shifting and squeezing as staff and family members jockeyed for position.

So when Marla, with Arlene Harwood at her side and Matthew in her arms, finally had an opportunity to talk with Dr Clara Moorehouse about her father's condition, there was little in the way of privacy. The discussion was held at Gill's side. His skin looked like concrete and his eyes were closed, but he was alive.

'Surely you can find a room for him somewhere instead of dumping him here,' Arlene said.

'We're doing the best we can,' Moorehouse said.

'You would think, for someone who was married

to the woman who used to run this hospital, that you—'

'Please, Aunt Arlene,' Marla said. 'It's okay.'

'The word we're receiving,' the doctor said, 'is that it's some kind of chemical poisoning. There's no treatment. We'll do everything we can for your father. But it's out of our hands. He's luckier than many, who clearly consumed much more water than he did. It's wait and see.'

'But he *might* make it?' Marla asked, shifting Matthew from one arm to the other.

The doctor said, 'I don't know if you're a religious person. I'm not. But if I were, I'd say a few prayers for him, because it's out of our hands. He might very well make it. But if he does, you need to know that there may be some permanent effects.'

Arlene put her arm around her niece. 'Thank you,' she said. 'Can we stay here?'

'Stay as long as you want,' Moorehouse said. 'If a room opens up, we'll move him, but I don't see that happening anytime soon. We may even end up transferring him to one of the hospitals in Albany. I'll let you know.'

The doctor excused herself to talk to some other equally anxious family members farther down the hall, including a woman wearing a hijab that covered her hair and neck who was attending to a sick man who looked Middle Eastern.

Matthew, who had been crying off and on ever since they'd arrived at the hospital, started up again.

'He's hungry,' Marla said. She took a sniff of him. 'And he needs to be changed.'

'You need to go home,' Arlene said. 'You need to look after Matthew and yourself. You must be starving.'

'I can't leave,' she said. 'What if they move Dad to another hospital? I have to stay with him.'

Arlene said, 'I have an idea. I'll call Don to come pick you and Matthew up and I'll stay here with Gill. If anything happens, I'll call you right away.'

Marla's face had grown long with weariness. 'I don't know. Maybe I—'

'Marla!'

She whirled around, and standing there in the middle of the hallway, his eyes red, arms outstretched, was Derek Cutter. The recently graduated Thackeray student and father of Matthew.

'I've been looking everywhere!' he said. 'I tried to call you, and I went to your house, and I didn't know what had happened to you or to Matthew and—'

Marla burst into tears, kept hold of Matthew with one arm, extended the other, and wrapped it around Derek. His hug encircled mother and child. But then he saw Gill, released Marla and Matthew, and said, 'Oh no.'

Marla said, 'He's hanging in there.'

'I'm so sorry.'

'What about you, and your parents? Are they okay?'

Derek nodded, said his parents were out of town,

and he'd heard the loudspeakers from a passing fire truck while still in bed. Marla filled him in on how her cousin had brought them to the hospital, what the doctor had said, how she was thinking of going home to change and feed the baby.

'I can take you,' he said.

Arlene thought that was an excellent idea. 'I'll stay here,' she said. 'Go.'

Marla made a token protest before allowing herself to leave. Derek, slipping an arm around Marla, whispered, 'I don't think . . . I didn't realize how big a part of my life you and Matthew are until I thought maybe I'd lost you.'

It was the first thing in several hours that made Arlene Harwood smile. She said to Gill, 'I don't know if you can hear me or not, Gill, but I think things are going to be okay with Marla. I really do.'

Gill's lips appeared to move slightly, although his eyes did not open.

'What was that?' Arlene said, bending over, putting her ear close to his mouth. The lips moved again.

Arlene reversed things, shifting her mouth close to his ear. 'I'll tell Marla no such thing. You'll tell her yourself when you're better. And she knows, Gill. She knows.'

She stood back, hoping he might open his eyes. She reached for his hand and gave it a squeeze.

At the far end of the hall, a man in his forties

who was standing over a silver-haired woman parked on yet another gurney caught sight of the woman wearing the hijab. She was speaking in whispers to the patient Dr Moorehouse had been attending to moments earlier.

The man raised a hand, pointed, and said, 'You've got your fucking nerve.'

He spoke loud enough that it was hard for anyone not to hear. Heads turned, looked his way. The woman in the hijab looked, too, and realized quickly she was the one being pointed at.

The man said, 'Being right here, among us. That takes some gall, lady.'

The woman, with a pronounced accent, said, 'Are you talking to me?'

'You see any other terrorists around?'

The woman clearly didn't consider that worthy of a response, and returned to comforting her loved one.

'You think we don't know what's going on?' the man said, taking measured steps up the hallway.

The woman turned her head again. 'Please leave us alone,' she said.

'You know who that is back there?' he said, pointing to the woman he'd been looking after. 'That's my mother. She's only sixty-six years old, and yesterday, she was the healthiest woman in this goddamn town. But now, she's just clinging to life. I don't know if she's going to make it or not.'

'This is my husband,' the woman said. 'And he is dying.'

265

'But isn't that what you people do? You sacrifice a few for the cause? Like when you send a woman into some public square with dynamite strapped to her chest?'

'Stop it!' Arlene said.

The man looked past the woman he'd been harassing to take in Arlene. 'Don't you see? They're hiding in plain sight. They're here – they're everywhere. This is how they're doing it.'

'Shut up!' Arlene shouted. 'Go take care of your mother and leave that woman alone.'

A door halfway up the hall opened and Angus Carlson emerged.

'What's going on?' he asked, glancing first in Arlene's direction, then at the man who was still pointing. Except now there was something in his hand that was not there before.

He was waving around a gun.

People started screaming. Those who had been standing next to gurneys either dropped to the floor or used their bodies to shield the sick, except for the woman in the hijab, who stood tall and straight and stared directly at her accuser.

Carlson immediately drew his own gun, and as he pointed it at the man, he shouted, 'Police! Drop your weapon!'

The man did not. He said, 'Arrest her!'

'Sir, you need to lower your weapon right now.'

'Don't you see?' he said. 'What's happened today? It's an attack! First it was the drive-in, and now this.' The man's eyes were filling with tears. 'My mother is dying.'

Carlson's voice came down a notch, but remained firm. 'Sir, you need to lower your weapon immediately. If what you're saying is true, then that's good, that's good, you bringing it to my attention.'

The woman glanced at him, anger and fear in her eyes.

Carlson met them for half a second, then said to the man, 'You can be certain a full investigation of your allegations will be made. If you turn out to be right, I wouldn't be surprised if they want to give you some kind of medal. But so long as you're waving that gun around, we can't get started on any of that.'

'They get off,' the man said. 'They always get off.'

'We'll have to make sure nothing like that happens.' Carlson moved closer, extended his left hand. 'Why don't you just hand your weapon over to me? Let's put this behind us. We're all under tremendous stress today. We're all on edge.'

The man's eyes darted back and forth between Carlson and the woman, but the gun remained trained on the woman.

And Angus Carlson had his weapon trained on the man.

'Please, sir. I don't know how good a shot you are, but if you pull that trigger, there's a chance you may hit someone else. Maybe someone else's mother. Or father. A son or daughter. And I have to tell you, if you pull that trigger, I'm going to have to do the same. I'll have to shoot you. And even though I've had training, there's a good chance I'll hit someone *I'm* not supposed to, too.'

Everyone was frozen. No one in the hall was breathing.

'Think about your mother. Think about when she gets well. She's going to need you. And how are you going to help her with her recovery if you're sitting in jail someplace waiting to go to trial?'

Arlene said, 'He's right. What would your mother want?'

Carlson gave her a look that said *I don't need your help.*

But Arlene continued. 'If my son shot an unarmed woman, for any reason, I would be ashamed of him.'

A silence that felt eternal followed. But it didn't go on for more than five or six seconds.

At which point the man said, 'I don't care.'

He raised the gun a quarter of an inch, looked at the woman in the hijab, squinted.

Carlson fired.

The shot was deafening, and in its wake came a chorus of simultaneous screams. The bullet caught the man in the upper thigh and blew him back, as though he'd been brought down by an invisible football player. As he fell, the gun slipped from his hand and clattered to the floor.

Carlson dived for it, scooped it up, then reached into his pocket for a set of plastic cuffs.

'You shot me!' the man said. 'Jesus Christ, you shot me.'

The screams lasted only a few seconds, and now some people, at least those who were not on gurneys, had switched to applause. Carlson holstered his own gun, tucked the man's into the pocket of his sport jacket, then, as blood streamed from the man's thigh, rolled him onto his side so that he could cinch his wrists together behind his back.

'The good news is,' Carlson said, 'we don't have to worry about how long it will take to get you to the hospital.'

A pretty good quip, considering his voice was trembling, and his heart pounding so hard it felt like it would come right out of his chest.

CHAPTER 29

Duckworth

Once the water treatment plant had been evacuated, I put a call in to Rhonda Finderman.

'If you haven't already,' I told her, 'you need to call the governor. If those Homeland Security guys who were here looking at the drive-in explosion can be called back, send them to the water plant. Tell them to bring their hazmat suits. The state has a spills response program for dealing with hazardous material, which is exactly what it looks like we've got here.'

'Is that the chief?' Randall Finley, who was several steps away from me, was trying to listen in on the conversation. 'Because I have a complaint!'

Finderman said, 'Who's that?'

'Never mind. Did you get what I said?'

'Yes,' she said. 'And I just got a call from the state environmental unit. They think they may have a handle on what's in the water.'

'Let me guess,' I said. 'Sodium azide.'

'Jesus, yes. How did you know?'

'It's spilled all over the floor in the plant, around where the fluoride tanks are.' I lowered my voice. 'I've been downplaying terrorism with all the shit that's been going on, but if this isn't a terrorist act, I don't know what is. But what the hell is sodium azide?'

'It's bad, bad stuff,' Finderman said. 'At least, when it's added to water, it is. They use it in automobile air bags, among other things. When it's triggered by an electrical charge, it turns into nitrogen gas and blows up.'

'Yeah, well, that's not how it's being used here.'

'It's got no odor or taste, and if it's added to water, it causes all the symptoms we've been seeing at the hospital. Convulsions, respiratory failure, dropping heart rate.'

'What can they do for it?' I asked.

'Nothing.'

'Say again?'

'*Nothing*, Barry. There's no magic pill, no antidote. You either live or you don't. Severity of symptoms depends on exposure, or how much is ingested. If what you swallowed didn't quite kill you, you could end up with permanent lung or brain damage.'

'Whoever put this into the water killed one of the workers here,' I said.

'Who?'

I told her.

'What's killing one guy when you're ultimately planning to kill hundreds, or thousands?' Finderman asked.

She had a point.

'What's the death toll?' I asked her.

'It's gone up. It was a hundred and twenty-three, but I just heard we're revising that up to one hundred and thirty-one.' A pause. 'I lost my niece. Esme. She was seventeen. My brother and his wife, they're beyond devastated.'

'I'm sorry,' I said.

'I want who did this,' Rhonda said. 'Whoever he is, or whoever they are, I want them.'

'There's more,' I said.

'More what?'

I told her about Lorraine Plummer, the murdered student at Thackeray College. 'I had to leave the scene,' I said regretfully. 'I couldn't get Wanda or anyone else to get there. We need a crime scene unit there.'

'We've had to bring in coroners from other jurisdictions,' the chief said. 'It's like we've had a flood, a hurricane, and locusts all at once. A few years' worth of bodies in a single morning.'

'The Thackeray thing, even in light of what else has happened today, is big, Chief.'

'Go on.'

'Our guy is back.'

'What guy? What – no, come on.'

'Wanda will have to do a full autopsy, but I had a good look at the body. The wounds are the same as on Olivia Fisher and Rosemary Gaynor.'

'Goddamn it, Barry. When are you going to let this go?'

'I'd be more than happy to take you to look at the body and let you judge for yourself.'

There was quiet at the other end. The Fisher and Gaynor murders were evidently still a source of friction between us, but I'd already admitted to myself there was plenty of blame to go around.

'Duncomb's dead, and Gaynor's in jail,' the chief said. 'Your two lead suspects.'

'Yeah.'

'Shit,' Finderman said. 'If you think it's the same killer . . . I trust your judgment.'

'There's nothing I can do here right now,' I told her. 'I can't even have anyone get near Tate Whitehead's body. The whole area has to be closed off until it's been given an all clear. I'm going to spend the next few hours working the college homicide.'

'Just keep in touch,' Rhonda Finderman said.

Finley, who'd been watching me this whole time, said, 'I want to talk to her! I want to talk to her right now!'

I put away my phone.

Finley waved a finger at me. 'You're going to be sorry when I'm mayor.'

'We don't agree on much, but I think you're right about that.'

'I don't forget.'

I closed the distance between us, put my face in his. 'I don't forget, either, Randy. I *never* forget. The other day, when you called me to check out all those dead squirrels, and you hinted around, wondering whether I had anything on anybody, I thought, no, I don't play that game. I don't have anything on anybody. Except maybe that's not true. Maybe I have something on *you*.'

He took a step back. 'Me? What the hell have you got on me?'

'I was on the phone a few minutes ago and learned something kind of interesting. Something interesting about you, Randy.'

'I don't know what you're talking about.'

'I heard you did your good deed before coming back up here. You set up by the falls and handed out hundreds of cases of bottled water.'

'Yeah,' he said, puffing himself up. 'I did. You should have come by. I'd've given you one even if you are a horse's ass.'

'It's kind of amazing how you were ready to go so fast.'

Randy shrugged. 'You do what you have to do when people are in trouble.'

'How'd you know?'

'How'd I know what?'

'How'd you know you were going to need so much bottled water?'

He was shaking his head. 'I don't know what the hell you're talking about.'

'You cranked up production this week. Before any of this happened.'

'Where the hell did you hear that?'

I'd heard it from David Harwood. A comment

just in passing. But it had been bothering me for a while now.

'Did I hear wrong?' I asked.

Finley's mouth opened like he was going to say something, but he hadn't figured out yet what it was going to be.

'Yeah, that's wrong,' he said.

'So it'd be okay if I started asking around, checked that out. Because if it's true, it raises a question. Why would Randall Finley, just as he's on the comeback trail, start bottling more of his famous springwater on the eve of a catastrophic poisoning of the town's water supply?'

'You fat fuck,' he said.

'You want to make life difficult for me?' I asked him. 'Go ahead. Meanwhile, I'm going to go whisper in the ear of one of those CNN or *New York Times* reporters swarming all over town. Then I wouldn't even have to start nosing around. I'd just let them do it for me. See how long it takes before someone puts a camera in your face and asks if you'd actually be willing to let hundreds of people die to advance your half-assed political career.'

'You son of a bitch,' he said.

'I didn't mind "fat fuck." I gotta admit, that's pretty accurate. But now you're casting aspersions on my mother.'

'You saying I did this?' he asked, pointing a thumb back at the plant.

'Did you?'

I should have been ready. I should have seen it coming. But I'm not as young as I used to be, and I'm the first to admit I could be in better shape. So when Randy charged at me, I didn't move as quickly as I could. I didn't take a defensive stance, like shifting my weight forward so he'd have a harder time taking me down.

But take me down he did.

He rammed his body into me, put his arms around me, and tackled me to the ground.

'You fucker!' he said.

We turned slightly as we fell, which was just as well, because it meant I hit the pavement on my side, my left shoulder taking a lot of the impact. If I'd fallen straight back, I'd have probably cracked my head open. And I'd already hit it on a curb a few days earlier when that Thackeray College professor had gotten the better of me.

Maybe I wasn't cut out for this anymore.

We rolled on the parking lot, a couple of overweight – Randy, less so, I admit – middle-aged guys duking it out. Not the sort of fight you could sell a lot of tickets to.

I was worried he'd go for my gun, which was holstered and attached to my belt on my left side. It wasn't that I believed Randall Finley actually wanted to murder me, but in heated moments, sometimes people lose their heads. So I had to deal with this quickly before things spiraled even more out of control.

He'd lost his grip on me when we went down,

so my arms were no longer pinned. I made a fist with my right hand, swung it as fast and as hard as I could, and aimed it where I thought it would do the most good.

At Randall Finley's nose.

Our former mayor's nose was something of a legend in Promise Falls. It had been punched before – at least two times that I knew of – and both times by his former driver, Jim Cutter. The second time, Cutter had broken it.

I connected. Not quite dead center, I'm afraid. A little off to one side. And I didn't hear the crunch of broken cartilage that I was hoping for. But it did the trick.

Finley yelped in pain, put both hands over his face. Blood trickled out from under them and from between his fingers.

'Jesus!' he screamed. 'Not my nose!'

'Should be used to it by now,' I said, getting to my knees, and then forcing myself back up onto two feet. Finley lay on the pavement, writhing.

'You didn't answer my question,' I said. 'Did you do it?'

'You're crazy, you know that?' he said, taking his hands from his face, looking at the blood as he drew himself up into a sitting position. 'Batshit crazy!'

'You know your way around this water treatment plant,' I said. 'Ottman told me. You drop by here regularly.' I dusted myself off. 'Is that what you did with Tate Whitehead? Jumped him? Before you went in there and poisoned the water?'

I didn't know that I believed what I was saying, but as the words came out of my mouth, I realized the man I was looking at was not just an asshole that I'd had more than enough of.

He was a suspect.

'It was for the summer!' Finley said.

'What was for the summer?'

'The increase in production! Demand goes up in summer, just when we have people off on holidays! We up production in the spring to be ready, you dumb fuck!'

'That's a good story,' I said. 'I guess we'll see how that holds up.'

I didn't offer to help him to his feet. And I didn't have the energy to charge him with assaulting a police officer. I could always do that later. So I left him there on the pavement and headed for my car.

I was going to take a short break from the Promise Falls water tragedy and go three years into the past.

It was time to think about Olivia Fisher. It was time to go back to the beginning. I just hoped Walden Fisher, whom I'd last seen in the emergency ward of Promise Falls General, was well enough to talk about what had happened to her.

CHAPTER 30

Theresa and Ron Jones were already living in the house next to Samantha Worthington's when she moved in with her son, Carl. Theresa and Ron had bought their place fifteen years ago, but the owner of the property next door rented it out, so they had seen people come and go over the years. There was a couple about ten years ago Theresa and Ron were pretty sure were dealing drugs out of the house, and they thanked God when that crew moved out after two years. There was that father and son who lived there for a while, who liked to repair motorcycles in the front yard. They sure weren't sorry to see them go, either.

But they had liked Sam and her boy. The most noise they ever heard coming through the shared wall was when Carl and his mother carried on conversations between floors, shouting at each other – not in an angry way, just trying to be heard – or when Carl was playing some war-type video game, explosions and machine-gun fire rattling the dishes in their cupboards.

Their front doors were not much more than

thirty feet apart, so they ended up seeing one another quite often, making small talk, chatting about the weather. But Sam Worthington never revealed much about herself, other than that she was raising her boy on her own, and that she managed a Laundromat. The little they knew about her life before Promise Falls, they had learned from short conversations with Carl.

The most interesting tidbit being that his dad was in jail back in Boston.

They also knew the two had been through quite a lot lately. There'd been something on the news about an attempted abduction, and a shoot-out – a shoot-out, for crying out loud! – at her place of work.

But even after all that, they saw Sam and Carl going in and out of the house, like, hey, life goes on.

Until two nights ago. Thursday night.

That was when they saw Samantha Worthington running in and out with three suitcases, jamming them into her car. Carl was lugging a heavy bag made of canvas that looked to Theresa like a rolled-up tent.

Ron Jones, watching some of this from the upstairs bedroom window, was pretty sure he saw a shotgun among the items Sam slipped into the car. She had tried to disguise it by rolling it up in a blanket, but he saw the tip of what looked like a barrel poking out the end.

'I'm going to just step outside and see what's going on,' Theresa said.

She acted as though she'd forgotten something in

the glove compartment of her old Chevy Astro van. She had the passenger door open, was rooting around in the folder that held her ownership and insurance, when Sam came by with another suitcase.

'You heading away early for the long weekend?' Theresa asked, just being neighborly.

Sam, hair hanging over her eyes, the base of her neck glistening with sweat, forced the case into the open trunk and glanced over. 'What?'

'I said, you going away for the weekend?'

Sam nodded. 'Yeah. We're off for a while.'

At which point Carl came out with a sleeping bag under one arm, a pillow under the other.

'Where you going?' she asked.

'Oh, we'll see where the road takes us,' Sam said, heading back into the house for another load.

But as was often the case, it was Carl who was a little freer with information. While he was dumping an overstuffed backpack into the car, and his mother was still in the house, he said to Theresa, 'We haven't gone camping in years, but Mom says we can do that till things die down.'

'Die down?' Theresa said.

Carl might have said more, but Sam was coming back out of the house with bags of groceries. It looked like she'd emptied out a cupboard. 'Go get the cooler,' she told her son.

'Did you put some Coke in it?' he asked.

'A couple. But I don't want you drinking soda nonstop.'

Carl ran into the house and emerged seconds

281

later with a cheap white Styrofoam cooler with a blue lid. He got it into the backseat. Sam locked up the house, the two of them got into the car, and they were gone.

Just like that.

So Theresa was not shocked when someone showed up at the door Saturday morning wondering where the neighbors had gone. Word was just starting to get around about the poisoned water, but luckily for Ron and Theresa, they'd slept in – ever since Ron had retired from teaching high school in Albany, and Theresa had finally decided to stop working in the accounting department at General Electric, they were no longer waking up every day at six, or earlier – and had tuned the radio to the local news before heading downstairs to put on the coffee.

When the chimes rang, she went to the front door, since Ron was out back doing battle with the dandelions.

'Hi. Sorry to bother you,' said the man on their front step. 'I'm looking for the folks from next door. Samantha and Carl?'

'Oh yeah,' said Theresa. 'Who are you?'

The man smiled apologetically, as though he should have introduced himself to begin with. 'My name's Harwood. David Harwood? I knocked on their door just now, and was by earlier, and they don't seem to be around.'

'They must have gone away for the weekend,' she said.

'Yeah,' the man said, unable to hide the disappointment in his voice. 'I really need to get in touch with them. Sam is – well, Sam and I have been seeing each other, and I'm worried that I haven't heard from her, that she isn't answering her cell phone.'

Theresa heard a noise at the back of the house. Ron coming in. 'Where are you?' he called out.

'Front door!' she said. When Ron showed up, a jar of weed spray in his hand, she said, 'This man's name is David Harwood. He was looking for Sam and Carl next door.'

'Hi there,' Ron said.

'Hi. I was worried, you know, because of the water scare, that maybe they were sick, but I looked in the windows, and it looks like no one's home. And the car's gone, anyway.'

'Yeah,' Ron said. 'I saw them packing up a couple of nights ago.'

'Did Sam say where they were going?'

Ron shook his head. 'I didn't talk to them.'

'I did,' Theresa said. 'Just for a second. All Sam said was they were going away. Just as well, considering what the town is going through today. Maybe she knows someone who has a cottage. That'd be the place to be this weekend.'

'Isn't that the truth? Well, I thank you for your trouble.'

'It's more likely they went to a camp—'

Theresa cut her husband off, saying, 'You want to leave a card or something in case she comes back? Someplace she can get in touch with you?'

'No, that's fine,' he said. 'You have a good day, now.'

Theresa closed the door, then leaned up against it with her back and placed the tips of her fingers on her chest, just below her neck. She took several deep breaths.

'Are you okay?' her husband asked.

'Why did you have to say that?'

'Say what?'

'What you were starting to say. That they might have gone to a campground.'

'Isn't that what you figured? They were putting sleeping bags and a tent into the car. Doesn't take a rocket scientist to guess they were going camping.'

'He might have heard you. I think he did.'

'So what?' Ron asked.

'So he might start checking campgrounds, that's what.'

'So what if he does? He said they've been seeing each other, him and Sam.'

'Yeah.' Theresa nodded. 'Sam *has* been seeing someone named David Harwood. I've seen him drop by the last week or so.'

'Okay. And?'

'And that wasn't him.'

CHAPTER 31

Once the coroner showed up – a woman named Wanda Therrieult – Joyce Pilgrim returned to her office.

That detective wanted her to review video from the college's security cameras for the hours before and after the time when he believed Lorraine Plummer had been killed. One of the rooms in the small collection of offices that made up the security division was devoted to tech matters, including several computer monitors linked into the cameras posted around the campus.

It had been Joyce's plan to head straight in there, but she felt there was something more pressing she had to deal with first.

She had to call Lorraine Plummer's parents, Lester and Alma. It was their call, after all, that had prompted her to go looking for the student in the first place. They were probably still by the phone, waiting to hear back.

But wait. Was it her responsibility? Should she be the one to give them the horrible news? Or was that up to the police? If this was a murder – which it clearly was – wasn't it more appropriate for the cops to break the news? Shouldn't it be Duckworth's job?

She knew what she was doing. She was looking for a way out. Joyce didn't want to make the call. She wanted a legitimate excuse not to have to pick up that phone.

Should she call Duckworth and ask if he'd done it? Had he even taken down contact information for the Plummers? She didn't think he had. The man was probably going out of his mind. How many Promise Falls families were getting bad news today?

Joyce knew this was something she had to do herself.

She picked up the landline, entered the number for the Plummers. The phone did not complete the first ring.

'Yes?' It was the mother, Alma.

'Ms Plummer?'

'That's right. Lester, get on the extension!'

A click, then, 'Hello?'

'You're both there?' Joyce said.

'Yes,' said Lester.

'Has anyone been in touch with you?' she asked.

'No,' said Lester. 'You mean about the water? We've been watching the news. About the poisoned water. When did that happen? Has that been going on all week? Is Lorraine sick?'

'Is she in the hospital?' Alma asked.

'Dear God, did she drink the water?' Lester Plummer asked.

'No,' said Joyce. 'She didn't drink the water. The college is on a separate water supply from the town, so we weren't affected here.'

She could hear both parents sigh in relief.

'I'm sorry,' Joyce Pilgrim said, 'but the news is still bad.'

When she got off the phone, she did not immediately go into the tech room. Instead, she sat stone-still in her desk chair and felt herself start to shake. She gripped the arms of the chair.

I will not lose it.

She took several deep breaths, fought back tears. She'd managed to hold it together through the rest of that phone call. If she could listen to two people be overcome with grief and not start crying herself, she could do anything.

Right?

She thought about calling her husband. She wanted to hear Ted's voice. But she was sure the moment he came on the line, she'd go to pieces.

She would talk to him later.

Joyce hoped the next time she talked with Duckworth, he wouldn't ask whether she'd quizzed Lorraine Plummer's parents about whether their daughter had ever mentioned a married man.

She couldn't do it. The people were too distraught. She'd broken the news to them. Duckworth could ask them his questions.

Joyce seated herself at the desk in the tech room, moved the mouse around, entered in the time period. She wanted to see footage from 11:20 p.m. through to 1:20 a.m. Duckworth had said he believed Lorraine had been killed about twenty minutes past midnight.

Cameras were posted on the road near the library and the athletic center. There were other cameras, too, although none close to the dormitory where Lorraine lived. But anyone driving onto the Thackeray grounds, headed for that building, would have had to pass either the library or the athletic center.

She brought up the video that had been taken from the athletic-center camera first. Set it up to begin at 11:20 p.m.

There wasn't a whole lot to look at. With so few students in attendance, there were no cars, and very few people walking about. At 11:45 a young man and woman, holding hands, walked across the screen.

At 11:51, a jogger. White male, late teens or twenties, pair of shorts, white T-shirt. Wires coming down from his ears. On-screen for maybe seven seconds. She made a note of his appearance, scribbled onto a pad: 'runner 11:51.'

At 12:02 a.m., he reappeared, going the other way. Joyce made another note.

She was able to fast-forward through the stretches where there was no activity. And there was nothing after that jogger's return trip on the athletic-center camera. At one point, she thought she saw something, rewound, started the video again at regular speed.

Something moving along the side of the road, up close to a building. Very low to the ground. Was it a person? Someone crawling? Was it someone who had been injured, or someone sneaking around?

She rewound, watched it again. It wasn't one moving object, but three, or possibly four.

Raccoons.

Joyce laughed. Her first laugh in some time.

Time to turn her attention to the other camera, the one mounted near the library. One corner of the library building was in the upper-right quadrant of the screen. A road bisected the screen horizontally. The upper left was wooded area, and below the street, sidewalk. The camera itself was mounted atop a student residence – not Lorraine's – across from the library. The building where Lorraine lived was offscreen, to the right, maybe a hundred yards away.

The library was closed, of course, that late at night, and only about a fifth of the usual lights were on. Most of the road illumination came from streetlamps.

Joyce started at 11:20 p.m., and again fast-forwarded until something caught her eye.

A car entered the screen quickly from the left, stopped dead center. Joyce noted the time: 11:41 p.m. The driver's door opened – the interior dome light flashed on – and a man jumped out carrying something square, and white.

A pizza box. It was a pizza delivery guy.

He ran toward the bottom of the screen, disappeared. Was he headed for the residence just out of view? Or could he have, once off closed-circuit, cut right and gone to Lorraine's building?

Had she ordered a pizza? Duckworth had looked at her phone. If he'd seen a pizza delivery call, wouldn't he have been all over that? But then again, she could have ordered it online, using her laptop. Or maybe she—

Hang on. The pizza guy was back, already. Only three minutes had passed. It was 11:44. He got behind the wheel, did a U-turn in the street, and tore off in the direction he'd come from.

Still, Joyce made a note.

11:45: nothing.

11:49: nothing.

11:55: nothing.

12:01: noth – *Hello. What's this?*

A vehicle nosed into the screen from the left. Literally, nosed. A bumper and about six inches of hood. The vehicle nudged its way into the scene, and stopped.

There wasn't enough vehicle showing to tell whether it was a car, an SUV, or maybe a pickup truck. The only thing it definitely did *not* look like was a van, where you would expect to see the hood sloping vertically up into a windshield.

Joyce hit pause, stared at the screen, brought her nose up to it, trying to tell what kind of car or truck it might be. But the image was grainy, the lighting inadequate.

She hit play, allowed the video to continue.

The headlights went out. For a few seconds, there was nothing.

Then, a flash of light from the left. Two seconds maybe. On, and off.

The dome light, she thought. Someone getting out of the car, then closing the door.

And then, a person.

He – Joyce was guessing it was a he – came around the front of the vehicle quickly, mounted the curb, kept walking in that direction and out of the frame.

Gone.

Joyce paused the video, rewound, then went through the next fifteen seconds in slo-mo. Headlights off. Flash of light. Man coming around front of car.

Pause.

What could she actually tell about him? He was little more than a blurry, dark figure. No hat, but she couldn't see his face well enough to know whether he was white, black, or brown. Anywhere from five-six to six feet, she guessed, which was not terribly helpful. That accounted for most men on the planet.

Pants, jacket. In other words, not naked.

'Shit,' Joyce said to no one in particular.

He was there, and then he was gone. A few seconds later, it was 12:02 a.m.

Joyce made more notes, then let the video continue. She resisted the urge to fast-forward. Her eyes stayed locked on the vehicle as the minutes ticked by.

At 12:07, a jogger.

Joyce was pretty sure it was the same jogger she'd seen from the other camera. He came in from the right side of the screen, ran to the left, and then he was gone. Instead of running on the sidewalk, he had chosen to run down the middle of the street.

She rewound, took a closer look at him. Same shorts, it looked like. And again, what looked like two strands of spaghetti running down from his ears.

Same jogger.

He'd run right past the parked vehicle. Within a few feet of it.

Joyce let the surveillance video play on.

It got to be 12:20 a.m., which was around the time Duckworth believed Lorraine Plummer had been killed.

Then it was 12:21.

12:22.

Joyce sat, eyes riveted.

He came out of nowhere at 12:34 a.m.

Coming from below the screen, running around the front of the car.

Two seconds of light as he opened the door, got behind the wheel, and closed the door.

Headlights on.

Drive forward, Joyce thought. *Drive forward and let me get a better look at your ride.*

The vehicle backed out of the frame.

'Fuck!' Joyce said, and banged a fist on the table hard enough to shake the monitor.

She kept the video rolling until 1:20, but there was nothing else to see.

Joyce leaned back in the computer chair, laced her fingers together at the back of her head, and again shouted, 'Fuck!'

She'd really wanted to see what that son of a bitch was driving. But then she realized that even if she couldn't see it, someone else had.

I have to find that jogger.

CHAPTER 32

Duckworth

I'd been through the Olivia Fisher file several times in the last couple of weeks. I knew the basic facts, which were these: She was a beautiful young woman, twenty-four years old, black hair to her shoulders, round, bright eyes. Five-five, 132 pounds. She'd been born right here, at Promise Falls General Hospital, and done all her schooling in the town. She had never lived away from home, although that might very well have changed.

Olivia was engaged to Victor Rooney, also twenty-four at the time, another Promise Falls born-and-raised kid, who had gone to Thackeray for two years before dropping out. School wasn't his thing. But he had, in the months prior to Olivia's death, gotten a job with the town fire department. He had, over the years, held other odd jobs. Some of those had also been with the town, in other capacities.

One, I now remembered from a conversation I'd had not long ago with Olivia's father, Walden, had been a summer position at the water treatment plant.

They were to be married in three months, at the end of August 2012. The hall had been booked, the invitations mailed. Olivia had just completed an environmental science degree at Thackeray, and was in line for a job at an oceanic institute in Boston. She was going to accept it, even though it would mean living away from Promise Falls, and her family, for the first time in her life. Victor was said to be sorry about leaving Promise Falls, but had planned to apply for a firefighting job anywhere in the Boston area.

None of that happened.

On Friday, May 25, at nine twenty p.m., Olivia Fisher was in Promise Falls Park, not far from the foot of the waterfall, waiting to meet her fiancé. He'd worked an afternoon shift with the fire department and was planning to grab a couple of drinks with his buddies after, at Knight's. He planned to leave there at nine and walk over to the park – it was only a few blocks from the bar, and he knew he probably wouldn't be in any shape to drive – but he lost track of time.

Had he left when he'd planned to, it was possible Olivia would not have been grabbed from behind. It was possible a knife would not have penetrated the left side of her abdomen. It was possible that knife would not then have sliced across Olivia to roughly the same position on the other side of her torso.

With that distinctive, signature cut. Curving down slightly in the middle, a crude smile.

The attack most likely took little more than a few seconds. But in that time, Olivia Fisher managed to scream. From all accounts, at least twice.

Two horrific shrieks.

The assailant immediately fled the scene. He did not sexually assault his victim. He did not take her purse, or remove anything from it.

The primary on the case had been former detective and now chief Rhonda Finderman. The incident had happened when I was out of the country, and I had not been involved in the initial investigation.

Rhonda's notes, however, were thorough. I could find no fault with them. My problem with Rhonda had been her failure to bring to my attention the similarity between the Fisher murder and that of Rosemary Gaynor. But I'd been over that before, and concluded I had to carry the can for that as much as anyone else.

I had learned things about Olivia on my own.

As with Lorraine Plummer, she had been a participant in the sex games of three couples: Adam and Miriam Chalmers, Peter and Georgina Blackmore, and Clive and Liz Duncomb. Excited to meet a published author – Chalmers – she had accepted an invitation to the man's house for dinner, where everyone else was present. While other young women who'd been brought to the home to be sexually exploited had been drugged,

Olivia, at least according to Blackmore, had been a more willing participant.

That had been a month before she died.

I'd considered that one of those six had been involved in Olivia's death, but nothing had panned out. Following Duncomb's death, I'd brought in for questioning his wife, Liz – a real piece of work – reasoning that she could have had the same motive as her husband for killing Olivia: the fear that she might talk about what had gone on in that house.

But I didn't believe Liz had the physical bearing to do what had been done to Olivia.

I'd briefly considered a doctor named Jack Sturgess – whom I'd once suspected in the Rosemary Gaynor murder – in Olivia's death, but that had been a dead end as well. And Bill Gaynor didn't look good for it, either.

And neither of them could have had anything to do with Lorraine Plummer's death.

So I was back where I'd started.

There were other issues with the Fisher crime.

The witnesses. Or, at least, the potential witnesses. There'd been so many of them. Twenty-two, according to Rhonda Finderman's notes.

Twenty-two people who heard Olivia Fisher's screams.

And did nothing.

Finderman tracked down more than half of them herself. The others, perhaps motivated by guilt and a wish to get things off their chest, came forward. Some were in other areas of the park.

Two were on the bridge that spanned the falls.

Several others were in an open-window coffee shop across the street from the park. Others were strolling along the sidewalk.

It was a lovely spring evening. The days had grown longer; winter was a quickly fading memory. The sun had set, but the air remained warm enough to manage without a jacket. There was the persistent dull roar of the falls in the background, but sounds carried.

Everyone would have heard Olivia.

There was a consistency to the interviews with those who had heard her cries.

'I figured a call to 911 would already have been made.'

'I would have done something, but I assumed someone closer would have.'

'I thought it was probably just kids goofing around.'

'I didn't hear anything after the first two screams, so I guessed it was nothing.'

'I leave this kind of thing to the professionals.'

And so on.

Promise Falls had, on that particular evening, suffered a collective lack of responsibility. A wave of not-my-problem.

For a period of time, it brought shame on the town. Promise Falls, in the words of one CNN commentator, was 'the town that didn't care.'

The town was smeared across social media. We earned our own Twitter hashtag: #brokenpromise.

We were, indeed, broken.

But as with all targets of social outrage, we were

298

soon forgotten as the world found others. A flip tweet from a PR person about AIDS in Africa. A comedian making a joke about tsunami victims. A congressman saying blacks were lazy.

Luckily for the twenty-two people who heard but did not act, their names were never made public. Police feared there might be reprisals. But they were all here in the files.

One, I recognized. It was, coincidentally, the father of someone I'd spoken to in the last couple of hours.

Don Harwood. Father of David.

Finderman hadn't tracked him down on her own. He came into the station to confess his sin.

'I was one of them,' he told Rhonda. 'I was one of the people who did nothing.'

Finderman, in her notes, described how the man had wept as he told her what he'd heard.

'I was just getting into my car. I'd gone into the smoke shop there to look for something on the newsstand.' He had built a model train layout in his basement for his grandson, Ethan, and was looking for the latest issue of a magazine about Lionel Trains. 'I found it, and when I came out, I heard the screams. They sounded like they were coming from the park, and I looked that way, and I thought about whether to do something, but I looked up and down the street and no one else was doing anything or calling anybody, so I guessed there was nothing to worry about. I'll never forgive myself for that.'

There was other fallout from the Fisher murder.

Victor Rooney started drinking heavily. He lost his job with the fire department and had been in and out of work ever since. He was racked with guilt, according to Rhonda's notes, over not being on time to meet Olivia. I had wondered, when I started looking into the case, whether the source of his guilt might be something different.

Like, maybe he'd killed Olivia. Nine times out of ten, it was the boyfriend or the husband.

But Rhonda had checked out his alibi. She had interviewed his drinking buddies at Knight's. He'd been there at the time of Olivia's death.

All of which left me nowhere.

Which was why I wanted to pay another visit to Walden Fisher. To see whether there was something we'd all overlooked.

The last time I'd seen Olivia's father, he'd been waiting at Promise Falls General for a doctor to have a look at him. Considering how many patients were up there, he might still be waiting.

If he wasn't dead.

Last I'd heard, Angus Carlson was still at the hospital talking to people. I phoned him, aware that if he was still in the ER, the call might not get through to him.

He answered.

'Hey,' he said. He sounded subdued, which probably shouldn't have surprised me, given what we'd all been dealing with.

'Hey,' I said back. 'I need you to do something for me.'

'I can't.'

'You haven't even heard what it is.'

'Don't you know?' Carlson asked.

'Know what?' I wondered if Carlson himself had taken ill.

'Some shit went down here at the hospital. I'm outside now, giving a statement.'

'What happened?'

'I shot a guy.'

'*What?*'

He filled me in.

'Jesus Christ,' I said.

'Yeah, I know. What next, right? A zombie apocalypse?'

It was a typical Carlson attempt at a joke, but I heard no levity in his voice. For maybe the first time, I felt for him.

'It sounds like you did the right thing,' I said. 'And you got lucky. You brought him down without taking a life. There's no telling what that guy might have done once he started firing.'

'Yeah, well. What was it you wanted, anyway?'

'It doesn't matter.'

'No, go ahead.'

'I want to talk to Walden Fisher. He was up there in the ER when I left. You seen him lately?'

A pause. 'No,' he said. 'I remember when you were talking to him, but I didn't see him around later.'

301

'Maybe he was admitted.'

'Maybe. And they're moving a lot of people out of here.' A pause. It sounded as though Carlson was talking to someone else. 'I'm going to have to go,' he said when he got back. 'What did you want to talk to Mr Fisher for?'

'Don't worry about it,' I said. 'You've got enough to deal with right now. Hang in there, okay, Angus?'

'Yeah,' Carlson said. 'Thanks, Barry.'

I could have returned to the hospital and hunted for Walden Fisher, but it would still be chaotic there – especially now that there had been a shooting there – and even if he was in the building, it could take a long time to locate him. I decided it might be more expedient to go by his house first, in the event that he'd been treated and released.

When I parked out front of his place, I could see through the porch's screen door straight into the house, the main door wide open. It didn't necessarily mean he was home. He probably hadn't taken time to lock up the house when he came running out, sick. What had he told me at the hospital? That he'd nearly been run over by an ambulance.

I scanned the surface of the road, and sure enough, I saw what looked like the remains of someone's stomach contents. The kind of deposit one often saw on the sidewalk outside any Promise Falls bar on a Friday or Saturday night.

I went up to the door, rapped lightly, and called through the screen, 'Mr Fisher?'

The sound of a chair being pushed back. I could see down a short hallway to the kitchen, and several seconds later, Walden appeared. He walked very slowly to the screen door, pushed it open.

'Oh,' he said. 'Hey.'

'You're home,' I said. 'How are you feeling?'

'Like I threw up a cow. They kicked me out of the ER, wanted me to go to Albany to get checked out.'

'You're back already?'

'Didn't go,' he said wearily. 'Didn't have it in me. I hadn't died yet, so I figured I wasn't going to, but I'm still kind of shaky.'

'Can I come in?'

'Uh, yeah, sure. I was just sitting in the kitchen staring out the window. I'd offer you a coffee, but I think that's what got me in trouble in the first place.'

As I followed him back into the kitchen, I asked, 'Did a doctor even look at you?'

'Some lady gave me the once-over. But there were people way worse than me, people keeling over dead, and she had to go tend to them.'

'You're feeling better?'

Walden nodded. 'Yeah. I only had a couple of sips of the coffee I'd made myself. Guess that's what saved me. I make kind of lousy coffee anyway, never drink all that much of it.' A weak grin. 'Bad coffee saved my life, I guess.' He waved his hand at the kitchen, the dirty dishes in the sink, an open cereal box on the counter. 'Place is a bit of a mess.'

'That's okay.'

'I got beer in the fridge if you'd like that, maybe a can of pop or something. Some lemonade? In a carton, not something with tap water in it.'

'I'm fine.'

'Do you know how long it'll be before we can drink the water again?'

I shook my head. 'No. Mind if I sit?'

'Be my guest.'

I pulled out a chair and dropped myself into it. Walden Fisher sat opposite me. A metal nail file sat on the table. He picked it up, slipped it into his shirt pocket. His fingernails looked ragged from biting. He'd said something to me once about his nerves being all shot to hell these last few years. Not very surprising.

'How'd you get home from the hospital?'

'Victor gave me a lift,' he said. 'So, did you come by just to see if I was okay, or is there something else on your mind?'

'We talked the other day, about Olivia,' I said. 'I wanted to talk some more.'

'Shoot,' he said.

'We haven't given up trying to find out who killed your daughter.'

Walden shrugged. 'So you say,' he said.

'I can't get into specifics, but there've been times when I thought I had an idea who it might be.

Individuals who were already in custody, or possibly even deceased.'

'Like who?'

'As I said, I can't get into that. But I'm less sure of that now.'

'What are you saying?'

'Just that. That he's not someone we've picked up for some other offense.'

Walden leaned in. 'Has he done it again?'

I shook my head. 'I'm sorry. The reason I've come to see you is to learn more about Olivia. Tell me about her.'

He leaned back. 'She was wonderful. She was smart. She was everything to me and Beth. She would have been somebody. She already was. But she'd have shown the world how amazing she could be if she'd been given the chance.'

'I'll bet.'

'Olivia was never mean to anyone. She never held a grudge. She was always happy when something good happened for someone else. You know how some people, they don't like it when someone else has a success. They're bitter or jealous or whatever. But she wasn't like that.'

'She grew up here?' I said, casting my eye about the kitchen.

'Yup. Beth and I were living here when we had her. This was the only place she ever lived. She didn't bunk in at Thackeray. Didn't make any sense, and it was a heck of a lot cheaper to live at home when she went to school.'

'Of course.'

'She's still got her room upstairs,' Walden said. 'Haven't touched it.'

'Really?' I asked. I might have sounded surprised, but I wasn't. Grieving families often left the rooms of those they'd lost untouched. It was too painful to go in there. Cleaning out a bedroom was a final acknowledgment of what had happened. And even if the bedroom could be used by another family member, who wanted to be the relative that moved into it?

'Beth wouldn't touch a thing in there, and since she's died, well, I haven't felt the need, either.'

I couldn't imagine that seeing the room would help me any, but I wanted to just the same. So I asked.

'Sure, why not?' Walden said. 'You might want to lead the way up the stairs. I'm still feeling pretty weak. I'll catch up to you. It's the first door on the left.'

I found my way.

The door was closed. I turned the knob, opened it slowly. The air inside was stale. Olivia's bedroom was maybe ten by ten, a double bed taking center stage. The walls were pale green, what Sherwin-Williams would probably call 'foam green' or 'seaweed.' Puffy yellow spread on the bed. One wall was dominated by a magnificent framed photo of a whale breaking the surface of the water.

'When she was a little girl,' said Walden, who'd caught up to me and was standing in the hall, 'she loved that movie *Free Willy*. You know the one? About this little boy who wants to free a killer whale from an aquarium because they're going to kill it?'

'I know it.'

'She cried every time she saw it. Had it on videotape, then on a DVD. Had the sequels, too, but even Olivia had to admit they were pretty lame. That was her word for them. "Lame."'

The other pictures on the wall were not as large as that one, but they all featured sea creatures. Photos of a pod – I think that's what they call them – of dolphins. A sea horse, an octopus, a photo of Jacques Cousteau.

'She hated *Jaws*,' Walden said. 'Just hated it. That shark, she said, was just being a shark. It was just doing what it naturally does. It wasn't a monster. That's what she said. Made her mad when people said they loved that movie.'

I noticed several unopened envelopes on the desk, some with the Promise Falls municipal logo in the corner.

'What's all this?' I asked, picking them up, leafing through them.

'She still gets mail,' he said. 'Like a credit card statement, or an ad, something like that. Companies that don't know what happened. Beth got so upset when something for Olivia came in the mail, she'd just put it there on her dresser like Olivia was going to come home one day and deal with it. And I haven't got the energy to tell those idiots that it's been three years. What really gets me is that the town doesn't even know.'

I held up one of the envelopes. 'What are these?'

'Warnings about paying a speeding ticket.' His face went red with anger. 'How can one part of the police department be trying to figure out who killed her, and another department is busy nagging her about a ticket?'

I shook my head. 'I'm sorry. It shouldn't happen, but it does.' There were three such envelopes, unopened. 'I'll take these, if you like, and make sure they stop.'

'I'd be grateful,' he said. 'Last time you were here, you sounded like you were going to talk to Victor.'

'I popped by,' I said.

'He's not in a good frame of mind. I think he's taking the anniversary harder than I am.'

I knew that in two days it would be three years since Olivia's murder.

'He's just so angry,' Walden said.

'Of course he is,' I said. 'It's a natural reaction to an act of senseless violence.'

'It's not the killer he's angry with,' Walden Fisher said.

I had a feeling where this was going. 'The others,' I said.

'The ones that heard her screams and couldn't be bothered to do a thing. That's what really eats at Victor. You know all about that.'

'I do.'

'He nearly started a fight with complete strangers

in a bar the other night, accusing them of being cowards.'

'Were they some of the people? Who did nothing?'

'Hell, no. No one even knows who those people were. But the way Victor sees it, the whole town's guilty. If those random citizens of Promise Falls would turn their backs on Olivia, maybe anyone in this town would have. Sometimes I think the anger's just going to consume Victor. He's drinking a lot. I worry about him.'

'You said he drove you home?' I asked.

'That's right. He came by the hospital, to see what was going on. Saw me there. The doctor said if I wanted someone to look at me, maybe I should go to Albany. I figured, I wasn't dead yet, so I might as well come home.'

'Was Victor sick?'

'No,' Walden said. 'He got lucky. He hadn't had any of the water to drink. But he was telling me his landlady died. Spotted her dead in the backyard.'

'That must have been rough.'

Walden nodded. 'Yeah. Like we haven't all been through enough.'

I scanned Olivia's room one more time, getting a small sense of who she was and what she cared about, but I wasn't coming away with anything useful.

We made our way back down the stairs. Walden stepped with me out onto the porch.

'There were twenty-two of them, you know,' Walden said.

'Yes.'

'Those are the ones Victor really blames. Well, those twenty-two and himself. I don't know that there's anyone he blames more than himself, for not showing up on time to meet Olivia.'

I thought about that.

Twenty-two, plus himself.

I could do the math.

CHAPTER 33

O nce he had left the water plant, Randall Finley decided to head back to the park, where his people were still handing out free flats of water from the backs of the Finley Springs trucks. Many of the trucks had already run out and been sent back to the plant for more.

Along the way, he put in a call to David. There might be some more photo opportunities, and he wanted David to be there.

David picked up on the first ring.

'My man,' Finley said. 'I'm going back to the park. Should be there in five. Meet me.'

'I can't,' David said.

'Come on, the good people of Promise Falls are counting on us.'

'I know, it's all about helping the people.'

'Am I hearing a tone?'

'Forget it,' David said. 'I've got something else I have to deal with.'

'What could be more important than helping people get good, clean water?'

'That Sam person you were asking me about before? I'm worried she and her son may be in trouble.'

Finley sighed. 'David, I gotta say, you need to get your head in the game.'

'Excuse me?'

'This town is in the midst of the biggest crisis it's ever seen, and you've got your shorts in a knot because some woman doesn't want to see you anymore?'

'That's not what it's about. It's more serious than that.'

'Is it more serious than people dropping dead all over town?'

'I can't talk about this, Randy.'

'You're not going to make employee of the month this way,' Finley said. His tone darkened. 'Let me ask you something.'

'What?'

'Have you been talking to Duckworth today?'

'Duckworth? Why would you ask that?'

'That's an easy yes-or-no question.'

'Okay, yeah, I was talking to him. I thought he might be able to help me with my situation.'

'Your Sam situation,' Randy said.

'That's right.'

'Is that all you talked about?' When David didn't answer immediately, Finley pressed on. 'Was it?'

'I don't remember. Mostly we talked about Sam.'

'Did my name come up?'

'I think it might have. I called him when he was at the water plant. He said he was going to arrest you or something, for getting in the way.'

'What did you tell him?'

'Tell him about what?'

'About me.'

'Randy, I have to go. I didn't say anything to him about—'

'Did you say something about how I'd increased production at the plant?'

Another pause. 'I think, just kind of in passing,' David confessed.

'Goddamn it, so it *was* you. What the fuck were you thinking, saying something like that?'

'When Duckworth said you were being arrested, I thought it had to do with the water.'

'That I'd somehow poisoned it?'

'I never said that. I never said I thought you'd poisoned the water. He was the one who said you'd been arrested. And then it kind of came together for me, at the time, that if you *had* done it, it made sense that you'd upped production.'

'And that would make sense why?'

'Because then you could be the big hero, coming to the town's rescue with fresh, clean water.'

'Is that what you think?' Finley asked.

'No,' David said. 'I don't . . . I don't think that.'

'You don't sound sure.'

'I'm pretty sure.'

'Fuck!' Finley said. 'Maybe we should put that on a campaign button. "I'm voting Finley because I'm pretty sure he's not a mass murderer."'

'I'd go with a T-shirt,' David said. 'That'd never fit on a button.'

'You think it's funny.'

'I don't think any of this is funny. Look, I've already told you what I think of you. You're a pompous gasbag, but do I think you'd kill hundreds of people just to look good? No. The bar's not set that high with you, Randy, but I think you're above that. If I've offended you, fire me. Or I can quit. I've offered before, and I can offer again.'

Now it was Finley's turn to go quiet. Finally, he said, 'I don't want you to quit. Thing is, as little respect as you have for me, I don't know that I could find anyone with more.' A long sigh. 'I'm not a bad guy, David. I swear.'

David's tone turned more conciliatory. 'There're still weeks to go before the election. I'll have time to do what you need me to do. But you decided to run just when a lot of shit's been going on in my life. That stuff with my cousin Marla, and then—'

'Yeah, yeah, fine, I don't need a recap. Do what you have to do and then check in.'

Finley took the phone from his ear and tucked it away as Promise Falls Park came into view. The convoy of Finley Springs trucks was there, but he wasn't going to be able to get a parking spot near them.

It was like Times Square at rush hour. Word had spread.

Cars jammed the road bordering the park. People were stopping in the middle of the street, running over to the trucks for free flats of water, then scurrying back to their cars with them.

'Son of a bitch,' Finley said to himself, followed by, 'Cheap bastards.'

There was a Promise Falls police car off to the side of the road, lights flashing, a female uniformed officer trying to direct traffic. Letting people grab their water, then making a hole for them to drive away.

Finley pulled his Lincoln half up onto the sidewalk, got out, and started walking toward all the commotion. Was that a TV crew? With a CBS logo on the side of the camera resting on one man's shoulder?

Maybe it didn't matter that David couldn't make it. There was a fucking national network here.

'Hello, hello, hello!' Finley said, reaching the first truck. Trevor Duckworth was handing out cases of water from the back of it as quickly as he could. 'Let me help you out there!' the former mayor said, nudging Trevor out of the way, grabbing a case, and handing it to a young, unshaven man standing there with a girl of about six.

'Here you go, sir!' Finley said, then looked down at the girl and patted her head. 'This your daughter?'

'Yup. Say hi, Martina,' the man said.

'Hi,' said Martina, extending a hand. Finley grinned and shook it.

'That's the man who owns the water company,' the girl's father said.

'Thank you,' the girl said. 'All the regular water is poisoned.'

'I know!' Finley said. 'Awful thing, just awful. Let's hope they get it back to normal real quick.'

'Thank you for all you're doing,' the man said, holding the water with two outstretched arms.

'No problem,' Finley said. 'How about you, ma'am? Can I help you?'

Trevor leapt into the back of the truck and shoved cases toward the door so his boss could grab one after another. A few people took shots with their phones. The CBS crew had figured out what was happening, and was shooting footage.

Finley offered everyone a smile, but not too big a smile. This was, after all, a solemn occasion.

People had died.

The CBS crew had grabbed a few shots but now was moving farther up the line of trucks. Finley got his phone out and said to Trevor, 'David's a bit held up, so I need you to take some video.' He handed the phone over to him. 'You know how to use this?'

'Yeah,' Trevor said.

'Just saw your dad up at the water plant.'

'Oh yeah.'

'Heck of a guy,' Finley said. 'Doin' a bang-up job. He's gonna get to the bottom of what's happened. You can take that to the bank.'

Trevor held the phone up in front of him, Finley filling up the screen. 'Rolling,' he said.

Finley continued to sling cases into the arms of Promise Falls residents. He wasn't registering faces. He figured he could go for a few minutes until he started to feel it in his back.

316

A plump woman with short hair, dressed in jeans and a dark blue athletic shirt that read 'Thackeray,' had come to the front of the line. 'Here ya go,' Finley said, but the woman didn't have her arms out to receive the flat of water bottles, and Finley had to hang on to it.

The woman said, 'You opportunistic bastard.'

Finley's eyes met the woman's. His face broke into a grin and he said, 'Why, Amanda Croydon. I thought you must be dead.'

The mayor of Promise Falls rested her hands on her hips and said, 'I'd gone to Buffalo for the weekend to see my sister. When I heard this morning, I drove straight back.'

'Well,' Finley said, handing the water to the next person in line, 'while you were cruising along the New York Thruway, I was rolling up my sleeves.'

'What the hell is all this?'

Finley glanced Trevor's way, wanting to be sure this was all being recorded.

'This,' Finley said, waving his hand before him, 'is what's called being there for the people.'

Croydon shook her head. 'No, this is called grandstanding. There are emergency systems in place. Thousands of cases of bottled water are on the way from the state as we speak. The governor's declaring a state of emergency.'

'Well, Amanda, as we speak, these people already have water. Sometimes, the private sector does a much better job serving the people than the public, and this turns out to be one of those times. Surely

317

you're not opposed to a private citizen pitching in where he can.'

The mayor's face reddened. She pointed a short, thick finger at Finley.

'It's a cheap stunt, that's what it is. These people are in true crisis and you turn it into a PR opportunity.'

Finley shook his head with disappointment as people began to gather and watch.

'If the good folks of Promise Falls should decide next time around to choose me to represent them in the mayor's office, and I certainly wouldn't presume that they will, but if they do, I can promise them one thing for certain. If and when another tragedy hits this town, I will welcome help from *anyone*, anyone at all, if it means the people in this town will be helped, even if that help ends up exposing my shortcomings on the job. Because these people' – and his voice began to rise – 'these people you see here today, mean more to me than any job or elected position.'

Finley resisted all temptations to look at Trevor and the phone.

'That's what I'm about,' he continued. 'I'm about the people, and I've been doing my best for them since this nightmare began early this morning. Nice of you to finally join us.'

'I'll have you know,' Amanda Croydon said, looking as though she might blow a fuse, 'I've already been up to the hospital and conferred with Chief Finderman and—'

'Oh, you've *conferred*,' Finley said. 'And here I almost accused you of doing nothing.'

'—*and* the governor, and the Atlanta Centers for—'

'And yet,' Finley said, cutting her off, 'you still have time to justify to me everything you've been doing. Listen, I'd love to chat longer, but I have water to distribute.' He grabbed another case, moved past the mayor to hand it to an elderly couple.

'You tell her!' the man said.

Amanda Croydon turned around and walked off into the crowd. Over his shoulder, Finley looked to make sure Trevor was still recording.

He wasn't. He was holding the phone down near his waist, looking at the screen, hitting a button.

'Trevor!' Finley said. 'This is no time to play Scrabble. Wait. Are you tweeting this? You putting it on Facebook?'

'You have a call,' Trevor said. He put the phone to his ear. 'Hello?'

'For God's sake,' Finley said, throwing a case of water back into the truck and extending his hand. He snapped his fingers.

Trevor handed him the phone.

Finley glanced at the screen long enough to see that it was a call from his home. 'Hello?'

'Mr Finley?'

'Yes, Lindsay, it's me.'

'I think there's something wrong with Bipsie.'

'Lindsay, I've kind of got my hands full here. What's wrong with the dog?'

'She's sick. She was throwing up and acting

319

weird and . . . and I think . . . Mr Finley, I think she might be dead.'

Finley kneaded his forehead with the fingers of his free hand. Then it hit him. 'Tell me you didn't let the dog drink out of the toilet.'

'She does that,' Lindsay said. 'She might have.'

'For Christ's sake, why didn't you put the lids down so the dog couldn't get into them? It's not just water coming out of the taps that's poison. It's any water that comes into the house!'

'The water is poison?'

For a second, he stopped breathing. 'Lindsay, what did you say?'

'You say the water is poisoned? How could that happen?'

'Are you saying you don't know?' He started shouting. 'Fucking hell, how could you not know?'

'You didn't say anything when you left.'

'I didn't know then! Haven't you had the radio on? The TV? You didn't hear them blasting warnings through the neighborhood?'

'Please don't yell at me,' Lindsay said. 'I've been reading, and I was in the basement doing laundry.'

'If Bipsie was thirsty, you should have given her some of the bottled! I can't believe this! Jane'll be devastated. Does Jane know?'

There was nothing at the other end of the line. 'Lindsay? Lindsay!'

After several seconds, she said, 'Oh no.'

CHAPTER 34

Cal Weaver had to decide whether to follow Dwayne or the man who'd given Dwayne the cash. He went with the latter. Cal knew who Dwayne was. He needed to find out more about the other guy, because there was obviously something fishy about meeting someone in an alley for a payoff.

The two men talked for about five minutes, some of their exchange appearing heated. At one point, Dwayne angrily jabbed his finger at the man's chest. His friend didn't much care for that, brushing his hand away and pointing in return. But nodding followed; an agreement of some kind seemed to have been reached.

Dwayne shoved the money deep into the front pocket of his jeans.

Dwayne came out onto the sidewalk first and headed back to his pickup truck. The other man held back about ninety seconds, then emerged. He went in the other direction.

Cal sat in the car, watched.

The man crossed the street half a block up and got into an old junker of a Ford Aerostar van. A two-tone, blue and rust. The van pulled out into the street, exhaust belching out the back, at which point Cal checked his mirror and moved into traffic.

He reached over to the glove box, popped it open, and grabbed a notepad. With a pen from his pocket, he scribbled down the license plate number. He still had a friend or two with the police – if not in Promise Falls, then elsewhere – who could run a plate for him.

The man made a stop near the park by the falls. Cal, who'd kept the car radio tuned to the news all day, had heard there was free water being given out there. He wasn't interested in facing the crowds – he'd live on beer and OJ for the next few days if he had to. But his new friend clearly wanted to take advantage of the offer. He left the van running in the middle of the street as he ran over for a case. When he returned to the van, he slid open the side door and tossed the pack of twenty-four bottles of water inside.

Once back behind the wheel, he headed north, then took a turn east that led in the direction of an industrial area, and beyond that, the now-mothballed Five Mountains amusement park.

Cal kept a couple of cars between the van and himself. The Aerostar wasn't taking a circuitous route. If it had been, Cal would have guessed the driver suspected he was being followed.

The van's left turn signal came on, then the brake lights. Cal and two cars ahead of him had to slow to a stop while the driver waited for oncoming traffic to clear. Once it had, he turned into an industrial park. The other cars, and Cal, moved forward. He glanced left as the van drove on between two large warehouse-sized buildings.

Oncoming traffic was thin, so Cal executed a swift U-turn, then sped back to where the van had turned off. He rolled onto the gravel shoulder and came to a stop. The van slipped into a spot between some other cars. The driver got out and went into a business directly in front of where he'd parked.

Cal turned in.

He drove down slowly between the two buildings, slowly enough that he could read the sign in the window of the place the driver had gone into without actually hitting the brakes.

SUPERFAST PRINTING, it said. Orders large and small. Business cards, letterhead, envelopes. Some work, the window sign promised, could be done while one waited.

Was the driver a customer, or an employee?

Cal parked the car and walked back to the storefront, but when he tried the door, it was locked.

He made a visor of his hand and peered through the glass door. A counter separated the waiting area from where the work was done. Cal could see several high-end, oversized copying machines, several desks with computers, and stacks of packages wrapped in plain brown paper. The place went back a long way, maybe sixty feet, and there was what looked like a garage door on the back wall.

Near that door, the man Cal had seen give money to Dwayne was moving some packages. He looked up, saw Cal, and waved him away. Shouted something that sounded like 'Closed!'

So Cal knocked.

The man shook his head, stopped what he was doing, and walked all the way to the front. He unlocked the door and opened it a foot.

'We're closed,' he said. He was wearing a small name tag that read HARRY.

'Sorry,' Cal said. 'I just saw you go in, so I thought you were open.'

'It's Saturday of a holiday weekend,' Harry said. 'So we're closed.'

'But you're working,' Cal said amiably. 'Listen, have you got, like, ten seconds to help me out? My company's moving to a new location soon, so we're going to need all new cards, letterhead, invoices, the whole nine yards. I was wondering what something like that would run me.'

Harry seemed to be weighing whether it would be easier to just help Cal out or close the door in his face.

'Fine,' he said, opening the door wider. 'Ten seconds.'

Harry took a position behind the chest-high counter as Cal approached and rested his elbows on it.

'Did you get your earlier stationery with us?'

Harry asked. 'If so, it should all be in the computer. We just change the address and print it all out. It saves you a little, because we don't have to do any designing for you, but most of the cost is in the actual printing.'

'No, it wasn't done here.'

'Well, like I said, it doesn't make that much difference anyway,' Harry told him. 'How much you need? Five hundred of everything? A thousand? Two thousand? Gets a bit cheaper as the numbers go up. And then, maybe you need more invoices than business cards, or letterhead. We can accommodate what you need.'

'Five hundred of everything would be what? Invoices, letterhead, envelopes, business cards.'

Harry did some scribbling on a notepad. 'You're looking at around four fifty.'

'How long's it take? I could wait for it.'

Harry shook his head. 'Not for an order like that. You're looking at about a week or—'

Two loud metallic bangs echoed out from the back. Someone had pounded on the metal garage door.

'What's that?' Cal asked. 'Just about gave me a heart attack.'

'Delivery,' he said.

'Everybody's working on Saturday,' Cal remarked.

'Why don't you come back on Tuesday? We open at nine.'

Another bang on the door, louder this time.

'Hang on,' Harry said, and bolted for the back

of the shop. He punched a big red button on the wall and the garage door began to rise.

There was a pickup truck backed up to the door. Cal recognized it immediately as his brother-in-law's.

As Cal turned to look out the front window, he heard the truck pull in, the garage door slide back down. Then hurried footsteps as Harry returned to the counter.

'Sorry, mister, but you really need to come back on—'

'That's fine, no problem. I'll do that,' Cal said, turning long enough to offer up a smile of thanks. He headed for the door.

Cal made the decision not to follow Dwayne at this point. From the industrial park he went back to his hotel, packed up his things, and checked out. By the time he got back to Dwayne and Celeste's house, Dwayne's pickup was there, backed up tight to the garage. Crystal was at the living room window, looking out.

Cal parked on the street and as he went around to the trunk to grab his bag, Crystal came out the front door with a slice of pizza in her hand.

'You're missing dinner,' she said.

Cal glanced at his watch. It was a few minutes past five.

'Looks good,' he said. 'What kind is that?'

'Hawaiian,' she said. 'With pineapple on it. But there're other kinds, too.'

'Really?'

'There's a pepperoni one. And a veggie one. And wings. He brought home lots of stuff,' Crystal said.

'You mean Dwayne?'

The girl nodded. 'I forgot his name.'

'That's okay. How are you doing?'

'I want my dad to come.'

'I know,' Cal said.

'Dwayne didn't want to watch the Weather Channel.'

'Not everyone finds it as interesting as you do,' he said. 'And it is Dwayne and Celeste's TV.'

She moved in close enough that her shoulder was touching the side of his waist, but she was looking down and beyond him.

'What happened to my mother?' she asked.

'The police came. They'll take your mom out. They'll look after things.'

'Was she still dead?'

'Yes.'

'I knew that. It was a stupid question.'

'No, it wasn't,' Cal said.

'I want to know what happens next,' she said.

'I don't know, exactly. That'll be up to your dad, mostly.'

'I mean, like right away,' Crystal said. 'Do they cut my mom open and stuff like on TV?'

Cal rested a hand tentatively on her shoulder. When she didn't flinch, he held it there more firmly.

'I'm not sure,' he said. 'There'll be an autopsy to be sure of the cause of death. You know what that is?'

'Yes.'

'So, yes, they might have to do some of that.'

Her shoulder pressed into him a little harder. 'You don't talk to me like I'm a little kid.'

'You deserve the truth,' Cal said. 'I don't know any way to get through this without being honest with you.' He patted her. 'Believe me, if I could find a way, I'd try.'

'My mom said your wife died. And that you had a son and he died, too.'

'That's right.' He paused. 'It was a few years ago. Before I moved back here.'

'Are you sad anymore?'

Cal tightened his grip on the girl's shoulder. 'Every minute of every day,' he said.

Crystal thought about that for a few seconds, saying nothing. Then, abruptly, she moved away from him and walked back into the house.

Cal followed. Dinner was being presented in the living room, in front of the television. There were three open pizza boxes and a container of chicken wings with hot sauce crowding the coffee table. The TV was tuned to baseball. Dwayne was on the couch, holding a gnawed wing between thumb and forefinger. When he saw Cal, he said, 'Just missed the end of a Toronto-Seattle game.'

'Don't watch much baseball,' he said.

'Hey, grab a beer and have some pizza!' Dwayne said amiably. 'We got veggie, which I got for Celeste, and Hawaiian and another one here with sausage and shit on it. Didn't know what the kid liked, but she seems to like the one with the pine-apple. And there're wings, too, but they're kinda messy.'

'Looks great,' Cal said. 'Where's Celeste?'

'In the kitchen,' he said, and went back to watching the television.

Crystal was eating her pizza at the kitchen table with a can of ginger ale. Celeste was at the fridge, taking out a beer for herself. She cracked the top, took a swig.

'Oh, hey,' she said, a smile on her face. 'Did you get some pizza?'

'Just about to.'

'Beer?'

'Why would I say no to that?'

She handed him one, then brought down a plate from the cupboard. 'Get some pizza. But the veggie is mine.' She gave him a look of mock fury.

'Like I'm gonna steal your veggie,' he said. 'Dwayne seems pretty upbeat.'

'I know,' she said, whispering. 'I'm trying not to make a big deal about it. It's just nice to see him happy for once.'

'Sure. He brought home a feast.'

Keeping her voice low, Celeste said, 'He got a deposit on a job. Or a retainer, or something. I think he said Walmart. They pay him a certain amount a month, and if they have any paving needs in their lot, they call him and he fixes it. So, some months he might do no work for them, but he still gets paid, and other months he might have a lot of potholes to fill or whatever, but it all balances out.'

'Sounds like a good deal,' Cal said. 'I'm gonna get something to eat.'

'Remember, hands off the veggie.'

'You couldn't pay me to eat that,' he said. He took his plate and his beer and went into the living room. He grabbed a slice of Hawaiian and a slice of pepperoni, plus half a dozen wings, and sat down on a La-Z-Boy chair.

'Don't get too comfy there,' Dwayne said, grinning. 'Soon as I'm done here, I'm dropping into that chair and not moving till bedtime.'

'I'll consider myself warned,' Cal said. 'Listen, this is a lot of food. Let me pay you back for this.'

'Don't worry about it.'

'At least let me contribute.'

A firm shake of the head. 'No fucking way.' He glanced around suddenly. 'Where's the kid? Celeste already told me not to swear in front of the kid.'

'She's in the kitchen.'

'Good.'

'Celeste told me about your good news. About the Walmart retainer.'

Dwayne fixed his eyes on the TV. 'Yeah, well, it's a good thing, no doubt about that.'

'Nice to have something to celebrate on a day like this,' Cal said.

Dwayne glanced his way, puzzled, as though he'd forgotten about all the people who had died in Promise Falls that day. 'Oh, right, for sure. You

330

know, they were handing out free water by the park today, but hey' – he raised his beer – 'who needs that stuff?'

Cal returned the salute with his own bottle.

'Remember what W. C. Fields said about water?' Cal asked.

'W. C. who?'

'Fields. A comic from years ago. Anyway, he said he didn't drink water because' – Cal lowered his voice – 'fish fuck in it.'

Dwayne laughed, slapped a palm on one knee. 'That's a good one.'

Cal set his plate and beer on a small table next to his chair, dabbed his mouth with a napkin, and said, 'Think I'll hit the can before I have anything else.'

'There's a plan,' Dwayne said.

Cal slipped out of the living room, but instead of heading upstairs, he quietly went out the back door, down the steps, and meandered in the direction of Dwayne's pickup. He'd backed it to within a foot of the garage door.

The pickup had what was called a tonneau cover over the bed, made of black vinyl. It kept items in the truck from falling out, and could be locked to foil would-be thieves. It could be tipped up at the back to allow an item to be dropped in, without opening the tailgate.

Cal went around to the far side of the truck and attempted to lift the cover an inch, testing to see whether it was locked. It was not.

He got out his phone, opened the flashlight app. There was still plenty of sunlight, but he wasn't planning to open the cover that far. He raised it about a foot, which cast light near the tailgate. Cal stuck the flashlight in, and there was just enough light to see that not only was there nothing near the end of the bed, but nothing was in there at all.

He dropped the cover back into place and put away his phone.

There was a regular door on the property line side of the garage, which, Cal was pleased to note, was out of sight from the house. He tried the door.

Locked.

Shit.

He wanted to know what it was Dwayne might have been picking up at the back end of that printing shop. He was willing to bet it was not several thousand invoices for his paving company.

There was a small window, divided into four smaller panes, in the side door. At first Cal thought the glass was simply too dirty to see through, then realized that something had been taped over it. A piece of black paper, or a garbage bag.

He had a set of picks hidden under the spare tire in his trunk. The state of New York frowned on the possession of burglar's tools, but sometimes they came in handy in his line of work. So he kept them out of sight.

He tucked the small satchel into his pocket and trotted back up the driveway. As he went past the house, he glanced at it to make sure Dwayne didn't happen to be looking out the back window.

Once he was hidden beyond the corner of the garage, he went down on one knee so he could be at eye level with the lock. He set the satchel on the ground and drew out two picks. The lock didn't look very challenging, and he thought he could defeat it in two to three minutes.

After three minutes, he concluded it wasn't going to be as easy as he'd first thought. But some locks were like that. Maybe this one would take him six.

Cal was so focused on what he was doing, and so confident he was out of sight, that he had failed to notice Dwayne standing down by the front end of his pickup truck.

'I thought you were going for a crap,' Dwayne said.

Cal's head turned abruptly.

'But then I happened to look out the living room window and saw you going to your car, and I wondered what the hell you were doing.'

Cal withdrew the picks, put them back in the satchel, and stood. He offered no apology as he looked his brother-in-law in the eye.

'What's in the garage, Dwayne?' he asked.

Dwayne walked slowly up the side of the truck, past the corner of the garage, and stopped when he was no more than a foot away.

'What's it to you?' Dwayne asked.

'I know where you got the pizza money, and it wasn't from Walmart.'

'What?'

'The guy at the printing shop. You met him earlier, got paid, and then made a pickup at the shop.'

The muscles in Dwayne's neck tightened. 'You've been following me?'

'I saw you in the alley, taking the money,' he said. 'Then I followed the other guy.'

'You fucking son of a bitch. Who are you working for? Or did Celeste put you up to this?'

Cal shook his head, ignored the questions. 'Just open the garage.'

'It was Celeste, wasn't it?'

'No. But she is worried about you. She says you've been gone a lot. Sometimes at odd hours. She senses something's going on, but she doesn't know what.'

'Whatever's going on is between her and me.'

'No,' Cal said. 'She's my sister. If you're into something bad, Dwayne, it could blow back on her. Open the garage.'

'I'm not opening the garage. You need to get in your car and get the fuck out of here and take that freaky little kid with you.'

'Does Celeste know what's in here?'

'You're not hearing me, Cal. Get off my property.'

'I suppose you could call the cops and have me arrested for trespassing.' Cal reached into his pocket for his phone. 'You want to make the call or you want me to do it?'

Dwayne's eyes blinked. 'You're sticking your

nose in where it don't belong,' Dwayne warned. 'Something bad could happen to you.'

Cal smiled and closed the gap between them by a few inches. 'You seem to be under the impression that I give a fuck. Everything bad that can happen to me has already happened. Open the garage.'

Dwayne slowly shook his head, dropped his chin down to his chest in defeat. He dug into his pockets and withdrew a set of keys. In addition to the big remote for the truck, there were half a dozen others.

'Just gotta find the right one here,' he mumbled, moving in front of the door. He'd settled on a key, had it ready to slide into the lock.

Cal saw it coming, but he was too late to stop it.

Dwayne turned abruptly, ran a fist straight into his gut. Cal doubled over and collapsed into the weeds and grass surrounding the garage foundation.

'Really sorry about this, man,' Dwayne said, making another fist and driving it straight into Cal's head.

This time, Cal went down all the way. Didn't even feel the sharp edges of gravel jabbing into his cheek.

Now Dwayne unlocked the garage door, and dragged Cal inside.

CHAPTER 35

Brandon Worthington had definitely heard what his ex-wife's stupid old neighbor was hoping he hadn't heard. When he'd said he thought Sam and Carl 'might have gone camp—'

Well, it didn't take Stephen Hawking to figure out what he was about to say was 'camping.' And the more Brandon thought about it, the more sense it made.

Back when they were first going out, and even after they'd been married awhile, they'd gone camping. They even did it a few times after they had Carl. Camping was about as cheap a vacation as you could take. No airline tickets, no expensive hotels. You just found a patch of land and pitched your tent.

Not that there weren't some costs. He and Sam didn't usually strike off into the middle of some woods somewhere. Fuck that. They tried that once, and it was no fun, unless your idea of a good time is hanging your bare ass over a log when you've got to do your business.

So after that experience, when they wanted to

go away for the weekend with the tent, they'd find a licensed campground. KOA or something like that. At least then you had some facilities. A big restroom with toilets and sinks and even showers. Brandon didn't mind cooking and sleeping under the stars, but when he had to deal with his morning constitutional, he wanted an honest-to-God toilet, thank you very much. He hadn't exactly grown up roughing it. His father, Garnet, had worked in the financial industry his whole career, and his mother, Yolanda, had inherited money – a pretty good chunk of it, too – when her parents died.

Which made it all the weirder when he decided to rob banks. Although, the way he looked at it, it wasn't all *that* weird. Once he and Sam were married, and living on their own, Brandon had just assumed his parents would buy them a house – and not some shitty starter home, either – and a decent car, maybe even a place on the Cape they could drive to on weekends in the summer.

Who knew his father was going to cut him off, insist Brandon make it on his own?

'You gotta have that fire in your belly,' his dad liked to tell him. 'You'll never get anywhere in life if I just hand everything to you.'

Not that Yolanda didn't try to do an end run around her husband. Whenever she could, she'd slip her son a hundred dollars, sometimes two hundred, sometimes even more. Always cash. She knew her husband reviewed all the checks she wrote, but she skimmed where she could.

But it wasn't enough. Not enough to live the way he expected to live.

Sam, however, wasn't troubled by living in a small apartment. She hadn't come from money, and she hadn't been left much after her parents died. Her father had been a midlevel manager at a big-box hardware store, and her mother had worked in a high school cafeteria.

'We're good. We're okay,' she so often told him. 'We've got each other. You've got a good job.'

Seriously? Working for the post office?

His perpetual anger and resentment poisoned the marriage. Brandon became abusive. He never actually beat her, but there was the time he shoved her a little too hard and she crashed into their piddly entertainment unit, knocking one of the small speakers off the shelf.

Landed right on her fucking toe.

If she hadn't walked around the place barefoot, she'd have been fine.

So now and then, Sam would move out for a few days at a time, taking young Carl with her, bunking in with a girlfriend. Brandon would apologize and swear it would never happen again and talk Sam into returning. He became convinced that if he had enough money, he could buy them a better life.

He figured there was a way to solve his financial problems and stick it to his father at the same time.

So he went into a sister branch to the one his

dad managed, and stuck the place up. Had the gun, the ski mask, the whole thing.

Just might have worked, too, if a cop wanting to exchange the fifties the ATM had given him for smaller bills hadn't wandered in at that very moment.

Sometimes you couldn't get a break.

Sam filed for divorce. Brandon went to jail.

Ed Noble, who of all of Brandon's friends was the one with the most screws that needed tightening, came under Yolanda's influence, started doing her bidding. Yolanda wanted Carl to herself. She'd lost her son to prison, but she was not going to lose her grandson, and she'd figured that with the right amount of intimidation, Samantha would give him up. She got Ed to do her dirty work.

It hadn't exactly worked out.

It wasn't just Brandon in jail now. Ed was there, too, awaiting trial. Garnet and Yolanda were facing multiple charges, and out on bail.

Then Yolanda went and had a heart attack.

At first, Brandon wondered whether she'd faked it, hoping to get some sympathy from the prosecuting attorney's office. But it was pretty hard to fake an EKG. She ended up in intensive care, and for a while there it was looking touch and go.

Yolanda asked to see her son.

'Bring me my boy,' she whispered to the doctor from her ICU bed. 'Don't let me die without seeing him.'

Arrangements were made.

Brandon stood at Yolanda's bedside, held her hand, looked sadly into her eyes. Yolanda whispered something he could not hear.

'I'm sorry. What was that?' he said.

She said it again, but he still could not make it out. So he leaned down, put his ear so close to her mouth that she could have kissed it.

Yolanda whispered, 'Find the bitch, get your son.'

And then that orderly came in. A guy about Brandon's height and build, maybe a little bigger. Brandon had spent a lot of time working out in prison, learned a thing or two.

He didn't even have to think. He just acted. Looped his arm around the orderly's neck and squeezed. The dumb bastard struggled, but Brandon just squeezed harder. Within seconds, the guy had passed out. Brandon stripped off his pants and shirt, pulled them on over his own clothes.

His mother smiled the whole time.

Brandon pushed the orderly under the bed, gave his mom a kiss good-bye, and walked right out of that ICU like he owned the place. Dumbass cop posted at the door was playing Angry Birds on his phone. Probably caught a glimpse of legs in pale green pants striding past him, never looked up.

Brandon flew down the stairs, came out into the hospital parking lot. He needed to find a car, but searching for one with the keys left in it would be a waste of time. No one did that anymore. He needed a car that was already running.

So he kept hoofing it until he got to a plaza where there was a 7-Eleven. Sooner or later, some idiot would leave a car running while he ran in for a pack of cigarettes. While he waited, he stripped off the scrubs and stuffed them in a garbage can. Half an hour later, a woman pulled into the lot in a little shitbox Kia. He wasn't going to be choosy. She parked right close to the door and got out, and as soon as Brandon noticed exhaust still coming out of the tailpipe, he made his move.

He stayed off the Mass Pike and the New York Thruway. So it took a lot longer to get to Promise Falls than he'd hoped. He was worried Samantha would hear that he was out before he got there.

Which was exactly how it had turned out.

But now he had an idea where she might have gone. A camping trip made sense. Once she'd learned he'd escaped custody, she'd have been looking for a place to go. But a hotel – even a motel – was going to be a strain on Samantha's budget, especially when she didn't know how long she was going to have to stay there. She didn't exactly get paid a hundred grand a year to look after a Laundromat. But finding a space to put up a tent in a nearby campground wouldn't cost her all that much.

And Brandon was pretty sure she still had the tent. One time, about a year back, when Carl's mother had allowed him to visit his father in prison, the boy had mentioned how much fun he and his mother had had on a recent camping trip.

So there you go.

All Brandon had to do now was a bit of research. See how many campgrounds there were within a short drive of Promise Falls. Odds were Sam had checked in at one of them, although there was the distinct possibility she wouldn't have done so under her real name.

He decided to check around the Lake Luzerne area first. It wasn't that far a drive, and there were a bunch of campgrounds up that way. Those places were usually gated, so he wouldn't be able to just drive in without registering. But he figured if he parked down the road, he'd be able to walk in. If anyone stopped him, he'd say he was already a guest, heading back to his campsite.

It worked like a charm at the first place, which was called Sleepy Pines. He strolled the entire campground, but never spotted the blue-and-yellow tent he and Sam and Carl had shared many nights years ago.

So he scratched Sleepy Pines off the list.

No luck at Canoe Park, either. But there were still plenty of places to go. Like Camp Sunrise, and Call of the Loon Acres.

All he wanted to do now was find Sam. Find her and Carl.

Have a little word with them.

A nice chat.

CHAPTER 36

Duckworth

I was on my way to Victor Rooney's place when Wanda Therrieult phoned.

'You saw what I saw,' she said.

'You tell me what you saw.'

'Well, I have to do a full autopsy, but I'd say this Thackeray student, this Lorraine Plummer, is the latest.'

'After Olivia Fisher and Rosemary Gaynor,' I said.

'Yeah.'

'That was my thinking, too,' I said. 'When will you get to the autopsy?'

'The body's being taken to the morgue now, but honestly, Barry, I don't know when I'll get to her. All those other bodies, we may think we know what happened to them, that they were poisoned by the water, but I have to do the due diligence. Every one of them has to be autopsied.'

'You're getting out-of-town help,' I said.

'Sure, but you're going to have to wait. And if I don't lie down soon, in a proper bed, I'm going to collapse wherever I'm standing.'

I knew how she was feeling. I'd been running on empty for several hours now. I wanted to go home, have something to eat – even a salad – then crawl into bed with Maureen and sleep till Christmas. Maybe, after I'd had a chance to talk to Rooney, I could do that. Even just a few hours of sleep would do me. I could be back at this by six in the morning, if not earlier.

'I hear ya, Wanda,' I said.

'Barry,' she said, 'you know me.'

'I do.'

'I'm a woman of science. I *believe* in science. My life is all about science. It's about facts and evidence and data. You know what I mean?'

'Yup.'

'There's nothing mystical about it. But these last few days, I can't help but wonder, are we being punished for something? Did we do something bad, and God's taking it out on us?'

'Maybe not God,' I said. 'But I get what you're saying.'

'I'll talk to you later,' she said.

I dropped the phone onto the seat next to me, and it hadn't been out of my hand for ten seconds before it rang again. I glanced at the screen, saw the name FINLEY come up.

'Fuck off,' I said out loud.

It rang ten times before he gave up. But a few seconds later, it started ringing again.

FINLEY.

Was he going to keep doing this until I answered? I reached for the phone and put it to my ear.

'What is it, Randy?' I said.

His voice was more subdued than I expected it to be. Shaky, too. 'Barry, can you come by my house?'

'What's this about?'

'I think . . . I think there's been a murder.'

'What? Randy, what's going on? Who's been murdered?'

'Jane,' he said. 'Jane's dead.'

'Randy, what happened to her?'

'She's dead. Lindsay killed her.'

'Lindsay?'

'She works for us. Looks after Jane, takes care of the house. She did it. She killed Jane. She killed our dog, too. Bipsie. Bipsie's dead. Lindsay killed both of them. I need you to come over. Barry, would you come over? Please, come over. She's still here. Lindsay's here. I told her she couldn't go home yet.'

'I'm on my way,' I said.

Finley was waiting for me out front. He walked up to my car, spoke to me through the open window before I even had my seat belt off.

'I want her charged,' he said. 'You need to charge her with murder.'

'Okay, Randy,' I said, getting out. 'Let me get up to speed.'

'I was handing out water. Lindsay called me to say that Bipsie was sick. She'd been drinking out of the toilet.'

'Okay,' I said.

'That's the same water that comes out of the tap,' he pointed out to me.

'I know.'

'So the dog started throwing up and died. And she called to tell me. And I said, "How could you let the dog drink out of the toilet when the water's poisoned?" and she says, "What are you talking about?" Can you believe that? She didn't know? How could she not know?'

'Tell me about Jane,' I said as we walked to the house.

'Lindsay poisoned her,' Finley said. He was moving slowly, as though he were pulling a concrete block with each leg.

'How did she do that?'

'Lemonade. She gave her lemonade. There're a hundred bottles of fresh springwater in the fridge, plus a watercooler. But that stupid bitch thought it was too much trouble to crack open a few bottles. I've told her a hundred times, use the bottled stuff for everything. Drinking, cooking. But she made the lemonade—'

'You talking about the frozen stuff? You add four cans of water?'

'That's right. I *always* told her, use the bottles. Because my water is *better*. Even before what happened today, my water is cleaner and better.

346

But she thought it was easier to make it with water from the tap.'

'She didn't know,' I said.

'That doesn't matter,' Finley said. 'It was murder.'

'Where is she?'

'She's in the kitchen, crying her eyes out,' Finley said.

'I meant Jane.'

'Oh.' He swallowed hard. 'She's upstairs, in her room. Since she got sick – not today, but in the last year – I've been sleeping in the guest room so I wouldn't disturb her with my snoring and turning over and all.'

'Sure,' I said. We were at the front door. 'Why don't you wait out here?'

'If Lindsay tries to leave, I'll stop her.'

'Okay.'

I went into the house. The stairs to the second floor were right there in the foyer, but I went into the kitchen first. Just as Finley had said, Lindsay was sitting, and crying, at the kitchen table, a box of tissues in front of her, a mound of used tissues surrounding it. She looked at me when I came in, her eyes bloodshot.

'Lindsay?' I said. She nodded. I told her who I was and showed her my ID. 'What's your last name?'

'Brookins,' she said, dabbing her eyes.

'I'm going upstairs, and then I'm coming back, and we can talk.'

'I didn't murder her,' she said. 'What he says, that's not true. I didn't know.'

Something dark and furry in the corner of the room caught my eye.

'The dog,' I said.

'Bipsie,' she said. 'I didn't know. I really didn't know.'

I nodded. 'I'll be back.'

I went up the stairs and found Jane's room without help. All I had to do was follow my nose. The woman was sprawled diagonally across the bed, facedown, her legs up by the pillow. The bedspread was awash in vomit. It looked as though maybe she'd been in the process of trying to crawl out of the bed before she succumbed.

On the bedside table, a tall, narrow glass with half an inch of pink lemonade in the bottom.

I made my way back down to the kitchen. Lindsay's version of events was not much different from Randy's.

She had taken Mrs Finley her lemonade around ten in the morning. Jane had said she was tired and probably going to go back to sleep. Lindsay returned to the kitchen to tidy up and start lunch preparations, then went to the basement to do laundry. It must have been around then, she said, when the fire trucks with their loudspeakers went through the neighborhood. She had heard some indistinct noises outside, but didn't pay any attention to them.

It wasn't her habit to listen to the radio or turn on the TV through the day. During her downtime, she read. She showed me a dog-eared, used copy of a John Grisham novel. I looked inside the front cover, where it had been stamped 'Naman's Used Books.'

'I was about to go upstairs and check on Mrs Finley,' she said, 'when Bipsie started to act weird.'

The dog was throwing up. She cleaned up after her once; then the dog was sick again. As Lindsay was wiping up after her a second time, the dog keeled over.

'I didn't know what to do, so I called Mr Finley to tell him. He said the water was poisoned. And then I thought, oh no.'

I nodded understandingly. 'Okay,' I said.

'He says I murdered her. I didn't murder her. It was an accident. I swear it was an accident. It's just, he is always telling me to use his water, and sometimes I do and sometimes I don't, because one time, his water had some brown flecks or something in it. A bad batch, he said. But ever since then, I don't use it all the time. When I make Mrs Finley lemonade, I just use the tap, but I didn't tell Mr Finley. If he knew the water was poisoned, he should have told me before he went out.'

It wasn't in my nature to come to Randy's defense, but I said, 'He probably didn't know then. And once he did, he probably didn't think he needed to call home. Because of what he was always telling you.'

She had both hands up to her mouth. 'Oh God, I *did* kill her. I did. But I didn't mean it.'

I went back outside, found Randy standing under a tree.

Weeping.

I came up on him from behind and placed a hand on his shoulder. 'I'm sorry, Randy.'

He had one hand on the tree trunk, supporting himself. He struggled to regain his composure, then said, 'You saw her?'

'Jane? Yes.'

'She looks so . . . she'd be so humiliated.'

'She'll be taken care of.'

'You talked to Lindsay?'

'I did.'

'What did she tell you?'

'It's an accident, Randy. She didn't know. It's not murder.'

Finley turned, put his forearm on the tree, and rested his head on it. 'I know.' He started twice to say something, then stopped. The third time, he managed. 'It's my fault. Soon as I knew what was happening, I should have called. I just thought – no, I just *didn't* think. I was so consumed with . . . with taking full advantage of what was going on. That was all I could see.'

I said nothing.

'It was a tragedy, I knew that. It's not like I didn't care. I *did* care. But I saw an opportunity, and I took it.' He turned his face around enough to see me. 'That's what I do.'

'I know. It's in your DNA.'

'I got so focused on that, I never thought about

. . . and the thing is, she's the whole reason I've been doing it.'

I took a step toward him. 'What do you mean?'

A self-effacing smile came over his face. 'You know what an asshole I am, right, Barry?'

Who was it who said 'never bullshit a bullshitter'?

'Sure.'

'I was trying to show I wasn't. Maybe not to you. I could never convince you. But after all the dumbass things I've done over the years, especially that stuff with the hooker a few years ago, I wanted to prove to Jane there was more to me than that. I was going to be mayor again, I told her. I was going to do some good. Some real good. I even had an idea to get some jobs here. I was working a deal with Frank Mancini. You know Frank?'

'I'm aware of him.'

'I mean, yeah, there was something in it for me, too, but he's going to build this plant on the site of the drive-in. Jobs. Maybe not as many as that private jail that was going to move in here at one point, but some. I wanted to get this town back on its feet. I wanted to show Jane. I wanted her to be proud of me again. I wanted to pay her back for all the shame I brought down on her.'

I nodded.

'You believe any of this?' he asked me.

'I don't know,' I said honestly. 'Maybe.'

He stopped using the tree to support himself and looked me in the eye. 'You think I did it.

That I somehow did this thing to the water, so I could rush in and be the white knight.'

'Maybe,' I said again.

'If I was going to kill hundreds of people to save my political career, you don't think I would have made sure my wife wasn't one of the casualties?'

I searched those eyes. I didn't know the answer to that question. It was possible he was telling me the truth.

It was also possible Jane was already deathly ill, her days numbered, and in Finley's mind, letting her go a little early was justifiable to advance his political objectives.

But for the love of God, he was only running for mayor of Promise Falls. This wasn't the goddamn presidency. How could someone want something that insignificant that badly?

On top of that, Jane's death really did come down to Lindsay going against her employer's wishes, and not being aware of what was happening in the town.

No, Randall Finley did not intend for his wife to die.

I held out a hand. He looked down at it, puzzled, then slowly took it in his and gripped it.

'I believe you,' I said.

CHAPTER 37

Joyce Pilgrim started with a call to the woman in charge of summer athletics. Thackeray ran a number of programs from May through September. They were open to any students taking courses during that period, as well as people from beyond Thackeray. In addition, Thackeray rented out its various fields to local baseball and soccer clubs through the summer.

The summer athletics director was Hilda Brownlee, and Joyce tracked her down at home.

'I'm looking for a jogger,' she said.

'A jogger?' said Hilda.

'Someone who likes to take a run around the campus late at night. I wondered if you have any students training for any track or long-distance running events.'

'I can't think of anyone off the top of my head,' she said. 'Can I get back to you?'

In the meantime, Joyce had compiled a list of all the young people who were living in Thackeray residences over the summer. There were seventy-three of them. She went through the list, name by name. Fifty-eight of the residents were female, fifteen male.

She made a list of the fifteen men.

Then Joyce went through the Thackeray student database and found the e-mail addresses for all of them, and prepared to send out a group message.

She had written something about trying to find the person who was running through the campus on the night of May 20 and into the morning of May 21. But before she hit the send button, she thought for a moment. Up to now, her suspicions were focused on the man in the car that had edged into the frame of the closed-circuit television footage. And she wanted to find the jogger who might have gotten a better look at that car, and the driver.

But what if, Joyce wondered, the jogger had killed Lorraine Plummer? What if the man in the car had nothing to do with it? She could hardly expect a possible suspect to write back and say: 'Yeah, that was me! I was running around at that time and have no alibi!'

Maybe an e-mail wasn't such a good idea.

So, name by name, she began researching the fifteen students. She started with Facebook, but she found only a couple of them there. It was Joyce's experience that while it was young people who'd turned Facebook into a social media phenomenon, now that all their parents and grand-parents were on it, posting pictures of their cats and grandkids and dim-witted sayings like 'Click

Like If You Love Your Niece,' it was no longer the place to be.

Joyce did broader Google searches on them all.

She didn't turn up much of interest on any of them, at least nothing that mentioned whether they were track stars or marathon runners. And the thing was, just because a guy went for a jog at midnight did not mean he was competing for the Olympics. He might just be out for exercise.

Joyce was at home, having a late dinner with her husband, when Hilda called her back.

'I don't have anything for you,' she said. 'I mean, I don't have anyone who's specifically in a track program who's attending Thackeray. I'd say eighty percent of the kids enrolled in summer stuff are from the town, anyway.'

Joyce decided she had to come at this from a different direction.

'I'm going back out,' she told her husband late that evening.

'Are you kidding me?'

She had told him about finding Lorraine Plummer, of course, but had decided not to dwell on it. She did not want to be the wife who came home and went to pieces about what had happened at work, even if discovering a murder was not the sort of thing that happened to most people encountered on the job.

'Do you want to talk about it?' her husband kept asking.

'No,' she said. 'I do not want to talk about it.'

What she found, oddly enough, was that she wanted to be at the college, not at home. When Clive Duncomb had been her boss, she hated every second she was there – the guy was such a sexist asshole – but now that she was in charge, she felt a new commitment. A responsibility.

Thackeray was – she almost felt embarrassed to say this to herself because it bordered on corny – her *beat*. She knew she wasn't a cop. Far from it. But she was in charge of security, and the death of Lorraine Plummer meant Thackeray wasn't *secure*.

She wanted to do something about that.

Joyce was certainly not going to try to track down a killer. If she found out anything, she would pass it along to the Promise Falls police. That Duckworth guy. But given what the town had been through today, she knew the Plummer murder wasn't going to get the attention it normally would.

At least the coroner finally showed up. Wanda Something. After she'd finished her examination of the body, she had a pretty grim look on her face. At first, Joyce figured in that line of work, everything you had to do put you in a foul mood. But Joyce could tell this was different. And when Wanda got on the phone to tell someone about what she'd found, Joyce listened in, and picked up a vibe that whoever had killed Lorraine, this was not his first outing.

Jesus.

Once the sun had set, Joyce indicated she was

heading back out to the campus. Her husband said he would come with her.

'No way,' Joyce said. 'Unless you'd like me to come to work with you on Tuesday morning. Hold your hand while you plaster and drywall.'

Soon after, Joyce Pilgrim was sitting in her car, parked on the street in the exact same place where that vehicle had been parked during the period Duckworth believed Lorraine had been murdered. She was, admittedly, early. If – and there were several ifs – this particular person did his run at the same time every night, she had several hours to wait. This was, of course, *if* he ran every night. And *if* he took the same route.

And, *if* all those *ifs* aligned, he'd be useful to Joyce only *if* he remembered seeing that car that night. Even then, he'd be useful only *if* he was good at telling one car from another.

Still, it was all she had at the moment.

Thackeray was a quiet place this time of year. The occasional student walked past. Once in a while, a car drove by.

Joyce was thinking she should have brought along some coffee, but that would mean, at some point, having to run to the nearest available bathroom. Just like when you're waiting for the cable guy to show up, the two minutes you leave the house to mail a letter, that's when he rings the bell.

At least she had music.

She had no way to run her iPhone through her

old clunker's stereo system, but she did have CDs. She opened up her folder of discs, found her favorite, and slipped it into the slot in the dash.

Stevie Wonder, *Songs in the Key of Life*.

Joyce loved Stevie. No other artist – not since the dawn of time – even came close.

She tapped her fingers on the steering wheel, bounced her shoe off the side of the transmission hump. She played the entire disc, popped it out, replaced it with *Original Musiquarium*, which was made up of hits from 1972 to 1980.

Joyce was halfway through *Journey Through the Secret Life of Plants* when she saw him.

It was nearly ten, and he was running toward her on the other side of the street. Not flat out. A steady jog, pacing himself. As he got closer, Joyce sized him up. Late twenties, early thirties. Too old to be a student, she thought, and a little on the young side to be a professor, although she had to admit there were a few on campus who'd never seen a first-run episode of *Star Trek: The Next Generation*.

She couldn't be certain this was the same guy she'd seen in the video, but it was certainly possible. He had the earbuds trailing down to a music player clipped to the band of his running shorts.

Joyce killed the music and got out of her car. She stood in the middle of the road, waved her hands at him when he got to be about sixty yards away.

He slowed, stopped about twenty feet from her, and pulled the buds from his ears. Between breaths, he said, 'You okay?'

'Yeah.' Joyce showed him her ID, told him she was with Thackeray College security.

'Am I not allowed to run here?' he asked. 'I didn't think it would be a problem.'

'You're not affiliated with Thackeray?' Joyce asked. 'Enrolled here, or work here?'

The man shook his head. 'No. But come on, it's not really private property, is it?'

Joyce smiled. 'I don't care about that. But I need to ask you some questions.'

The man glanced at his watch. 'I've been trying to beat my previous time.'

'I'm sorry, but it's important. So you don't live on campus?'

'No, I live in town. But I like running through here. It's pretty. And I only just kind of started doing it. I used to run years ago, but I'm trying to get myself back in some kind of shape. More exercise, less drinking, if you know what I mean.'

'Sure, yeah. Listen, were you running here the other night? Around midnight?'

The man asked her which night, exactly, and she told him.

'Yeah,' he said. 'That was my first or second night, I think. How would you know that?'

Joyce pointed to one of the buildings. 'Security camera up there.'

'Oh,' he said.

'Anyway, that night, around that time, do you remember seeing a car parked right where mine is now?'

The jogger shrugged. 'Not that I . . . I don't really recall.'

'It was there for about an hour. A man got out, went in that direction, then returned to the vehicle, and then backed up that way. Turned around, I guess, and drove off.'

'So you're looking for that car?'

Joyce nodded.

'And that guy?'

She nodded again.

'What are you looking for him for?'

Joyce said, 'It's just important that I find him.'

The man appeared to be thinking. 'Actually, yeah, I do kind of remember seeing somebody around then.'

'Really?'

'Maybe.'

'Okay,' Joyce said, starting to feel excited. 'Listen, I didn't even ask. What's your name?'

'Rooney,' the jogger said. 'Victor Rooney.'

CHAPTER 38

David Harwood had felt a little stupid when Cal Weaver had asked him whether he'd spoken to Samantha Worthington's neighbors about where she and Carl might have gone. David was no licensed private detective, but he had been a reporter, and he'd done some investigative journalism over the years – particularly back before the *Promise Falls Standard* started slashing staff and could still afford to do that sort of thing – so not to have considered something as basic as asking the folks who lived on either side of Sam if they'd seen her packing up was pretty embarrassing.

David decided to chalk it up to having too much on his mind.

Now he was going to do what he should have done the first time.

He was back at Sam's place. He'd hoped that maybe when he got here, she'd be back. That he would find her car in the driveway, that she and Carl would be fine.

But the car was still gone when he parked on the street in front of her house.

361

He rang the bell on the house to the right first. It took a second ring to draw out a woman in her eighties, who, it turned out, lived alone, and had not seen Sam or Carl, and did not, in fact, even know who lived on either side of her.

Then he tried the house on the left.

It didn't take long before a woman came to the door, opened it wide, and said to him, 'I was wondering when you'd show up.'

'Excuse me?' David said.

'You're here looking for Samantha and her boy?'

'Uh, yes, I am.'

A man appeared, standing behind the woman. 'What's going on?' he asked.

The woman looked over her shoulder and said, 'This is the real one.'

'Oh,' the man said. 'You figured he'd get here sooner or later.'

'I have no idea what you're talking about,' David said.

'I'm Theresa and that's my husband, Ron,' she said. 'Jones.'

'Okay.'

'And you're David Harwood, right?'

David nodded. 'How do you know that?'

'I've seen you dropping by to see Sam and I recognized you. From the TV, and the paper, back when you were having all that trouble with your wife.'

'That was years ago,' David said.

'Well, I remember,' she said.

362

'What did you mean,' David asked Theresa, 'when you said "the real one"?'

'You're not the first one named David Harwood to come to our door today,' she said.

David felt his stomach drop. 'Who was here?'

Theresa told him about the man who'd come around earlier in the day looking for Sam and Carl. How he'd identified himself as David.

'That had to be her ex-husband,' David said. 'He just got out of jail. I mean, he fled. They didn't let him out on purpose.'

'Good Lord,' Theresa said. 'We had no idea.'

Brandon Worthington probably knew all about him, David thought. His parents would have filled him in. That David had been seeing Sam, that he was the one in the picture having sex with her in her kitchen, that he was the one who'd fucked up Ed's attempt to grab Carl at the school that day. Sam might have spoken about David, in a favorable light, to her neighbors. Or maybe Sam had told the Joneses that if someone named David came around, it would be safe to tell him where she'd gone.

Except, because Theresa Jones knew Brandon wasn't who he claimed to be, it didn't work. And besides, Sam hadn't told her where she was going, anyway.

But it had looked, Theresa Jones told David now, like they were off on a camping trip.

'Good thing you didn't tell him that,' David said.

'Well,' Ron Jones said slowly, 'that's where I might have let the cat out of the bag. Just a bit.'

So it was possible Brandon had figured out his ex-wife and son had packed their sleeping bags and planned to live in a tent until his recapture. But even if Brandon had put that much together, he wouldn't have any idea which campsite they might go to.

But David did.

What was it Sam had said to him? She'd been talking about how, once their relationship had progressed to the point where they didn't care if the boys knew they were sleeping together (which, let's face it, they had probably already figured out), it would be fun to take them on a camping trip.

Sam had said that she and Carl had gone camping a couple of times since moving to Promise Falls. It was something she'd done back when she was married to Brandon, and she'd enjoyed it more than he had. Carl loved everything about it. Exploring the woods, cooking over a fire, burning the marshmallows until they were black ash.

'There's a nice place up around Lake Luzerne,' she'd told him.

David said to Theresa and Ron Jones, 'Thanks very much for your help. I appreciate it more than you can know.'

When he got back into his car, he got out his phone and opened a Web browser. He couldn't remember the name of the campsite Sam had mentioned. But he thought if he could find a list of places in the Lake Luzerne area, he'd recognize it when he saw it.

It didn't take long.

Camp Sunrise.

He was sure that was the place.

David considered driving up there now. But it would be dark by the time he got to Lake Luzerne, and he didn't know where, exactly, Camp Sunrise was. Traipsing around the campsite late at night, surprising Sam and Carl in their tent when they were probably worried about Brandon finding them – assuming they were actually at Camp Sunrise – might not end well.

David could very well end up with a shotgun in his face once again. This time, it might go off.

First thing in the morning. That was what he'd do. He'd head up first thing in the morning.

CHAPTER 39

Duckworth

I stayed for a while with Randall Finley.

First, I went back into the house and took a more formal statement from Lindsay. She related the events of the day a second time, and her story held together. I don't know why I felt the need to apologize on Randy's behalf, but I told her he'd been upset, and he understood she had not set out to murder Jane. I suppose I did it for her more than him. Still, Lindsay remained distraught, and I wasn't convinced she could drive herself home safely. She called her twenty-year-old son, who took a taxi over, then drove his mother back to her place in her car.

I asked Randy, who had dropped himself into a wrought-iron chair outside near the front door, if he wanted me to do anything with Bipsie. He shook his head sorrowfully and asked if I could put her into a garbage bag until he decided what to do with her. He muttered something about burying her in the backyard next to Jane, given how much she loved that dog.

Gently, I told him town bylaws prevented him from burying Jane on the property.

'I don't even know what I'm saying anymore.'

I said I would bag the dog's body and leave it in the garage out back, but Randy asked me to leave her in the downstairs laundry room for now.

And that was what I did.

I explained that it might be some time before anyone could come and deal with Jane.

'Maybe I'll go up and sit with her,' he said. I wasn't sure he appreciated how unpleasant it was in that room. He added, 'I could start getting Jane ready. You know, get her cleaned up and all.'

With as many euphemisms as I could muster, I cautioned him against meddling with his wife's body.

'I understand,' he said, and went back into the house.

I wanted to give the place another walk-through before I left. Through the kitchen, the basement, out back. As I was getting ready to leave, I could hear a voice on the second floor.

As I ascended the stairs, I could hear Randall Finley talking softly and continuously, not pausing to formulate thoughts. At the top of the stairs I could just see into Jane's bedroom.

Randy was in a chair by the bed, an open book on his lap, seemingly oblivious to the stench that enveloped him.

He was reading to his wife.

★   ★   ★

I'd planned to pay a visit to Victor Rooney on my way home. I'd only spoken to him once, several days ago, and I wanted to pick his brain some more about Olivia Fisher, the woman he'd been going to marry.

But there was more to my visit than just that. It was what Walden had said, about how angry Victor was. With himself, and those twenty-two Promise Falls citizens who might have responded to Olivia's cries, but did nothing.

Those twenty-two, and himself. Twenty-three people who, had they behaved with a greater sense of community, might have made the difference between life and death for Olivia. Maybe none of those twenty-two people could have saved Olivia's life. By the time she was screaming, she was probably as good as dead.

But if they had acted, if they had done *anything* when they heard what was happening in the park by the falls, they might have seen her killer. They might have been able to provide a description. They might have seen his car, recalled part, or all, of a license plate.

If they had done any of those things, the police might have caught him.

And Rosemary Gaynor would be alive.

And Lorraine Plummer would be alive.

Just how angry was Victor Rooney about this town's failure to measure up? Angry enough to get even somehow?

Angry enough to start sending out messages?

Like twenty-three dead squirrels strung up on a fence? Three bloody mannequins in car '23' of a decommissioned Ferris wheel? A fiery, out-of-control bus with '23' on the back? And then there was Mason Helt and his hoodie with that same number on it, and what he had supposedly told the women he'd assaulted. That he didn't mean to harm them, just to put a scare into them. That it was a kind of gig.

And finally, there was today's date. May 23. A day Promise Falls would never forget. In a year or two or even less, someone would suggest a memorial in the town square with the names of everyone who had died this day.

So, the plan had been to see Victor Rooney.

But by the time I was done at the Finley house, I was exhausted. I was weak, I had a headache, and my feet were killing me. I needed a recharging before I asked anyone else a single question.

I pointed the car home.

There were familiar voices as soon as I stepped into the house. But I already knew Trevor was there by the Finley Springs truck parked in the driveway. I found him and Maureen at the kitchen table.

The smell of something wonderful was in the air. Something from the oven. If I was not mistaken, it was lasagna.

They pushed back their chairs in a chorus of squeaks and came to greet me. Maureen put her arms around me first. 'I didn't know when to

369

expect you,' she said, 'but I put something together just in case.'

I held her tightly in my arms. Behind her, Trevor stood, waiting. When Maureen released me, my son gave me a strong hug, several pats on the back.

'Hey, Dad,' he said, and there was this collective feeling that we were all just on the edge of losing it.

I think, at that moment, we were all glad to be alive. We were all okay, and we were together at a time when in so many other houses in Promise Falls, there was only grief and unbearable sorrow.

'I was never able to find Amanda Croydon for you,' Maureen said.

'She turned up,' I said. When I was driving home with the radio tuned to the news, I heard some snippets of a shouting match between her and Randall Finley where he'd been handing out free water.

'I didn't know you were looking for her,' Trevor said. 'I was there, saw her fight with Randy. I was recording it on his phone, but then he got a call from home. His dog died or something.'

I filled them in on how much worse it was than that. Maureen shook her head sadly.

Trevor said, 'I wonder if he'll pack it in. The whole running-for-mayor thing.'

I said it was probably too soon to tell. He reached into the fridge to grab a beer for me, but I waved him off. 'Have to go back out.'

'Are you sure?' Maureen said. 'You're not the only cop in town.'

It took all the energy I had to smile. 'I'm not so sure about that.'

'You know you haven't been breathing normally since you walked in here,' she said.

'What?'

'Yeah,' Trevor said. 'You keep taking really deep breaths.'

'I'm fine,' I said. 'I'm just tired, that's all.'

'You think that's all it is?' said Maureen, donning mitts and taking the lasagna out of the oven.

'I'm positive,' I said. They weren't wrong in their observation. I was taking in deep breaths, then letting them out over several seconds.

Exhaustion.

'I just have one more thing I want to do,' I told them. 'Then I'll come home and go into an eight-hour coma.'

Maureen did up three plates. A garden salad on the side. Trevor hoovered his in seconds, and I wasn't far behind him. But halfway through my serving, I put down my fork.

'What?' Maureen asked.

'It's nothing. Just a little light-headed.' I laughed. 'I think all the blood's rushing to my stomach, and that's a demanding area to service.'

No one laughed with me.

'I'm fine, really.' I wanted to change the subject by saying to Trevor, 'I hear you guys handed out thousands of cases of water today.'

'We did.'

'That must have felt good, doing that.'

Trevor shrugged. 'Yes and no. I mean, it was good to help people, but some of them were really ugly about it. You kind of wanted every family to get a case, but some people tried to come back and get extra cases, more than their share, you know?'

'Yeah.'

'And the whole thing was the Finley Show anyway.'

'Yeah,' I said again.

'He was just soaking up the attention. I mean, it cost him a fortune in product, but it was the kind of advertising you can't buy, you know?'

I nodded.

'All day I wondered if he did it.'

Maureen looked stunned. 'What are you saying?'

I broke in. 'For a while, I entertained the idea, too, that he'd done something to the water so he could come to the rescue. But for God's sake, all that to be mayor of Promise Falls? And wouldn't he have made sure his wife didn't end up becoming one of the casualties?'

'A dead wife just buys him even more sympathy,' Trevor said.

'Oh, that's awful,' Maureen said. 'No one would do that.'

I let dinner settle before I went back out again. We moved into the living room, where I dropped into my favorite chair. Maureen tuned in one of the national newscasts to see what they had on Promise Falls; then Trevor grabbed the remote and channel surfed to see what the other networks had done.

The entire country knew all about Promise Falls.

One of the networks had turned us into a back-drop headline: THE CURSE OF PROMISE FALLS. They'd folded in material on the drive-in collapse, a look back at the Olivia Fisher case.

Sometime later, I felt someone nudging me in the shoulder.

'Barry,' Maureen said. 'Barry.'

I had fallen asleep. 'Shit,' I said, stirring suddenly. 'How long was I out?'

'It's okay. I didn't want to bother you. You needed to rest.'

'What time is it?'

'Nearly ten thirty,' Maureen said. 'Trevor asked me to say good-bye for him. He was pretty tired, too, and left about half an hour ago.'

'Jesus,' I said, pushing myself out of the chair. 'I have to go.'

She didn't argue. She'd spent enough years with me to know there was no point.

I slipped on my jacket, grabbed my keys, and was out the door. Once I was behind the wheel and had the engine going, I gave myself a minute. Heading out of the house so quickly after waking up hadn't given me time to gain back my equilibrium. I was woozy.

But I was fine.

I headed for Victor Rooney's house. Save for one light over the front door, the place was in total darkness when I got there.

I knocked on the door anyway. Hard.

'She died.'

I turned around. A man was standing on the sidewalk, watching me.

'Pardon?' I said.

'The lady that lives there. She was one of the ones what died this morning.'

I didn't know, but there was no reason to be surprised that Victor Rooney's landlady – it took me a moment to call up the name: Emily Townsend – would be among the dead.

'The water,' I said, since it was always possible she had died of something else. A heart attack, a fall down the stairs.

'Yep. They found her in the backyard.' He pointed to a house down the street. 'Mr Tarkington didn't make it, either. His wife's probably going to live, but their daughter says she could have brain damage.'

'Awful,' I said.

The man pointed to the house north of the one I was standing in front of. 'I live next door. Me and the wife heard the warnings before we drank anything. Ms Townsend wasn't so lucky. They came for her late this afternoon. She was lying out there for hours.'

I said, 'My name's Duckworth. I'm with the

police. I was actually looking for the man she rented to. Victor Rooney.'

'Oh yeah,' the neighbor said. 'I've seen him around. But I guess he's not home.'

'I guess not,' I said.

But I tried banging on the door one more time, just in case. There was a part of me that was grateful. Anything I wanted to ask Victor tonight I could just as easily ask him tomorrow morning.

I went home. I had nothing left. I went up to bed and slipped into that coma I'd promised myself.

CHAPTER 40

Crystal found Celeste up in the main bedroom where she slept every night with Dwayne, folding clothes on the bed, putting things into drawers.

'Where's Cal?' she asked, clipboard and paper in her hand as always.

'I don't know, sweetheart,' Celeste said. 'I haven't seen him in a while. He's probably in the living room watching TV with Dwayne.'

'No, he isn't.'

'Well, I'm not sure. Look around. I'm sure he's somewhere.'

Crystal went back downstairs. The television was still on, tuned in to some sports channel that Dwayne had wanted to watch. But Dwayne was not there watching it. She went into the kitchen, then down into the basement. She looked in the furnace room, and a dingy rec room with a Ping-Pong table that had no net, and a small workroom where Dwayne kept his tools and had a workbench.

Crystal went back up two flights and entered the main bedroom again, but Celeste was not there. She found her in the bathroom, putting up fresh towels.

'I still can't find Cal,' Crystal said.

'Darlin', it's been two minutes since we last talked, and I haven't seen him in that time. Didn't you look in the living room?'

'Yes. And I looked in the furnace room and the workroom and the kitchen and the other bathrooms and a room with a lot of tools in it and I didn't find him anywhere.'

'Did you ask Dwayne?'

'I didn't see Dwayne,' Crystal said.

'How could you go in every room of the house and not see Dwayne?'

Crystal said, 'I don't know.'

'Maybe they're both outside.'

'It's dark now.'

'Well, if it's dark, just turn on the outside lights. They're right by the door. I just want to finish a couple of things up here and if you haven't found Cal by then, I'll help you.'

Crystal turned around and left without saying anything.

She went to the front door, looked outside, where Cal's car was still parked at the curb. She turned on the light, took one step out onto the porch, and looked around.

No Cal. No Dwayne.

She walked through the house to the back door and turned on that light, too. She saw Dwayne, standing by his pickup truck, talking on his cell phone, but there was no sign of Cal.

Crystal went outside, headed directly to Dwayne,

and even though he was in the middle of a conversation with someone, she asked, 'Where's Cal?'

He raised an index finger toward her and turned away ninety degrees. Crystal changed position so that she was in front of him again and asked, 'Where's Cal?'

Dwayne looked angrily at her and said, 'I'm on the phone.'

'Where's Cal?' she asked.

'Are you deaf? I am *on* the *phone.*'

'Where's Cal?' Crystal asked.

'Do you see him? I don't see him. Go look in the house.'

He turned his back to her and continued his phone conversation, speaking in low tones.

Crystal raised her voice. 'I looked all over the house! He's not there.'

Dwayne spun around. 'Goddamn it, I'm trying to do some business here. Maybe he went for a drive.'

'His car is here.'

'Maybe he went for a walk.'

'Where would he walk to?'

'How the hell should I know? Around the block maybe.'

'Why would he walk around the block? He didn't even finish his pizza. He didn't finish his beer, either.'

'Go ask Celeste,' Dwayne said. He walked toward the middle of the yard, waving his free arm behind him, as though trying to ward off a swarm of mosquitoes.

Crystal followed and pulled at his shirtsleeve. 'I asked Celeste. She told me to ask you.'

'Yeah, well, I'm telling you to go ask her again because I don't know.'

Crystal stood there a moment, as though pondering whether this was a sound strategy. Then she started heading for the back door.

'No, wait. Hang on,' Dwayne said. 'Hang on, kid.'

'My name is Crystal.'

'Yeah, okay, Crystal. Just hang on.'

Dwayne spoke into the phone. 'I'll call you back in a couple of minutes. It's the kid.' He shoved the phone down into the front pocket of his jeans, let out an enormous sigh, and said to Crystal, 'Okay, fine, you have my undivided attention.'

'I just want to find him.'

'Sure, of course, yeah. Okay, well, let's have a look at the street. Maybe he's out there having a smoke.'

'I don't think he smokes.'

'Well, if he quit, having to look after you might have driven him to take it up again.'

'Why?' Crystal asked.

'Huh?'

'Why would looking after me make someone smoke?'

'It was just a joke.'

'I don't get it.'

'Never mind. Come on.' He led her away from

the garage, toward the street. 'He had a pretty stressful day, you know? He might have come out here just to have a few minutes to himself.'

'But he likes me,' Crystal said. 'Why would he come out here to be by himself?'

'What makes you think he likes you?'

'He's nice to me.'

Dwayne nodded. 'I guess.'

'He's nicer than you.'

'What's that supposed to mean?' Dwayne asked. 'Who brought home pizza and wings tonight? Huh? Who was that?'

'That was you.'

'You don't think that was pretty nice of me? I was thinking about you when I got that mess of food.'

That gave Crystal pause. 'Oh.'

They'd reached the street and were standing next to Cal's Honda. 'You're right – his car's here, so he can't have gone far,' Dwayne said.

Without warning, Crystal shouted at the top of her lungs, 'Cal!'

'Jesus,' Dwayne said, making a show of putting his fingers to his ears. 'You nearly busted my eardrum when—'

'*Cal!*'

'Dial it down, kid.'

'*Cal!*'

She'd started off down the sidewalk. Dwayne ran to catch up to her, grabbed her by the shoulder. 'You can't be screaming like that.'

'I want him to hear me.'

'You don't even know where he is. You can't go around the neighborhood screaming for someone like they're a lost dog.'

'Why?'

'You're not normal – you know that?'

She looked up at him with wide eyes. 'That's what everyone says.'

'Okay, look, why don't you go back in the house and I'll look around for him? When I've found him, I'll let you know.'

'If we both look, we'll find him twice as fast,' she said.

'Not necessarily. If we—'

'Cal!'

Dwayne glanced around the street nervously, as though expecting people to start coming to their doors.

And someone did.

Celeste.

'What's going on?' she said, coming down the porch steps and across the yard.

'Nothing,' Dwayne said. 'We're just talking.'

'No, we're not,' Crystal said. 'We're trying to find Cal.'

Celeste put her fists on her hips. 'You still haven't found him?'

'No,' Crystal said.

'His car's still here,' Celeste said.

'You're a regular Sherlock Holmes,' Dwayne said. 'Look, like I told Crystal here, I'm sure he's just gone for a walk or something. If he's not back in an hour, I'll go looking for him.'

'I need him,' Crystal said.

Worry washed over Celeste's face. 'I think we need to find him now. It's not like him to just walk off.' Something occurred to her. 'You know what? I'll just call him.'

'What?' Dwayne said, now looking pretty worried himself. 'Is that a good idea?'

'It's a very good idea,' Crystal said.

Celeste took her phone from her back pocket, made a couple of taps on the screen, then put it to her ear.

'It's ringing,' she said.

Crystal stood stock-still, and Dwayne appeared to be holding his breath.

'He's not picking up,' Celeste said. 'I'm going to let it go a few more . . . okay, it's going to message. Cal, hey, it's Celeste, and we're wondering where the hell you are.'

She ended the call but held on to the phone rather than put it away.

'Call him again,' Crystal said.

'Sweetheart,' Celeste said, 'let's give him a minute to hear the message.'

'No, I think I heard the phone.'

'What?' Dwayne said. 'I didn't hear anything.'

'Call him again,' Crystal repeated.

Celeste made the call. While she held the phone to her ear, Dwayne said, 'I didn't hear a damn thing. You must be hearing—'

'*Shh!*' Crystal said.

No one made a sound.

Crystal pointed toward the garage. 'It's coming from over there.'

'I already looked there,' Dwayne said.

But his wife and Crystal were already moving up the driveway and past the house. The phone was still pressed to Celeste's ear. 'It's still ringing.'

As they reached the garage, Crystal said, 'Don't you hear it? It's in there.' She pointed to the door. '*Cal!*'

'Okay, I heard it, too,' Celeste said, and put her phone back into her pocket. She went to the smaller door at the side, attempted to open it but found it locked.

'*Cal!*' Crystal had her mouth right up to the door.

'Have you got the key?' Celeste said to Dwayne.

'I don't know why the hell he'd be in there. I always keep the door locked.'

'Do you have the key?' his wife asked again.

'Um,' he said, 'it might be in the house.'

'Check your pockets,' she snapped at him. 'You never go out of the house without your keys.'

'*Cal!*'

He took a long time hunting for them in his jeans. 'I've got my truck keys, but I don't know if the garage key is on—'

'Of course it is. Give them to me.'

Dwayne, looking like a man who'd lost all hope, handed the keys over to his wife. There were half a dozen of them on the ring, and he didn't bother to single out the right one for her.

The third key did the trick.

She opened the door, flicked on the light. Crystal managed to duck under her arm and got into the room first.

Cal was on the floor, on his side. Duct tape was wrapped around his ankles and knees, and had been used to secure his wrists together at his back. There was another strip slapped across his mouth.

'Oh my God!' Celeste said, and dropped to her knees.

Cal was conscious, and rolled onto his stomach to allow Celeste to release his hands more easily. But after picking at the tape for several seconds, she turned to Dwayne, who was still standing in the doorway, and asked for a knife.

'Uh, sure,' he said, and reached into his other pocket for a small jackknife. He extracted a blade, then carefully put it into his wife's hand. 'He's probably going to say some crazy shit, but you need to keep in mind that he might have been hit on the head or something.'

'What are you talking about?' Celeste said, focused now on cutting through the tape on Cal's wrists without nicking him and drawing blood. Crystal was working at the tape on his ankles. She managed to cut through it with her nails, and was now working on the tape that bound his knees together.

Once Cal's wrists were free, he rolled back over into a sitting position and worked the tape off his mouth himself, his eyes on Dwayne the entire time. He wadded the tape into a ball and flicked it his way.

'Pretty smart move, leaving me with my phone,' Cal said.

'I don't know what you're talking about,' Dwayne said.

Celeste's eyes darted back and forth between them. 'What the hell happened here? What's going on?'

Cal helped Crystal free his knees, at which point she threw her arms around his neck and held him tight.

'I couldn't find you,' she said.

'I'm okay,' Cal said, pulling her arms from around him. 'Thank you for tracking me down.' He struggled to his feet, picking up a two-foot-long scrap of two-by-four at the same time.

'You should put that down,' Dwayne said. 'We need to talk about this.'

'We can talk in a minute,' Cal said, and then, his face flushed with an instantaneous rage, swung the board as hard as he could into Dwayne's right leg above the knee. Dwayne wasn't able to move quickly enough to avoid it, but when Cal looked like he was ready to take a second swing, he stumbled back and out of the way.

'Jesus!' he said, grabbing his leg. 'I think you broke it!'

'No,' Cal said, holding up the board and inspecting it. 'It's fine.'

Celeste got between them and screamed, 'Stop it! Stop it!' She pushed Cal back, then turned to her injured husband. 'Did you do this? Did you do this to my brother?'

'I'm hurt,' he said. 'I'm hurt bad.'

Celeste, shaking her head in disbelief, looked back at Cal and asked, 'Did he do this?'

But before he could answer, something beyond him caught Celeste's eyes. A large black plastic tarp was draped over something in the middle of the garage floor.

'What is that?' she asked.

Cal turned around to see what his sister was looking at. Celeste walked to the middle of the room, reached down, and took hold of a corner of the tarp and started to pull.

'No,' Dwayne said. 'Don't.'

Celeste gave the tarp a strong tug to reveal what had been hidden beneath.

Dozens of boxes of stereo components. Receivers, mostly. By Sony, Denon, Onkyo. A box marked '3-D Projector.' Several more boxes filled with Blu-ray disc players.

'Where the hell did those come from?' Dwayne said.

CHAPTER 41

Angus Carlson said, 'They've pulled me off active duty until the investigation is over.'

'I'm sorry,' Gale said, slipping an arm over his shoulder to comfort him. They were sitting on the curb out front of their house, under a streetlamp. 'But you did the right thing.'

He shrugged. 'I don't know. It seemed like it at the time. At least the guy isn't dead. I shot him in the leg.'

'You did what you had to do. And you've got all those witnesses in the hospital. They'll all back you up.'

'The gun was empty.'

'What?'

'The guy who was waving a gun around at the woman wearing the hijab—'

'Which one is that?'

'What?'

'There're the hijab and the niqab and the burka,' Gale said. 'Right?'

'The burka covers everything, and the niqab is like that, but you can see the eyes.'

'Then which one is the hijab?'

'That's the scarf that goes around the head, covers the hair, but you can see the face.'

'Is that what the woman was wearing? That one?'

'Yeah. I was trying to tell you about the gun.'

'I'm sorry,' Gale said.

'When they checked the guy's gun, there were no bullets in it. I just hope they don't use that against me. I mean, he was waving it around, acting like a crazy person.'

'You couldn't know his gun wasn't loaded,' she said. 'It's not like you have X-ray vision. I mean, lots of people have been shot by the police for waving around toy guns. It wasn't a toy gun, was it?'

'No, it was real. But when something like this happens, they look at everything. The other guy, he'll probably get a lawyer who'll say somehow I should have known, that I shot him needlessly, that I could have defused the situation some other way. But I talked to the chief, and she told me not to worry.'

'Then don't.' She paused. 'How long are you off duty?'

'I don't know.'

'Will they still let you be a detective?'

Angus shook his head. 'No idea. Probably, but I don't know. This kind of thing, you think you're in the clear, and then they find something to nail you on.' He laughed derisively. 'Wouldn't my mom just love to hear about this?'

'Angus.'

'It's been great telling her how good I'm doing, how things have turned out for me, despite all the shit she put me through. But now, this happens, and—'

'Don't talk about her,' Gale said. 'I hate it when you bring her up. Just don't do it.'

Angus became sullen. 'Fine.'

They were both quiet for a minute. Finally, Gale said, 'The hijab-niqab-burka thing got me thinking.'

'Thinking about what?'

'Actually, it doesn't really have to do with that. But it's just the way things link in your mind, you know. Anyway, it's probably totally nothing.'

Angus Carlson closed his eyes and dropped his head. 'Gale, just tell me.'

'I went for a walk this morning. I had to get out of the house, just to do something, you know?'

'Yeah.'

'So, you know Naman's?'

'The bookstore?'

'Yeah, he sells used books. He doesn't carry just-published stuff.'

'He got firebombed the other night,' Angus said. 'Someone threw a Molotov cocktail through his window.'

'I didn't know that. If I'd known, I wouldn't have bothered, but I went down there looking for a book.'

'What book?'

'It doesn't matter,' she said.

'Come on, what book?'

Now it was her time to sigh. 'I wanted to see if there were any books about couples. You know, like us. Couples who don't have children, and why that is, and why one partner might want a child and the other doesn't.'

'Gale.'

'You asked me what I was looking for and I told you. But listen to me.'

'Okay, go on.'

'So I walked down to the store, and it was all boarded up, but Naman was there, inside, kind of going through the damage. It was just awful. Books that didn't catch on fire were all water-damaged from when the fire department got there, but even so, there were some books that weren't damaged that much at all, except for smelling like smoke. I slipped inside and I talked to him and I felt so bad for him.'

'Sure.'

'I mean, people were blaming him just because he's Muslim or whatever he is. Thinking he had something to do with the bombing at the drive-in, or what happened to the water.'

'People can be like that,' Angus said. 'They don't know what to do with the anger, and they racially profile, and then that kind of thing happens.'

'Which is why I feel really bad to even mention this, but . . .'

'But what?'

'There was a book in his store, on the floor, right there in front of me, about poison.'

Angus stiffened, turned his head toward his wife. 'A book?'

Gale nodded. 'I can't remember the exact title. But it was a kind of guide, of all the poisons that are out there. All these ways that you can kill people.'

Angus appeared to be thinking. 'Just because he had a book like that doesn't mean he's the one who poisoned the town's water.'

'I know. I know that.'

'Did you say anything?'

She nodded. 'I picked it up and handed it to him. This was right after he'd made some comment about people being suspicious of him. And I made a bad joke of it, I guess, saying something like "Well, I guess you better not let anyone see you with this, then."'

'You said that.'

'Yeah.' She screwed up her face worriedly. 'You think I shouldn't have said that?'

'I don't know. Like you said, it's probably nothing.'

'You're right. It probably is.'

'Unless,' Carlson said, 'it *is* something.'

'That's kind of what I was thinking, too,' Gale said.

DAY II

CHAPTER 42

David set out Sunday at daybreak. He could make it to Lake Luzerne in under an hour, he figured. And if Sam and Carl were at Camp Sunrise, that'd be fantastic, because checking all the other campsites could take several hours.

'Where are you off to so early?' his mother asked him when she found him in the kitchen. She and Don were always up before David, so it was a surprise to find him there.

'Just something I have to do,' he said.

'Is it something for Mr Finley?' she asked.

'No.' That got him thinking that he really needed to get in touch with Randy. The man had, after all, hired him to do a job, and David had not exactly been giving one hundred percent. Despite the contempt David felt for him, he felt some measure of guilt that he wasn't earning his salary.

He didn't want to call and wake the man, so he decided to send him a text that Finley could discover whenever he got around to looking at his phone.

Will be away much of today but hope to connect late afternoon. Sorry about this.

David sent the text.

He was about to put his phone away when he saw the telltale dots that told him Finley was writing a reply.

Fine.

That didn't sound like the Finley David knew. Where was the outrage? The bluster? The guilt-tripping?

Maybe, David thought, he'd been terminated. Maybe Finley's short response meant he had found someone else to work for him. David wasn't sure whether to be hurt or relieved. He didn't like working for the man, but he also needed the job.

David phoned him.

'Am I fired?' David asked when Finley answered.

'I don't know,' Finley said.

'Look, I know I've had some things going on, but I'm hoping to get them all sorted out. I've got to take a run up to Lake Luzerne today, but once I'm done up there, I can—'

'Jane's dead.'

Finley filled him in. A stunned David didn't know what to say beyond that he was sorry.

'I may pull out,' Finley said. 'I'm thinking, the hell with it.'

'Don't make a decision right away,' David

396

counseled. 'Take care . . . of what you have to take care of. Give it some time. Then decide.'

'You don't understand,' he said.

'Don't understand what?'

'She was the reason,' Finley said.

David started to say something else but realized Finley had ended the call.

'What happened?' Arlene asked as Don came into the room.

David shook his head and asked, 'Can you look after Ethan today?'

Don asked, 'Can we have coffee today or is the water still going to kill us?'

Arlene asked her son, 'Do you know? Is the water safe yet?'

'They should have it fixed by now,' Don said. 'I don't know why the hell they can't have it fixed by now. They should have been able to flush the system. I've half a mind to go over to the plant myself and see what the hell they're doing.'

'Yes,' Arlene said. 'I'm sure they'd welcome your input.'

If I don't have a job, David thought, *I'll be losing this house and moving back in with them.*

'Can you look after Ethan?' he asked again.

'Of course,' Arlene said.

David was out the door.

David didn't have GPS built into his car, or even one of those stick-on mini-nav systems that could be put atop the dashboard. But he had looked up the location for Camp Sunrise on his phone's map app. He wasn't expecting it to be difficult to find.

He was there in just over an hour, and along the way he had to think about just what the purpose of this trip was. Was his search for Sam solely motivated by concern for her, or was this more about him?

About half-and-half, he concluded.

He was, without a doubt, worried for her safety. Brandon was looking for her, and he wanted to be sure Sam and her son were safe, that Brandon had not found them. But he also realized Sam was no fool. The fact that she'd gotten herself and Carl out of town so quickly was evidence of that.

But that wasn't enough for David. He had to *know*.

And, he admitted to himself, he wanted Sam to know he cared enough to look for her.

When he reached Camp Sunrise, he found a small, tollbooth-like structure between the entrance and exit lanes. It was designed to look like a mini log cabin, with wooden gates in the raised position on both sides. There was no one in the booth, so there was nothing to stop him from driving straight in.

It wasn't even nine in the morning yet, and the camp was a sleepy place. Few people were out and about, but as he drove the narrow, winding roads that led through the forested grounds, he noticed exceptions. There was a man frying up some bacon on a Coleman stove set up on a picnic table. At another campsite, a woman was running an extension cord from an electrical post to a cappuccino maker resting on the top of a stump.

'Roughing it,' David said under his breath.

David didn't see any empty campsites. This was a long weekend, and it seemed a safe bet that the place was filled to capacity. There were tents, small trailers, and those hybrid tent-trailer things, with two wheels and a metal chassis, that opened up to sleep four or more people.

Driving slowly through the camp, David did not see Sam or Carl anywhere, and even if they were still sleeping in their tent, he saw no car that looked like hers. He made his way back to where he'd turned in off the main road, and saw that there was now someone in the booth. He pulled up alongside it and powered down the window.

'Help ya?' said a man – no, more like a kid about seventeen – at the window.

'I'm not staying here,' David said. 'I'm trying to find somebody.'

'Okay.'

'Samantha Worthington,' he said. 'She probably checked in Thursday night. She's with her son, about nine or ten, and they'd have pitched a tent. They don't have a trailer or anything like that.' He thought maybe he needed a reason to be looking for them. 'There's kind of a family emergency back home and we've been trying to locate them.'

The kid appeared to be consulting a book, or maybe a laptop. David couldn't see from where he sat.

'I don't have anything here. No Worthington,' he said. 'When did you say they arrived?'

'Thursday, probably.'

'Did they have a reservation?'

David was betting Samantha had not made one. If she'd just found out about Brandon's escape, there wouldn't have been time. She'd have thrown everything they needed into the car and just taken off.

'I doubt it,' David said.

'Well, if they didn't, they wouldn't have been able to get in. All the sites had been booked ahead by Wednesday.'

David felt deflated. He'd played a hunch and it had been wrong. But just because Sam wasn't here didn't mean she couldn't have tried another campsite in the area.

'Thanks,' he said to the kid. He drove out of the park, then pulled over onto the shoulder of the road to consult the Web browser on his phone, thinking he'd get the names and locations of other nearby campsites.

Except he couldn't get online. He had no bars on his phone.

He couldn't get cell service here.

Maybe that was why Samantha hadn't taken any of his calls, or tried to get in touch with him. He felt simultaneously discouraged and encouraged. He believed he was on the right track, but was still no closer to finding them.

He got out of the car and walked back to the booth.

'If you're full up, where might you send someone to try next?'

The kid in the booth didn't hesitate. 'Probably Call of the Loon.'

'What?'

'I know, seriously. A pretty dumb name for a place. Call of the Loon Acres. About five more miles up the road that way. They try to squeeze in extras even when they're booked solid.'

'Thanks,' David said, and ran back to the car.

CHAPTER 43

Duckworth

When the alarm went off at six, I was dreaming. It was more a nightmare than a dream, but no one ever says they were nightmaring. But that's a more accurate word for what I was doing when the clock radio started to beep.

I'm in the park by the falls. It's dusk and I am standing on the sidewalk by the road that runs parallel to the park.

I hear screaming. It seems to be coming from all directions. I turn and look one way, thinking that is where the screams are originating. But I no sooner spin around than the screams seem to be coming from behind me. I keep spinning round and round, and pretty soon it's as though the screams are coming from everywhere.

I am turning and turning to the point of dizziness. Finally I stop, pretty sure the screams are not all around me, but near the base of the falls. I start walking in that direction; then I feel a tap on my shoulder.

I spin around suddenly and there, directly in front of me, is Olivia Fisher.

She is looking at me quizzically, an almost naive expression on her face. She says, 'Didn't you hear me?'

'I did,' I say. 'I just couldn't tell where the sound was coming from.'

'It was coming from here,' she says, opens her mouth wide, and points into it. But her mouth has opened unnaturally wide, as though her jaw is no longer hinged.

And blood begins to pour from her mouth, like water gushing from an opened fire hydrant. Blood spills over me, and I look down and see that within seconds it is up to my knees.

Even though her mouth is flowing with blood, I can still hear her speaking to me. 'Do you know what my favorite number is?'

'No,' I say.

'Twenty-three. Do you know why?'

'Tell me.'

'You already know. You've figured it out.'

'No, I haven't. I'm not sure. I—'

'Oh, dear,' Olivia says. Her mouth is back to normal now, no blood flowing from it. But she has her hands over her stomach, where her entrails are spilling out. She is attempting to stuff them back in.

'How will I explain this to my mother?' she asks.

The alarm wakes me before I can offer her a suggestion.

Maureen sat up in bed as I reached over to kill the alarm. 'If that hadn't gone off, I'd have woken you up,' she said. 'You were starting to shout things. You were having a nightmare.'

'Yeah,' I said, throwing back the covers and putting my feet on the floor. I had a headache and my mouth was dry.

'I can make coffee,' Maureen said. 'I got bottled water yesterday.'

'You went down to Finley's circus?'

'I got it at the Stop and Shop.'

I checked my phone, which was recharging on my bedside table. I hadn't muted it when I'd turned out the light, in case someone tried to reach me in the night. But there was a text message on the screen.

'I never heard this come in,' I said.

'You were out cold,' Maureen said. 'When did it show up?'

I looked. The text was from Joyce Pilgrim, and she'd sent it at eleven forty-five p.m. About half an hour after I'd lost consciousness. I told Maureen.

'I hadn't come to bed yet,' she said, 'so I never heard it, either.'

I read the message: Call me when you get this. Might have something.

'Shit,' I said.

Maureen threw back the covers and headed downstairs as I texted back to Joyce: Just got this. If you're up, phone me.

I took the phone with me into the bathroom,

404

placing it on a shelf just outside the shower. And thought: *Is it safe to take a shower?*

I'd had one the morning before with no ill effects. Maybe water laced with sodium azide was enough to kill you if you drank it, but its effects were negligible when it washed over your skin. Those granules I'd touched the day before had made my finger itch, but hadn't burned through my skin or anything.

I made a call to the station to see what the latest updates were. The state health officials believed the contaminated water had moved through the system, but to be on the safe side, they were recommending against drinking anything from the taps for at least another forty-eight hours. Water for nondrinking purposes was believed to be safe. In the case of a shower, they advised, let it run for a good five minutes before stepping in.

Well, that was a relief. The idea of taking a bath with several bottles of Finley Springs water did not appeal to me.

I turned on the water and let it run.

After five minutes, I stripped out of my pajamas and stepped under the hot spray. I was rinsing shampoo out of my hair while soaping up my ample belly when my cell phone rang.

'Goddamn it.'

I turned off the shower while still soapy, reached out for a towel to get my hands dry enough to pick up the phone without dropping it, then, still in the stall, put the phone to my ear.

'Yeah?'

'It's Joyce. I got your text.'

'Okay,' I said. 'Sorry. I was asleep when you sent yours. Just saw it.'

'I figured.'

'So what have you got?'

'A witness. Maybe. Not a great one, but a witness.'

'Go on,' I said, using my free hand to wipe away some shampoo that was trying to find its way into my eye.

'So I did what you asked. I reviewed the surveillance footage.' She told me about seeing a car park near Lorraine Plummer's residence around the time of her murder, a man getting out and returning.

'What did he look like?'

'You can't tell a thing from the video,' she said. 'And you can't get any kind of a good look at the car, either.'

'Well, still, that's something. Maybe we can get someone to enhance the video, or maybe there are some other cameras along the way to Thackeray we can check. But what's this about a witness?'

She told me about the appearance of the jogger in the video. How he'd run right past the parked car.

'So last night, I camped out there, thinking maybe this was a regular run this guy takes, and I'd get a chance to ask him whether he noticed that car or not.'

I felt my pulse quicken, which took my mind

off the fact that I was freezing as soapy water clung to me. Maureen stepped into the bathroom, looked at me standing naked in the shower with a phone in my hand, gave me an up and down, and left without comment.

'And?' I said.

'He came by. I got out of my car and stopped him and got him to think back to the car and whether he remembered anything.'

'Ok-k-ay.'

'Something wrong?'

'Nothing. Just felt a chill, is all.'

'So I tried to jog his memory, no pun intended, and it kind of came back to him.'

'You're kidding.'

'No. He said the car was a four-door sedan. Hard to tell at night, but dark blue or maybe black. He was a little fuzzy on the make, but he thought North American. Like a Ford.'

'Plate number?' I knew, even as I asked it, that it was a long shot.

'No, he didn't take any notice of the plate. At least, not the numbers. But he thought maybe it was out of state. He thought it might have been green.'

Green. Vermont plates were green, and Vermont was not very far away.

'Okay,' I said. 'So we've got a bit to go on with the car.'

'He says he saw the guy,' Joyce Pilgrim said.

I gripped the phone a little tighter. 'Tell me.'

'White, about six-three, ball cap – for the Yankees, he thinks – running shoes, dark blue Windbreaker, maybe a hundred and eighty to two hundred pounds.'

'He must have got a long look at him to get that kind of detail.'

'He says he only saw him for a second. And he didn't see him near the car. Saw him farther away, near the building where Lorraine Plummer was killed. But he was figuring it must have been the guy whose car it was, since there wasn't anyone else around.'

'This is amazing, Joyce. This is really terrific work.' I took one step out of the shower and reached for a towel. I rubbed it over my soapy hair, tried to blot myself where I could with one available hand. 'You got a name for this witness?'

'Yeah, hang on, I wrote it down. Here's the phone number. It's—'

'I can't take it down right now. I can call you back in a couple of minutes. What about the name?' I stepped out of the shower all the way, my feet on the furry white bath mat.

'Rooney,' she said.

'What?'

'Rooney. Victor Rooney.'

The towel slipped out of my hand.

I said nothing. I was trying to grasp the significance. The boyfriend of Olivia Fisher just happened to be running past Lorraine Plummer's building at the time of her murder.

Maybe his description of the mystery man was so good, right down to the Yankees cap, because he wanted us to have someone else to look for.

Maybe someone he'd never seen at all.

'Thanks, Joyce,' I said. 'I'll be getting back to you.'

Maureen appeared again, looked at me standing there, stark naked, towel around my ankles, phone still to my ear.

'Coffee's ready,' she said.

CHAPTER 44

There had been a lot of screaming and yelling before things had quieted down the previous evening. Celeste had been yelling at Dwayne to explain how Cal had come to be tied up in the garage. Dwayne was shouting back that he had no idea. Cal had cried 'Bullshit!' on that. Then Celeste turned her anger on her brother, shouting that he had very likely broken her husband's leg when Cal went at him with the two-by-four.

And then Crystal had started screaming hysterically at no one in particular.

At that point, Cal moved to calm her. He tried to bring the girl into his arms, but she was reluctant at first, standing rigidly, arms tight to her body. He knelt down next to her, spoke softly to her, but not before telling Celeste and Dwayne to go into the house.

'Don't think about hightailing it out of here,' Cal had warned his brother-in-law. 'Because I'll find you, and when I do, I'm gonna be mad.'

Dwayne had said nothing as he retreated from the garage. But as he and his wife headed back toward the house, they could be heard arguing again.

'I'm okay,' Cal had told Crystal. 'I really am. I've got a bump on the head, but otherwise I'm fine.'

'There wouldn't be anybody to look after me till my dad gets here,' she said, 'if you were dead.'

'I'm not dead.' He'd put his hands on her upper arms, squeezed. 'I'm sorry you had to see all that. You've been through enough.'

'I heard the phone.'

Cal smiled. 'You saved me.'

'Celeste phoned you, but I heard it. Dwayne said he didn't hear anything, but I was sure. He was lying.'

'Yes, he was lying.'

'Are you going to kill him?'

Cal had shaken his head. 'I don't think so.'

'But you might.'

He was reminded that Crystal was not good at detecting irony or sarcasm. 'I will definitely not kill him.'

'Because I'm okay with it if you do.'

'Celeste would be very upset with me.' He'd given her shoulders another squeeze. 'You were there for me. I don't know what might have happened if you hadn't found me.'

Crystal had moved into his arms, put hers around him. 'I love you,' she'd said.

Other than Crystal, no one had had any sleep by the time the sun came up.

411

Dwayne had finally come clean on what was going on. His friend Harry at the printing operation – a guy he had, years ago, gone to high school with – was part of a gang that was ripping off electronics stores. They'd stolen from parked trucks and broken into several stores over the last eighteen months and had acquired a lot of product.

Harry said they were starting to worry the police might be onto them, and they needed a few places to hide the merchandise. Harry knew that Dwayne wasn't making much money these days, what with the town canceling many of his paving contracts, so he approached him. 'Hide this stuff for us,' he said, 'and we'll give you a thousand bucks.'

Dwayne wrestled with it for a while. He convinced himself he wasn't really doing anything wrong. He hadn't stolen the goods. He wasn't in on any of that. He hadn't planned it, he hadn't driven the truck, and he hadn't broken into any places. All he was doing now was hanging on to some stuff for a friend. He told himself he didn't really know for sure where it had come from. Harry could have been making up a wild story just to sound more important.

Sure.

So he started hiding stuff for Harry. He'd been doing it for the better part of a month. Celeste wasn't sure whether to be horrified or relieved. At least she knew now that when her husband was gone at odd hours, he wasn't having an affair.

Although, if you got caught sleeping with another woman, you weren't likely to end up in jail.

When Cal guessed correctly that something was going on in the garage, Dwayne panicked. Once he'd knocked him out, he didn't know what else to do but tie him up and hide him in the garage until he figured out his next step.

He was on the phone with Harry, trying to come up with a plan, when Crystal appeared, determined to find Cal.

'What was Harry's plan?' Cal asked.

Dwayne was hesitant. 'We hadn't really come up with anything.'

'Was Harry's plan to kill me?'

Dwayne, who was sitting across the kitchen table from Cal, holding an ice pack to his thigh, couldn't look his brother-in-law in the eye. 'There was no way I'd let that happen. *No way.*'

'But Harry put it out there.'

'And I shut it down.'

'Oh my God,' Celeste said, pacing the kitchen floor. 'How can this be happening? How is it possible? What the hell were you thinking?'

'I know,' Dwayne said sheepishly. 'I fucked up.'

'Fucked up?' Celeste said. 'Is that what you'd call this? A fuckup? A fuckup is when you back the truck into the mailbox. This – I don't even know what to call this – this is a *catastrophe.* How could you have gotten us into this? This is my *brother*! You actually discussed with this asshole the idea of killing my brother!'

'I told you, that never would have happened.'

'What if Harry decided you wouldn't be part of it? He'd just do it anyway?'

Dwayne looked blankly at his wife.

Cal said, 'What if Harry decided you were as much a liability as me?'

That made him blink. 'No. I mean, we go back. Harry and me go way back.'

Cal sighed. Celeste was about to light into her husband again, but her brother raised a calming hand. 'We're going to figure this out.'

'Figure it out?' she said. 'How? By you laying charges against my husband? Because if I was you, that's what I'd be thinking of doing. I'd want to send this son of a bitch to jail – that's what I'd want to do.' But then her face began to crumple. 'But tell me you're not going to do that.'

Cal slowly shook his head. 'I'm not going to do that.' He looked at Dwayne. 'But that doesn't mean you still couldn't end up in prison. You've got a garage filled with stolen merchandise. You need to get rid of it.'

'I can't just do that.'

'Why not?' Celeste asked.

'Are you kidding? Harry and his buddies expect to get it back when they think it's safe. And there's the matter of the money. They've paid me to do a job.'

'How much?' Celeste asked.

'So far, nineteen hundred.'

'So give it back.'

Dwayne lowered his eyes. 'It's already all gone.'

Cal was very quiet. Thinking.

Celeste said, 'What are we going to do, Cal? What the hell are we going to do?'

He said to his brother-in-law, 'Call Harry. Set up a meeting. Tell him we want to do a return.'

CHAPTER 45

Samantha Worthington had taken the call Thursday afternoon while working at the Laundromat. It was someone in the prosecutor's office in Boston, who'd been involved in the trial against Brandon.

'He's on the loose,' the woman said. 'During a hospital visit to see his mother. He got away. Thought you should know.'

The first thing Sam did, after going into the bathroom to throw up, was call the owner of the Laundromat and tell him she was gone. Right then, right now. She was walking out the door and she didn't know when she would be back.

Didn't even lock up. There were three customers in the middle of doing their laundry. Clothes agitating in washers, spinning round in dryers. Sam walked out the back door, got in her car, and headed straight for her son's school.

Classes would have been over in another ten minutes, but Sam felt there was no time to spare. Her ex-husband had escaped the night before. That gave him plenty of time to get to Promise Falls. Granted, he might have a few challenges in that regard. He'd have to find transportation. He'd have to get out of the Boston area without being seen.

But what if he had someone helping him? Ed Noble was in jail, but maybe another one of Brandon's idiotic friends had stepped into the breach. Maybe he was in Promise Falls already. Maybe he was waiting for her at her house.

She parked illegally at the school's main entrance, went to the office, and said she had to pull Carl out now.

The office secretary said, 'The bell will be going in just seven minutes, Ms Worthington, so—'

'Now!'

Carl was dismissed from his class and showed up in the office two minutes later. 'What's going on?' he asked.

'Get in the car,' she said.

By the time they were almost home, she'd told him what she knew. They had to get out of town before his father got there.

'How do we even know he's coming?' Carl asked.

'Are you kidding me?' his mother said. 'After all the shit his parents pulled? What do you think he's going to do? Go to Disneyland?'

But she couldn't shake the fear that he might already be in the house. Carl had an idea.

'Drop me off a block away,' he said. 'I'll sneak up and peek in the windows and see if he's there.'

Sam didn't want to put her son in a risky situation. 'Not a chance.'

'I can *do* it,' he said. 'I've done it before.'

'What?'

'Like, one time – you won't get mad, okay?'

Sam, with some reluctance, said, 'Okay.'

'I found this dead cat on the road. It had been hit by a car, but it hadn't been split open or anything, and me and my friends wanted to have a closer look at it, you know? So we put it in a bag, but then no one else wanted to take it home and they wanted me to do it, so I said okay, but I knew you'd freak out if you saw me come into the house with a bag filled with a dead cat, so before I came in, I peeked in the windows and saw you were in the kitchen, which gave me just enough time to get in the front door and up to my room.'

Sam was speechless.

'Anyway, I had it for like a day in my closet and it was starting to smell, so I put it in the garbage.'

Sam was going to ask Carl just when this had happened, then decided it did not matter.

'Okay,' she said. 'I'll let you out here. I'm going to sit in the car, right here in this spot. You go find out if he's in the house.'

Carl bolted from the car and almost instantly disappeared, ducking between houses half a block from their place.

Four minutes went by. Then six. Sam was starting to worry. The kid wasn't as smart as he thought. Brandon must have been in the house and had spotted him. Grabbed him. Now she had to decide whether to call the police or—

Carl opened the passenger door, jumped in. 'All clear,' he said.

Sam gave him his marching orders. Pack a bag, fast. She'd dig out the camping supplies. She'd find that cheap Styrofoam cooler and dump food from the fridge into it. They'd raid the cupboard for other stuff, then throw everything into the car as quickly as possible.

One of the last things she put into the car was the pump-action shotgun.

You just never knew.

She'd wrapped it up in a blanket, placed it on the floor of the backseat, the barrel propped up on the hump. She'd put three shells in the chamber, pulled the fore-end back to cock the hammer and load a shell, moved the slide back forward. All she'd have to do was pull the trigger.

'Do *not* touch that,' she told Carl.

Just before hitting the road, she went to a bank machine and took out five hundred. Her daily maximum withdrawal, but it wouldn't have mattered if she'd been allowed to take out more. Once she'd made the withdrawal, all that was left was thirty-four bucks.

She headed north to Lake Luzerne. It wouldn't take long to get to Camp Sunrise. Brandon knew she and Carl still went on camping trips, but she was pretty sure he didn't know the name of their favorite campsite.

But when she got there, the place was fully booked. The kid in the booth suggested they try

419

Call of the Loon Acres. There might still be some vacant campsites if they moved fast.

They got the second-to-last spot.

She and Carl pitched the tent, brought in their sleeping bags, set up the Coleman stove on their picnic table. If you were going to hide out, you might as well have some fun doing it. This, at least, was a hideout Sam could afford. She had enough cash to stay here for a week or more. They'd live on the food they'd taken from the house, and when that ran out, they'd hit a local grocery store.

No restaurants, no fast-food joints. Too expensive. Sam didn't know how long they'd have to stay here. She figured the police would be out in force looking for Brandon and would have him back behind bars before too long.

Sam parked her car around the back of the tent. She hadn't wanted to keep the shotgun in the tent with her. Didn't want to take that kind of risk with Carl in there. But she had left it on the backseat of the car, the blanket no longer wrapped around it, but covering it loosely. So, if need be, she could run to the car, open the back door, and have that shotgun in hand in seconds.

She felt bad about David.

Carl had asked her, 'Are you going to call him?'

She wanted to. But hadn't she involved him enough in her problems? David had already rescued Carl from Ed. Did she want him having to rescue them from Brandon? Shouldn't she be able to handle her own shit?

420

The truth was, David was better off without her. Samantha Worthington, she told herself, was bad news.

About as bad as it got.

By the time they'd set themselves up at Call of the Loon – seriously, how did they come up with *that*? – it was something of a moot point. There was almost no cell service there. And Sam was starting to think she was safer with the phone turned off completely. She didn't want anyone triangulating her position. Not that Brandon was likely to have the means to do that, but who knew? Maybe he had a friend somewhere who could do something like that.

Not worth taking the chance.

So now it was Sunday morning. They'd spent three nights sleeping in this tent, and the novelty was wearing off. The first couple of days had been, considering everything, fun. They'd gone on some hikes, seen a deer, if not a loon. The park bordered on the lake, and while it was still too early in the year to swim – the water was freezing – they'd wandered out onto the docks, skipped some stones.

But the night before, as they were bunking down for the night, Carl had said, 'Can we go back tomorrow?'

'I don't know.'

'This has been fun, but I don't want to do it anymore. I want to go back. I want to see my friends. I want to see Ethan. I want to be in school Tuesday. I don't know what I missed on Friday. I'm going to have to catch up. If we're gone for lots of days, I'm going to get way behind and then I won't get into the next grade.'

'I don't know if it's safe to go back. Tell you what. Tomorrow, we'll take a ride someplace where we get cell reception, and I'll make a call. See if the police have found your father.'

'Would it be so bad?' he'd asked.

'Would what be so bad?'

'If he found us?'

She could hardly believe what he was asking.

'Your father – and I'm sorry to say this – is a convicted criminal, Carl. He robbed a bank. He knocked someone out in the hospital. He's a bad, bad person.'

Carl had thought about that. 'I know.'

'And now he's an *escaped* convict. A person like that is pretty desperate. There's no telling what he might do.'

'But doesn't Dad love me?' Carl had asked.

Sam had felt the tears welling up in her eyes. 'Yes, he loves you. For all his faults, he loves you.'

'He never beat me or anything.'

'I know. He never did that.'

'If he was a really bad man, he'd have beat me. And you. Did he ever beat you?'

Sam hadn't wanted to get into the times Brandon had scared the hell out of her. Had he ever actually, deliberately hurt her? There was that time he'd knocked the speaker off the shelf and it had landed on her foot, but he couldn't have known that would happen. But he'd shaken a fist at her

422

more than once. She'd seen him start to take a swing, then stop himself.

She knew he had it in him.

'Go to sleep,' she'd finally said.

They both slept well. Sam looked at her watch, saw that it was nearly nine. Carl was still sleeping soundly. She got dressed, laced up her shoes, then slowly raised the front flap zipper without waking her son. Sam slipped out, stood, did some stretches. Sleeping on the ground was not all it was cracked up to be. The truth was, she wanted to be home as much as Carl did.

She fired up the Coleman, filled a small pot with water from a nearby tap. Some of the other guests had mentioned something about the water in Promise Falls being contaminated. Maybe getting out of town had its benefits.

She put the pot on the stove. She spooned out some instant coffee from a jar of Nescafé into a paper cup. Once the water was boiling, she'd pour it in. It wasn't exactly Starbucks, but it would have to do.

Sam filled the cup, tossed the rest of the boiling water onto the dirt, turned off the flame on the stove. She blew on the coffee, then took a tentative sip.

'Ahh,' she said.

'You always did like your cup of joe in the morning.'

The voice came from behind her. She whirled around so quickly she dropped the coffee onto the ground.

'Hi,' said Brandon. 'It's great to see you, Sam.'

423

CHAPTER 46

Duckworth

I finished up in the bathroom, got dressed, and headed downstairs. Maureen, aware that I was in a hurry to get out of the house, had a breakfast ready for me. Coffee made with bottled water, a bowlful of blueberries and strawberries, and some kind of bran-granola mix that looked like something we'd put out in the bird feeder, with a small container of milk alongside.

'Okay, I'll admit, the berries look delicious,' I said, 'but what is this?'

'I promise it won't kill you.'

'I might want to drink town water after the first mouthful. Did this come out of that bag of stuff you give to the starlings?'

'It's not bad. Trust me,' Maureen said. 'You've said you've felt better. I'm trying to help.'

I sat down, attacked the berries first. They were sweet enough that they didn't need any sugar sprinkled on them. But I did it anyway. I poured the milk over the cereal, got some on my spoon, and put it in my mouth.

'Mmm,' I said. I couldn't think of a discreet way to spit it out. I washed it down with some coffee.

I hadn't been able to stop thinking about Joyce Pilgrim's call. I'd already been planning to visit Victor Rooney today. I'd wanted to ask him about his feelings of antipathy toward Promise Falls. Someone had it in for the town, and Victor had as good a reason as anyone else I could think of.

The people of Promise Falls had failed Olivia, and by extension, they had failed him.

I'd learned from Olivia's father that Victor knew his way around machinery. He had the smarts to start up a mothballed Ferris wheel. He could probably figure out how to make up some basic explosives powerful enough to bring down a drive-in movie screen. He had even worked at the water treatment plant one summer in his teens. He could have known Mason Helt – this was something I'd want to check – and persuaded him to scare female Thackeray students in a '23' hoodie.

And it didn't take a genius to trap twenty-three squirrels and string them up on a fence, or get a bus out of the town compound and set it on fire.

But now that I knew he'd been in the vicinity of Lorraine Plummer's building at the time of her death, my mind was exploring all kinds of possibilities.

Rooney'd had an alibi for the time of Olivia's death. But was it conceivable he killed Rosemary Gaynor and Lorraine Plummer in a similar fashion as a way of making Promise Falls pay for its sins?

My mind circled back to the 'twenty-three' business. I could imagine Victor wanting to take action against the twenty-two people who did nothing when they heard Olivia's screams. But would he really include his own inaction, bringing the number of those who'd failed to be responsible citizens up to twenty-three? Did that make any sense? Was I reaching?

I was so busy thinking it through that I got to the bottom of the cereal bowl without realizing what I was eating.

'I'll have to make you that again,' Maureen said.

I finished off the berries and downed half my coffee. 'I'm off.'

I slipped on my sport jacket and was out the door. Just as I was slipping the key into the ignition, a car stopped at the end of the driveway, blocking my path. A Lincoln.

I got out. Finley got out of the Lincoln and met me halfway up the driveway.

'Randy,' I said.

He didn't look much better to me than he had the day before at his house. 'Barry,' he said. 'You got a second?'

I wanted to say no, but what came out of my mouth was, 'Sure.'

'I did put the squeeze on your son,' he said. 'You already know this, but I'm telling you, you got it right. Whatever Trevor told you, it's true. About his ex-girlfriend, and the thing that happened between them. I used that against him to get him

426

to tell me stuff he heard you talking about. How Finderman didn't do her job right.'

I didn't say anything.

'That's me. That's how I operate. I did it.' He paused. 'I've come to apologize.'

'Okay.'

'I'm not going to ask whether you accept it or not. If I was you, I probably wouldn't. But I'm telling you I'm sorry, just the same.'

'I hear you,' I said.

'That's not all,' Randy said. 'I want to help.'

'You've been doing that,' I reminded him. 'Yesterday, when you were handing out water.'

'Oh, that,' he said. 'That was for publicity. I mean, don't get me wrong. I was happy to help people. But I wanted to stick it to Amanda Croydon, and I did a pretty good job.' He managed a smile for about two seconds. 'But it doesn't matter anymore.'

'Why's that?'

'I'm going to withdraw. I'm not going to run for mayor.'

The last thing I wanted to do was discourage him from dropping out. I didn't want him in charge of Promise Falls again. But I wondered if he was packing it in for the right reason.

'Because of Jane?' I asked.

He nodded. 'I wanted to prove something to her. I can't now.'

'I guess you know what the right thing to do is.'

'But like I said, I want to help. I want to help

you find out who poisoned this town. I want to help find out who killed all these people.'

Was I being conned? Was this a performance? Was Randy really pulling out, or was this an even more brilliant publicity stunt than handing out the water? I could imagine him going before the cameras to withdraw, to declare that helping the police was more important than his political future.

'If I need your help, I'll be in touch,' I said. I started to turn to get back into my car, but Randy grabbed my arm.

'Don't you get it?' he asked. 'You think I'm playing you, don't you? That this is some new stunt I've dreamed up. Barry, this son of a bitch, whoever did this, he killed my wife.'

He wouldn't let go of my arm. 'He killed Jane. He killed my Jane.'

Gently, I freed myself from his grasp. 'I know.'

'I'll be looking for you,' he said. 'Anytime I see you around town, I'm going to be bugging you, seeing if I can help. I'm going to be a huge pain in the ass.'

It was impossible not to smile. 'Randy, you've always been that.'

Even he smiled. 'You're a straight shooter, Barry. Always have been. When I said you'd make a good chief, it was for real. You know how they say even a busted clock gives you the right time twice a day? Well, even when you're a nonstop bullshit artist, occasionally the truth slips out by accident.'

CHAPTER 47

David Harwood made a couple of wrong turns, but eventually found his way to Call of the Loon Acres. There was no formal gate similar to the one at the previous campsite, but there was a sign directing guests to a parking lot. It read: ONE VEHICLE PER SIGHT, ALL OTHERS HERE. PLEASE LIMIT YOU'RE DRIVING THREW THE PARK.

He pulled into the graveled lot and parked among a dozen other vehicles. He did not see Sam's among them, and figured if she was staying here, she was parked by her tent. Once out of the car, he marveled at how quiet it was. The odd chirping of birds, muffled voices of some early risers drifting out from the woods.

The smell of smoke and bacon.

He and Sam had talked about taking their boys, together, on such a trip, and it had sounded like such a good idea. But being here now neither relaxed David nor gave him an appreciation of the great outdoors.

He was wired. He'd had no coffee but felt as though he'd overdosed on caffeine. Aside from those troubles a few years ago involving his late

429

wife, and his recent entanglement in his cousin Marla's tragedy, David had little experience with dangerous people. Okay, years ago, there was that hired killer, but that hadn't exactly ended well.

But he'd never come up against an escaped convict before. And he was hoping he wouldn't now.

His only goal at the moment was to find Sam, and be reassured she was okay. He hadn't thought about what the next step might be.

Would he stay with her, either at the campsite or back in Promise Falls, until Brandon Worthington had been caught and returned to prison? Be her protector? Her bodyguard? And was he kidding himself that he could play that role? Did he think he was Liam Neeson or something?

He would be happy to put her and Carl up at his house, where they might feel less vulnerable. It'd be crowded, what with his parents there, but their own home was supposed to be ready for them to move back into any day now.

He also knew Sam might tell him to mind his own business. He could hear her saying, 'I can look after myself, thank you very much.' After all, she'd left without telling him where she was going.

Next to the sign for the parking lot, there was a map of Call of the Loon Acres, which showed a tangle of roads, the location of the bathrooms, the lake, a store where you could buy ice and other provisions.

David started walking.

He trekked up a road that was little more than two ruts with a strip of grass in the center. About every fifty feet on either side, nestled back in between the trees, he saw a tent or a trailer, plus a car.

David didn't know the shape or color of Sam's tent, so he was looking for her car.

It turned out he didn't need to know that either.

He saw Sam. And a man he'd never seen before, but was pretty sure he recognized from the Boston TV news report he'd found online.

He heard voices first, about fifty yards up the road. That was when he stopped.

The man was standing just off the road, about thirty feet from a picnic table where a woman was working at a camp stove. They were having a conversation.

Brandon had found her.

David underwent a brief paralysis, a weakness in the knees. How should he respond? Stride right up? Find the camp office and get someone to call the police? But if he did the latter, and Brandon did something in the meantime – like attacking Sam, or making a grab for Carl – David wouldn't be there to help.

Shit, shit, shit.

He needed to get closer, hear what was going on without Brandon knowing he was there.

David ducked left, off the road and into the woods. He was three or four campsites away from where Sam had pitched her tent. He tiptoed past someone else's tent trailer and went into thicker forest, twigs snapping and leaves rustling under his feet. Using the trees as cover, he worked his way as quietly as he could until he was behind Sam's tent. Parked behind it was her car.

He crouched as he emerged from the woods, blocked by not only the tent but by the car, too. He could see neither Sam nor Brandon, but he could still hear them talking. He wasn't able to make out anything they were saying.

He poked his head above the sill of the back window of Sam's car, but all he could see was the tent.

Something in the backseat caught his eye. Something extending out from under a blanket.

Four inches of a shotgun barrel.

The same shotgun Sam had pointed at him the first time he had knocked on her door.

David reached up for the door handle, lifted, and pulled, testing to see whether it was locked. It wasn't.

Slowly, he opened the door, worried that it would creak or squeak. He needed to get it open only a few inches. He got it as far as he needed to without making any noise. He slid the blanket off the shotgun, took hold of the barrel near the end, and slowly pulled it toward him.

He realized he had the barrel pointing straight at his chest, so he shifted a few inches to the left so that he wouldn't kill himself if the damn thing went off.

He didn't even know if it was loaded. But then, maybe it wouldn't have to be.

Just having it would be enough to defuse the situation, if it came to that.

He got the weapon all the way out, held it in his arms, got a sense of its heft.

David didn't know a lot about guns. But didn't you have to – what did they call it – rack it? To put a shell in the chamber, if there were any shells in it to begin with?

But he didn't see anything to rack. There was something under the barrel that looked like you had to slide it back and forth.

He decided not to touch it. Just waving the gun around would be threatening enough, wouldn't it?

Sweat was beaded on his forehead, running into his eyes and stinging. His heart was pounding. It was a drum beating in his ears.

Take a breath, take a breath, take a breath.

He could do this. He could save Sam.

All he had to do now was get into a position where he could see what was going on.

CHAPTER 48

The meeting was set up on a lightly traveled road that ran behind the Five Mountains theme park.

Cal had picked the spot because he could see the better part of a mile in each direction. If Harry was followed to the location, they'd know.

He was in the passenger seat of Dwayne's pickup, Dwayne behind the wheel. His leg was swollen where Cal had hit it, but the bone wasn't broken and he was able to drive.

'I really appreciate this,' Dwayne said. 'Considering.'

Cal's eyes kept moving from the road ahead to the oversized mirror bolted to the passenger door. He was looking for the rusted blue Aerostar van he'd seen Harry driving the day before.

'Like I was saying,' Dwayne said, 'I'm really grateful that—'

'Yeah, I got it,' Cal said. 'I'm not doing this for you. I'm doing it for Celeste.'

'I know,' he said quietly. 'I don't think Harry is going to like this.'

Cal, looking in the mirror, said, 'This might be him.'

Dwayne glanced in his own mirror. 'Yeah, I think – he's pulling over onto the shoulder.'

'Let's do this,' Cal said, and opened his door. They were both out of the truck, standing by the back bumper, as Harry's van rolled up on the gravel. The van stopped five feet behind Dwayne's truck.

Harry got out, looked at Cal.

'I know you.'

Cal nodded. 'Don't worry about those business cards.'

'Jesus,' he said nervously. 'Are you a cop?'

Cal shook his head slowly.

'What's going on?' Harry asked Dwayne. 'Is this the guy? The one snooping around your place?'

Dwayne said, 'Yeah. Look, Harry, I'm really sorry, but the thing is, I really can't be—'

Cal cut in. 'He's not going to hold on to your shit any longer.' He patted the vinyl cover over the pickup bed. 'It's all here. You're taking it back.'

Harry said, 'No fucking way. They might be watching me.'

Cal looked up and down the road. 'Doesn't look like it to me. Open up your van. We'll get this stuff moved over.'

Harry raised his hands. 'Whoa, whoa. Hold on.' He pointed at Dwayne. 'We had a deal. I paid you for a service.'

Cal reached into his pocket, pulled out an envelope, and slapped it into Harry's hand. 'That should cover everything you paid him, plus some interest.'

Harry peered into the envelope. 'I don't know about this.'

Cal said to Dwayne, 'Open the tailgate. The two of you move the stuff. I'll keep an eye out.'

Harry threw the envelope back at Cal. It bounced off his chest and landed on the gravel. No one moved to pick it up.

'No fucking way,' Harry said.

Cal moved his tongue around inside his mouth, poking out one cheek and then the other. 'Can I have a word with you privately, Harry?'

'Huh?'

'Just for a second.'

Without waiting for Harry to decide, Cal stepped forward, put a friendly hand on the man's shoulder, and led him down the side of the van, out of sight of any passing traffic. Out of the corner of his eye he saw Dwayne pick up the envelope. In the distance, beyond a fence, stood a motionless Ferris wheel and roller coaster.

'Him and me had a deal,' Harry said.

'I understand that,' Cal said. 'I'm gonna be honest with you. Dwayne there, he's my brother-in-law.'

'Yeah, he mentioned.'

'He's married to my sister. I love my sister very much. And while Dwayne is a bit of a dickhead, basically he's an okay guy, and he's been pretty good to my sister all these years, so I'd hate to see things go south for them.'

'I'm helping him. I did him a *favor*.'

'I'm sure you see it that way, and no doubt about it, these have been tough times for him. But he's going to have to find a way out of his financial problems without you.'

'Look, I don't give a fuck,' Harry persisted. 'And I got people to answer to, you know?'

'You're going to have to work it out with them.'

'I don't know about that.'

'What do you know about *me*, Harry?'

'Huh? I don't know anything about you.'

'Let me tell you. I used to be a cop.' Harry's eyes went wide. 'Right here in Promise Falls. But I'm not anymore. You know why?' Harry shook his head. 'I lost it one day. I smashed the head of a hit-and-run driver into the hood of his car. So they cut me loose. A few years went by, I tried to get my life back on track, but that didn't go so well. Had a wife and a son, but they're both gone now.'

'What's any of that got to do with—'

Cal held up a finger to let him know he wasn't done.

'I don't know who you're working with. You're not ripping this stuff off on your own. I know that much. You need two, three guys, at least. I don't know if you're a bunch of amateurs, or whether you're actually good at this stuff. I don't know whether you're working with bikers or drug dealers or what, but I don't care. This is what I do know. I know where you live. I know where you work. I know your wife's name is Francine. That you've

437

got two kids. Boy and a girl, both teenagers. And I can find out more if I need to. I'm telling you that you are going to take back this shit Dwayne's been holding for you, that you're going to take back the money, that you are never going to talk to Dwayne again, that if you see him on the street, you're going to cross to the other side, that if anything ever happens to him or my sister, if one of you even mentions him to the cops if you ever get caught, I am going to find you and I am going to put a bullet in your head, because I don't give a fuck about anything anymore except making sure my sister and her husband are safe.'

Harry blinked.

'Do you understand what I'm saying?'

Harry nodded.

'That's good. So can you now help Dwayne move that stuff from his truck to yours?'

'I can do that,' he said.

When it was done, and Dwayne and Cal were driving back to the house, Dwayne said, 'I'll find a way to pay you back the money.'

'Shut up, Dwayne,' Cal said.

CHAPTER 49

Duckworth

Victor Rooney was sitting on the front step, shirtless and barefoot but wearing a pair of jeans, when I pulled up in front of the house. I parked at the curb, got out.

'Mr Rooney,' I said.

He was eating a piece of buttered toast, and made no attempt to get up.

'Yeah,' he said.

'How are you today?'

'Oh, I'm just peachy,' he said. 'Got the whole house to myself as it turns out.'

'I heard. Your landlady, Ms Townsend, was one of the casualties.'

He took a bite of toast. 'Found her yesterday morning in the backyard. Dead as a doornail.'

'I'm sorry,' I said. 'That must have been quite a shock.'

Victor nodded. 'Not the sort of thing you see every day.'

'You didn't see her getting sick?'

'I'd slept in. By the time I came downstairs,

439

she was already toast.' He glanced at what was in his hand. 'Maybe that's not the best choice of words.'

'So she'd had water from the tap, but not you.'

His head went from side to side. 'Yeah, I mean, no. I mean, she'd had coffee, and I hadn't had anything. I mean, other than some juice from the fridge. But it was okay.'

'Lucky,' I said.

'I guess. Mr Fisher was lucky, too. I mean, he got pretty sick, but at least he didn't die.'

'Yeah,' I said. 'There might be long-term effects. They don't know yet.'

'Huh,' he said. 'So, Walden, he might end up brain-damaged or something.'

'Let's hope not.'

'I don't know exactly what happens now,' he said, glancing back at the house. 'I mean, she owned the place, but who gets it now? She's probably got next of kin or whatever you call it, but that's not my responsibility, is it?'

I shrugged. It wasn't, technically. 'You might want to look through her address book, something like that. If she had out-of-town family, they may hear about what happened here and make inquiries. That'll get the ball rolling. Failing that, the police will get to it eventually. They're a little backed up right now.'

He nodded, took another bite of toast.

'I think I might just move, anyway,' he said. 'I think I'm done here.'

440

'Why's that?'

He looked at me as though I was slow-witted, and there were times when I thought I was. 'You gotta be kidding me.'

'I can understand why you might want to put this town behind you,' I said, 'but I'd have thought you'd have done it three years ago.'

'Sometimes it takes a while to get your act together.' He finished the toast, wiped his mouth with a paper napkin, balled it up, and tossed it onto the porch. He leaned back, arms outstretched, palms on the porch boards. 'You just come by to shoot the shit?'

'I heard from Joyce Pilgrim,' I said.

His face screwed up. 'Who?'

'The security chief at Thackeray.'

'Oh yeah, sure.' He nodded. 'I talked to her last night. Why'd she call you?'

'Why?' I'd have thought it was obvious.

'Yeah. I mean, what's the big deal if some guy parked illegally or something?'

'So she didn't say why she was asking.'

He shook his head.

'Can you tell me again what you told her? About the car and the man you saw?'

He repeated what Joyce had said to me on the phone. The man he'd seen was white, over six feet tall, maybe two hundred pounds, tops. He was wearing a Yankees baseball cap, a dark blue jacket or Windbreaker, and running shoes.

'Was the car parked under a streetlight?'

'I don't think so.'

'And the car itself?'

'I think it might have been a Taurus. An older one, with the big bulbous fenders.'

'Color?'

He shrugged. 'Black, blue? Don't know.'

'Ms Pilgrim said you thought the plate was green.'

'I'm not as sure about that, but maybe,' he said. 'That'd make it Vermont, right?'

'Could,' I said.

'Why the big deal about this?'

I pressed on. 'You have pretty good observational skills.'

'I don't know. I guess.'

'I mean, late at night, that car not being under a streetlight, and you managed to get a pretty good look at that guy, right down to the ball cap.'

'You make it sound like a bad thing.'

'Not at all. What you saw could be really helpful.'

'Helpful for *what*?'

The murder of Lorraine Plummer had probably made the news, but it had been overshadowed by the deaths from poisoned water. It was possible Victor didn't know about her death. Or was pretending to be uninformed.

'Around the time you were jogging through the campus grounds,' I said evenly, 'a young woman was murdered. A summer student.'

I watched his reaction closely.

'Jesus,' he said. 'That woman – Pilgrim? – she

never said anything about that. So then, this guy she was asking about, he could have been the guy who killed her?'

I waited a second. 'Possibly.'

'Wow. I didn't know that. Wish I'd taken an even closer look.'

'Don't feel bad about that. You saw and remembered more than most people would. Quite a bit more.'

Victor's eyes narrowed. 'There it is again.'

'What?'

'That sounds more like an accusation than praise. I'm trying to help out and you're making me feel like I did something wrong.'

'Sorry if that's how I came across,' I said. 'Do you jog around there every night?'

'I kind of went back to running just recently, in the last week or so. I thought it'd be a way to get myself back together.'

'You mean back in shape?'

'Partly, but mentally, too, you know.'

'I guess,' I said. 'I'm not much of a health nut.'

'No kidding,' he said.

'So tell me about the mentally part.'

'I've kind of – I don't know – let myself go. Been hitting the drinking too hard. Haven't been able to find a job. It's taken me a long time to get over things.'

'Olivia.'

'Yeah. But you can only go on like that so long. You have to move on, you know?'

'And taking up running was part of that?'

'Yeah. I thought, if I felt better physically, maybe I'd start feeling better mentally.'

'How's it going?'

He grinned. 'It may be too early to tell.'

'Part of that plan includes moving away?'

'Maybe.'

'And maybe this is just when the town needs you,' I said. 'After what happened yesterday.'

'I don't know about that.'

'Maybe the town had it coming,' I said.

Victor Rooney studied me. 'Say again?'

'I said maybe the town had it coming. For how it failed Olivia.'

'I'm not following.'

'Have you ever felt that way? That those twenty-two people who heard Olivia's screams and did nothing, that they were representative of the entire town? That they were a kind of a cross section? That if they'd do nothing, nobody here would?'

'Twenty-two?' he asked. 'Was that how many people it was?'

'I think you already know that. Don't you think sometimes there're actually twenty-three people to blame?'

He stood. 'I got stuff to do.'

'Don't you blame yourself, too? For not meeting Olivia when you were supposed to?'

Victor stepped up onto the porch, grabbed a T-shirt that had been tossed onto a wicker chair. He slipped it on, and as his head popped out the top, he said, 'I don't know where you're going with this.'

'If you blame yourself and the whole town, you didn't end up paying quite as high a price for your failure as more than a hundred others did.'

There was a pair of low-rise sneakers under the chair. He slipped his feet into them, not bothering to do the laces.

'You know any place in this town where I can get an actual cup of coffee?' he asked. 'If I have to, I'll drive to fucking Albany.'

'Why do you think someone would do it?' I asked. 'Why would someone poison the water?'

'Who says *someone* even did it?' Victor said. 'Maybe there was some kind of contamination. Sewage, nuclear waste. Something like that.'

'You know a little bit about it, don't you?' I asked.

'Huh?'

'You worked there one summer. At the water treatment plant.'

'That was a long time ago. Just for a couple of months.'

'Long enough to know how the place runs, though.'

'Are you accusing me of something?'

'What'd you take in school, Victor? Engineering? Chemistry? Wasn't that it? That's pretty helpful stuff to know. You'd have thought you could find a job with that kind of background. But you ended up at the fire department for a while, right?'

'I didn't get my degree,' he said.

'But even so, you'd have learned a few things. Like, how to start up a Ferris wheel, say. Get a bus from the town compound going.'

'Bus?' he said. 'You talking about that bus that was on fire?'

I kept on. 'Or how to acquire sodium azide. A pretty large quantity.'

'I don't know what the fuck you're talking about.' He dug into his pocket for some keys. 'I'm going out.'

He came down the steps and started walking toward the garage. I followed.

'If we review more security footage from Thackeray,' I said, 'will we find you running through the campus other nights, or just that one?'

'Leave me alone.'

'Because if it was just the once, that's quite a coincidence. That you'd happen to be running there the night that girl got killed.'

'You already know I was there at least twice. That woman found me there last night. I went through there a lot. Christ, is there anything you don't think I've done? You think I've got something to do with the poisoned water, and that bus, and now you think I killed that girl?'

In my mind, jigsaw puzzle pieces floated about. Victor Rooney jogging around Thackeray at the time of Lorraine Plummer's death. Lorraine Plummer, one of the women assaulted by a man wearing a hoodie with '23' on it. Mason Helt,

446

wearing said hoodie, killed while attacking Joyce Pilgrim.

Connections. Degrees of separation.

But all I really knew was that Helt had attacked Pilgrim. I didn't know, for certain, that he'd attacked the others. Was it possible he'd had a partner? Rooney's admission that Thackeray was part of his jogging route had me wondering.

I didn't know that Rooney was linked to the man Clive Duncomb had fatally shot, but it didn't stop me from asking, 'How did you know Mason Helt?'

If the question in any way unnerved him, he hid it well.

'Who?' Rooney said.

'Mason Helt. A Thackeray student.'

'I don't know anyone by that name.'

He turned the handle on the double-wide garage door and swung it upward. Inside was an old, rusted van that had been squeezed in between shelves and assorted piles of junk.

He unlocked the van door, got in, slammed it as I stood there by the back bumper, off to the side. As he turned the ignition, black exhaust belched from the tailpipe. I took a step back, waved the fumes away from my face.

The van backed up until it was fully on the driveway, at which point Victor got out, left the driver's door open and the engine running, and walked back to draw the garage door back down.

But before he did, something on one of the shelves caught my eye.

'Hang on,' I said, raising a hand.

'What?'

'What's that?' I asked, pointing.

The garage was cluttered, so it was possible Victor's puzzlement was genuine.

Already my mind was wondering about the legality of a search. This was not Victor Rooney's garage. It belonged to his landlady, who was deceased. But would a court see the garage, where Victor had parked his van, as his property?

It would be better if I had his permission.

'Do you mind if I go in here?' I asked.

'I guess not,' he said cautiously.

'You're sure?'

'Yeah.'

I wished I had a witness, but there you go.

'What is it?' he asked.

I led him over to a set of metal shelves that were littered with paint cans, winter car brushes, garden supplies, coiled hoses, even a box filled with old long-playing records. The back wall of the garage was a mess of stacked wood scraps. Partial sheets of plywood, posts, some scraps of Styrofoam board used for insulation. But right now, I was focused on the shelves.

One shelf in particular.

'What's that?' I said.

It looked like a wire cage, dimensions similar to those of a loaf of bread. About a foot long, five inches tall and wide. At one end there was a funneled opening. It would be easy enough to stick your hand in – if it was small enough – but when you pulled it out, you'd get caught on the pointed wire ends of the funnel.

I was pretty sure I knew what it was. I wondered whether Victor knew. And if he did know, whether he'd admit it.

He shook his head. 'Emily kept a lot of shit out here.'

'So you don't know what that is?'

Victor shrugged.

'Beats me.'

I said, 'I think it's a trap.'

'A trap?'

I nodded. 'For squirrels.'

'No shit.'

And then something else caught my eye. Something poking out from behind one of the scrap plywood sheets leaning up against the back wall.

CHAPTER 50

'Jesus, Brandon, what the hell are you doing here?' Samantha asked when she turned around and saw her ex-husband.

He smiled. 'I bet you thought I couldn't find you.'

Sam said, 'Are you out of your mind? Breaking out of jail?'

Brandon shook his head. 'I didn't break out. I was on a trip to see my mother in the—'

'I know,' she said. 'Same difference.'

'She had a heart attack,' he said. 'She's in intensive care.'

'Shit, I never sent a card.'

Brandon sighed, took a step toward her.

'Don't come near me,' she said. 'Stay right there. If you get any closer, I'll start screaming. I swear to God.'

He raised his hands defensively and took a step back. 'Okay, okay. Don't have a hissy.'

'A hissy? Really? After what your parents did? And your dumbass friend Ed?' She had reached for the empty pot that was sitting on the Coleman. It wasn't much of a weapon, but it would have to do. The one she really wanted was in the car, behind the tent.

What a smart idea that turned out to be.

'Do you have any idea the shit they pulled?' she asked him, her voice starting to rise.

Brandon glanced left and right. 'You're going to wake up all the other campers.'

'You think I care?'

'Look,' he said, 'I know what they did. I heard all about it. The police came to interview me, in jail. They wanted to know what I'd had to do with it.'

Sam cocked her head to one side, waiting for an answer.

'Nothing,' he told her. 'I had absolutely nothing to do with it. I had no idea what was going on.'

'Bullshit.'

He nodded understandingly. 'I don't blame you for saying that.'

The tent flap opened. Carl stuck his head out, saw his mother first, and said, 'I thought I heard—'

His eyes landed on his father and he said, 'Dad!'

'You stay in there!' Sam said to her son.

'I just wanted to see—'

'Hey, sport,' Brandon said, not moving. 'How's it going?'

'Okay,' Carl said warily. 'You're supposed to be in jail.'

Brandon grinned. 'Yeah, I know. I'm sort of playing hooky.'

That made Carl laugh. But the laughter was cut

short when his mother said, 'I told you to get in there and you pull that zipper down.'

'Okay, okay,' he said, drawing his head back in like a frightened turtle.

'Wait,' Brandon said. 'There's something I want to say, and I want Carl to hear it, too.'

All that was sticking out beyond the edge of the tent now was Carl's nose, but his face remained visible.

'He can hear anything you have to stay with the tent zipped up,' Sam said.

Brandon looked at his ex-wife imploringly. 'Please. Five minutes. It's all I ask.'

Sam was weighing the request. Her eyes moved between Brandon and Carl. She was afraid for herself, and afraid for him, but Carl did not show any signs of fear. He looked like he wanted to hear what his father had to say.

'Five minutes,' Sam said.

Brandon nodded slowly, took a breath, as though getting ready to make a speech. 'So, you need to know why I came here, why I tracked you down. I didn't know I was going to get a chance like this. That kinda just happened. When they let me out to visit my mom—'

'I hope she dies,' Sam said.

Brandon wasn't flustered. 'I get that. Anyway, when they let me visit her in the hospital, I had a chance to get away, and I took it. Because I wanted to see you, and Carl. To talk to you. I mean, I figured any letters I wrote, you'd just throw them out. Anything I wanted to tell you, you'd never know. I figured it would be better if I could talk to you face-to-face.'

'You nearly killed that guy in the hospital.'

'No, I didn't. I just choked him enough to make him pass out, is all. He's fine.'

'Four minutes,' Sam said.

'So, once I slipped away, and, well, you know, stole a car, I started heading this way. Because I wanted to say I'm sorry.'

The word hung there for a few seconds.

'Sorry,' Sam repeated.

He nodded. 'That sounds kinda short of the mark, I know. I don't quite know what else to say. My mom, I know she's crazy. She's a nasty, vindictive . . . well, she's a piece of work, no doubt about it. That's what she is. And she's mean enough and scary enough that she makes others go along with what she says. It's not that big a surprise that she got Ed to do what she wanted. He's just dumb. He was my friend, I admit it, but he hasn't got the smarts of a beanbag. What's scary is that she gets my dad to go along with so much of her crazy shit.'

He looked down, scraped his foot across the dirt. Carl's entire head was out of the tent now.

'They told me all the stuff they did. Trying to grab Carl at school, then Ed coming to where you work and, well—'

'Trying to kill me,' Sam said.

'Yeah, that. I didn't know, and if I did, I'd have

done everything I could to stop it. And even if you believe me, even if you accept what I'm telling you, I'll understand if you don't forgive me. Not asking for anything like that. Fact is, if you'd never gotten mixed up with me, you'd never have gotten mixed up with my fucked-up family and friends. I'm the cause of all your troubles, when you get right down to it.'

He looked at his son.

'I've been just about the worst father in the world for you, for all the same reasons.' He chuckled weakly. 'You didn't pick so good when it came to dads.'

'You can't really pick your dad,' Carl said.

'He's trying to be funny,' his mother said.

'Oh,' Carl said. 'I get it.'

'I've done a lot of thinking while I've been in jail,' Brandon said. 'Sorting out the mistakes I made while I was still outside. How I expected everything to come to me without working hard for it. I get that now. When I get out—'cause, let's face it, I'll be going back in, and for probably a lot longer – I hope I'm gonna be a different kind of man. Someone who takes responsibility for things. Who doesn't blame others.'

'One minute,' Sam said, folding her arms across her chest.

'Okeydoke,' Brandon said. 'I'm going to leave now. I'm going to find the office and have them call the cops and I'll sit and wait for them to come. I'll never bother either of you again. If you ever want to get in touch' – and here he looked straight at Carl – 'I'll be most grateful to hear from you. I would like that a *lot*, to be honest. If you ever want me in your life, I'll be there, but you gotta be the one that takes the first step. I'm not gonna push it.'

Brandon took a long breath.

'I'm sorry. I truly am. I did what I set out to do. Now I can go back to Boston.' He grinned. 'I'm sure there're plenty of cops happy to give me a lift.'

He bowed his head, turned, and started to walk away.

'Wait!' Carl shouted, and Brandon spun around.

Carl shot out of the tent, arms outstretched. His intention was clear. He wanted to give his father a hug good-bye. But in his rush to come out, his foot caught on a stretch of upturned canvas that ran across the bottom of the open tent flap.

He went flying. His arms went out to break his fall. He hit the ground hard and yelped in pain.

Brandon, instinctively, suddenly charged toward his son.

Sam, still standing there, wielding the pot by its handle, also started running toward Carl.

David brought the shotgun up to his shoulder and aimed.

CHAPTER 51

'You didn't sleep at all, did you?' Gale asked her husband in the morning.

Angus Carlson was sitting on the edge of the bed, elbows on his knees, head in his hands.

'No,' he said.

'You're going to be okay,' she said. 'They're going to decide you did the right thing.'

'Probably,' he said, getting up and walking naked into the bathroom. 'But it could still go all to shit. A cop does a righteous shoot – then they turn the facts all around later.'

'We should do something today,' she said, propping herself up in bed, rearranging the pillow at her back. 'Something fun. We should just get in the car and get out of this town. Try to forget everything that's happened.'

She could hear a familiar trickle. Once she had heard the flush, she continued. 'I know it's hard to do, but we need to try to put all these things out of our heads, even if it's just for a few hours.'

'I don't know,' he said from the other room.

'Why don't we . . . I've got it. Why don't we drive to Montreal? It's not that far. I could throw

456

some things into a bag, have us ready to go in an hour. We could be there by the afternoon. I could find us a hotel online. I'm already off today and tomorrow, and I could call in sick Tuesday and Wednesday, or maybe they'll just give me the time off anyway. What do you say?'

Nothing from Angus.

'Or do you have to be available?' she asked. 'Like, even if you're on leave, do you have to go in and answer questions about what happened? Haven't they kind of got enough to deal with right now? In fact, I can't believe they're making you take a leave of absence when there's so much going on.'

She could hear the sound of teeth being brushed.

'Are you listening to anything I'm saying?' Gale asked.

Angus Carlson reappeared. He walked naked across the room, opened a dresser drawer, grabbed a pair of boxers, and stepped into them.

'I've been thinking about what you said,' Angus said.

'About going to Montreal?'

'No. What you said last night.'

She looked blank. 'Which thing? What?'

'About when you went to the bookstore,' Angus said. 'To Naman's.'

'Yes?'

'The book about poison that you saw there.'

Gale threw back the covers, crawled forward, and perched herself on the bed in a kneeling position. She was excited. 'Yes? You think it means something?'

He was buttoning up a shirt. 'I don't know if it does or not. But I'm not sure it's the kind of thing that can be ignored. I mean, it might really be nothing. But if it turns out Naman did have something to do with all this, we'll be kicking ourselves later if we didn't bother to check it out.'

'Oh my God, you really think he could be behind it?'

Angus pulled on a pair of jeans. 'There're all kinds of these things happening. These lone-wolf, rogue terrorists who get inspired by jihadists overseas. They're not linked to any actual terror group. They're acting totally on their own. He could be one of those.'

He sat down on the edge of the bed, close to his wife. 'What if this Naman guy blew up the drive-in? Maybe that was just a warm-up for what happened yesterday.'

'That's terrifying,' Gale said, 'that there could be someone like that, just living among us. It could be someone you know, someone you live right next door to, and it turns out they're some kind of monster.'

'I know,' Angus said. 'That's what always happens, when they finally arrest some killer or terrorist. Turns out, he was a member of the chamber of commerce or he was a Scout leader or he played on the local hockey team. These kind of people, Gale, are like you say. They're among us.'

458

'So what are you going to do? About Naman? Are you going to tell Detective Duckworth what I saw?'

Angus thought about that. 'I don't think so.'

'Why not?'

'I don't know how it would look.'

'What do you mean?'

'Like, I get put on leave, and then call in with a tip. Like I'm trying to impress them, wheedle my way back in. I'm not going to do that.'

'But if Naman actually had something to do with this—'

'I'll do it myself,' Angus said.

'Go on,' Gale said slowly.

'I'll go over there and talk to him. Not as a cop, but just someone dropping by, seeing how he's managing after the place got firebombed.'

'Can you do that?' she asked.

'Why not?'

'And then,' Gale said, 'if you do find something, if you really do believe he might have had something to do with it, *then* you'll go to Duckworth?'

'Exactly,' he said.

Gale threw her arms around him. 'I'm so proud of you.'

'It's no big deal,' Angus said.

'No, it is, it really is. I love it when I see you excited about something like this. Because sometimes . . .'

'Sometimes what?'

'Nothing,' she said.

'No, sometimes what?'

'All I was going to say is that sometimes, you know, you get in this very dark place. And I get that. We all have moments when we get down. But I worry about you when you're like that, when you start obsessing—'

'Obsessing?'

'That was the wrong word.'

'No, no, it's the right word. I know that's how I can be when it comes to my mom.'

'I really see you moving forward,' Gale said. 'Like, right now, you're in a different place altogether.'

'I am,' he said.

Angus leaned in close to his wife, kissed her lips. She slipped her arms around his neck and pulled him into her. They tumbled over onto the bed.

'I love you,' she said.

'I have to go,' Angus said. 'I have to do this thing.' He untangled himself from her. 'But later, when I get back home, we'll talk about Montreal.'

'Really?'

'Sure. You're right. We need to get away. I'm starting to wonder why anyone lives here at all.'

CHAPTER 52

Duckworth

'What's this?' I asked Victor Rooney, pointing to the back wall of the garage. 'What?' he said, the engine still running and the door to his van still open. He was standing with me, just inside the garage, where we had been looking at the squirrel traps on the shelves that lined one wall.

I was pointing to something wrapped in dark plastic sheeting sticking out from behind a sheet of plywood that was leaned up against the wall. There was about two feet of it showing, whatever it was, and it was shaped roughly like a rolled carpet. But at the end there was something sticking up.

Like feet, I thought.

I became very aware of the gun at my side, that at any moment I might be reaching for it.

'I don't know what that is,' Victor said. 'She kept all kinds of stuff out here.'

'You want to move that piece of plywood for me?' I asked. 'I want to get a better look at it.'

461

I'd have attempted to move it myself, but I wanted my hands free.

'Why should I do that?' he asked.

'I just thought you'd want to help.'

'I've got things to do,' he said. 'You should get out of the garage. I want to close the door.'

'You asked me in, remember?' I said. 'Just give me another second. Do you mind?' I pointed to the plywood.

Hesitantly, he walked over to the sheet, put a hand on each side, and lifted it out of the way.

That rolled carpet was about six feet long. But it got broader in the middle, and there was something round at one end.

What we had here was a mummy.

'Jesus,' Victor said. 'That looks like a person.'

Indeed it did. But who? Who was missing? My mind raced back through the last few days.

A kid. Not a kid, really. A young man. George something. George Lydecker. Angus Carlson had been working on it. A recent grad from Thackeray. Could that be who was wrapped up tight here?

I turned and faced Victor, felt my heart starting to pick up speed. 'Mr Rooney, I need you to lie flat on the floor with your arms behind your back.'

'What?'

'Flat on the floor, hands behind your back. I'm placing you under arrest.'

'I don't have anything to do with this,' he protested. 'This isn't even my garage. I just park my van here. This is total bullshit.'

'Mr Rooney—'

He pointed to the object wrapped in plastic. 'Is that a fucking dead guy? Because if it is, I'm as surprised to see it as you are. I don't ever remember seeing anything like that before. Or any of that other shit.'

He nodded toward the squirrel traps. I glanced back for half a second, and spotted something I had not seen when I'd looked that way earlier.

A hand.

Turned sideways, palm out, it was poking out from behind some paint cans.

'Don't move,' I said to Rooney, and shifted toward the shelves. As I got closer, the hand looked shinier and less lifelike.

It was from a mannequin.

I'd just won the lotto.

I looked back at Rooney. There was panic in his eyes. I'd reached into my pocket for a plastic cuff, just like the one I had used to secure Randall Finley to the door at the water treatment plant.

'This is the last time I'm going to ask nicely,' I said. 'On the floor, hands behind your back.'

He bolted.

He went straight for the van. With the door open and the engine running, it wasn't going to take him long to get away.

I brought out my gun.

'Freeze!' I said, arms outstretched, both hands on the weapon. Victor had very little interest in doing what I asked.

I wasn't going to shoot him. My life was not in jeopardy, and I had a lot of questions for him. I did not want him dead. So as Victor got behind the wheel and threw the van into reverse, I aimed for the tires.

That's the sort of thing they do all the time in the movies, but a tire doesn't present as a large target, especially when you're not standing beside the vehicle. Which was why I didn't hit the front right tire until my third shot, by which time Rooney was halfway down the driveway. The van lurched to one side, but Rooney wasn't slowing down as the wheel rim dug into asphalt. He was going so quickly in reverse the transmission was whining in protest.

I aimed for the other front tire as he reached the sidewalk. Took out a headlight.

I started running.

Once Rooney hit the street and cranked the wheel, the side of the van would present itself to me. I'd have a brief opportunity to take out another tire. With two out, he wouldn't get far. I'd be on the phone in thirty seconds and police all over town would be looking for him.

As it turned out, he didn't get much past the end of the driveway.

The moment the van emerged onto the street, there was a tremendous, teeth-rattling crash.

A fire truck broadsided Rooney's van.

It couldn't have been answering an urgent call, because there'd been no sound of sirens. But the

Promise Falls Fire Department was still making regular rounds of the city, looking for people in trouble, still reminding them it was not yet safe to drink the water.

The truck – it was a pumper, not a ladder truck – hadn't been going all that fast, probably no more than thirty miles per hour, but there's a lot of weight to a truck like that, and it pushed Rooney's van a good forty feet up the street before the driver behind the wheel of the truck had fully applied the brakes.

I had my phone out, ready to call 911, then figured, What the hell?

The fire department was already here. Chances were they were putting in a call for an ambulance.

I hoped so. Because at that moment, I felt a stabbing pain in my chest.

CHAPTER 53

From where David had been sitting in the woods, he could see Sam, and he could see Brandon, but he could not see Carl anywhere. He had a view of the back and the side of the tent. David didn't know whether Carl was still inside it, or had gone off to use the central bathrooms, and he didn't know which would be worse. If Carl was in the tent, it might be tricky for Brandon to try to drag him out. But if Carl had gone to the bathroom, he might end up walking back into the middle of this confrontation at any moment.

He could hear only a little of what they were saying. Brandon was doing most of the talking. But he wasn't always speaking directly to Sam. His eyes were moving from her to the tent and back again.

Carl, David guessed, was in the tent, maybe looking out. Yeah, that was it. Sam turned to look at the tent at one point and spoke sharply. Loud enough that David could hear. She'd told him not to come out.

In Sam's hand was a small cooking pot. The

way she was holding it, David surmised she was intending to use it to hit Brandon when and if she had the chance.

What she needed was what David had in his hands now. He was crouched down, the shotgun raised up to eye level, left hand supporting the barrel, right hand, and finger, poised over the trigger.

He was at least forty feet away. He was squinting down the barrel and had Brandon, more or less, in his sights. But what the hell did he know about shooting a shotgun? If he fired this thing, would the shot go wide and end up hitting Sam? Or tear through the tent and hit Carl?

Even if he did have some experience with a shotgun, was he really going to shoot Brandon if he tried something?

Probably not.

What would he tell the police? It sure wouldn't be self-defense, what with him off hiding in the bushes.

No, he wouldn't fire the shotgun. But that didn't mean he couldn't use it. If Brandon threatened Sam or Carl, he could run out and, with that shotgun in his hands, scare Brandon off.

That seemed like a sound strategy.

So long as Brandon didn't have a gun.

If he did, he hadn't pulled it out. He was standing there in jeans and a shirt. If he had a gun, the only place he could be hiding it was behind his back. That would mean he had it tucked into his belt. David was thinking that'd attract a lot of attention, some guy wandering through the campsite with a butt sticking out of his butt.

So maybe he didn't have a gun.

Jesus, I hope he doesn't.

David did not want to get into a gunfight with this guy. So if by some chance he did have a gun, walking into things waving a shotgun might just be the dumbest thing David could do. It would get Brandon riled up. Once everyone started shooting, there was no telling who'd end up dead.

What he should have done, David now concluded, was find the office and call the police. He'd considered it earlier and decided against it. Now he was sorry.

Now he was here, in the trees, shotgun in hand.

He could abort. He could set the shotgun down, sneak back through the woods the way he'd come, and make the call. It wasn't too late to handle the situation sensibly. If Brandon made a grab for the kid, the police could be there before he got out of the campsite.

Brandon's car – he must have stolen or borrowed one from somebody – had to have been in the parking lot where David had left his own wheels. If he had known which one it was, he could have slashed a tire or two.

He wasn't cut out for this. Any other time he'd been in a tough situation, it hadn't taken him long to come to that conclusion. What was wrong with him that he didn't learn?

David gently set the gun in the grass. He was ready to sneak back to the campsite entrance.

But hold on.

Brandon looked like he was getting ready to walk away. Was that possible? Had he really decided to slip out of that Boston hospital and find his way up here just so he could have a chat?

That didn't seem likely.

David got back into position, picked up the shotgun again. Trained it in the general direction of the tent. Brandon, who had started walking away, suddenly pivoted. He started running flat out toward the small canvas enclosure.

Sam was booting it in the same direction, the metal pot still clutched in her hand. It looked to David as though her intention was to cut Brandon off.

Brandon had to be going for Carl.

David was already certain the boy had been at the door to the tent. It looked pretty clear to David that Brandon was going to grab his son and make a run for it.

What am I going to do?

He brought the shotgun up to his shoulder, eyed down the barrel. Could he take a shot? By the time he was even asking himself that question, Brandon had vanished. He was obscured by the tent. He was probably crawling into it now, going for Carl, hoping to grab an arm or a leg.

David couldn't do anything about what he couldn't see. So he sprang up from his crouching position and ran toward the tent, the shotgun angled across his chest.

'Hey!' he shouted. 'Get away from the kid!'

Sam, just outside the tent door and still visible, stopped and looked in the direction of the voice. When her eyes settled on him, her jaw dropped.

'David?'

'Get back!' he shouted.

Now Brandon's head popped up above the top of the tent. He saw David running toward them brandishing the shotgun.

Brandon quickly grabbed Sam around the waist and dragged her to the ground. The pot fell from her hand. She tried to say something, but all that came out was a scream.

David was almost to the tent. He made a wide approach, moving around the far side of the picnic table. He'd moved the shotgun into a firing position, holding it slightly above waist level.

What happened next happened very quickly.

Brandon grabbed the pot Sam had dropped.

David shouted, 'Hold it!'

Sam screamed, 'Brandon, it's okay, it's—'

Brandon, coming out of a crouch like a runner shooting out of the blocks, pot raised menacingly, yelled at Sam and Carl, 'Get down!'

David felt his finger on the trigger of the shotgun.

Sam cried, 'David, no!'

Carl wailed, 'Dad!'

David fired.

Brandon, already closing the distance between himself and David, spun hard to the right and went down. His right hand went to his neck. Blood came streaming out between his fingers.

'Don't move, don't move, don't move!' David yelled, standing over Brandon.

Carl started to run toward his father, but Sam grabbed the boy and straitjacketed him with her arms.

'No!' Sam said. 'God, no!'

David looked at her and said, 'Are you okay? Did he hurt you?'

'You idiot!' she yelled at him over the cries of her son. 'You stupid fucking idiot!'

'But . . .'

'He was sorry!' she said. 'He came to say he was sorry!'

David, numb, lowered the shotgun. 'What?'

The blood pouring from Brandon's neck soaked into the forest floor and began to puddle by David's shoes.

CHAPTER 54

Arlene Harwood got off the phone and said to her husband, Don, 'Good news.'

They were sitting in the living room of their son David's house. 'Lay it on me,' Don said.

'That was Marla.'

Gill was recovering. At the very least, he was holding his own. He'd ended up staying in the Promise Falls hospital instead of being moved to Albany, where so many other patients had been taken.

Most of Gill's symptoms had receded. He had regained consciousness, although he was some-what disoriented. He was no longer sick to his stomach and his vision did not seem to be seriously impaired.

'He's not out of the woods yet,' Arlene said. 'They still want to do tests to see if there's any kind of permanent damage, but this is such good news.'

Derek Cutter and his family had stepped in to help. They'd been chauffeuring Marla back and forth to the hospital for regular visits. Derek's parents had offered to take Matthew during these

472

periods so Marla could concentrate on her father. Derek had been with her almost nonstop, and his folks had, with Marla's permission, stayed overnight in her father's house, with her, to help out where they could.

'That's all good news,' Don said.

'You don't look happy.'

'I am, I really am. That's all good. You heard anything from David?'

'Nothing since he took off this morning looking for Sam and her boy. What's Ethan doing?'

'Beats me.'

Arlene called out, 'Ethan?'

A shout from upstairs: 'Yeah?'

'Where are you?'

'Upstairs!'

'What are you doing?'

'On my computer!'

'Jesus, could you all stop shouting?' Don said, sitting in his recliner.

Arlene looked at him. 'You've been out of sorts all day.'

'I have not.'

'Oh, please.'

Don picked up an old *People* magazine from the table next to him, leafed through it, put it back down.

'Talk to me,' Arlene said.

Don's lips moved tentatively. 'I'm going to go see him,' he said, finally.

'You're going to see who?'

'Walden.'

'Walden Fisher?'

He nodded. 'Yeah. I'm going to talk to him.'

'Talk to him about what?'

'You know.'

'Don, are you sure that's such a good idea?'

'The other day, when he came over here, and he went with me to the school to get Ethan, and we got a bite to eat?'

'I remember,' Arlene said. 'That was the day I fell.'

'Yeah, well, that was horrible. I felt sick every second I was with him. Couldn't wait to get home. I just felt . . . I just felt so guilty.'

'You shouldn't feel that way.'

He looked at his wife. 'I did nothing.'

'You weren't the only one. There were lots of people who reacted the way you did. Everyone probably thought someone else was going to do something.'

'I should have been the one who thought different,' he said. 'I can still hear it.'

Arlene winced. She knew what he was referring to.

'I can still hear the scream. Olivia, in the park, screaming her last breath.'

'You weren't even that close,' Arlene said. 'There were lots of people who were closer to the park than you were. And suppose you *had* done something. What would it have been? What could you have done, beyond taking out your phone and calling the police? By that time, the poor girl was gone.'

'I know. That's not the point. I know it might not have made a difference. But I didn't know that then. And maybe there were other things I could have done. I could have run in the direction of her scream. Even if I couldn't save her, I might have gotten a look at who did it. But no, I just stood there, assumed someone else would do something, listened for another scream, and when I didn't hear one, I got in my car and I came home.' He paused, studied Arlene, his face questioning. 'What kind of man does that?'

'You're a good man,' she said.

He looked away. 'I want to tell Walden I'm sorry.'

'All that does is open old wounds for him,' Arlene said. 'Are you doing this – this unburdening of yourself – for Walden? Or are you doing it for you? Because if you're doing it for you, then it's selfish. Spare Walden the pain.'

'Walden's been through so much pain he probably doesn't even feel it anymore,' Don said. 'I'd be doing it because it's the right thing to do.'

'Think on it,' Arlene advised. 'It's been three years. Another day thinking about it one way or the other won't make any difference.'

'I hear her in my dreams sometimes,' he said. 'Screaming.'

Arlene shook her head sadly.

He asked her, 'What would you do?'

'Me?'

'If you were me? No, wait. You wouldn't have gotten yourself in the fix I'm in. You'd have done the right thing. You'd have called the police or run to help. But let's say you're me. What would you do today? What would you do now? Wouldn't you feel it was time to offer an apology? Isn't a late apology better than no apology at all?'

She still had nothing to say.

He moved forward in his chair. 'What would you have me tell Ethan?'

'You don't have to tell Ethan anything.'

'If he ever hears this story, I would hope by then that at least there'd be a postscript, where I tried to make it right.'

'You can't make it right,' Arlene said. 'If you rented one of those skywriting planes and wrote out "I'm sorry" over Walden Fisher's house, it wouldn't make anything right. What's done is done. You can't change anything. You want to confess? Become a Catholic. They've got a place where you can do that sort of thing.'

Don stood up out of his chair. 'There's no talking to you,' he said, and wandered off into the kitchen.

CHAPTER 55

Duckworth

'It only lasted a second,' I told the female paramedic.

'Describe it for me again,' she said.

'I was running down the driveway, and when the van got hit, I stopped, and that's when I felt it. But it only hit me for a moment. I'm fine.'

She was wrapping a blood pressure cuff around my arm, then squeezing the bulb. 'I want to check you out.'

'How's the guy in the van?' I asked. 'Rooney?'

'They've taken him to PFG,' she said. 'He wasn't conscious, but he was alive.'

She was tending to me on the front porch of the house where Victor Rooney rented his room. The fire truck and the van it had crashed into were still there, as were three police cars and the second ambulance to the scene. The first had already left with Rooney. No one in the fire truck had been injured.

'Really, I'm okay,' I said. All I could think about was what was in the garage. I'd already put in a

477

call for a crime scene unit. They'd go through the place inch by inch, speck by speck. I'd warned them that they might want to bring along their hazmat suits. They'd probably have been wearing them anyway, but now there was the added possibility of sodium azide traces.

The paramedic wasn't listening to my protests. 'Your blood pressure is okay,' she said, 'but I think you should come in and get checked out.'

'Later,' I said. 'I'll come in later.'

I was more excited about what we were going to find in that garage than I was worried about my health. 'I think it was just muscular,' I told her. 'Go. I absolve you.'

She didn't look very happy with me, but she finally withdrew. By the time she was getting into her ambulance, the crime scene unit had arrived, as well as Wanda Therrieult.

'You okay?' she asked.

'Fine,' I said. 'Never better.'

'What are we looking at?'

I pointed to the garage. 'One body. I think it may be a missing Thackeray student named George Lydecker.'

An unmarked car raced up the street and squealed to a halt out front of the house. Rhonda Finderman got out.

'Chief,' I said.

'Bring me up to speed.'

I gave her the broad strokes.

'This is our guy? This is the guy that poisoned the water?'

'I don't know,' I said. 'It's not nailed down. If they find traces of sodium azide in there, that'll help do it. But there's a lot in that garage that connects to my number-twenty-three theory.'

Finderman said, 'What did you find?'

I told her about the squirrel traps, the mannequin parts. I'd even noticed a can of red paint, which I was betting matched the 'YOU'LL BE SORRY' warning on the Ferris wheel at Five Mountains.

Rooney, I told Finderman, had a motive for harming the people of Promise Falls. The twenty-two people who'd ignored Olivia Fisher's cries.

'You're one short,' Finderman said. 'You're saying all that stuff in the garage links to your Mr Twenty-three.'

'He's the twenty-third,' I said. 'He blamed himself, too.' I felt a little uneasy as I said it, though. Like trying to squeeze that proverbial square peg through a round hole. I wanted things to fit.

Finderman looked skeptical. 'Maybe so. When Rooney wakes up – if he wakes up – let's hope he'll fill us in on a few things. At the very least, he's a major suspect in a series of tragedies in this town.'

'As well as the murder of whoever's in the garage,' I said.

'We need to set up a news conference,' she said.

'I'm not sure,' I said. 'I mean, what we've found here, it looks promising, but there's still a lot of work to do.'

'Barry, the town's completely on edge. We need to give people *something*. We need to let the people know we've made a significant discovery.'

I didn't see any way out of it. Maybe she was right.

'Okay,' I said. 'Let's set it up for this afternoon. We'll know even more then. Like if that's George Lydecker in there.'

Rhonda thought that was fine. But she would put the word out to the media that something was coming.

'What about the others?' the chief asked me. 'Rosemary Gaynor, and this latest one, at Thackeray. Lorraine Plummer?' She was doing better at keeping herself up to speed.

'I honestly don't know,' I said. 'It's very possible all these dots connect, but I don't know how.'

'Okay. I'll let you know when we set a time to face the cameras.' She smiled and rested a hand on my shoulder. 'Nice work, Barry. Really, really nice.'

I got back to the station two hours later. By that time, we'd pretty much confirmed that the deceased was, indeed, George Lydecker. I knew Angus Carlson was on leave, but I put in a call to him anyway, since he'd investigated the student's disappearance.

I got him on his cell.

'Sorry to bother you,' I said.

'It's okay.'

'We found George Lydecker. And very possibly our water poisoner.'

Angus told me Lydecker had a reputation for sneaking into unlocked garages and snooping around, stealing things. That got me wondering whether George had simply found himself in the wrong place at the wrong time. If Victor had discovered him in that garage, and feared George might tell the police what he'd seen – even at the risk of getting himself into trouble for the break-in – Victor might have seen no option but to kill him.

One small tumbler falling into place.

'How you managing?' I asked Angus.

'Okay. I just want them to realize I had a good reason to shoot that guy.'

'I haven't heard anything that suggests anyone feels you didn't. This is just how it is in an officer-involved shooting. Things have to run their course.'

'Got it.'

'What are you doing today?' I asked. 'I mean, look at the bright side. The whole town's going to hell and you got yourself a day off.' When Angus didn't say anything right away, I said, 'Okay, not funny.'

'Might visit my mom,' he said.

'Well, hang in there,' I said.

'Barry?' Angus said quickly before I ended the call.

'Yeah?'

'Why'd he do it? Why'd Victor want to kill the whole town?'

'Not sure,' I said. 'My guess is payback.'

'What do you mean, payback?'

'For Olivia Fisher. The town wasn't there for her.'

'Jesus Christ,' Angus said.

'Yeah, I know.'

When we were done talking, I leaned back in my chair. Rubbed my chest. I was pretty sure it was nothing, what had happened in Victor's driveway. A sharp pain that had lasted only a second. Probably cramped up somehow when I started running. I'd get myself checked out when the dust settled.

If it ever did.

The phone rang. I snatched up the receiver. It was reception.

'There's a Cal Weaver here to see you.'

'Send him in,' I said.

I got up, leaving my sport jacket on the back of my chair, and met him coming down the hall. We shook hands. 'Good to see you're okay,' I said.

'Never had a chance to drink the water yesterday,' he said. 'Had a fire at my place a few nights ago and was staying out of town.'

'What's up?' I asked.

'Got somewhere we can talk?'

I led him into an interrogation room and closed the door. We sat down opposite each other.

'I remember this room,' he said.

'Feeling wistful?'

'I didn't spend much time in here. Never made it to detective.'

'Until you left.'

'Yeah,' he said. He put his palms flat down on the table's cold, metal surface. 'You haven't closed the Miriam Chalmers thing.'

'No,' I said. 'I like Clive Duncomb for it, but he's dead. So we're not exactly in a position to lay charges. Why?'

Cal gave that some thought. 'You know my involvement. I'd been working for Adam Chalmers's daughter after that thing at the drive-in.'

'Yeah,' I said. 'Lucy Brighton.'

'That's right. Lucy.'

'Does she have some information that might help us?'

'She's dead,' Cal said. 'Yesterday. The water.'

'Shit,' I said. 'I haven't seen a complete list of casualties yet.'

'Her daughter phoned me after she found her mother on the floor of the kitchen. Crystal. She's eleven. She's been through a lot.'

I shook my head. 'I still don't know why you're here.'

He ran his hand across the surface of the table. 'Like I said, I wondered if you had enough on Duncomb to satisfy you he was the one. He was bad news. He was a bad cop before he became a bad security chief.'

'Yeah,' I said. 'No argument there.'

'It's not going to hurt his reputation any if he gets saddled with Miriam's murder.'

I leaned in. 'What's going on?'

'I just wanted to know if the investigation was more or less at an end.'

'Not if there's someone else out there who needs to be brought to justice,' I said.

'There isn't,' Cal said. 'If Duncomb's a good fit for this, that's fine. I wouldn't want to do anything that messes that up.'

'Cal.'

He smiled. 'They talk a lot about victims of crime, and with good reason. The family members who have to deal with the loss of a loved one. They give victim impact statements at sentencing hearings. They get to tell the judge how their lives have changed. But there are other victims of crime, ones you don't hear about so much. The relatives of perpetrators. Their lives get turned upside down, too. They're not responsible for what happened, but they get blamed. They get shunned. They have to live with the shame of what someone with their blood did. They have to move away, start over again. Even though they go through a tremendous amount of pain, no one much gives a shit about them.'

I waited.

'Sometimes,' Cal said, 'in a perfect world, under

the right circumstances, it would be better if they never knew in the first place.'

He pushed his chair back, stood. 'It was good to see you, Barry.'

'Yeah,' I said. 'We should grab a beer sometime.'

He smiled, slipped past me, and left the interrogation room.

When I got back to my desk, I noticed the ends of two envelopes sticking out from the inside pocket of my sport jacket. They'd been jammed in there since yesterday. I grabbed them, tossed them onto my desk. They were the reminders from the Promise Falls police to Olivia Fisher to pay her speeding tickets. I'd taken them from Walden with the hope that I could get the town to stop sending them after all this time.

I slit the envelopes, pulled out the notices, and tossed them onto my desk as the phone rang again.

'Son of a bitch,' I said, dropping into my chair and grabbing the receiver at the same time.

'Ten minutes,' Rhonda Finderman said. 'Presser's going to be out front of the building.'

'Got it,' I said.

That meant making myself presentable, and that meant finding a mirror. I stood, threw on my jacket, and opened my bottom desk drawer to find a tie. I usually wore one to work but hadn't bothered today. I found a blue-and-silver-striped one that looked more or less clean, if wrinkled, and took it with me into the men's room.

I stood before the mirror, did up the tie, folded my collar back down over it. Ran my fingers through my hair. Checked for anything between my teeth. I wished Maureen were here. Not in the actual men's room, but at the station, to give me the once-over before I went before the cameras. A few years ago, she'd recorded me on the six o'clock news when I'd made a statement for the press about the death of Thackeray College's president.

She'd played it for me when I got home, paused it at just the right moment.

'You see that?' she'd said.

'See what?'

She'd gone right up to the screen and pointed to my mouth.

'That,' she said, 'is a donut sprinkle.'

So ever since, I'd made an effort when I went before the cameras.

I came back to my desk. I still had another five minutes before I had to go outside. I sat down and unfolded the two notices to Olivia Fisher. As I was reading through them, I picked up the phone and entered the extension that would connect me to the traffic department's fine collection office.

'Traffic, Harrigan.'

'Hey,' I said. 'It's Detective Barry Duckworth. I'm wondering if you can do a favor for me.'

'Let me guess. You got a parking ticket.'

'No,' I said. I explained that notices of an unpaid fine were still being sent out to a homicide victim.

'Oh, shit, that's awful,' Harrigan said.

'Yeah,' I said.

'There should be a number on the top of the notice there – that'd be the ticket number. You see that?'

'Yeah.'

'You want to read that off to me?'

I did. 'Will that cover both notices?'

'Yeah, we can put a stop to those.'

'That's terrific,' I said, my eye scanning down the page at the other information that had been included. The make and model and year of Olivia's vehicle, which happened to be a 2004 Nissan Sentra.

'I hardly knew what to say when this person's father showed me these—'

I stopped midsentence. I'd come upon another bit of information from the original ticket that stopped me cold.

'You there?' Harrigan said.

'I'm here,' I said.

'Is there anything else I can do for you?'

My mind had suddenly kicked into overdrive. I was trying to bring up a conversation from a few weeks ago.

When I'd been talking to Bill Gaynor.

Right after the discovery of his wife's body.

What was it I'd asked him? Right. Had his wife ever been in any kind of trouble with the law? Was she in any way known to the police?

What was it he'd said?

'Are you serious? Of course not. Okay, she got a speeding ticket a week or so ago, but I'd hardly call that being in trouble with the law.'

Yeah, that was what he'd said.

'Detective Duckworth?' Harrigan said.

'Yeah, I'm here. Listen, can you find a more recent ticket in the system if I give you a name? I haven't got the ticket number or anything like that. But it would have been for driving over the posted speed limit.'

'Sure.'

'Rosemary Gaynor.'

'Spell it.'

I did. In the background I could hear several keystrokes.

'Yeah, okay, I think I have it here. This would have been on April twenty-two. Does that sound about right?'

'It does. Read me every single detail off that ticket.'

Harrigan obliged.

'Anything else?' he asked.

'No,' I said. 'That's good. Thank you.'

I hung up the phone, trying to get my head around what I'd just learned. Wondering if it meant anything. Wondering if it was just a coincidence.

The phone rang.

'We're on,' Rhonda Finderman said.

'You're on your own,' I told her.

CHAPTER 56

'I need more stuff,' Crystal said to Cal about an hour after he and Dwayne got back to the house. Cal had made a quick visit to the police station, and now was sitting on the porch of his sister and brother-in-law's place.

'What stuff?' Cal asked.

'I need more paper and pencils and my home-work and more clothes,' she said. 'They're all in my house. I need to go to the house and get all that stuff. Is my mom still there?'

'No,' Cal said. 'She's not.'

'Did the funeral people take her away?'

'More or less,' he said. 'I can check into that for you.'

Crystal appeared to be thinking. 'Did they do anything with what happened in the house when they took my mom away?'

Cal guessed what Crystal was referring to. Her mother had been violently ill in the kitchen and the bathroom. 'They didn't,' he said. 'But it's been taken care of.'

What Cal had not told Crystal was that, on his way back with Dwayne, he'd called the morgue to confirm that Lucy's body had been removed from the house. Then he'd told Dwayne there was a way he could pay him back for getting him out of his arrangement with Harry.

'You name it,' Dwayne had said.

'It won't be fun.'

They went to Lucy's house and cleaned up. 'Jesus,' Dwayne had said when he saw what they had to do.

'I'll find cleaning supplies,' Cal had said.

It took them the better part of an hour to get the job done. Cal opened most of the windows to let fresh air blow through.

Anyone who came into the house now, Cal believed, wouldn't know what had happened.

Except for Crystal, of course.

'So all the throw-up is gone?' Crystal asked.

Cal nodded.

The girl did some more thinking. 'I want to go back over.'

'I'm not so sure that's a good idea.'

'I have to get things. And you won't know where everything is.'

'Still, I think—'

She looked up into his face. 'I can do it.'

Cal put his palm to her cheek. 'Okay. Do you want to go now?' Cal tipped his head in the direction of his car, parked at the curb.

'I guess,' she said.

'I'll let Celeste know.'

Cal went into the house and found his sister upstairs, sitting alone in her bedroom.

'Heading out for a while,' he told her.

'Thank you,' she said softly.

'You don't have to keep saying that.'

'I feel like I can't say it enough. You really got Dwayne out of a mess.'

Cal nodded. 'I won't save him again,' he said.

'It won't happen again,' Celeste said. 'He's not a bad man.'

Cal looked her in the eye. 'Maybe not. But he's a stupid one. And that can be just as dangerous.'

'You think I should leave him.'

'The risks he takes ultimately become your risks. When he enters into business with bad people, he's taking you along for the ride. He does something like this again, it won't be the other guy I take it out on.'

On the way over in the car, Crystal asked, 'Do you believe in ghosts?' She was looking down at her clipboard, sketching something, not watching the world go by as they drove to her house.

He glanced over at her. 'No,' he said. 'Why?'

'Will my mom's ghost be in the house?'

Cal shook his head. 'No. But your memories of her will be. And that's okay.'

'I don't want to live there all by myself.'

Cal tightened his grip on the steering wheel. 'You won't be doing that. It's against the law for someone your age to live by herself. You have to be eighteen to live on your own.'

'Eighteen?'

'That's when the law considers you an adult,' Cal told her.

'Oh.' She drew some more lines, then turned the pencil at a sharp angle and moved it back and forth furiously. Shading.

'My mom owned the house, right?'

'I would imagine so. Unless she was renting it from someone.'

'She used to talk about a mortgage.'

'Okay,' Cal said. 'Then she owned it. She paid money each month for you to live there. That was the mortgage.'

'How much did she pay?'

'I don't know.'

'Would it be like a million dollars?'

'No, it wouldn't be that much. It would be something she could afford, based on what she made at her job at the school.'

They pulled into the driveway. Crystal got out quickly, leaving her artwork on the floor in front of her seat. She got to the door first and waited until Cal got there with the key.

'You're sure it's okay?' she asked.

'I think so,' Cal said.

He inserted the key and pushed open the door. Crystal tentatively stepped inside. She stopped, raised her head, reminding Cal of an animal stopping to pick up any dangerous scents.

Slowly, she walked deeper into the house, and stopped again at the base of the stairs. Her eyes went up to the second floor, but she didn't move.

Cal stood patiently behind her and, after a few seconds, rested his fingers on her shoulders.

He felt Crystal's muscles twitch in the millisecond before she made the decision to go up. She got to the bathroom door, which Cal had deliberately left wide open when he and Dwayne had finished cleaning. She stood outside looking in for about ten seconds, then went to check the other rooms upstairs. She popped her head into her own room, then entered her mother's.

'You okay?' Cal asked.

She said, 'This could be your room.'

'Crystal.'

'Does everything my mom owned go to me?'

Cal had no idea what arrangements Lucy had made with her ex-husband, but he said, 'More or less.'

'So if this is my house, can I give it to you? Because you don't have one. So you could have this room, and I'll sleep where I always have. Because I don't want to stay with your sister and Dwayne.'

Cal said, 'Why don't you start grabbing the things you need?'

'Why can't I just stay here now? Why do I have to go back? I don't like Dwayne. He did bad things to you.'

Cal started considering options. He didn't think it was appropriate for him to stay in this house, just the two of them. Not even for a night.

Even though he couldn't think of anything he'd like more.

'I don't know about that, Crystal. You see—'

'Hello?'

A voice from downstairs. A man's voice.

'Anyone home?'

Crystal looked at Cal for half a second and, without saying a word, scooted down the stairs to the front door.

Cal heard the man say, 'Crystal!'

And he heard Crystal say, 'Daddy!'

'Oh, sweetheart, I got here as fast as I could.'

Cal reached the bottom of the stairs and found the man on his knees, arms around his daughter. As soon as he saw Cal, he got to his feet.

'Gerald Brighton?' Cal asked.

'That's right.'

Cal extended a hand. 'Cal Weaver. We spoke on the phone.'

Gerald Brighton nodded. 'Yes, that's right.'

'It's good that you're here.'

'Hit up everybody I knew for money for the flight. Didn't know I had that many friends.' He smiled as he looked at his daughter. 'Got a ticket for you to come back with me.'

'Well,' Cal said. 'Mr Brighton, I'm sorry for your loss.'

The man gave Crystal another hug, kissed the top of her head. 'Everything's going to be okay. Daddy's here. I'm going to get everything sorted out. You're going to live with me now. You'll really like San Francisco.'

'Okay,' she said, her voice muffled, her face pressed into his chest.

'She has some things at my sister's place,' Cal said.

'We'll come by later, pick them up,' Gerald Brighton said. 'I'll give you a call to let you know we're coming.'

'Of course,' Cal said.

'Thank you for all your help.'

'Don't mention it.' He smiled. 'She's a great kid. A real lifesaver. Good-bye, Crystal.'

'Good-bye,' she said, still clinging to her father.

Cal walked out, got into his car, and saw that Crystal had forgotten her clipboard and drawing paper. He reached down into the passenger foot-well and grabbed it.

Crystal had drawn a house, complete with driveway, windows, smoke coming out of the chimney.

She'd drawn faces in two of the windows, and attached labels to them. One read 'Crystal' and the other said 'Cal.'

He drove back to his sister's place. Gerald and Crystal could pick up the drawing and the clipboard when they came for the rest of her things.

CHAPTER 57

Duckworth

I didn't give Rhonda Finderman an opportunity to object to my bailing on the press conference. I put down the receiver and started heading for the door. Once I was in my car, I got out my phone and made a call to Angus Carlson's cell phone.

The phone rang several times before it went to voice mail.

'You've reached Angus Carlson. I can't take your call right now, so why not leave a message at the tone?'

After the beep, I said, 'Hey, Angus, it's Barry again. I know I shouldn't be bothering you with shit right now, but there's something I'd really like to bounce off you. It's urgent.'

I ended the call, kept the phone in my hand, and sat there for several seconds, pondering my next move. Placed another call to the building I was parked behind.

'Dispatch.'

'It's Detective Duckworth. I need an address and home phone number for Angus Carlson.'

I heard several keystrokes before I was given the information. I scribbled it down on a small notepad, then phoned Carlson's home. After three rings, a woman answered.

'Hello?'

'Hi. It's Detective Duckworth calling. Who's this?'

'Hi, Detective. This is Gale. Angus's wife. How are you?'

'Good, thank you, Gale.'

'Angus has lots of nice things to say about you.'

'Gale, is Angus there?'

'No, I'm afraid he isn't. Have you tried his cell?'

'I have. He didn't answer.'

'Oh,' Gale said. 'Well, if I hear from him, I can tell him you called.'

'I really need to speak with him. Do you have any idea where he might be?'

Gale didn't say anything right away. 'Well, he just went out a little while ago.'

'Where did he go?'

'I really . . . I don't want to get him in any trouble.'

The hairs went up on the back of my neck. 'What kind of trouble?'

'It's just – okay, you know about what happened yesterday?'

'At the hospital,' I said. 'Yes.'

'And he's on leave while the shooting is investigated?'

'That's right,' I said. 'I'm sure that will go in his favor.'

'Yeah, that's what we're both hoping. The thing is, he's sort of working today.'

'What do you mean, working?'

'He kind of had an idea – actually, it was my idea, and I wasn't even sure there was anything to it – but he had this thing he wanted to check out.'

'About what?'

'About the water being poisoned.'

'What was he checking out?'

'Okay, he's going to be mad if I tell you this, but I think I should do it anyway.'

'Gale, please.'

'You know that used bookstore? Naman's?'

'Yes. Someone torched it the other night.'

'That's the one,' she said. 'So, I dropped by there yesterday, and I didn't even know that had happened, and the owner, Naman – he's Muslim or something like that, you know – he was cleaning the place up, and I saw a book there that got me thinking.'

'A book.'

'A book all about poisons. How to make them.'

'Really?'

'And I thought, it's probably nothing. But I told Angus, and he thought it might mean something, so he decided to look into it.'

'He's gone to the bookstore?'

'That's what he said. I guess he thought if he found out who poisoned the water, that'd look really good on him when this hearing into the shooting comes up.'

'Thanks, Gale,' I said. 'Thanks very much.'

There were plenty of available parking spaces out front of Naman's Books. I was thinking I'd look for Angus's car, then realized I didn't know what he drove. The shop was boarded up with plywood sheets, but I could hear noises inside. I tried the door and found it open.

'Hello?' I said, poking my head in.

'Who is it?' someone called out from the back of the shop.

'Police.'

Footsteps approached. A man with coffee-colored skin opened the door wide.

'Naman?' I said.

He nodded. 'Mr Safar, yes. I am Naman.'

I showed him my ID. 'May I come in?'

'What is this about? I am very busy. I'm still trying to clean this place up.'

'Sorry to bother you. May I come in?' I asked again.

He shrugged. It was as close to an invitation as I was going to get. I didn't know how bad the shop had looked initially, but there was clearly more work to be done. Swollen, water-damaged books remained scattered on the floor, and the smell of smoke was powerful. I could see through to the back of the shop, where light streamed through an open door. The edge of a Dumpster was visible.

A couple of floor lamps had been set up inside the store, powered by extension cords that led out the back door.

'Have you people found out who did this yet?' he asked me as he gathered damaged books into a blue Rubbermaid container.

'I can't say what progress is being made,' I said. 'I haven't been involved in the investigation. But I can look into it for you.'

'Never mind,' he said.

Halfway down the shop was another open door. I glanced in as I walked by it, saw that it led to a basement.

'Lots of damage down here, too?' I asked.

'Water had to be pumped out,' Naman said. 'Now it has to dry. That'll take weeks.'

Hours earlier, I was fairly certain we had our poisoner. There was still plenty of work to do, but Victor Rooney was looking like our guy. There hadn't been anything to point to Naman Safar. One damaged book about poison didn't make him a terrorist. And during my brief call to Angus to ask him about George Lydecker's habit of breaking into garages, I'd told him we might have our guy.

So maybe Angus wasn't convinced. If Angus thought there was something to what Gale had seen, had he already been here? Had he already talked to Naman?

'Did another Promise Falls detective come to see you today?' I asked.

'What? No. No one. I keep thinking someone will come and tell me what is going on, but you are the first today.'

'You're sure?' I asked.

Naman looked at me like I was the stupidest member of the Promise Falls police he had ever encountered, and maybe he was right. 'I think I would know if a police officer had been here.'

'Of course you would,' I said. 'Forgive me.' I peered farther into the doorway to the basement. 'Mind if I look down here?'

'What for?'

'Just wanted to see how bad the damage is.'

'I told you. Everything down there is still wet.'

'Let me just have a look. Is there a light?'

'They have still not turned the electric back on.'

'That's okay,' I said, took out my phone, and turned on the flashlight app. 'This isn't great, but it'll do.'

Naman stared at me.

I descended a set of open-back wood steps. It wasn't a deep basement. When I reached the bottom, the ceiling was just brushing the top of my head. I held up the phone, casting light around the room.

I glanced back up the stairs. Naman was silhouetted in the doorway, watching me.

'There was an inch of water down there after the fire,' he said.

The water was gone, but the concrete floor still looked damp, and the air was musty and rank.

The room was pretty much empty, save for a few wooden skids on the floor, and a furnace off in the corner. If I'd been thinking, in the back of my mind, that Angus had been here, and Naman had knocked him out and thrown him down the stairs, then that thinking had been wrong.

Except I'd yet to look behind the furnace.

'What are you doing down there?' Naman asked. 'I had to haul boxes and boxes of books from down there and throw them out. It is cleaned out.'

'One second,' I said.

I held the phone with my arm extended as I moved toward the furnace. That was when I heard steps behind me. I turned, saw Naman was halfway down the stairs.

'Please stay there, sir,' I said.

'What are you looking for?' he said, taking another step down.

'Sir, I won't ask you again. Please stay there.'

Naman stayed.

I reached the furnace, crouched under some ductwork, and looked behind it.

There was nothing – and nobody – there.

I crossed the room and said, 'Let's go back upstairs, Mr Safar.'

'Fine,' he said, and trudged his way up the steps. Once we were both back in the shop, I said, 'What's upstairs?'

'Apartment,' he said.

I realized I knew that. 'Mr Weaver,' I said.

'That's right. He had to move out because of the smoke and everything. So now, in addition to everything else, I have lost a tenant.'

I walked through the store, out the back door, and into the light. I peered over the lip of the Dumpster, which was filled with destroyed books and cardboard and other refuse.

I gave the man one of my business cards. 'I'm sorry to have troubled you. If a Detective Carlson comes by, please call me.'

He looked scornfully at the card and said, 'Whatever.'

I drove to the Carlson house. On the way, I tried Angus's cell phone once more, but he did not pick up. I was hoping that maybe, in the time I'd gone to the used bookstore, he'd returned home.

Gale came to the door and said, 'Detective Duckworth.'

I nodded, extended a hand. 'Hello, Gale.'

'Did you find him?'

'No,' I said. 'May I come in?'

'Yes, sure. Can I get you something? A coffee?'

'That's okay.'

'He wasn't at the bookstore?'

'No. And I don't think he'd been there, either.'

'That's weird,' she said. 'That's where he said he was going. After you left, I tried calling him, but he didn't answer.' Gale, suddenly worried, said, 'What do you think's happened to him?'

'I don't know that anything has happened to him,' I said. 'Can you think of anyplace else he might have gone?'

She shook her head. 'Not really.'

'What about his mother?' I asked. 'Does she live around here? Do you think he might have gone to talk to her about what he went through yesterday?'

Gale's face crumpled. Her lips turned into a jagged line.

'Oh, dear,' she said.

'What?' I said. 'What did I say?'

'Angus wouldn't have gone to see his mother.'

'Why not?'

'She's dead. She's been dead for years.'

CHAPTER 58

Duckworth

'His mother is dead?' I said. 'I don't – earlier today I asked him what he was going to do and he said he might visit her.'

'No,' she said, shaking her head.

'Why would he say he might see her, and why would he act like he was talking to his mother on the phone, if she's dead?'

'It's something he does. It helps him. When he was in therapy, it was something that was suggested to him. That when he was stressed-out, when he was angry, he could verbalize his feelings. That it would help him, help release the tension.'

'Let's sit down,' I said, and steered her into her own living room. We took chairs across from each other, a coffee table between us. 'When did his mother die?'

'When he was seventeen,' she said. 'Nearly twenty years ago.'

'What happened to her?'

'She killed herself. Jumped off a bridge onto the

interstate. She wasn't right in the head, if you know what I mean.'

'Depression?'

'That, and other things. Angus's father walked out on them when Angus was eight, and his mother raised him until she passed away.'

'Sounds like a rough childhood,' I said.

'She was . . . she was not a very good mother to him,' Gale said.

'Abuse?'

She nodded. 'Not just physical, but psychological, too. She wasn't always that way. When he was little, she was pretty happy and normal, for the most part. But then something happened to her after her husband walked out. She changed. Like, her mind completely changed. It's amazing that Angus turned out to be as well-adjusted as he is. You know, for the most part.'

'What do you mean, for the most part?'

'He has this thing . . . he has this thing about us never having children. He doesn't want to have them. Like he's afraid I'm going to turn into the kind of monster his mother was.' Her eyes filled with tears as she leaned forward. 'I would never become that kind of person.'

'Of course you wouldn't,' I said. 'Since he couldn't have gone to see his mother, are you sure you have no idea where he might be?'

She shook her head. 'None.'

'You say you tried phoning him, but he didn't answer?'

'That's right.'

'What about texting him?'

'I didn't do that.'

'It's easy not to answer the phone, but a person almost always looks at a text. I want you to send him one.'

She got up, went to the kitchen, and returned with a cell phone.

'What do you want me to say?'

'Something that will make him call home. Something he can't ignore.'

Her lower lip began to quiver. 'What's going on? Why do you need to talk to him so badly?'

'Text this to him. *Call me.* Put an exclamation mark after that.'

'What's going on?' she asked again.

'Just do that, but don't send it yet.' With one thumb, she typed the two words. 'Okay, now what?'

I tried to think of something that would make any man call home immediately. Besides an invitation to sex. Or, in the case of someone like me, cake.

'Say there's a leak under the sink. Water everywhere.'

'But there is no—'

'Please.'

'I don't like lying to him,' she said. 'It's not right.'

'I'll tell him I made you do it. I'll explain. The important thing right now is that we get him to phone you. Soon as the phone rings, hand it to me.'

Gale took two deep breaths, then typed what I'd asked.

'Send it,' I said.

She hit the button.

'Now we wait,' I said.

We sat there across from each other, not saying a word, counting the seconds. Ten, fifteen, thirty.

A full minute went by.

When the phone rang in Gale's hands, she jumped, as though it had the power to electrocute her. I extended my hand and she placed the phone in it. I hit the button to accept the call.

'Angus,' I said.

A pause, while he dealt with the surprise. 'Barry?'

'That's right.'

'What's – what's going on? I just got a text from Gale about a busted pipe or something. Are you there?'

'I'm here, with Gale.'

'How bad is it? Which sink?'

'There's no leak, Angus. I'm sorry. It was a trick. I made Gale do it, so you'd call. I've been trying to get in touch with you.'

'Jesus, what the hell?'

'Yeah, I know. I didn't want to do it. I went looking for you at the used bookstore.'

'The what?'

'Naman's. Gale said you were going there.'

'She shouldn't have said anything. I was just checking out a possible lead. Probably nothing.'

'But you never went.'

A pause at the other end. 'It's my next stop.'

'Where are you now?'

'Just driving around. What is it you want, Barry? What's so goddamn important?'

'There's something I need your help on. I wouldn't have pulled a stunt like this if it wasn't important.'

'Fine. Go ahead.'

'Not over the phone, Angus. It'd be easier to talk face-to-face.'

'What is it? Just tell me.'

'Seriously, Angus, this is a conversation I'd rather have with you in person.'

There was a long pause from Angus. Then, 'I don't think so. If you can't give me some idea what it's about, it'll just have to wait until the next time we run into each other.'

I ran my tongue over my front teeth. 'Okay, then,' I said slowly. 'Did you know that about a week before Olivia Fisher died, and a few days before Rosemary Gaynor died, they each got a speeding ticket?'

A long pause. Then, 'No. How would I know that?'

'Because you wrote them,' I said. 'Both of them.'

'I suppose that's possible,' he said. 'I was in uniform. I drove around. I wrote tickets.'

'And you interviewed Lorraine Plummer just days before she was murdered.'

An even longer pause at the other end. 'Yeah, of course I did. I told you all about it. I don't know what you're getting at, Barry.'

'It seems odd you never thought to mention that you'd met Fisher, and Gaynor, too.'

'I write a lot of tickets, Barry. Do you remember everyone you gave a ticket to when you were in uniform?'

Gale was watching me, her eyes wide.

'I'm struck by the fact that you came into contact, one way or another, with each of these three women shortly before they were all killed. I'm trying to get my head around that. That you never thought to mention it in the cases of Fisher and Gaynor.'

'What did I say just five seconds ago? I didn't remember. I *don't* remember.'

'We need to talk. Face-to-face. Let's sort this out. I'm sure it can all be explained away. What do you say?'

I waited for a reply.

'Angus?'

He'd ended the call.

I looked at Gale, saw a tear running down her cheek. 'I don't understand,' she said. 'I don't understand what's happening.'

It was then that my eye caught a framed picture on the mantel over the fireplace. It was a portrait shot, faded over time, of a woman in her thirties. Good-looking, with dark eyes and black hair that fell gently to her shoulders. She looked, at a glance, not unlike Olivia Fisher or Rosemary Gaynor or Lorraine Plummer.

'Who's that?' I asked Gale.

She followed my gaze, sniffed, and said, 'That's Angus's mother.'

CHAPTER 59

Angus had never intended to pay a visit to Naman.

He'd put very little stock in Gale's suspicion that the used bookseller might be involved with contaminating the town water supply just because he had a book on poisons. What had been done to Promise Falls was not the work of some guy who got the idea out of the pages of a book. It had been done by someone with a working knowledge of the town's infrastructure. That sure didn't sound like Naman. And from what little Duckworth had told him in their first conversation of the day, Victor Rooney sounded like someone who fit that profile.

But interviewing the bookseller was an excellent pretext to get out of the house, to leave Gale on her own.

He had seen another one.

Someone else who bore a striking resemblance to his mother.

It was happening more now than it used to. Was that because he was seeing more women who fit the profile? Or was the need greater?

Did it matter?

After Olivia Fisher, he'd gone three years before doing it again. But then he'd pulled over Rosemary Gaynor for doing sixty in a forty. There was something about her, something in her eyes, something in the way her dark hair fell to her shoulders, that made him think of her.

If he'd known she already had a child, he might have given her a pass. But there was no baby seat in the back of her car, nothing that immediately gave away that she was a mother. It was only after he'd killed her that he learned there had been a baby boy asleep upstairs.

There was no point in killing them after they'd given birth. It was too late then. You had to get them *before*.

With Lorraine Plummer, it had been much easier to get it right. She was a student. No serious boyfriend, no imminent marriage. Motherhood might be years away.

Perhaps that was why the *need* struck him again so soon after Rosemary Gaynor. Because he'd gotten it wrong.

But she certainly looked the part. She looked so much like *Leanna*.

They'd been having regular chats lately. Somewhat one-sided, of course. That therapist he'd been seeing way back before he and Gale even moved to Promise Falls from Ohio suggested them. *Give a voice to your feelings*, he'd been told. *Even if she can't hear you, you get to hear yourself. Let the feelings out.*

At times, it seemed to make a difference.

Sometimes, he'd talk to her, phone in hand, like he had a toll-free line to hell. Or he'd talk to her while driving, as though she were in the seat next to him. Other times, he would look at her picture on the mantel in the living room. Tell her what was on his mind. Give it to her straight.

Gale didn't understand. She thought it was crazy. Asked him not to do it.

Move on, she said. *It's over. She can't hurt you anymore.*

Easy for her to say.

Let's start a family of our own, Gale kept saying.

She just didn't get it.

He was always very careful to make sure they took all the necessary precautions, and not just when it came to sex. He'd been careful to choose a girl who looked nothing like his mother. Different hairstyle, facial structure, body type. He wanted her to be as unlike his mother as possible.

After all, he'd hate to think that he might have to kill Gale.

Angus *loved* Gale.

They were, he believed, a perfect couple. He'd always been able to talk to her. He'd told her all about his childhood. How things got so much worse after his father left. How his mother had slowly descended into a kind of madness at times.

Angus hadn't told Gale everything his mother had done. Some things he couldn't bring himself to say aloud. Only his therapist heard the grisly details, and even in the privacy of the doctor's office, there was one story Angus had always held back.

He'd told Gale of the lesser offenses. The relentless criticisms. That he was an accident. She'd never intended to have him. He was dumb like his father.

First came the insult. And then, when his lip would begin to quiver, she'd frown and say, 'Oh, come, now. You have to learn to take these things. I'd be doing you no favor not to point out your shortcomings.'

And then she'd lean in, nose to nose, and say, 'Give your mom a smile. A good boy always gives his mom a smile.'

A smile.

But being a good boy was an unattainable goal, as his mother constantly reminded him.

Good boys didn't roughhouse or run through the living room. Good boys walked on the stairs, never jumped. Good boys didn't get their clothes mussed up. Good boys didn't make farting noises. Good boys didn't get bad marks at school.

Good boys didn't look at dirty magazines and do nasty things with themselves under the covers.

That was one of the stories he'd never been able to tell Gale. The night, when he was thirteen, when his mother burst into his room and caught him in the middle of doing that.

How she'd whipped the covers off the bed, exposed his nakedness, his withering hardness.

He'd made a grab for the covers, but she held them firm.

'I thought you were a good boy,' she said.

'*Please!*' he whimpered, trying to get her to let go of the bedcovers. *'Leave me alone!'*

'If you think that's such a smart thing to do, if you're so proud of that kind of behavior, then go ahead and finish,' she said. 'I'll wait.'

He rolled onto his side, curling up into a ball, as though shielding himself from an imminent lashing. But her taunting had a much greater sting.

'I'm waiting,' she said.

He wrapped his arms around his knees, pulled them in closer to his chest, felt a tear run down his cheek to the pillow.

'Just as I thought,' his mother said. 'Even those most basic tasks you can't finish.'

And then she leaned in, kissed him on the forehead, and said, 'All right now, let's move on. Give your mom a smile.'

Pulling up the corners of his mouth felt like lifting a set of five-hundred-pound dumbbells.

After his mother died, he went to live with Aunt Belinda for two years. It just about killed him when she said to him one day, 'I know my sister wasn't the best of mothers, and it tore me apart watching how she treated you, but what could I do?'

She could have saved him, he thought. That's what she could have done.

He thought, often, how much better it would

have been if his mother had never had him. A life that never was would be preferable to what he'd endured.

That life seemed to turn around when he met Gale. Kind, loving, ego-boosting. After a stint in police college, he landed a job with the Cleveland force. Gale got work as a kindergarten teacher's aide.

But a perfect life with the perfect woman was not enough to turn things around.

Charlene Quint was his first. (Well, not *technically*.) A Cleveland waitress. Twenty-seven. Engaged. Pulled her over for failing to signal a turn. When she turned her head just the right way, he could see Leanna in her. He had her address, made a house call a week later.

It had simultaneously felt like the right thing to do and the wrong thing to do. But it had also felt *good*.

When he accepted a job with the Promise Falls police, and he and Gale moved away from Cleveland, and he was no longer exposed to the geographic markers of his formative years, he thought the feelings would dissipate.

Several years passed before Olivia Fisher. He had pulled her over near the Promise Falls Mall. She was doing seventy in a forty. A serious offense, but he knocked the ticket back to fifty. Not before, however, engaging her in enough chitchat to find out she was graduating from Thackeray, that she was engaged, that she did not yet have any children.

Several days later, he staked out her address. She was still living with her parents, Elizabeth and Walden. He saw her leave by herself in the same car she'd been driving when he'd ticketed her. Followed her to downtown Promise Falls. She parked the car and wandered into the park, not far from the falls.

It was getting dark, and there were no other people nearby.

He walked right up to her. Smiled, said, 'Ms Fisher?'

She didn't recognize him. Angus got that a lot. People meet you when you're in uniform, then run into you another time when you're in your street clothes, and they can't place you. You're out of context.

She said, 'Uh, hello?'

'I'm sorry,' he said. 'Happens all the time. I'm not in uniform. I was the mean old cop who gave you a speeding ticket the other day.'

'Oh, yes.' She smiled. 'You're right. I knew you looked familiar, but I couldn't place where I'd seen you.'

Angus nodded his understanding. 'I hope you'll forgive me.'

'What?'

'For the ticket. It's my job.'

'Oh, I know. Don't worry about that.'

'What are you doing here?' he asked.

The knife was already in his right hand, down at his side, the blade hidden against his pant leg.

'Just waiting for my boyfriend.'

Angus looked beyond her shoulder. 'The falls are gorgeous tonight, the way the lights on the bridge reflect in them.'

Olivia Fisher turned to look.

It was all the time he needed.

Left arm around the throat. Body pulled tight to his. Right arm around the front to her left side. Blade in. Then pull hard to the right. Down slightly in the middle.

Like a smile.

She let out such a scream.

He should have gotten his hand over her mouth, kept her from making such a noise. Not much he could do about it now.

He pulled out the knife, let her drop to the ground.

No time to savor the moment. That scream was sure to draw people. He ran. Bounded up a set of concrete steps that led up to the bridge that spanned the falls. He scaled them two at a time, tossing the knife into the falls along the way.

Rosemary Gaynor had gone more smoothly. He was in her home, didn't have to worry about being seen, or heard. He'd parked two blocks away. Went right to the front door, rang the bell. When she opened it, she recognized him, even though he was not in uniform.

'Officer?' she'd said.

Angus made the motion of tipping an imaginary hat. 'So sorry to bother you,' he said. 'It's about the ticket I wrote you the other day. I've been instructed to do a follow-up with you, and I didn't get to it while I was still on my shift, so I thought I'd pop by on my way home.'

'A follow-up?'

'In fact, they've sent me here to tear it up. I didn't realize that the zone where I clocked you was before the actual point where the speed limit drops.'

'You're kidding,' she said, and laughed. 'How often does *that* happen? Won't you come in?'

'That's very kind of you.'

The rest was easy.

And now, here he was, the Sunday of the Memorial Day weekend.

A new opportunity had presented itself.

He was more rattled than usual this time. He figured that was due to the shooting at the hospital. Killing people in secret was one thing, but an event that public, with implications for his job – his future – was quite another.

He needed to try to put that aside and concentrate on the task at hand. But complicating things further had been that call from Detective Duckworth.

Duckworth had connected the dots.

Angus believed it was all going to be over very soon. There might only be time for one more.

Sonja Roper.

The nurse at Promise Falls General. In their short conversation he'd learned she had no children. Not yet. But she had a boyfriend – a pilot who wasn't due home until tomorrow – and they were certainly planning to have children in the future.

So there was still time to save those kids.

To spare them inevitable lives of torment and misery.

It hadn't taken Angus any time at all to figure out where Sonja Roper lived. A quick call to the hospital confirmed she was off today. He parked a couple of blocks from her home. He'd slapped the stolen green Vermont plates on the car shortly after he'd left home.

She'll be my fifth, he thought.

But then he corrected himself mentally. *Sixth*.

He often forgot to count his mother.

Everyone thought she must have been depressed when, late one night, she leapt off that overpass straight into the path of a transport truck heading south on I-90.

There were some stories you didn't share even with your therapist.

CHAPTER 60

Sonja Roper had ended up working not just a double, but a triple shift the day before at Promise Falls General Hospital. Well, almost. She had arrived for a seven-hour shift that began at six in the morning, and by half past, the patients were starting to turn up. Things hadn't slowed down by the time her shift ended at one, so she hung in. By midafternoon, word had spread that the water was contaminated, and admissions had slowed to a trickle, no pun intended. For the most part, anyone who was going to get sick had gotten so. Her second shift would have ended at seven, but they still had their hands full treating the people who'd been admitted. She put in another three hours, and went home at ten.

Sonja had never seen anything like it in her life.

Not that she'd been around forever. She'd been working at the hospital for only two years. But still, that was not the kind of day you ever wanted to see. They trained for it – they did their best to be ready – but hoped and prayed they'd never have to deal with that kind of emergency.

When she was finally able to go home, she was

not sure she'd be able to keep her eyes open for the drive. One of the orderlies was leaving at the same time and offered her a lift home. She could come back for her car on Sunday.

She and her boyfriend, Stan, were renting a small house on Klondike. She was sorry he wouldn't be there when she got home. He was spending the night in Seattle, and if she remembered correctly, he'd be in Chicago Sunday night, flying home Monday.

Sonja just wanted to crawl into bed with him and fall asleep in his arms.

They had managed to talk on the phone around six. She told him how bad things were in Promise Falls, and he told her how proud he was of her, doing her part to help people through such a horrible time.

'I love you, Stan,' she said.

'I love you, too,' he said.

The good news was that she was asleep thirty seconds after her head hit the pillow. The bad news was her dreams were all about what she'd seen that day in the emergency ward. People throwing up, collapsing, dying right in front of her. The anguished cries of relatives who were powerless to do anything.

She woke up a couple of times but quickly went back to sleep. When she opened her eyes in the morning and looked at the clock, it was fifteen minutes past eleven.

'Wow,' Sonja said.

She thought about having a shower. Word was that a shower was safe. But she liked to do a four-mile run three mornings a week, and this struck her as a good day to clear her head. She got up, slipped on some sweats and running shoes, clipped an iPod Shuffle to her collar, and worked the buds into her ears.

When she opened the front door, the morning sun blinded her.

She did a few stretches on the front lawn first, set her iPod to play the best of Madonna, and headed out.

Sonja loved the feel of the warm sun on her face, the fresh air entering her lungs. This was exactly what she needed.

By the time she got back, she was drenched in sweat; her legs were numb and her lungs aching. She'd really pushed that last half mile.

But she felt good.

She unlocked the front door, stepped inside, pulled the buds from her ears, and dropped the iPod into a decorative bowl with her keys. She went into the kitchen and turned the tap on full blast, letting the water get cold.

Then it hit her. 'What am I thinking?' She turned off the tap and took a bottle of Poland Spring water from the refrigerator and took two long gulps.

There was a knock at the door.

'Just a second!' she said.

She put the bottle down on the counter, walked briskly to the front door, and opened it wide.

'Ms Roper?'

The man smiled, nodded respectfully.

'I know you,' she said slowly.

'We met yesterday at the hospital. I was asking—'

'You're the policeman,' Sonja said. 'I remember you. But I'm sorry. I've forgotten your name.'

'Carlson,' he said. 'Angus Carlson.'

She gestured down at herself. Her running clothes were dark with perspiration. 'You have to excuse me. I just did a run. I'm sweating buckets. Pretty dumb, huh, when I don't even know if the water's safe to shower with yet?'

'For what it's worth, I've heard it is. But I'm sorry. Should I come back later?'

'No, no, it's okay.'

'They say we need to wait another day or two before we drink anything from the tap, but for cleaning, showering, the crisis is over.'

'Really? That's some good news, I guess. Because if anyone ever needed a shower, it's me. So what's up?'

'We're still, of course, actively investigating the cause of the water contamination, and we're reinterviewing people who might have noticed something – anything – that might be helpful.'

'What could I have seen?' she asked.

'Well, we think it's possible that whoever did this – and we do think it was an individual with an agenda, and not some kind of environmental accident or something – he might very well have come to the hospital to see the results of his handi-work, actually see the people being ill.'

'Oh my God, that's just awful,' Sonja Roper said.

'I know. That's why I wanted to ask you if you noticed anything unusual yesterday. Anything at all.'

'Are you kidding? It was *all* unusual.'

Carlson nodded understandingly. 'Of course it was. But what I'm thinking is, did you notice anyone who didn't seem to belong? Someone who was just hanging around, not actually with anyone? Someone who was lurking?'

'I'd have to think about that a second. God, where are my manners? You want to step inside?'

'I suppose. Thank you.'

'I'm so rude. Forgive me.'

'Not at all,' Angus said.

CHAPTER 61

Duckworth

'What kind of car is your husband driving?'
I asked Gale Carlson.
'A Ford. A Fusion.'
'Color?'
'Um . . . dark blue,' she said.
'Plate number?'
She spluttered, 'I have no idea.'
'Year?'
Gale remained flustered. 'I think, 2007. We bought it used.'

I got out my phone, entered a number. 'Hey, I need you to look up a registration. I need a plate number on a dark blue 2007 Ford Fusion, registered to Angus Carlson. Yeah, *that* Angus Carlson. Call me when you have it.'

Then I called Rhonda Finderman.

'Barry? Jesus, why the hell did you bail on me?' she said, answering after one ring.

'Chief, I need you to—'

'I wanted you beside me when I did that conference. Everyone turned up. All the major networks.

CNN was there, the Albany media. They had a lot of questions and a lot of them I just had to wing. It would have gone a lot better if you'd—'

'Listen to me. Call whoever we call when we need to track a cell phone.'

'What?'

'Take this down.'

I gave her Angus's cell phone number and service provider. 'We need to see if they can triangulate his location.'

'Why, Barry? What's happened to Angus? Does this have something to do with the shooting at the hospital?'

'No.'

'Barry, talk to me.'

I moved away from Gale, far enough to be sure she would not hear me. 'Angus just moved to the top of the suspect list in the Fisher, Gaynor, and Plummer murders.'

For about three seconds, nothing. Then, 'What the fuck are you talking about?'

'I can't get into it now. I need to find him.'

'Jesus, Barry.'

'I know. Can you do the phone thing?'

'Leave it with me.'

'Tell me what's going on,' Gale asked me after I'd ended the call. 'Please tell me what's happening.'

'We have to find Angus,' I told her.

'Why were you asking him about those women who'd been murdered? You were acting like you thought he had something to do with it.'

'Gale, talk to me about him.'

Her face was crumpling. 'I don't understand what you're asking. He's my *husband*. I *love* him.'

'How's he been lately? Has he been moody? Has he seemed different?'

'He's always been moody,' Gale said, shaking her head, as though trying to shake off my questions. 'It's the job. It's being with the police. It's hard on him. And then what happened yesterday, he's very stressed-out about that.'

'Before yesterday,' I said. 'How has he been?'

'He's damaged,' she said. 'He's always been damaged. It was what drew me to him in the first place. He had so much pain. You have no idea. I wanted to help him with that. And I've been doing it, every single day. I know he comes across as funny sometimes, always making jokes, the wisecracks. It's an act. It masks the pain. Why were you asking him about those women?'

I wondered whether, deep down, she'd always suspected something. Maybe, maybe not. Often, it was the people closest to you that you knew the least about.

My phone rang.

'I've got a plate for you,' my contact said.

I wrote down the information, ended the call, then made another, to the Promise Falls police dispatcher.

'We need to find this car,' I said. I provided a full description, with plate number. 'It's Angus Carlson. We need to find him immediately.'

'Is he in trouble?' the dispatcher asked.

'Yes,' I said. But not the way the dispatcher meant, so I added, 'He needs to be approached with caution.'

'What?'

'Get the word out,' I said, and slipped the phone back into my pocket.

'He wouldn't hurt anyone,' Gale said. 'He wouldn't.' She turned away, wringing her hands.

I said, 'Text him. Tell him to come home.'

She tapped away on the phone. 'I'm telling him I love him. I'm telling him I need him.'

We waited for the three little dots that would indicate he was forming a reply, but there was nothing.

'This is all my fault,' she said.

'What do you mean?'

'I've been asking him lately – I've been asking him a lot – about our having a child. Trying to get him to warm to the idea.'

'I don't think this has anything to do with that,' I said.

'It might, it really might,' she said pleadingly. This was what she wanted it to be about. It was less horrific than the other possibilities that had to be going through her mind.

'Why?' I asked.

'He had such a horrible upbringing. After his father left, his mother . . . like I said, she changed. Angus didn't want to have children because there's such a huge risk that the parents will turn out to be monsters. I'd say to him, "Do you think that's what I could turn into? A monster?" And he'd say you just never know with people. We have these long talks about it, me trying to convince him that I'd never be like that, no matter what happened. Maybe he was worried about himself, that he had the potential to transform from a wonderful father to a bad one. But I know that would be impossible.'

She found a tissue, dabbed her eyes.

'Sometimes he would say . . .'

I waited. When she wouldn't continue, I said, 'Sometimes he would say what?'

'Sometimes he would say it'd be a better world if no more children were brought into it. At all. Period.'

She picked up the phone, looked expectantly at the screen.

'I should tell him,' she said, her thumb poised over the screen.

'Tell him what?' I asked.

CHAPTER 62

'Could you give me two seconds to freshen up?' Sonja Roper asked Angus Carlson. 'Sure, of course,' he said.

'I just want to splash some water on my face,' she said. 'But it felt good, to run off some of that tension from yesterday. I hope I never, ever see another day like that.'

Angus believed he could help her with that.

But he felt he was working against a deadline. The clock was ticking. Duckworth would be trying to find him. He was probably putting out a BOLO right now for his car. He'd have gotten the plate for his Ford, but they weren't going to find it that way, not with that stolen green Vermont plate slapped over his own. But that would slow them down for only so long.

On top of that, Sonja Roper wanted to freshen up, maybe get changed. Which meant she was probably heading into the bathroom and, if she had any smarts at all, locking the door. He couldn't kick the door down. That would give her time to respond, to get into a defensive position.

'Let's hope none of us ever see another day like

that,' Carlson said. 'It was the worst day in the history of this town, that's for sure.'

'It's kind of like what I imagine a plane crash would be like, although I hate to even say that, considering what my boyfriend does for a living. All those casualties, all at once. But with a crash, it'd be all kinds of physical injuries. Missing limbs, lacerations. With a mass poisoning, there wasn't blood, but it didn't make it any less horrifying, but it was different, you know?'

'Yes,' he said.

Maybe he could corner her in the kitchen before she went to the bathroom.

'Who would do such a thing?' she asked. 'Why would someone want to do that?'

Angus shook his head.

'I just don't know.'

Except now he did know, or at least had a pretty good idea. When Barry Duckworth called to ask him what he knew about George Lydecker, who'd been found in Victor Rooney's garage, he'd disclosed what he believed Rooney's motive had been.

Payback.

Rooney may have been taking revenge on a citizenry that did nothing to help Olivia Fisher. Which meant the deaths of more than a hundred Promise Falls residents led right back to Angus Carlson.

He was having a hard time getting his head around that.

He wasn't sure how he felt.

Angus was selective about those who had to die. He did not kill men. Men did not bear children. Yes, of course, they had a role to play in the reproductive process. But women were the ultimate givers of life. So all those men who had died the day before – it was a terrible thing. All the elderly, of both sexes. All the children, even the girls, who should have been entitled to at least a few more years.

It was wrong. So unnecessary.

That's a very, very sick person, Angus thought.

He rejected the notion that he was somehow liable for all that. Every individual had to be held responsible for his or her actions. Like when some nutcase said a movie made him kill. Was it the director's fault? The studio's? Should the screenwriter be charged? No, Angus thought. It was the fault of that nutcase, plain and simple.

Wasn't he willing to take responsibility for what he was doing? Of course he was. His mother played a role in his motivations, but in the end, it was up to him.

And right now, it was up to him to kill Sonja Roper.

She excused herself, walked down the hall, and disappeared into a room. Carlson heard the door close and lock. Seconds later, the sound of water running in a sink.

His cell phone vibrated in his pocket. He wasn't taking any more calls. He wasn't going to be tricked by Duckworth again. But it might be a text, and he was curious to see what it was.

It was, as he'd guessed it would be, Gale.

I love you. I need you. Please come home.

He shook his head sadly. That was probably Duckworth's doing. Telling her what to write.

Angus turned his attention back to Sonja.

He could position himself on the far side of the bathroom door. When she came out, she'd probably head back toward the living room. She'd exit the bathroom and turn left. He could wait to her right. The second she emerged, he could grab her from behind, pull her close to him, do it quickly.

Make the smile.

He got up, went down the hall. Stood against the wall just beyond the door. He could hear her moving around in there. A toilet flush. He reached down into his front pocket, where he kept the knife. It was an automatic, a blade just over three inches. One touch of the button and the blade would emerge. Short handle with a strong grip. Expensive. He'd hated throwing one away every time, but it was the prudent thing to do. In the case of Olivia Fisher, imperative.

You didn't want to be caught with a bloody knife on your person.

He took the weapon from his pocket, extended the blade.

Inside the bathroom, no more running water. He sensed she was ready to come out.

He was ready, too.

And then it hit him.

Stupid, stupid, stupid.

He needed to have done more than mute his phone. He should have turned it off completely. Duckworth might be trying to track his location.

Angus reached for his phone with his free hand, and as he did, it vibrated again.

Another text.

He decided to look at it before powering the phone down.

It was another one from Gale. It read:

Im pregnant.

CHAPTER 63

Duckworth

'What did he say?' I asked after Gale sent her most recent text message.

'He hasn't said anything,' she said.

When Gale told me she'd learned, three weeks ago, that she was expecting a child, I thought maybe the news would be enough to jolt Angus Carlson into coming back to the house.

'Wait,' she said. 'He's writing something. Here.' She turned the phone so I could see it.

I dont believe you.

Gale typed: It's true. Please come home.

Another stretch of time without a reply. Maybe a minute, which felt like an eternity in the world of texting. Then: Dworth made you say this.

Gale replied: He wanted me to tell u. But it is true. Have known for 3wks. Afraid to tell u.

My cell phone rang. It was Chief Finderman.

'We have an approximate location on the phone,' she told me.

536

'Where?'

'Klondike Street. Near Rossland.'

'If they can pinpoint it any better, let me know,' I said. 'Start having cars focus on that neighborhood. I'm heading there.'

'I hope you're wrong about this,' Rhonda said.

'Me, too,' I said, but wasn't sure I meant it. If Angus Carlson was our serial killer, I wanted him caught. If it reflected badly on the department, and Rhonda Finderman in particular, so be it.

I finished with Rhonda and looked at Gale, who was still staring at her phone. 'Anything else?'

She held the device up to me. Angus had written: Should have told me.

'Tell him the two of you need to talk about it. Right now.'

She tapped. I heard the *whoosh*.

'You're coming with me,' I said.

'Where are we going? Do you know where he is?'

'Roughly,' I said.

'Just tell me what it is you think he's done,' she said, not moving. 'You kept mentioning those women who'd been killed. Did Angus make some kind of mistake? Did he screw up the investigation? Is that why you're mad at him?'

I thought maybe she'd already figured it out, but was clinging to the hope that her husband wasn't a killer.

'I need to talk to him about those investigations, yes,' I said.

Gale swallowed hard. It looked like a marble

working its way down her throat. 'You think it's him.'

'I don't know that,' I said.

'It might be him,' she said.

'Gale.'

'He said something to me last night. Just before we went to sleep. I could tell he was thinking about something. He said he'd been talking to a nurse at the hospital, that she was getting married soon, that they wanted to have kids.' She paused. 'How it made him sad.'

I felt my blood starting to run cold. 'Did he mention a name?'

'No.'

'Anything else about her?'

Gale shook her head. Suddenly, she let out a short scream. Her phone had buzzed in her hand.

'It's Angus. He says he has to think.'

I'd already stepped out front. I called the hospital, asked to be put through to the emergency ward. Someone picked up and said, 'Emergency. Nurse Fielding.'

I identified myself. It took a little convincing, but she finally remembered me from when I was there the day before. 'I'm trying to track down someone who works in the ER who was there yesterday—'

'*Everyone* was here yesterday,' she said.

'This nurse probably was in her twenties or thirties, dark hair, and she might live on Klondike Street.'

'Oh, that's probably Sonja,' Nurse Fielding said.

'Sonja? Can you spell that? And do you have a last name?'

She spelled the first name, and then said, 'Roper.'

'Thanks,' I said. 'Is she there today?'

'No, she did a double and a half yesterday.'

'Do you have a contact number, and an exact address?'

'Hang on a second.'

While I waited, I said to Gale, 'Anything else from him?'

'No,' she said.

I had my notepad out, waiting for Nurse Fielding to report back. A few seconds later, she came on.

'Okay, Sonja lives at 31 Klondike,' she said.

Shit.

'And do you have a number for her?'

She gave me one. 'I think it's a cell,' she said. 'I don't think she has a landline.'

I ended the call and said to Gale, 'Let's go.' On the way to the car, I dialed Sonja Roper's number.

CHAPTER 64

When Gale texted him the news that she was pregnant, Angus became so fixated on the phone, staring at the words, that he lost track of what he'd come to Sonja Roper's house to do.

How could she be pregnant?

How could Gale have betrayed him that way?

Angus wondered, first, whether she was telling him the truth. But if she was, how had it happened? Of course, no method of birth control was one hundred percent effective. But he thought they'd been careful, unless Gale was deliberately *not* being careful.

He slipped the knife back into his pocket, wrote Gale back, accusing her of lying, then said she should have told him as soon as she'd known.

What would he have done had he known? he wondered.

Would he have killed Gale?

No, no, he wouldn't have done that. That was unthinkable. He'd have had her go to a clinic. He'd have made her terminate the pregnancy.

He was almost sure that was what he would have done.

Except . . . now he was overwhelmed with the idea that he might actually be a father. That a child of his was growing inside Gale.

How did that make him feel? In the first few seconds after she'd texted him, he was angry. Then confused. Then—

The bathroom door swung open.

Sonja Roper stepped out, dressed in jeans and a T-shirt, hair wet. Her feet were bare.

'Shit!' she said when she realized Angus was hovering right by the door, phone in hand. She jumped, spun around to face him, and backed her way into the living room. 'What were you doing there?'

'I was . . . I was just on my phone. Texting.'

'Why were you hiding outside the door there?'

'I wasn't – I didn't mean to startle you.'

'What kind of creep are you?'

'I didn't look in. I didn't try the door.'

'Look, I don't know what questions you've got, but you should leave.'

'My wife is pregnant,' he said.

'What?'

'She just texted me. She's pregnant.'

Sonja, bewildered, said, 'Well . . . that's just great. But it doesn't explain why you were creeping around outside my door.'

'She didn't tell me. She's known for three weeks.'

'I guess you should talk to *her* about that,' Sonja said. 'Like, right now would be a good time.'

A cell phone began to ring. The sound was coming from the kitchen.

'Don't answer that,' Angus said.

'Excuse me?'

'I said don't answer it. We have to talk.'

'Get out,' she said as the phone continued to ring. 'I want you out of here right now.'

Angus slowly started walking down the hall toward her. 'What do you think I should do?' he asked her.

'What?' Sonja said, glancing behind her with each backward step she took.

In the distance, the sound of sirens.

'What should I do about my wife being pregnant?' He looked at her plaintively. 'I'm not sure how to handle it. It's all feeling a bit overwhelming. There's only so much one person can do. I came here to solve one problem, but now another's overtaken it. But *is* it a problem?'

'You're off your nut,' Sonja said, turned, and ran.

She pushed the front door open with both hands and burst out of the house as though there'd been an explosion as two police cars raced up the street, lights flashing, sirens wailing. Sonja waved her arms as she ran across the lawn.

Angus came out the door after her, but once on the front step he stopped. He saw the cars screaming toward the house.

He got out his phone and texted to Gale: **Guess I will come home now.**

He stared at the screen as the police cars screeched to a halt out front of the house.

Coming to you, Gale wrote back.

A female officer was out of the first car. Sonja Roper was talking to her, pointing to Carlson.

'Detective Carlson!' the officer said. 'Are you Detective Carlson?'

He typed: **Ok.**

Then he looked up and said, 'Yes, I'm Carlson.'

Another car, plain black without markings, rounded the corner. Carlson recognized it immediately as an unmarked Promise Falls police car. He was pretty sure that was Barry Duckworth behind the wheel.

With Gale in the seat next to him.

Gale threw open the door as Duckworth brought the car to a stop.

'Gale!' Duckworth said. 'Wait!'

But she wasn't going to wait. She ran past the marked cars, ignored the female officer's call to stop, and ran directly to her husband. He stood there, waited. She got to within a foot of him, and when she stopped, he smiled.

'Maybe it's a good thing you didn't tell me,' Angus said. 'I don't know what I might have had to do.'

Gale suddenly went weak and dropped to her knees in front of him.

CHAPTER 65

Duckworth

Rhonda Finderman sat in on the interrogation. Angus insisted he did not want a lawyer. Once he'd signed off on that, and we were ready to record his statement, he told us everything, with plenty of corroborating detail.

About Olivia Fisher, and Rosemary Gaynor, and, most recently, Lorraine Plummer. There was a murder in Cleveland, too. Once I had the details on that, I'd be getting in touch with the Cleveland police so they could move that one to the solved column.

Angus explained to us how he was saving unborn children from a life of misery.

'I screwed up with Rosemary Gaynor,' he said. 'I didn't realize she already had a child.'

'And it wasn't her child,' I pointed out. 'Rosemary Gaynor couldn't have children.'

He grimaced, looking like a kid who'd gotten only an A when he was expecting an A-plus.

Chief Finderman didn't say a word through the whole thing. Bad enough that one of her own was a serial killer. This was the man she'd moved up to detective status. I didn't envy her when she went before the cameras on this one.

'I want your thoughts on something,' Angus said at one point.

'About what?' I asked.

'Well, it's about Victor Rooney and the poisoning of the water. I want to know if you think that's my fault.'

'I don't think my opinion on that matters, Angus,' I said.

'No, really, I'd like to know. I value your opinion.'

'Why don't you tell me if you think it's your fault?'

'At first, I thought maybe it was. But I think Victor has to own it. It was his decision. Regardless of what I did, or those other people who did nothing, he made the choice to do what he did.'

'I see.'

'You don't agree?' he asked.

'Like I said, my opinion doesn't matter here,' I told him. 'But let me ask you this. If you hadn't killed Olivia Fisher, would more than a hundred people have died in Promise Falls this weekend?'

Angus Carlson gave that some thought. 'I suppose that's one way of looking at it.'

'Yeah,' I said.

'Thank you for your kindness toward Gale,' he said.

'Sure.'

Angus shook his head slowly and sighed. 'Given that what's done is done, I hope it's a boy.'

★ ★ ★

Finderman and I left Angus in the interrogation room to confer.

'What a mess,' she said. 'And please don't say it is what it is.'

'That's not one of my sayings,' I said, steering her toward the coffee machine. 'But it's kind of apt.'

'God, Barry. One of our own.'

'It'll be bad,' I said. 'We just have to ride it out.'

'I'm the one who has to ride it out. You found a killer. I promoted one.'

'You think we might try to find a silver lining here?' I said, grabbing two mugs, glancing into them to ensure that they were at least remotely clean. 'We caught a serial killer. We've solved three homicides. And maybe another one or two for the folks in Cleveland. Did you notice, when I asked him about his mother's death, how uncomfortable he got? I think they should be taking another look at that, too.'

It was difficult for Finderman to see an upside at the moment, but she tried. 'In the course of one day you've found the guy who poisoned the town's water, and exposed a multiple murderer. Christ, they'll be making a movie about you.'

'You heard anything about Rooney?' I asked, pouring coffee into the two mugs. I held up the container of cream, but she shook her head. I handed her a mug.

'He's in the ICU,' Rhonda said. 'That fire truck hit him good. But he's far from a goner. They think he might regain consciousness before too long.' She took a sip of the coffee. 'I'm always amazed that this is not terrible.'

I nodded. 'Let's hope he'll be as forthcoming as Carlson was about why he did what he did.'

Rhonda turned her back to the wall and let it hold her up. 'I'm beat, but you look about a hundred times worse.'

I smiled. 'Yeah. I'm tired.'

'I heard you had some trouble at Rooney's house. When the paramedics came. You had some chest pain.'

I waved a hand. 'It was nothing. I was running. It only lasted a second.'

'Promise me you'll get yourself checked out.'

'I will.' I paused. 'I did. Saw the doctor a couple of days ago. She said – get this – I need to lose some weight.'

'Ridiculous,' the chief said, doing a good job of keeping a straight face.

'Tell me about it. Maureen's been trying to kill me with vegetables.'

'Wear a wire,' Rhonda said. 'We record her telling you to eat them all up, we swoop in, we arrest her.'

I was too weary to laugh. 'I'm sorry about the other thing.'

She didn't pretend not to know what I was talking about. 'It happens.'

'I was talking to Maureen. It was a private conversation. Trevor heard it, told Finley. Finley had something on Trevor – nothing huge, but enough – and put the squeeze on him.'

'It's not that it came out,' Rhonda said. 'It's that you believed I fucked up.'

I nodded. 'I thought so at the time, but it was frustration. In the last month, since the shit started hitting the fan by the bucketful, I've made more fuckups than I can count.' I paused. 'Maybe I'm done.'

'No.'

'It's twenty years.'

'Seriously?'

'May 'ninety-five, I came on. Slightly younger, and a whole lot thinner.'

'I didn't know. We should do something. Some kind of party.'

'I think I'll celebrate with sleep,' I said.

'Can you stay awake long enough for another press conference? One you'll actually show up to?'

I nodded. 'Yes. But there's something I have to do first.'

Her eyebrows went up slightly. 'Go on.'

'I don't want Walden Fisher to learn about it on the news. I don't want him turning on the radio and finding out we've got the guy who killed his daughter. He needs to hear it in person before everyone else does.'

Rhonda Finderman nodded. 'Okay.'

'I'm gonna head over that way now. Then I'll make a call to Lorraine Plummer's parents, and I guess Bill Gaynor deserves a heads-up as well, even if he is in jail.'

'I'll tell him,' Rhonda said. 'And I'll get the paperwork going on the official charges against Carlson.'

I nodded a thank-you. I poured the rest of my coffee into the sink and left the building. I thought I was going to make a clean getaway, but Randall Finley was standing by my car.

'I thought these were your wheels,' he said. 'I was just going to come in and look for you.'

'Hi, Randy.'

'Is it true?' he asked.

'Is what true?'

'Rumors are going around that you've got someone. In those murders. Of the women.'

'There'll be a presser later today.'

'And I already heard about Victor Rooney. God, Barry, you're having some kind of day. It was you, right? In both cases? You figured it out?'

There wasn't the usual forced enthusiasm in his voice, which I attributed to grief. I was detecting what sounded like genuine admiration, but I was too tired to appreciate it.

'It's been a day full of developments,' I conceded. 'But there's still a lot to nail down.'

'I meant what I said earlier. You should be the chief. You're the man for the job.'

'We have a chief,' I said. 'And she's doing just fine. I haven't forgotten the shit you pulled.' But there was no anger in my voice. 'Besides, I don't know what this has to do with you anymore.'

'I've reconsidered,' Finley said.

'You've what?'

'I'm still running. After a suitable period,' he said, and lowered his head in memory of the dead, 'I'll be back at it.'

'Why the change of heart?'

'What else am I going to do, Barry? Just sit around and put water into bottles? I'll go out of my mind. I have to do more than that. I have to make a difference.'

He said it with such a straight face, I felt he believed it.

'I guess you have to do what you have to do,' I said, opening my car door and getting in.

'So what I'm saying is, if you hear anything a guy in my position might like to know, it's in my nature to return the favor.'

God, we were right back where we'd started when he found those damn squirrels.

On the way, I phoned Maureen, filled her in.

'I wonder if any of the stores are open today,' she said.

'Why?'

'I might buy you a cake.'

'I accept.'

I thought she'd say something, but her voice had gone quiet.

'Maureen?'

'I'm here. I'm just . . . I've been just barely holding it together all day. There's a list online.' She paused. 'Of the dead.'

'Oh.'

'Some of them are people we know. Alicia, who I work with?'

'Right?'

'She lost both her parents. At one of the nursing homes. They said on the radio that there were forty-two fatalities in facilities for the elderly. They died before anyone could even get them to the hospital. It brings the number of dead to over two hundred.'

The scale of the tragedy had gotten so big I'd become numbed by it. I had lost the capacity to be shocked.

'I have a couple of things to do yet,' I told her, 'and then Rhonda and I are going to make a statement about Angus Carlson's arrest, and then I'll be home.'

'I love you,' Maureen said.

'I love you, too.'

By the time I'd mounted the steps to Walden Fisher's porch and rapped my knuckles on the door, I wasn't sure I had anything left. I could feel the exhaustion washing over me. It was just as well Walden took the better part of thirty seconds to come to the door. I needed that much time to keep my head from spinning.

'Hello?' he said as he swung the door open. Then, recognizing me, he said, 'Oh, Detective.'

'Mr Fisher,' I said, extending a hand.

He had been rubbing the tip of his right thumb

with his index finger. He spotted something scraggly on the nail and quickly bit it off. 'Sorry,' he said. He offered that same hand and I took it with some reluctance.

'May I come in?'

'Yes, yes, of course,' he said, and made way for me. 'I was thinking you might come by.'

Had he already heard about Carlson?

'Really?' I said.

'It was on the news. About Victor. My God, I just can't believe it. It's – it's unthinkable what he did.'

Of course. That much had become public.

'I apologize for not coming by to tell you about that,' I said. 'I should have. But there's been another development, something even more important to you.'

He looked at me expectantly. 'What?'

'I wouldn't mind getting off my feet,' I said.

We took seats in the living room. Walden was on the edge of his, leaning forward. Next to him, on an end table, was a picture of his wife, Beth, and daughter, Olivia, taken, I guessed, when Olivia was around twelve years old.

Both smiling.

I said, 'We have someone in custody in connection with Olivia's death.'

His mouth dropped open an inch. 'Victor?'

'No, not Victor. It's a man named Angus Carlson.' I drew a breath. 'A member of the Promise Falls police.'

Walden sat back in his chair, stunned. 'Carlson?'

'That's right.'

'But I met him. Yesterday, at the hospital.'

I nodded. 'That's right. Carlson has confessed to Olivia's murder, and two others here in Promise Falls. There may be more, in Cleveland, that happened before he moved here.'

'Dear God,' he said. 'He just came in and confessed?'

'No,' I said. 'There were things that led to him. In fact, you played a role there, when you gave me those letters the town had sent to Olivia. We found Carlson just before he was going to do it again, I think. There's going to be a statement this afternoon, but I wanted you to be the first to know about this.'

He shook his head slowly, still disbelieving.

'Why?' he asked.

I told him what Angus had told us. 'I can't say that it makes any sense.'

'In his mind it did,' Walden said.

I nodded. 'You never really know what's going on inside people's heads.'

He was mulling it over, trying to take it in. 'They're going to show up at my door, aren't they?'

'They?'

'Reporters,' he said. 'Soon as you tell them about this, they'll be swarming around out front.'

'That's a reasonable expectation,' I said. 'We can ask them to give the families – people like you – some space, but they don't tend to listen.'

He looked down at himself. His plaid flannel shirt had several minor stains on it.

'Beth would kill me if I went before the cameras looking like this,' he said with a sad smile. 'I should throw on a clean shirt. They might show up any minute.'

I didn't think that was so, but then again, Finley had already heard about Carlson. Someone might have phoned in a tip to the media.

'It's possible,' I said.

Walden stood. 'Give me a minute,' he said. 'I'll be right back.'

I stood as well as he crossed the room and went up the stairs.

Suddenly, I felt woozy.

It was a bit like how I'd felt when I'd chased Victor Rooney down the driveway, before the pain in my chest.

I took a few deep breaths. Oxygen, I thought. I needed oxygen.

The wooziness passed after several seconds, but there was a lingering feeling that I might be sick to my stomach.

There was probably a bathroom on the first floor. I walked in the direction of the kitchen, passed one door I thought might be a powder room, and opened it, only to discover it was a closet. But I got lucky with the second door.

I stepped into the two-piece bathroom, left the door open. There was a white porcelain pedestal sink next to a toilet. Behind me, a towel rack and a shelf with some knickknacks. What I wanted to do was splash some water on my face. I still wasn't going to drink it, but if it was safe enough to shower with, I could splash some on my cheeks.

I turned on the cold tap, held one hand under it until the water was good and chilly, cupped my palms beneath it. I closed my eyes tight, tossed the water on my face.

Did it again.

I turned off the tap, reached behind me for the hand towel hanging there, and dried my face off.

I needed to take some weight off my feet. I placed my hands on both sides of the sink, and inadvertently knocked something off the side.

I looked down between the sink and the toilet and saw that I had knocked Walden's metal nail file to the floor. About six inches long, with a clear blue plastic handle. It had landed next to a plastic wastepaper basket. I was worried the blood would rush to my head when I bent over to pick it up.

I needed a second.

While I was looking down, something in the trash basket caught my eye. Amid a few wadded tissues there was a small bottle, the kind that might contain cough syrup. But a glance at the label told me it was not cough syrup.

Bracing myself against the sink with one hand, I reached down into the basket with the other. Got my fingers around the bottle and brought it up to eye level.

I read the label.

Syrup of Ipecac.

I didn't even know they still made that stuff. I remembered back when I was a kid, it was in most people's medicine cabinets. But it had, over the years, fallen out of favor.

I certainly hadn't forgotten what it was for.

It made you throw up. Violently.

I sensed someone standing just outside the door. I turned, the bottle of ipecac still in my hand.

Walden Fisher, wearing a nice, crisp white shirt, was staring at me.

CHAPTER 66

*O*h, shit.

CHAPTER 67

Duckworth

'I was feeling dizzy,' I told Walden. 'Came in here for a minute to pull myself together.'
Walden said nothing.

I held up the bottle. 'What's the story on this, Walden?'

'That's ipecac,' he said.

'I know. I can read. I haven't seen this in a long time. But this looks like a relatively new bottle.' I took a closer look at it, turned it sideways. 'Empty, too. Where'd you get this?'

'I bought it. Had to go to a few places before I found it.'

'It makes you throw up,' I said.

'Yeah,' Walden said.

'So why did you want it?'

'In case I ever needed it.'

'You must have used it very recently,' I said. 'I mean, it was right there in the trash. So you must have had some in the last day or so.'

'That's right,' he said hesitantly. 'Yesterday morning. When I heard about the water being poisoned.'

His voice lacked conviction. I'd been in this line of work long enough to tell when someone was lying to me.

'At the hospital,' I reminded him, 'you said you'd had some coffee? Ran out into the street, throwing up, just as the ambulance was coming by.'

'Is that what I said?' he asked.

I nodded.

'Then maybe I had some of that after I got back home,' he said. 'I'm a little cloudy on the details.'

But things were coming into focus for me.

'Walden,' I said, 'did you drink this stuff *before* you ran out into the street?'

'Like I said, so much has happened in the last day or so.'

'Why would you do that?' I asked. 'Everyone else was sick from the tainted water, but you were sick from *this*. Walden, it's almost like you wanted people to think you were made ill by the poisoned water, when maybe you weren't.'

Walden moved his jaw around.

'Why would you do that, Walden? Why did you want everyone to think you'd been poisoned?'

That jaw kept moving around.

'Walden?'

'I took too much of it,' he said. 'I just wanted to appear sick, like everyone else. But I swallowed so much, I really did a number on myself. Threw up so violently, my heart started palpitating. Actually thought I might die for a while there.'

'Jesus, Walden, why—'

He came at me fast, palms forward. He slammed them into my chest and I went into the wall hard enough to get the wind knocked out of me. I was about to reach for my gun, but instead I raised my hands to defend myself from the fists that were pounding my head.

Walden was in a blind fury, his fists driving into me faster than I could deflect them. I felt a cheekbone collapse; then the vision in my left eye went blurry with blood. We weren't that different in age, but he was in better shape than I was, by a lot.

I started sliding down the wall. When I was on the way down, a fist went into my gut like a piston.

I was close to passing out.

He let me continue my slide until my butt was on the floor, my legs arranged haphazardly in front of me. Walden crouched down, found my gun, and unholstered it. By the time I was able to focus with my right eye – the flesh around my left was already puffing up and obscuring my view – he was standing over me with my own weapon pointed at my head.

I tasted blood in my mouth. My bottom lip was ballooning.

I said, 'Walden.'

'You didn't have to die,' he said. 'You got lucky yesterday. You didn't drink the water. You didn't have to be one of them.'

'Jesus, Walden . . . put the gun down. . . . Let's talk about this.'

'There's nothing to talk about,' he said.

I mumbled, 'If it was you . . . Victor . . . you must have set up Victor. . . . How could you set up someone who loved your daughter?'

'Just shut up,' Walden said. 'I have to think.'

'The squirrel trap, those mannequins . . .'

'I moved it all last night,' Walden said. 'When he went to do his run.'

'And the boy,' I said. 'That Lydecker kid.'

'That wasn't supposed to happen. I caught him snooping.'

I swallowed, felt blood trickling down my throat. 'You did it . . . for the same reason you had me believe Victor did it. Same motive, different person.'

'We felt the same way,' Walden said. 'I just felt it more. This town failed Olivia. It had to be taught a lesson.'

'Twenty-two bystanders, and Victor . . .'

'I hoped he'd drink the water,' Walden said. 'He was late. He was late and Olivia died. I wanted him to die, too. But now they'll think he did it. At least . . . at least for a while.'

'What . . . what do you mean, for a while?'

Walden took several breaths before he spoke. 'I thought . . . I thought I'd feel some satisfaction. That I would feel . . . vindicated. Something. But I don't. I don't think enough have been made to pay. I'm thinking . . . You know the Promise Falls Autumn Fair?'

Blood obscured my view of Walden. I blinked a few times, and said, 'The fair?'

'In October,' he said. 'I'm thinking, by then, everyone will feel safe again. They'll have let their guard down. They'll all believe it was Victor. Maybe a bomb . . . at the fair.'

'Walden . . . listen to me. You can't—'

'You know I have to kill you,' he said. 'I think you're a good man, but that doesn't matter. There was a time, back when I started planning this, when I thought, once I'd made my point, I'd turn myself in. But now I see there's more to do.'

I gurgled something.

'What?'

'Twenty-three,' I said. 'All of that was you.'

'I was sending a message,' he said. 'That justice was coming. I wanted people to be afraid. I was so pleased when I saw you were figuring it out. That's why I phoned you that time.'

'You're an engineer,' I said. 'You had the smarts for everything. The Ferris wheel, the bus, blowing up the drive-in. But Mason Helt . . .' For a moment there, things had gone dark. 'Helt,' I said.

'He took theater. I approached him, said he was going to be part of a study, something sanctioned by the college. About fear and paranoia. He was skeptical, but a thousand bucks went a long way to convincing him. After, I knew it was a mistake, actually meeting with a third party, bringing someone else into this. I caught a break when he ended up dead. I might have had to kill him myself if that hadn't happened.'

I mumbled something else.

'What's that?' Walden said.

'Tate. Tate Whitehead.'

Walden nodded. 'I knew there'd only be one person at the water plant, and that it would be him. I couldn't be interrupted. It took a long time to bring in what I needed.'

'Sodium something.'

'Azide,' he said.

'Yeah,' I said. 'That's it.'

'It took a long time to acquire what I needed. More than two years. I was stockpiling it, knowing I'd use it someday. I just didn't know when. I knew I'd never do it while Beth was alive. I couldn't run the risk of being sent away while she was still with me. But when she passed away, I knew it was time to move forward.'

'Walden . . . please don't kill me. . . . Turn yourself in. Your first instinct was the right one. Tell everyone why you did what you did. Make them understand how they failed you, how they failed Olivia.'

He looked at me solemnly. 'I'm sorry. But no.'

'Walden, listen to me. You—'

There was the sound of a loud knocking.

Walden's head whipped around. 'Jesus.' Panic washed over his face.

'Walden?' someone shouted. 'You home?'

I thought I recognized the voice, even with blood finding its way into my ears. I had a feeling that if I could stand, and look in the mirror, I'd be horrified by what I saw.

'Walden? It's Don! Don Harwood!'

I was right. I did know the voice. David's father.

Walden shouted: 'Just a second!'

He leaned in close to me, the gun inches from my bloodied nose. 'I'm going to talk to him,' he whispered. 'If you make one sound, even a peep, I will kill him. I'll shoot him with your gun. Do you understand me?'

I nodded.

'You have those cuffs,' he said.

'What?'

'Don't you carry those plastic cuffs around?'

I barely managed a nod.

'Get them out,' he said. Then, shouting: 'Be right there, Don!'

I struggled to get a hand into my pocket. I brought out one plastic cuff. Walden took one step back, keeping the gun trained on me. He was afraid to cuff me himself, probably fearing I'd try something. Which I would have.

'Put your hand up against the leg,' he said. He was pointing to the thick porcelain leg that supported the pedestal sink. 'Cuff your wrist to that.'

That would keep me here in the bathroom, as opposed to cuffing my wrists together.

I did as I was instructed, and secured my right hand to the leg. Both my hands were bloody, and I was leaving red handprints on the floor as I shifted my body. I had gone from a sitting position to being stretched out on the floor, my head between the sink and the toilet.

'Remember,' he said. 'One peep, and Don has to die, too. As it is, it only has to be you.'

He turned on the tap and rinsed his and my blood from his hands, dried them off, then slipped out into the hall and closed the door.

I lay there, 280 pounds of pain. With my free hand, I reached into my jacket and found my phone. I turned onto my side, blinked several times to get the blood out of my eyes so I could see the screen.

The door reopened.

Walden reached down and snatched the device from me. 'I can't believe I forgot that,' he said, and shut the door again.

I closed my eyes, rested my head on the cold tile floor. My ear was not far from the crack at the bottom of the door, allowing me to hear what was going on.

'Don, hey, how are you?' Walden said. 'Sorry it took me so long.'

'No, it's okay. Am I catching you at a bad time?'

'Well, I'm about to head out. Otherwise I'd invite you in.'

'Oh, okay, well,' said Don, 'I'll try to make this quick, although it's kind of a hard thing to say in a hurry.'

'What's hard to say?'

A long pause. 'Well, Walden, the thing is . . . I wanted to tell you this when you came by the other day. When I had to go to the school and pick up my grandson? It's something that's been eating at me for a long time.'

'What?'

'You see – God, this is hard to say – but you see, I was one of them.'

Now it was Walden's turn to pause. 'One of them?'

'I was down by the park that night. The night, you know, that Olivia . . . that she died.'

'You were there?'

'I heard what was happening. I don't even know that there's anything I could have done. I wasn't close. But I could have done *something*. I could've called the cops, or I could've run into the park. I keep playing it over and over in my head, wondering what I could have done that might have made a difference. I don't honestly think I could have saved her, Walden, but maybe, if I'd been a better person, if I'd done *something*, maybe I'd have seen the son of a bitch who did it.'

'Why are you telling me this?'

'I have to get it off my chest. It's eating me up, Walden.'

I thought about screaming. I thought about calling out for help. But I'd be killing Don Harwood. I couldn't do that to him.

Although I wondered, given what Don was confessing to, whether Walden would decide to kill him anyway. I was hurting so much on my side that I shifted to my stomach, my free hand sliding across the tile, coming into contact with something.

I pulled on the leg of the sink, testing it, thinking maybe I could make it break free, that I could slip my hand out from the bottom. But the sound of the sink crashing to the floor was going to get Don killed as quickly as if I cried for help.

Walden said, 'It's okay.'

'No, Walden, it's not okay. I'm not asking you to forgive me. I'll understand if you don't, but I—'

'Really, it's okay. It was good of you to come by, Don.'

'That's it?' Don Harwood said.

'Don't give it another thought.'

'Seriously? All this time, I've felt sick about this, and you don't care?'

'They caught the man today,' Walden said.

'They did?'

'I just – I just got a call from the police. They've caught someone.'

'Well, I'll be damned. I had no—'

A cell phone started ringing. Don said, 'Hang on.' Then, 'Hello? *David?* David, slow down. . . . What happened? You got *what?* You got shot? . . . No, *you* shot someone? Oh God, David, no . . . They couldn't do anything? . . . Where are you? Tell me where you are. I'll get your mother, and we'll—'

'Don,' Walden said.

'David, hang on a second.' A pause, and then, 'Walden, I have to go. Something awful's happened.'

'Sure. It was good of you to come by.'

'Yeah, well,' Don said. 'I have to go.'

I heard the door close.

I had no idea what Don's phone call was about, but whatever it was, it wasn't a priority for me.

Would Walden shoot me? Would he kill me with my own gun? Unlikely, I thought. It would make too much noise. It would leave a bullet hole in the bathroom to be repaired. He'd have to do it another way. Strangle me, maybe. Suffocate me. Disable my other arm and hold his hand over my mouth and nose until I was dead.

There'd be less mess that way.

The real challenge would be getting rid of me. I was probably a hundred pounds heavier – at least – than George Lydecker. If this bathroom had a bathtub, he could dump me into it once I was dead and cut me into pieces. But if he wanted to treat me like a side of beef, he was going to have to move me someplace else to do it.

Plus, there was the matter of my car out front. What was he going to do with that? I was hoping Don might have recognized it, asked Walden where I was. Then again, that probably would have gotten him killed. And now it sounded like Don had something else to worry about.

I heard steps coming back down the hall. The door opened.

'Did you hear that?' Walden asked. The gun was in his right hand. He must have hidden it when he was talking to Don.

'I heard,' I said.

'Everybody's got problems,' he said offhandedly. 'And you're my latest one.' He looked at the way he had instructed me to cuff myself. 'I screwed that up, didn't I? I should have had you put both hands around the leg and hooked them up together. You have another cuff?'

'Yes,' I said.

'Take it out of your pocket.'

'I can't reach it with this hand. It's in my other pocket.'

Walden sighed. 'Try.'

I attempted to reach across my body into my opposite pocket, but I was like O. J. trying on the glove. I made it look a lot harder than it actually was.

'I can't do it,' I said.

'Okay, don't try anything funny,' he said. 'Shift over that way.'

I rolled back onto my other side to allow Walden to get into my pocket. My free hand went under my body, where I'd kept the item my hand had brushed past while he'd been talking to Don.

He still had the gun in his hand, but it was pointed at the toilet and not at me. He fumbled around in my pocket with his left hand.

I rolled.

I rolled fast, and hard, and brought up my free hand, with the six-inch nail file clutched in my fist.

I swung my arm with all the strength I had left in me and plunged it into Walden Fisher's neck.

Walden screamed and tumbled, then hit his head on the sink. The gun fell out of his hand.

'Jesus!' he shouted.

I pulled the nail file out and jammed it into him again, this time catching him at the base of his neck, just above the rib cage.

And again.

And again.

Walden keeled over, his head hitting the opposite wall, a hand to his throat, his mouth wide, blood coming from everywhere. He stirred slightly, made one feeble attempt to grab for the gun that was just out of reach, made a noise that sounded like nuts and bolts rattling around in a can, and then he was gone.

I lay there for several minutes, catching my own breath, waiting to see if he'd take another.

He was dead.

I shifted over as close as my tethered arm would let me, patted him down, trying to find my phone. As best I could tell, it wasn't on him. So I crawled back to my original position, laid out on the floor on my back, one arm stretched out above my head, still attached to the sink.

Someone would come, eventually. Or maybe, once I had some strength back, I'd yank that sink right off the goddamn wall.

I closed my eyes, listening to my own breaths and the pulsing of my heart in my temples.

Thought about Maureen. Thought about Trevor.

Thought about cake.